ASHES OF INNOCENCE

PHIL PRICE

First Published by Phil Price
Republished by SpellBound Books 2022

PRINT ISBN: 978-1-7399975-7-1

1

AFGHANISTAN : 2005

John leaned against the armoured vehicle in the dusty marketplace as the sun kissed the mountains to the west of their position. He felt sick, waves of nausea washing over him as he stared at the corpse in front of him. It was human, but only just. The head, limbs and genitals had been crudely removed, the remaining torso littered with puncture wounds and smeared blood. Around him, more bodies lay, swarms of flies invading orifices and crawling over cooling flesh in search of food. They were fallen Taliban fighters, cut down by machine gun fire a few minutes before. Around them, haphazard low-rise buildings built of mud and wood formed a ring around the Royal Marines who stood on the baked earth. Many of the walls were pock-marked with bullet-holes, splashes of blood adorning their facades. He looked away, the lukewarm Afghan afternoon heading into another cold night, high up in the mountainous plateau. Their position was on the outskirts of Marjeh, a few hours' drive from their base, Camp Bastion. To John, it felt like a million miles away as he looked around the desolate space on the edge of the small town.

A soldier approached, designer sunglasses framing his bearded face. "Heli is five minutes out. Once we load up, we're moving out, back to base."

"What a way to go! Being killed in battle is one thing, James. Being tortured and cut up by the locals is something else. Did we really sign up for this shit?"

"I know, John. That's why the Russians shipped out. They couldn't handle them. We all know why we're here though, to liberate the people of Afghanistan from their violent oppressors, blah blah blah. The world has certainly changed. Flying planes into skyscrapers will do that."

"I preferred the world before *9/11.*"

"You're not alone, mate. I think we're in for the long haul. *Al Qaeda* is running amok, both here and around the world. Even if we kill Bin Laden, another one will take his place. Another nutcase hellbent on carnage. Come on, let's get our shit together, Captain."

"Roger that, Major," John replied, walking around the armoured patrol vehicle as the dull beat of a helicopter drifted towards them. He took one more look at the corpse on the ground, inwardly shivering. *I can't wait to go home,* he thought, shouldering his assault rifle.

Three hours later, John sat on his bunk, leafing through letters and photographs as troops went about their business. His boots hung off the bunk, never really leaving his feet unless he was in the shower. Even when he was asleep, they were loosely fastened, ready for action. He smiled as he came across his favourite picture. His wife, Lucy was sat on the edge of a slide, his daughter, Lottie happily perched on her lap. They were both smiling at the camera, a carefree look on their faces. His wife's dark locks were blowing in the autumn breeze, his daughter's blonde hair, similarly ruffled. They were the spitting image of each other, their first-born daughter retained his mother's creamy complexion. John was different, his chestnut brown hair and freckles were all his own.

"Wilson. You coming for some scran?" a fellow soldier said.

"I'll be there in a minute. I'll just square my stuff away. What's on the menu?"

"Lasagne," the soldier replied.

"Okay. Save me a seat, mate. I'll be five minutes." The soldier nodded, leaving John alone in the tented dormitory. The Afghan wind howled outside, making its way through gaps in the canvas sheeting.

So bloody cold tonight, he thought as he packed the pictures and letters away, placing them in his non-descript green metal locker. He didn't bother closing the door. The men and women around him were as much a part of his family as the loved ones back home. He glanced in the mirror, rubbing the fresh growth on his chin. *I'll let it grow a bit,* he thought. *Might make me blend in with the locals?* He walked from the dormitory, past similar looking awnings that reminded John of a *Star Wars* set, the dark desert backdrop forlorn and unwelcoming. A few hundred yards later, he was shivering as he entered the mess hall, glad to be out of the howling wind, laced with sand. As he walked towards the counter, the smell of lasagne and garlic bread assaulted his nostrils, making his stomach growl in protest. Men and women sat at trestle tables, chatting and laughing after a hard day at camp and out on manoeuvres. Muscled-arms, adorned with tattoos and designer sunglasses, were on display as the troops ate dinner like they were at home with loved ones. It all felt so very normal to John, who took a steel tray from the side of the counter, his mouth watering at the heady aroma inside the tent.

He found his seat next to Lieutenant Gittus, who was sat, elbows on the table as he polished off his dinner, mopping up the creamy sauce with a slice of garlic bread. "Blimey, you didn't waste any time?"

"Bloody starving, mate. I'll pop back for seconds in a minute."

"I'm surprised you're not the size of a house, lucky bastard," John replied.

"It's all that shagging I'm doing. Burns calories."

"Shagging! Out here? What are you shagging? Camels?"

Gittus snorted, rocking back on the chair legs as he let out a laugh. "The camels are better looking than the locals, mate."

"I wouldn't know. I'm not here to work my way through the Afghan female community. I have more than enough at home."

"Lucky you. How is Lucy?"

"All good, mate. Gonna give them a call in a bit."

"Send her my love. Tell her if she wants a younger model, I'm still on the market."

"In your dreams. And anyway, I'm only thirty-one!"

"Like I said, you're getting on a bit. How old is the wife?"

"Thirty."

"Perfect!"

John jabbed his friend on the shoulder. "I'll send her your regards."

"Good. How is the little `un?"

"She's doing great. She'll be starting school in September. Growing up fast. Proper little princess."

"Bet she's looking forward to Christmas."

"Hmm," John replied, his face dropping slightly. "I just wish I could be with them, mate. It's a long time until February. I really miss them."

"I'm sure you do. That's why I'm glad I'm single. I've got no one to miss, except Mum and Dad. February will be here before you know it. Then you can get jiggy with it again."

John smiled. "Nice to know you've got your priorities in line, mate."

"Always. Now, I think I need some more carbs," Gittus countered, rising from his chair.

An hour later, John was sat on his bunk, his laptop resting on his thighs as he attempted to put a call through to the UK. "C'mon," he uttered, becoming frustrated as the dial tone rang out across the dormitory.

"Hello, babe," a female voice said through the speakers as a digitised picture appeared on the screen.

"Hey, sweetheart. I can see you, just about."

"Same here. You're breaking up a bit, but I can hear your voice pretty good."

"How're things there? I miss you."

"We miss you too," she replied as another figure jerkily appeared on the screen.

"Hey, poppet," John chirped happily. "How's my little princess?"

"Hello, Daddy," Lottie squeaked excitedly, her face beaming.

Through the jerky resolution, John could make out her blonde curls, bouncing in jerky fashion as the internet struggled to keep up with the connection. Tears streamed down John's face, his chest constricting. "I miss you, Lottie," John said, his voice trembling with rising emotions.

"Miss you too, Daddy. We're going to the shops tomorrow. Mommy's gonna buy me Iggle Piggle and Upsy Daisy!"

"Lucky you. Can I play with them when I get home?"

"Yes, Daddy," Lottie replied matter-of-factly. "We can play with them in the servatory."

"She means conservatory," Lucy cut in gently. "It's her new word of the week. Well, almost. We're going into Birmingham in the morning, to do some final Christmas shopping. Can I get you anything?"

"Some more hiking socks and boxers. Mine are not lasting well and it's only been a few months since you'd sent the last lot."

"That bad?"

"Pretty much, sweetheart. I miss you both terribly. I cannot wait to see you."

"We miss you too, babe. Roll on February!"

"Tell me about it."

"How are things?"

"Not great. I can't say too much, but this place is something else."

"I worry about you so much. Why couldn't you just be a plumber or a salesman?"

"Salesman? Me? I'd be the worst salesman in history. I'd end up owing money, not making it."

Lucy smiled, the screen freezing for a few seconds, giving John an uninterrupted view of her face. He hit *print screen* on his keyboard, hoping to paste the image to a word doc after the call had finished. "How long have you got?"

"Not long. Internet is sketchy at best. I will call again on Monday."

"Okay, babe. Your folks came around today. They say hi."

"Are they both okay?" John responded, making a mental note to call them.

"They're fine. Your dad's putting in for retirement."

"About time too. Driving forklift trucks around a cold yard is no job for a man in his sixties."

"He said the same thing. They are making people redundant where he works, so he's taking it. He reckons he'll get a decent payoff."

"Oh, I'm sure Mum will be heading to the travel agents as soon as the cheque clears," he pointed out mischievously.

"Probably. They haven't been away for years. Neither have we, come to think about it."

John instantly felt guilt seep over him. "I know, babe. Tell you what, why don't you pick up some brochures tomorrow while you're out? Then we can start planning for a holiday next year."

"Really? That would be nice. Okay, you're on, mister."

John smiled, the resolution on the screen becoming more digitised. "Look, babe. My time is nearly up. I'll give you a call next week. Then you can fill me in on where you fancy going."

"Okay, babe," she said warmly. "You take care out there. We love you and want you home soon."

"I love you both, too. I'll be home before you know it. 'Bye, my love."

"'Bye, Daddy. Love ya," the young voice echoed down the line.

More tears formed in John's eyes, a low whimper of pain escaping him. "Night-night, poppet," he croaked, his voice thick with emotion. "Daddy loves you."

"'Bye, my love," Lucy replied. "Speak to you soon." John ended the call, wiping tears from his eyes as he closed the laptop heavily. He stowed it under his bed before staring up at the green tarpaulin above him. His mind was awash with thoughts. He could see his wife and daughter, happily splashing around in a swimming pool, its crystal-clear waters inviting. Shells erupted a few miles away. John rolled over onto his side, pulling the slim pillow around his ears as exhaustion quickly overcame him. He slept, fitfully.

2

BIRMINGHAM - ENGLAND

Watery sunlight filtered through the blinds as the two boys sat watching the movie. On the screen, a small figure with a garish smile painted on its plastic face plunged a knife into its victim. The boys, both redheads, watched in rapt concentration as the movie's main character stabbed at the young girl as she tried to crawl across the dusty cellar floor, a wet smear of blood following her pitiful escape. After dispatching its victim, the evil doll stood over her, its messy blonde hair and yellow coat splattered with blood.

"That's fucking sick," the younger boy said, as he picked his nose.

"Stop doing that!" his older brother admonished, wrinkling his freckled nose in disgust.

"Sorry," he replied suitably humbled by his sibling.

"You'll never get a girl if you keep doing that."

"I don't eat them," he countered defiantly. "And anyway, I don't want a girlfriend. Girls are weird!"

"Why?" he questioned, the movie forgotten.

"They just are," he stated, not really knowing what else to say.

"Well, one day you'll think differently, Luke. They have tits and fannies. What more could a man want?"

He wrinkled his nose, also adorned with freckles. "No thanks. I don't like girls that way!"

"Are you queer? Do you like cock instead?" the older brother asked, piercing grey eyes staring at the younger sibling.

Luke looked at his brother, a look of horror on his face. "Fuck off! No. I don't like boys or girls."

"Well, you'll have to decide one day. I get plenty of action at school when I'm there. The girls are proper into me."

"In your dreams. What girl would want action with you?"

"Plenty. I'll let you smell my fingers next time," Sean said, holding his hand under his younger brother's nose.

"Get off!" he roared, shoving the offending hand away. "It smells of shit!"

"Well, I've been scratching my arse too." The older brother looked around the lounge, noticing the time on the wall clock. "What shall we do today?"

"We could go over to the shops? I have a few quid in my wallet. Fancy an ice cream?"

"Erm, it's December, and I don't eat ice cream. That's for kids. I prefer vodka."

"Maybe we could take a bottle out of the cupboard and take some of Mum's fags?"

"You mean her joints?"

"Yes. Some of that skunk stuff."

"Okay. Let's do it."

The brief silence was broken by a loud bang on the front door. Luke walked over to the window, peering through the slatted blinds to see a figure on the front step. "It's Jerome," he said as he padded out into the hallway, pulling up his joggers.

The man regarded the boy for a few seconds before speaking after the youth had opened the door. "Where's Mandy?"

"She's upstairs, asleep," he replied, eyeing the man's attire. He was tall, dwarfing Luke as he stepped into the hallway. His coffee-coloured skin was pock-marked, his dreadlocks almost touching his waistband.

"Go into the lounge," the man ordered abruptly. "Where's Sean?"

"Here," Sean countered, ushering his brother into the living room.

Jerome slouched next to the doorframe, regarding the teenager. "Did you drop that stuff off?"

"Yes, just like you asked me to."

"Good boy," Jerome said, the term *boy* irking Sean somewhat. He pulled a roll of cash out of his pocket, peeling a twenty-pound note from it. He thrust it into Sean's hand. "Pop by tomorrow. I may have another job for you."

"Okay," Sean nodded, not really knowing what to add. The man made him nervous, his height was intimidating.

"Laters. I need to speak to your mother," he said as he began ascending the carpet-less staircase.

Sean walked into the lounge, smiling at his younger brother as he showed him the banknote. "Quids in, bruv."

"What's that for?" Luke asked inquisitively.

"None of your business, Lukey," the elder brother huffed. "And don't tell Mum, for fuck's sake." They both looked up at the ceiling as raised voices filtered from upstairs. "What are they rowing about this time?" The light fitting above them started to sway gently. The brothers were transfixed by it.

"Dunno," Luke replied. "Mum told me not to get involved with her friends." He walked over to the cupboard, easing a small metal container off the shelf. He opened it gently, pulling out two large rolled-up cigarettes and a box of matches. "Here we go. We'll only take two or Mum'll notice and wallop us, again."

Upstairs, the shouting had ended and a creaking noise drifted into the kitchen. Sean smiled, pointing up at the ceiling. "They're doing it," he exclaimed. "C'mon. Let's take a look."

"No, Sean! Mum will flip out."

"Come on," he replied, a wicked smile spreading across his face. "We can do one if she sees us." They crept into the hallway as more sounds filtered through the house. The boys tried not to laugh as they ascended the staircase, shuffling soundlessly across the small landing to the wooden door that was open a few inches. Sean placed his fingers to his lips, Luke nodding in compliance as the older brother opened the door.

Luke's eyes opened wide at the scene beyond the door. His mother was on all fours on the bed, her black Playboy dressing gown pushed up until it almost covered her head. The man was behind her, sideways on to the boys as he rutted and bucked behind her, his dreadlocks swaying in time with his movements. Despite the coolness of the room, sweat peppered his brow as he increased the intensity of his movements.

The door creaked on its hinges, the man looking to his right, spotting his spectators. He smiled, revealing uneven teeth, one of them gold. He slowed, taking his hands from the women's hips.

"Come on, Jerome," Mandy panted. "I'm close."

"We have visitors," the man replied, sliding himself out the woman on the bed. Both boys watched in morbid fascination as the man stood facing them. Their eyes were drawn to his midsections, Luke blinking rapidly at the sight of the man's hardness. He looked away as a female voice hollered across the bedroom.

"GET THE FUCK OUT OF HERE YOU LITTLE BASTARDS!" she screamed, pulling the gown over her naked body. The boys scarpered, taking the stairs two at a time before heading out of the kitchen door, vodka and cannabis safely stowed as they made their way, laughing, out of the back gate that led to an area of garages and abandoned cars.

"We'll be for it later," Sean stated, his breath slowly returning.

"I know. Mum will be more pissed that we've taken her vodka and skunk, though."

"Oh well, we can stay out as long as possible. Shall we go to the Fort?"

"Why not?" Luke responded, zipping up his winter coat as the first drops of rain fell from the leaden clouds above them. They walked across the gravelled earth, Sean kicking small stones against the metal garage doors. They came out onto a busy road, traffic flowing past them as they walked hurriedly to a pedestrian crossing with the rain falling steadily from above. As the green man signalled them to cross, they skittered across the main road towards their destination. Industrial units littered the suburb. The M6 motorway was just a few hundred yards ahead of the boys and traffic was trundling by on the busy Saturday morning. Ten minutes later, the boys skirted the huge car park as cars and shoppers made their way to the various outlets that formed a horseshoe around the perimeter.

"Look," Sean pointed out as they walked towards a mobile phone shop where shiny handsets were on display behind toughened glass. "I want that one."

Luke stared at the latest Nokia handset, shaking his head. "And how are you going to afford that? It's over a hundred quid."

"Who said I have to buy it?" Sean countered, his face defiant. "But not today. Anyway, all the phones on display are dummies. Liam at school knows where to get the one I want." As they moved away from the shops, Sean unscrewed the vodka. "Here, you go first," he offered, thrusting the bottle under his younger brother's nose.

Luke took a sip, trying his best to look cool and mature. It lasted a split second as he coughed violently, almost spitting the contents of his mouth down his front. He looked at his brother, trying to regain his composure. "It went down the wrong way," he croaked, taking a heftier swig. Tears stung his eyes as he fought to keep himself in check, the vodka burning the back of his throat.

"Give it here, bruv," Sean replied, lifting the bottle to his chapped lips. He took a swig, savouring the heady feeling that wafted over him as he smiled at Luke. "Let's go and have some fun."

They wandered around the shopping complex, Sean nodding at various youths who slouched next to shop entrances, looking for an opportunity. They carried on walking, heading into a large sports outlet, the frontage adorned with the latest football tops. "I want the new Villa top," Sean stated, pulling his younger sibling into an aisle where multitudes of clothing hung on chrome rails.

"Have you got enough to buy one?"

"Keep up, bruv. Who said anything about buying one?"

He winked at his brother as a large man dressed in black approached. "Can I help you?" he asked.

Both brothers turning around, startled.

"Just looking," Sean huffed indifferently.

"I've seen you in here before," the man replied as he loomed over them.

"Not me," Sean countered as Luke slunk behind him. "Never been in here before, mate."

"I think you have. And I think you should be on your way," he ordered, pointing towards the exit.

"Twat!" Sean spat, as he pushed past the large security guard. "Come on, Luke. There's a bad smell in here. Let's do one." A minute later, they were standing next to a large white van, watching throngs of shoppers going about their business. "Come on, bruv. Let's go and get wasted," he said, heading away from prying eyes. They walked away from the shops, hoping to find some fun elsewhere. They had no idea what was to unfold in the next hour.

3

BIRMINGHAM

"Hi, Mum. You okay?" Lucy asked as she cradled the cordless phone to her ear.

"Hello, love. I'm good. How're things over there?"

"All good. We're heading out in a bit, as soon as madam is ready."

"Where are you going?"

"To the Fort. I need to grab a few things and John needs some stuff sending over."

"Socks and jocks?"

Lucy smiled as she walked into the cosy lounge. "You got it in one. He's running low, so I will grab a few pairs and post them off tomorrow. Do you need anything?" She smiled down at Lottie, who was struggling to put her boots on. She looked up at her mother, her blonde curls bobbing. Lucy reached down and stroked her head, drawing a smile from her daughter.

"No thanks, love. I'm okay. Why don't you pop over after you've been to the shops? I'm not doing much today, just pottering around the place. The toilet cistern is playing up again. I'm just about to take a look. It's times like these when I miss your father."

Lucy's smile faded, an image of her late father appearing in her mind. He'd died suddenly six months before, leaving his family and loved ones at fifty-seven years old. "I miss him too, Mum."

"I know you do. I think about him every day. He'd have fixed the cistern in five minutes. He was good like that."

"Yes, he was," Lucy replied, dark clouds appearing on her sunny horizon. "I could take a look with you when I get there. I'm sure we can figure it out, somehow."

"Well, I'll take a look now. If I draw a blank, we can take a look later. Deal?"

"Deal," Lucy replied, trying to lighten the mood. "We won't be there too long. Probably be at yours for about one."

"Okay, sounds good. I've not seen Lottie for a few weeks. Be lovely to see her."

"I know, Mum. You really should think about moving closer to us. There isn't much to keep you in Tamworth anymore." She regretted making her statement sound so sombre.

"I know, love. Maybe after the New Year I'll have a think about it. The buses around here are not great. It takes me half a day just to get into town and back."

"Well, let's make a plan in January. Your house is immaculate. It will sell in no time."

"Okay, love. Let's do that."

"Great. Okay, well I'll see you in a few hours, Mum. Love you."

"Love you both too," Judy replied.

Lucy ended the call, walking over to the settee to pull her brown leather boots on. "Do you need help, princess?"

"No, Mummy. I did it," Lottie proclaimed happily.

"Clever girl. Now go and get your coat from under the stairs."

"Okay, Mummy," the girl replied, skipping out of the lounge. She returned a moment later as Lucy finished zipping up her boots. "I got my coat on, Mummy."

Lucy looked at her daughter, smiling. "Well done. You look lovely. Stand over by the fireplace," she urged as the girl happily skipped over to the far wall. Lucy pulled her phone out of her back pocket, selecting the camera. "Big smile for Daddy," she said. Lottie produced a huge grin as Lucy snapped a few pictures. "Perfect. Daddy will love that."

"When's Daddy coming home?" Lottie asked, her face suddenly serious.

"He'll be home very soon, Lottie," Lucy replied, trying to sound positive.

"At Christmas?"

"No, my love. But he will be home just after the New Year. He really misses you."

"I miss Daddy, too. He's funny."

"Yes, he is," Lucy replied rising emotions threatening to boil over. "Come on then. Let's go to the shops."

"Yay," Lottie exclaimed, hopping on the spot. "I want Iggle Piggle."

"I know. We'll find him, and Upsy Daisy, too." Five minutes later, Lucy's red Vauxhall Astra was reversing off the driveway, heading towards Birmingham city centre and the large shopping mall that lay a few miles to the north.

"How much have you got?" Sean hissed as he gripped the teenager's throat.

"Nuffink, man," the youth replied.

"Bullshit. You Pakis always have plenty of dosh. Did you steal some from Daddy's till? Come on, fucking hand it over." Sean reached down, twisting one of the boy's nipples, making the Asian boy cry out in anguish.

"Fuck off!" he screamed, drawing a few looks from passers-by. "My brother is in Boots, man. He'll fuck you up when I tell him what you've done."

"Bring it on. I'll sort your pussy-ass brother out as well." He reached down, pulling a few notes out of the teen's joggers. "Twenty quid. That will do nicely." He let go of the teenager, who slumped against the wall next to the car park.

"You're fucking dead, man," he shouted.

Sean advanced a few steps, firing a right jab that caught the boy on the bridge of the nose. "Take that, Paki prick," he spat, laughing as the boy grabbed his nose and doubled over. He watched as blood started splattering on the paving slabs, his brother hanging back a few feet, keeping a look out for security staff or police officers.

"You wait. You're a dead man," the Asian boy retorted, as he staggered towards the main shopping area.

Sean watched him go, pocketing the notes. "Not bad for a few minutes' work."

"Did you really need to punch him?" Luke asked.

"What? You heard how he spoke to me? I'm not having some stinking Paki talk to me like that."

"He said his brother will sort you out, Sean?"

"Nah! He's probably on his own. Come on, let's go and have a spliff."

A few minutes later, the brothers were standing next to the car park pay machine. Sean watched as his brother tried in vain to enjoy their mum's finest skunk. "You need to hold it in," Sean instructed as he watched his brother's face contort. "Don't cough it out, we only have two of them," he ordered, taking another swig of vodka.

Luke managed to control himself, drawing the strong cannabis into his lungs. His first attempt had ended in a massive coughing fit, with the younger brother grabbing the vodka bottle off Sean. After a large swig, the coughing fit had intensified for a few moments until the boy was finally ready for his second attempt. He rested against the stone wall, blowing a steady stream of smoke into the air, his eyes appearing glazed. "Wow. That's mad. My head is spinning."

"Give it here, bruv," Sean said, as a steady stream of vehicles passed close by, heading into the retail park. Behind them, the motorway loomed over them, heavy goods vehicles trundling along its length, heading both north and south on the dreary Saturday morning. The older brother took a long toke, drawing the smoke into his lungs, his own head swimming slightly as the drug took hold. He took a sip of vodka, watching Luke sway on his feet. "Is it messing with your head yet?"

"Not sure. Give me some more." Sean obliged, handing the younger sibling the half-smoked roll-up. Luke took it, taking another long drag as a red hatchback passed close to where they were standing. "Fuck!" Luke exclaimed. "Did you see that?"

"No. What?"

"In that car. It looked just like the evil doll in that movie we've just watched."

"Fuck off!"

"I'm serious, Sean," Luke pleaded, his vision becoming more and more enhanced as the drug took hold of him. "Same hair, same coat."

Sean watched as the red car headed towards the shops, the alcohol and cannabis blurring his judgement. "Come on. Show me this evil doll," he said, taking one last swig of vodka before stowing the bottle in his coat pocket. "Don't get too close though, bruv. It may stick a knife in ya."

"Follow me," Luke replied, his steps wayward as he almost tripped on the paving slabs. They headed towards the main shopping area, an evil doll in their drug-induced sights.

4

"Hold Mummy's hand, princess," Lucy asked as she led her daughter towards the shops.

"It's cold, Mummy. Can we have a hot chocolate?"

"Of course, poppet. There is a coffee shop over there. Let's get a few things from the shops first, then we can have a treat before we go over to see Nanny."

"Okay," the girl replied happily, her leather boots skipping over puddles. They walked into a large toy shop, both mother and daughter perusing the shelves before Lottie found what she was looking for. She skipped happily to the tills, tightly holding the two soft toys as if her life depended on it. They left the shop, heading towards the car to deposit the toys, much to Lottie's annoyance. However, her bad mood did not last long as she walked alongside her mother, captivated by the shiny shelves and Christmas decorations that filled every outlet. As her mother held a dress up to her body, deciding whether to try it on as she appraised herself in a full-length mirror, Lottie caught sight of a boy smiling at her. She smiled back, liking his red hair and freckles.

"Come on, Lottie," Lucy said. "Mummy needs to try this on." She led her daughter towards the rear of the store, Lottie turning and waving at the boy, who had now disappeared. Ten minutes later, mother and daughter were heading back out into the rainy afternoon, a large shopping bag bumping rhythmically against Lucy's hip as they strolled towards Costa. They ordered their drinks, Lucy choosing two large chocolate cookies, one dark the other white before finding a small table towards the back of the coffee shop.

"I like my cookie, Mummy," Lottie stated happily, as she gently sipped at her warm drink.

"Me too, princess," Lucy replied, watching as her little girl ate her cookie and sipped at her hot chocolate in as dignified a way as possible. Lucy chuckled as Lottie dabbed at her mouth with a burgundy napkin, placing her warm hand over hers. "Daddy will be very proud of his little girl. You're such a lady?"

"What's a lady, Mummy?"

Lucy had to consider the question. "Well, it's someone who does things properly. Like eats nicely, or has good manners."

"Do I have manners, Mummy?"

"Yes, poppet. Most of the time, anyway." They sat in silence for a few minutes, mother and daughter enjoying their early afternoon treat. As she finished her drink, Lucy checked her watch. "We should make a move. I just need to pop to the loo. Finish your cookie first, though."

"Okay, Mummy."

A minute later, they walked across the dark tiled floor, towards a door marked *Toilets*. They headed through into a small corridor with two doors, one female, the other male. "Hmm. No baby-changing toilets? That's not great," Lucy huffed, slightly perturbed. She opened the female door, about to usher Lottie inside until she saw the size of the cubicle. *Shit. She won't fit in here with me,* she thought, noticing a puddle of dirty water around the bottom of the pan that was slowly seeping towards her. She thought about finding another toilet, not wanting to leave Lottie outside. Her bladder protested as she turned around, making Lucy's mind up. "Sweetie. Can you stand here while Mummy pops to the toilet?"

"Yes, Mummy," the little girl replied, nodding her head in agreement.

"Good girl," Lucy replied, kissing the top of her head before closing the door. The lock reminded her of the type found in hospitals, a long chrome handle that is turned vertically to lock the person inside. As she struggled with the wobbly handle, two things happened at once. Firstly, the door handle came away in her hand, locking Lucy within the small confines of the toilet. Secondly, the fire alarm in the coffee shop sounded, a commotion filtering through to where she was stood. "Shit!" she exclaimed, trying to fit the lock onto the bolt that would open the door. As she exerted pressure on the bolt, the handle on the other side of the door fell off, clanking on the tiled floor. "Fuck!" Lucy called out, a sense of panic spreading over her as she thought of Lottie, who was only a few feet away. "Lottie. Can you hear me?"

"Yes, Mummy. What's the noise for?"

"It's the fire alarm." She was about to continue, when she heard the door to the main area open. She banged on the door, a cold sweat peppering her brow as her anxiety ramped-up several notches. "Help! I'm stuck in here. Somebody get me out!" Lucy could hear customers moving chairs against the flooring, muffled voices filtering under the door. "HELP ME!" she screamed as she heard the outer door open.

"Hello?" a male voice replied.

"Thank God! Hello. I'm stuck in here. The handle came off. Can you get me out, please? Lottie, are you still there?"

"Yes, Mummy," her daughter replied, her voice almost drowned out by the fire alarm.

"Hang on," the male voice replied. Lucy heard a metallic sound followed a clunking noise as the man tried to fit the bolt and handle onto the door. "You need to line up your handle. Can you do that?"

"What's going on, Steve?" a female voice asked.

"Someone's locked in the toilet. Her daughter is here with her."

"I'll take the daughter outside while you try and open the door," the female voice responded firmly.

"No," Lucy shouted. "She stays here with me!" Tears began running down Lucy's cheek as sense of panic spread through her.

"I'll look after her," the woman responded calmly. "Steve, hurry up and get her out of there."

The man turned towards the broken lock as the first vestiges of smoke began seeping under the outer door. "Can you line up the handle?" Steve asked, his voice strained.

"Hang on," Lucy replied as she bent down to retrieve the discarded handle, her hands shaking. After a few minutes of trying to get it to fit, the door came open and she stumbled out into the small corridor, almost bumping into the man, a kind-looking fifty-something with thinning grey hair.

"Come on. We need to get out. There's a small fire in the kitchen."

"Thank you," Lucy replied, noticing the smoke as she tugged at the outer handle before striding across the deserted coffee shop. Through the glass, she could see a large group of people, standing by expectantly in the light drizzle. Within seconds, Lucy was amongst them. "Has anyone seen my daughter? Lottie! Lottie, it's Mummy. Where are you?"

Customers started looking around themselves as Lucy bustled around them. "Lottie!" she shouted, tears beginning to form at the corners of her eyes. "Where are you? *LOTTIE*?"

Steve came to her side, calling the female who'd escorted Lottie outside. "Diane, where's the little girl?"

A middle-aged woman, a few inches shorter than Lucy, with a closely-cropped grey hair and steel-rimmed glasses, pointed behind her. "She's…" The little girl was not there.

"Lottie!" Lucy yelled, her panic levels increasing with every heartbeat.

"She was just there," Diane stated. "One of the customer's took a tumble. I told the girl to stand still. She can't have gone far?"

"How old is she?" a young woman asked.

"She's four. She's got blonde hair and a yellow coat."

Another woman pushed through the crowd towards Lucy. "I've just seen her. She was walking towards the car park with two boys."

"Where?" Lucy urged, grabbing the older woman's shoulder, the strength of her grip making the other woman wince slightly.

"That way?" she replied, pointing towards the motorway. "Only a few minutes ago?"

Lucy broke through the crowd of patrons as the fire alarm inside the coffee shop was cut off abruptly. "Lottie!" Lucy cried, a tumult of emotions running through her body. She approached a pay station, catching sight of yellow hair several hundred yards ahead. *That's her,* she thought, not wanting to cry out and potentially alert anyone who had abducted her. She'd recently watched a movie on TV, where a father had called after his son as he was being led away by a paedophile. The son had eventually been killed, the father's call making all the difference. She kept quiet, racing between parked cars as a red fire engine made its way into the retail park, its blue lights pulsing against the darkening skies above. *Where are you?* Her stomach was churning as she ran on towards the main dual-carriageway that led towards Birmingham and Castle Bromwich.

A few minutes before, the three figures came to the same stretch of road. "I want Mummy," Lottie stated matter-of-factly.

"Don't worry," Sean soothed, his vision swimming as he pulled her towards a steel flyover that spanned a dual-carriageway next to a disused rail yard. "We're taking you to her now."

"But she's in the shop," the little girl replied insistently. "I want Mummy."

"Sean," Luke said. "What are we doing?"

"Shut it," the older brother hissed. "You said she was the evil doll. She looks just like her." She'll probably slit our throats if we let her."

"I'm not a doll," Lottie countered. "I have lots of dollies at home."

"It's okay," Sean replied, taking another swig of vodka to dull the rising panic he now felt. "We have some dollies over there," the teenager pointing towards the rail yard. The brothers were unsteady on their feet, as they had consumed the second joint a few minutes before the girl had come walking out of the coffee shop with a throng of customers. Both brothers had seen the likeness to the doll from the horror movie, their addled minds twisting reality before they led her away.

"Sean. We're gonna get in trouble for this. If people find out we've taken her, the police will be after us and you've already been in trouble with them."

"Shut it. I know what I'm doing. No one knows we've got her." They came down the other side of the flyover as traffic still trundled past on the nearby motorway. A footpath led off in either direction, hugging the dual-carriageway that was devoid of traffic. "We need to get off the road. Someone will spot us any minute."

"I want my Mummy!" Lottie shrieked, trying to pull away from Sean's grip.

"Shut the fuck up!" he shouted, his piercing grey eyes glaring at her. Lottie flinched before the tears began. She wailed in his grip as a car appeared a few hundred yards away, its headlights fighting against the dreary afternoon. "In there," Sean barked, pointing towards a gap in the steel fencing that led to the disused rail yard. The brothers ducked through the hole, dragging the protesting four-year-old with them.

"Make her quiet, Sean," Luke hissed. "She's driving me mad." He placed his hand over her mouth to quieten her. Lottie responding by biting the boy's little finger until she broke the skin. "FUCK!" he screamed, yanking his hand away. "Little bastard," he hollered, inspecting the damaged finger. He kicked out at the little girl, catching her on the thigh, making Lottie cry out in pain.

"Come on," the older brother urged as he dragged Lottie through a chain-link fence. "This way." In front of them, rusted railway lines lay beneath tufted grass. An old boxcar stood off to one side, its windows smashed. A few yards past the lines, a small building site sat quietly underneath the motorway above, hundreds of concrete pillars filling their vista. The entrance gates were locked, signage warning of prosecution to any unauthorised visitors. "We can fit through there. Then we'll be out of sight."

Sean squeezed through the poorly-fitted gates, dragging Lottie with him. She went down, landing on all fours in a puddle, making her cries more intense and persistent. "Shut the fuck up, you little bitch," Sean spat as he dragged Lottie to her feet.

"You're not nice. My mummy will tell you off," the little girl replied defiantly, sticking her tongue out at the teenager before aiming a well-placed kick at his shin.

Something deep inside Sean snapped. He stepped forward and shoved the girl against an orange cement mixer. Lottie banged her head on the lip of the hopper, falling sideways, her skull bouncing off a concrete block. She lay there immobile as a trickle of crimson seeped into the grey breeze block underneath her blonde hair. "Not so tough now, are ya?"

"Sean. You've killed her," Luke blurted as he cradled his hand, staring down at the crumpled form, her yellow coat dirty and torn.

"She's not dead, bruv," Sean replied confidently.

"But you've hurt her. Her mum's probably looking for her right now. We need to get back home quickly. We're in enough trouble as it is. She could identify us. Like in the movies."

Sean was thinking as best he could with vodka and cannabis clouding his judgement. He had done many bad things over the past few years. Beating people up, stealing cars, breaking into houses and shoplifting were incidents that had already alerted the police and his school. This was a step up. And Sean knew it. *I'll end up in a young offenders' if anyone finds out what I've done,* he thought, as his eyes settled on a stack of broken white pallets. An idea quickly formed in his addled mind. "Luke. The pallets. Let's pile them on top of her."

"And then what?"

"We burn them. No one will find her after that. We'll be in the clear," Sean said, as he dropped a pallet next to the unconscious girl.

"Sean, you can't do that. That's murder!" the younger brother argued.

"No, it ain't. She fell over and banged her head. That cement mixer was leaking petrol," he replied, unscrewing the cap and toppling it over. Pink liquid sloshed out over the pallets, Lottie's coat becoming quickly sodden by the fuel. "We can leave the nub end of the joint that I've still got. Some druggie must have set fire to the pallets by accident, y'see? We'll be in the clear."

"We can't do this. She's just a baby!"

"If the law finds out what we've done, we'll both end up in borstal.

Do you want that? It's full of mean bastards. Not even your brother will be able to help you."

"Just hurry. The longer we stay out here, the more chance we'll get caught." Luke urged, his voice quivering with fear as he looked around himself. "My head hurts, Sean. My eyes feel funny."

"Stop fucking about, bruv. Come on!" They dragged the pallets towards the prone figure lying on the floor, positioning them above her like a makeshift bonfire. Sean pulled the lighter out of his jeans pocket, walking back over to the pile of wood as a scream echoed through the building site.

"*LOTTIE*!" Lucy screeched, scrambling through the gates. She ran towards the pile of pallets, pulling them off her before picking up her daughter. "What the fuck have you done to her?"

"Nothing," Sean stated. "We found her here."

"You fucking liar! I saw you both leading her away from the shops. I followed you. What the hell were you going to do to my daughter?" she bellowed, eyeing the lighter in Sean's hand.

"Nothing. We were just about to light a fire to keep her warm."

"Bullshit!" Lucy spat. "KEEP AWAY FROM HER!" She looked at both brothers, noticing the glazed expressions on their dirty faces. She placed the unconscious Lottie on a dry pallet, away from the rest, tears streaming down her face when she saw the blood on her fingers. "I'm calling the police." She fished her mobile out of her jacket pocket, the sleeve of the dark coat torn at the elbow. She dialled *999* as the brothers looked at each other, Luke beginning to cry. "Police please," Lucy urged as the call was connected.

Sean reacted, snatching the phone out of her hand. "You're not calling anyone," he spat, turning away from Lucy with the phone in his hand. He ended the call quickly, his hands shaking.

"Give me that back!" she shouted, trying to wrestle the phone from the teenager's grip. She grabbed a handful of ginger hair, yanking it towards her with force, making Sean wince in pain. He lashed out, back-handing Lucy across the face. She stumbled backwards, tripping over the pallets, her head connecting with a block of wood with a large nail protruding from it. The spike embedded itself just below her ear, her fingers splaying out in shock for a few seconds until she lay still, Lucy's left foot twitching on the wet ground.

"Someone's coming," Luke urged, as the noise of a vehicle could be heard close by.

"Let's get out of here," Sean replied, tossing the lighter on top of the pallets. The naked flame caught quickly, becoming a conflagration within seconds. The fire covered Lucy, melting her clothing, her dark hair disappearing as the flames consumed it ravenously. She lay there twitching, mercifully unconscious from the impact a few seconds before. Her life had already darkened to a blackened void before the fire did the rest. Lucy's life was snuffed out in seconds, her last instinct being to protect her daughter against her abductors.

The two boys scarpered out of the building site as a white van pulled up at the entrance. A rotund security guard bustled towards the gates, keys in his hand. He could see the flames but had no idea as to who or what lay in the middle of them. As he flung the gates open, he noticed a little girl in a yellow coat lying on a white pallet, the flames licking at her feet.

"Bloody hell," he blurted, lifting the girl into his arms, carrying her back to his van. He laid her out on the bench seat, placing his spare coat over her before heading back out to the fire. As he drew closer, his eyes widened in horror. Poking out of the flames were a pair of legs, the leather boots catching fire as he stood, frozen in horror. "Oh, my God!" he exclaimed, pulling his mobile out of his pocket. He knew that whoever was lying there was beyond hope. He stuttered and stumbled over his words as the call was connected to the emergency services. He blurted a garbled message, tears streaking his face, partly from the flames, but mostly from the gruesome scene that unfolding before him. "Someone's dead. She's on fire. Send someone quick!" He fell to his knees, vomiting onto the floor, the little girl forgotten as sirens began wailing in the distance.

5

AFGHANISTAN

Lieutenant Colonel Vince Trueman put the phone down, pinching the bridge of his nose with thumb and forefinger. He sat, staring at the green canvas wall in front of him, his face expressionless. In his late forties, with three days' beard growth and dark hair, Vince was an experienced soldier. He'd completed tours in the Balkans, Iraq and now two tours in Afghanistan. He'd seen it all, yet the phone call he'd just received brought tears to his eyes.

The flap in front of him opened and a tall, thin, middle-aged man in combat fatigues entered the small room. Brigadier Chris Sidaway caught the look in his Lieutenant Colonel's eyes, stopping in his tracks. "Vince. What's up? You look like you've seen a ghost."

Vince opened his drawer, pulling out a bottle of rum, along with two shot glasses. He unscrewed the cork, pouring two fingers of rum into each glass before handing one to Sidaway. "Just had a call from Whitehall. Sit down, Chris."

The Brigadier did so without questioning his subordinate. He'd served with Vince for five years. Even though he was the Lieutenant Colonel's superior, they talked like they were equals, such was Vince's presence and command. Chris considered the younger man a friend. One of his family. He could trust him with his life. "And?"

"Captain John Wilson's wife and daughter were attacked this afternoon in Birmingham. We don't know all the details yet, but the little girl is in intensive care. His wife, Lucy, is dead." He consumed the drink in one go, the burn in his throat feeling good. Feeling real.

"Good God!" Chris exclaimed before downing his rum. The two men sat there for a few moments, letting the gravity of the situation sink in. "Where is he now?"

"Out on manoeuvres," Vince replied, picking up the phone. "Hello. Where's Captain Wilson?" He listened to the reply, nodding his head. "Radio through. He's to return to base immediately. Tell them to head home." He replaced the receiver, pouring two more measures of rum. "I've seen some shit, Chris. We both have. We've seen some fucking horrors over the past ten years. Headless babies raped by tribal leaders. Soldiers blown to bits by RPGs. But I've never had to tell one of my own that their family back home had been murdered." A single tear escaped his eyes, dripping quickly into his dark beard.

"Do you want me to do it?" Sidaway replied gravely.

"It's okay, Chris. I should do it. Jesus! John's a good bloke, and a damn good soldier, too. His little girl is only four, for fucks sake! What the hell happened to them over there?"

"Who knows? I'm sure whoever did it will be rounded up soon."

"Rounded up then strung up, if I had my way. Four years old. Same age as my granddaughter, Mollie. If anyone laid a hand on her, I'd skin the bastards alive."

"Make sure he's taken care of. Whatever he needs. He's one of our own," Sidaway replied as he stood up. He turned, walking out of the makeshift office, his gait stiff. His shoulders sagging.

Vince sat there, looking at the picture on his desk. His daughter and granddaughter smiled back at him, carefree expressions beaming out of the framed picture. He poured one more glass of rum, downing the fiery liquid once more, hoping that it would prepare him for what lay ahead.

John crouched behind the bonnet of the vehicle as machine gun fire traced a line in the dirt next to his position. The sun was setting, the mountain passes and valleys quickly becoming shrouded in darkness as the ambush continued. They'd received a communication to return to base immediately. As their vehicle had rounded a bend in the road, they had come under a barrage of bullets from above. He looked over at Gittus; the younger man's face appeared clammy, almost grey. Blood seeped from a wound on his thigh, his fatigues darkening as he tried to bind it with his rifle strap.

"Stay there," John called. "It looks like a lone wolf, high up on the left-hand side." He looked around the vehicle, spotting Second Lieutenant Jones, who was hunkered down behind the vehicle's door. More bullets peppered their position, John edging around the Jackal MWMIK until he was next to the larger man.

"How shall we do this?" Jones sat as a stray bullet whizzed past his helmet. They both moved around towards the vehicle's bonnet, trying to get a fix on their target.

John looked at the terrain, noticing a small gulley to his left that disappeared into the sandstone wall. "Stay here. I'll head over there and flush him out. Don't be a hero. Return fire if you can. But make him think we're out of options." John readied himself, preparing to launch across the six-foot gap into the relative safety of the small gulley. "Return fire once he lays down a volley."

"Okay," Jones replied, his assault rifle held easily in his meaty hands. The windscreen of their vehicle shattered, splinters of glass covering the two men. Jones rose up, bringing his weapon to bear in one fluid motion, unleashing half a magazine at the unseen foe. As he ducked back down, John was gone, lost from sight. "Go get the bastard, Wilson," Jones shouted, as he looked over at his injured comrade.

Inside the gulley, John shouldered his SA80 assault rifle, traversing the confines as he edged towards a right turn. He flattened himself to the sandstone, his desert boots edging him closer to the turn. The narrow passageway was littered with objects. John screwed his nose up when he almost trod on a pile of human faeces. He skirted it carefully. There were discarded bottles and Coca-Cola cans, along with spent shells and the remains of cooking fires. He took a portable mirror stick out of his utility belt, extending it slowly. He angled it, enabling John to see the gulley ahead. It was deserted, rising slowly before veering left and out of sight. A few seconds later, he came around the bend, his rifle pointing ahead, his index finger resting lightly on the trigger. More gunfire erupted close by, followed by suppressing fire from Jones. *Keep them occupied, mate,* he thought as he rounded the bend.

His already elevated heartbeat ramped up a notch as he came to another right turn, the darkening sky above already littered with far-off stars. Close by, John could hear a male voice, slightly muffled. He edged closer, unclipping a grenade from his tactical vest as another voice announced itself. It was clearer than the first voice. It was also male, lighter than the other. *Possibly father and son,* John surmised as he rounded the corner. He crouched down, peeking around the next bend, spotting a gap in the sandstone wall to his right, along with several holes in the rock a few inches off the ground. He slid himself silently up dusty stone as more gunfire erupted beyond the wall. The tang of bullets hitting metal was unmistakable, John hoping that his brothers-in-arms were holding out.

John was tall, just over six feet. He looked at the divots in the rock, guessing that he could use them as a foothold to peek over the wall. It would only take a second to see what was on the other side. He slid his boot into the cleft, bracing his thigh for the push. Time seemed to slow down as his head came up over the summit. Two men were facing away from him, their crude rifles aiming down into the gorge. Both wore wearing Khetpartugs, a small, brightly coloured embroidered waistcoat popular amongst Pashtun men. John knew what he had to do. He pulled the pin from his grenade with his middle finger, holding the device close to his chest. He closed his eyes, working out how he would toss the grenade, factoring in the delay, remembering exactly where the enemy combatants were positioned. An image flashed through his mind. His daughter appeared, her blonde hair bobbing up and down as she bounced around on her bed. John smiled thinly, moving the image of his little girl out of his mind. There was business to take care of. Lives depending on it. He opened his eyes, his thumb moving away from the spoon, which came away, its spring ejecting it with a muted click. He caught the slither of metal, not wanting to make a noise as he moved around the improvised doorway, bowling the grenade underarm towards the Afghan men. He ducked back behind the wall, closing his eyes as a voice rang out.

"Yadawia!" John braced himself as the grenade detonated, the blast kicking him away from the wall. He switched his assault rifle to fully automatic, counting down from three, ready to make his move. He shot into the opening, surveying the carnage that greeted him. Both men were down, blood splattering the walls. He aimed, firing a short burst into both men's skulls. John kept his distance, wary of explosive vests and possible booby traps. Satisfied both combatants were dead, he made his way deliberately back to the vehicle, relaying a message to Jones to saddle up. Five minutes later, Gittus was loaded into the rear of the vehicle and John was behind the wheel with Jones manning the turret, scanning the gorge ahead for further attacks. None came. The soldiers arrived back at base as a full moon cast its silvery glow across the Afghan plateau. John started wondering, *why did they ask us to return to base immediately?* His answer would be waiting for him. An answer not even his worst nightmares had presented to him.

6

The fiery liquid inside Vince's bottle was quickly diminishing. He looked across at John, suddenly feeling very old and very small. His back ached; however, he put that to one side, staring across at the picture of utter desolation in front of him. "Take a drink, John," Vince said softly. "You're in shock. The rum will at least feel real."

John looked up at him, his eyes red-rimmed, his face streaked with tears. "Lucy."

"I know, mate. I have no words for you. No one has. Is there anyone that you want to call?" John looked about the makeshift office, his mind a tumult of random images. His wife flashed before him, a carefree smile on her face. It was followed by an image of her laid out on a slab, blue and cold. "John!" Vince repeated, unusually patient. "Do you want to call someone?"

John nodded. "Judy. Lucy's mother."

Vince pushed a pad across the table. "Write her number down. I will put you through." John tried to recall the number. It took a few seconds to remember it as his mind was elsewhere, locked somewhere between hell and a nightmare that he hoped to wake up from. He reached over and grabbed the shot glass, his fingers clumsy and awkward as he lifted the glass to his lips. He downed the rum, the burn in his throat the only thing that felt real in his life. "Here you go, mate. I will give you some space." Vince stood, patting John on the shoulder before leaving him alone.

"Hello?" a choked voice replied from almost five thousand miles away.

"Judy. It's John." His voice cracking with grief as he began sobbing.

"John." His mother-in-law on the other end of the line crumbled, racking sobs rendering her speechless for almost a minute. John cried too, searing pain spilling out, his vision blurred with tears. "They. Took. My. Girl," Judy blurted, her voice harsh and raw, her breathing laboured.

"W-what happened?" he stammered.

He waited for a few moments while his mother-in-law tried to compose herself. "Two youths snatched Lottie from the Fort. Lucy chased them."

"Snatched Lottie? Why? Oh God! Is she, okay?"

"No, John. I'm with her at the hospital. She's in intensive care."

John felt dizzy. His entire world had fallen apart within five minutes. His wife was dead, his daughter fighting for her life. "What did they do to her?" he asked, not really wanting the answer.

"We still don't know, John. She's suffered a head injury. The boys that did this have been arrested. I've been in touch with the police. I'll have to call them back in a bit to let them know that I've spoken to you. They tried to call you, but your phone was off. So, they found my number in Lucy's phone. Oh God, John!" she cried. "They killed my little girl!"

John placed his hand on the desk, preparing himself for the next question. "Judy, how did Lucy die?"

He waited whilst his mother-in-law tried to regain her composure. Through hacking sobs, she managed to answer him. "They burned her, John. They burned my baby." More sobs came through the receiver.

John closed his eyes, his whole body shaking. *Lucy. No, no, not my Lucy.* The phone receiver shook in his hand, his knuckles turning white as he gripped the green plastic tighter and tighter. "What hospital are you in?" John asked, his pulse throbbing in his temples, trying to hold it together.

"Heartlands Hospital. I'm outside Lottie's room. She looks so helpless, John. Christ! How could this happen? They were just out shopping."

He broke down, almost dropping the phone to the floor. He could hear Judy crying uncontrollably on the other end of the line, magnifying his pain. His vision was filled with Lucy. Her laugh, the way she looked at him. His mind was tearing itself apart. "What have the doctors said?"

"Not much yet. I am waiting for the doctor to arrive. We've only been here an hour or so and the doctor who initially saw her was only a locum. Another one is expected any minute."

"This is unbelievable," John replied, his voice hollow. "I only spoke to them last night. They were both so happy. And now, this." More tears fell, on both ends of the line.

"John, the doctor is here. I will call you back when I have an update."

"Send me a text and I will call you back, Judy."

"Okay, love. Will you be okay?"

"I don't know. I honestly don't know what to think or do. I will speak to my C.O. I need to come home."

"Yes. I think that Lottie will need her daddy. I'll text you. Love you, John. Stay strong."

"You too, Judy," John said before replacing the receiver. He sat there, staring at the floor for what seemed like hours until Vince popped his head around the tarpaulin.

"Can I come in?"

"Yes," John replied, his voice monotone.

Vince walked around the desk, sitting down heavily. He poured another rum, refilling John's glass. "I'm so sorry, John. I don't know what else to say. What news of your little girl?"

"She's in intensive care. Head injury. They killed my wife. Burned her body."

Vince looked into John's eyes, watching as the life ebbed out of him. "Jesus Christ!" He downed his rum, wiping his lips with the back of his hand. "What do you need?"

"I need to go home, sir."

"Yes. I know you do, mate. There's an A400M heading home in a few hours, via Frankfurt. I'll make the necessary calls to get you on it. Go and get your kit ready. And John, for what it's worth, I'm so sorry."

"Thank you, sir," he replied, rising on unsteady legs.

Vince walked around the desk, embracing his captain. "Anything you need, just let me know. You're family, after all."

John looked at Vince, swallowing down his tears. "Thank you, sir. I'll be in touch." He turned and walked out of the office.

Once he was alone, Vince walked over to his desk, picking up the phone receiver. He dialled a number from memory, waiting a few seconds until his daughter picked up the phone, half a world away.

"Dad?"

"Hello, love," Vince replied.

"What time is it there?"

"Just after ten. You all okay?"

"Yes, Dad," Angela Trueman responded. "Just cooking tea. Do you want to speak to Mollie?"

"Is she there?"

"Yes. Hang on." The line crackled as Angela called out to her daughter. "Mollie. Grandad's on the phone." Vince sat, staring straight ahead, the phone crackling once more.

"Hello, Grandad Vinny," his granddaughter chirped. Her voice was light, full of life.

Tears streamed down his face at the sound of her voice. "Hello, princess. Are you being good for Mummy?"

"Yes, Grandad. She's making me pizza for din-dins."

"Pizza! My favourite. What flavour?"

"What flavour, Mummy?" Vince heard his daughter in the background, answering cheerfully.

"Ham and pineapple, Grandad."

"I could," he changed his choice of words, in light of recent events, "demolish a pizza right now. Are you and Mummy sharing it?"

"No, Grandad. Mummy is having Sketti Bol-nese."

Vince smiled, his mood lightening ever so slightly. "Well, you enjoy your din-dins, princess. Can I speak to Mummy for a minute?"

"Okay, Grandad. Love you."

"Love you too, Mollie," Vince replied, swinging his boots onto his desk.

The phone crackled briefly before another voice came through. "You okay, Dad?"

Vince sighed. "I've been better. I've just had to tell one of my guys that his wife and daughter have been attacked in Birmingham."

"Shit, really! Hang on, I heard something on the radio earlier. Two yobs snatched a little girl and killed the mother. It's all over the news here. Jesus! Is that one of your guys?"

"Yes. He's heading home. It's rocked me sideways, love. I don't normally cry, but I've shed a few tonight."

"I bet you have. The world's going to shit!"

"You're not wrong." Vince paused. "Have you heard from your mother?" he asked tentatively, asking after his ex-wife out of courtesy rather than interest.

"She's okay. She popped round last week. Not seen much of her lately. She's got a new fella, apparently."

"Poor bastard!" Vince said playfully, burnt bodies forgotten momentarily.

"I agree with you. I know she's my mum, but she's hard work."

"Unlike me," he replied dryly.

"Well, you're always overseas, Dad. It would be nice if you were back home in Derby."

I know, sweetheart. I will be home soon. Anyway. I'd better let you go. Got a few things to do before I turn in. Love you both."

"We love you too, Dad. Stay safe."

"'Bye, sweetheart,"

"'Bye, Dad."

Vince ended the call, leaning back in his seat. He felt weary, wanting nothing more than a hot shower and his bunk. However, he had one more call to make. He needed another one of his family to return home. On a plane, bound for the UK.

7

Fourteen hours after boarding the plane in Kandahar, John touched down at RAF Brize Norton in the UK on a damp December day. He walked down the ramp, a large green pack slung over his shoulder. He walked like a man twenty years his senior. His chin had two days growth on it, his dark hair was unkempt. Twenty minutes after touching down, John was seated in the back of an unmarked saloon that took him quickly home. It was early afternoon as the UK countryside passed John by and the car ate up the motorway miles, dropping him at his house just over an hour later. The only conversation he had in the car was with his parents, who were expecting him home. John kept the call short and succinct, not wanting his emotions to boil over in the back of the car for the unknown driver to witness.

The driver popped the boot as John climbed out, and stayed in his seat as the captain hefted his pack onto his shoulder while two middle-aged people climbed out of a small hatchback a few yards away. The large saloon pulled away, heading away from John who turned to face his parents. His pack slipped to the ground, the soldier folding to his knees as his mother and father tried to embrace him.

"Oh John," his mother choked. "What have they done?" Margaret

Wilson buried her head in the crook of her son's neck as her husband tried to lift him off the pavement.

"Let's get inside, Son," Derek Wilson urged, his voice thick with emotion. Wintry winds blew across the quiet street in south Birmingham, assaulting what grey, wispy hair the older man had left. His ruddy complexion was streaked with tears as he hefted his son to his feet, pulling his wife with him. He embraced the younger man, sobbing openly as curtains began twitching nearby.

"They killed my Lucy," John croaked, almost toppling over his fallen pack. His mother picked it up off the wet slabs and walked with the two men towards the modest semi-detached house. A minute later, they were in the lounge as strengthening winds pummelled the double-glazing. John slumped onto the sofa, his head in his hands as his resolve deserted him completely. His mother pulled him sideways into her embrace and John went willingly. He was a tough soldier who had killed for Queen and country, yet he welcomed his mother's embrace as if he was a little boy whose favourite pet had just died.

Derek stood in the doorway, slipping off his leather loafers. "I'll put the kettle on. I don't know what else to do."

"Okay, love," Margaret said, seeing the pain etched on her husband's face. She turned her attention back to her son as her husband plodded silently into the hallway. "Oh, John. I don't know what to say," she blurted, stroking her son's dark, tufted hair. "I can't believe this is happening."

John sat up, his face a tear-streaked mess. "I need to get to the hospital, Mum. I need to see Lottie."

"Yes, love. We'll take you. As soon as we've drunk our tea. Do you want to take a quick shower and get changed?" she asked, eyeing his worn fatigues and desert boots.

"I'll go like this, Mum."

"Okay, love."

John looked around the lounge, seeing pictures of Lucy and Lottie on display. He forced himself to look at them, drinking in the sight of his family, even though it made him ache inside. "I need to call Judy," he said, rising stiffly from the sofa. He suddenly felt weary, the last few hours quickly catching up with him. He walked into the small conservatory, watching the bare trees in his back garden bowing under the increasing winds. Time seemed to slow down. He heard the kettle boil in the kitchen, followed by the clinking of teaspoons and the closing of the fridge door. A grey squirrel ran along the fence, furtively looking out for danger before disappearing into the conifers. He was home. But it didn't feel like a home to John. It felt like a brick shell, devoid of life and love.

He pulled his mobile phone out of his pocket, scrolling through his contacts until his mother-in-law's number appeared on the screen. He dialled, subconsciously holding his breath as the dial tone chirped in his ear. "Hi," he said, walking over to the bay window and peering out onto the bleak day. John listened for a few moments, nodding as his mother-in-law passed on information. "Okay. My phone's about to die. We'll be heading over in five minutes. Love you." He hung up the phone. As he walked out of the conservatory back to the dark sofa, his mother looked at him expectantly.

"Any news?"

"No change. She's still in intensive care," he replied, as his father walked in with three mugs of tea.

"Here you go, Son. Get that down you."

"Thanks, Dad," he said, before walking over to the rear window. He took a sip, leaning on the window ledge as he looked at his parents. "I still can't believe this is happening. I only spoke to her two days ago."

"We know, Son," Derek replied sadly, wanting nothing more than to gather his son in his arms and somehow take away his pain. He'd loved his daughter-in-law beyond words. They had a special relationship, where Derek would regularly rib Lucy on many a subject. His wife had loved her too, often defending her daughter-in-law's honour when her husband decided to poke innocent fun at her. It was all good-natured though, the three of them holding a special bond. A bond only outmatched by the one they had for Lottie. Derek looked at his son, the pain in his chest almost making him wince. He was proud of him, in ways that words simply could not quantify.

An only child, John had grown up in a happy home, the relationship with his parents as strong as the platinum band he wore on his left hand. He momentarily forgot his own pain, looking at his beloved parents, seeing the anguish and hurt that was washing over them. John took a swig of his tea, enjoying the burn as it hit the back of his throat. Walking over, he sat in between them, wrapping his arms around their shoulders. "I'm sorry," he said. "This must be tearing you both apart, too."

Derek broke down, falling sideways onto the arm of the settee, racking sobs escaping him. Margaret was there in a flash, pulling him into her arms. John watched, tears streaming down his face as his parents' lives fell apart before him. He did the only thing that came to mind, placing his hands on their shoulders as he cried with them, head bowed. They sat there, tears mingling as a police car sped past the front of the house, its siren wailing, blue light flickering throughout the lounge for a split second. John pulled himself to his feet, his heavy legs barely propelling him towards the bay window once more. The flashing lights diminished into the distance.

John watched the patrol car round a bend before being lost to sight. "Shall we go?"

"Yes," Margaret responded sombrely. "Lottie needs us."

"Are you okay, Dad?" John asked.

The older man wiped the tears from his eyes with a blue handkerchief, blowing his nose loudly. "Not really. But we have to be strong. For Lottie and Judy's sake. Come on. Let's go see them. And then let's find out what bastards did this."

8

They sat in the car in silence, Derek navigating his way through the busy Monday traffic. Christmas was approaching and shoppers were out in force, clogging up the streets of Birmingham. John sat in the passenger seat, his head leaning against the window as his mother took a seat behind him. He'd not been home in months and he could see changes as they made their way through Northfield. New shops appeared as people streamed in and out of them, bustling for position. A few pubs that John had visited over the years were now boarded up, their facades gently crumbling under leaden skies. They left Northfield, heading down the Bristol Road South towards Selly Oak. John had never liked the suburb, which lay next to Edgbaston to the north, Harborne and Stirchley to the east and west. He always felt it was too busy, barely able to cope with traffic. A prestigious university lay at the edge of the sprawling mass, hundreds of students walking up and down the main street that led towards the city centre. Derek flicked on his wipers as a gentle rain began to fall.

They cut across the city, driving towards Small Heath and Heartlands Hospital that lay a few miles further on. John looked at the clock in the centre of the dashboard. It was getting on for three and the skies above were beginning to darken as the plucky Ford Focus weaved its way in and out of traffic. The city seemed to change, with Asian people milling around shop doorways that displayed Halal meat and Islamic fashions. He rarely ventured to this part of the city, preferring the leafy south of the city, where he'd been born and raised. They pulled up at a barrier and Derek buzzed down his window to take the ticket before they eventually found themselves a tight parking space a few hundred yards from the main building.

They filed out of the car, bracing themselves against the harsh English weather as they made their way towards the Accident and Emergency entrance. Outside the double doors, a large group of white and Asian men stood smoking, kicking their heels as wives and partners sat with loved ones inside. As they squeezed past, John noticed a man with a camera who was standing a few yards away. He was older than John, possibly in his early forties, his large black coat offering protection against the elements. As the soldier turned back towards the entrance, the man snapped a few pictures, before heading around the rear of a parked ambulance.

"She's in ward fifteen," John stated, as he tried to get his bearings.

"There." Derek nudged his son with his elbow. John nodded, turning right, with his parents following a few steps behind. They walked for a few minutes, passing patients in gowns who were walking ponderously in the opposite direction. John felt uncomfortable. He'd never liked hospitals, hating the sterile environment with its white walls and clinical smell. His footsteps sounded loud on the blue linoleum flooring, the noise amplified by the stark surroundings. As they drew nearer to the ward, John noticed a policewoman stationed on the other side of the entrance doors, with her hat removed. He walked up to the intercom, pressing the button.

"Hello?" a crackly voice squawked through a speaker on the wall.

"Hi. I'm here to see my daughter, Lottie Wilson," John replied, feeling emotions rising inside him. He was flanked by his parents, his mother's hand resting on his shoulder.

"Come through," the voice replied, before the door released its magnetic lock.

John pulled the door open, walking past the policewoman who

regarded him with a quizzical eye. "John!" Judy exclaimed, appearing out of a side room at the bottom of the corridor.

He went to her, his footsteps quickening until John embraced his mother-in-law. Tears fell and both of them sobbed in each other's arms as they were joined by his parents. They wrapped themselves around John and Judy, forming a tight circle that appeared unbreakable. After a minute, John pulled away, looking at the older woman. He'd always thought that his mother-in-law was an attractive woman. Her steel-grey hair was always immaculate, just reaching Judy's shoulders. She was much shorter than her daughter, just cresting the five-foot mark, with a curvy figure. She was approaching fifty, but John could see that the last twenty-four hours had aged her. There were dark smudges under her eyes and her face was devoid of makeup. She looked exhausted, both physically and mentally.

"How is she?" he asked, dreading the answer.

"No change, love. She's still unconscious. The doctor will be checking in on her shortly. I told the nurses that you were on your way." She looked at Margaret and Derek, fresh tears forming in her eyes.

"Come here, love," Margaret urged, embracing the other woman. Judy began sobbing, causing hospital staff and the policewoman to turn around.

"They took my girl," she rasped, her voice cracking.

"I'm so sorry. I don't know what else to say." They stood there, mothers and grandmothers alike, joined in grief. The two men stood near them, feeling empty and lost. Derek watched as his son walked towards the open doorway, wanting to go with him, but sensing that he needed to let his son do this on his own terms.

John walked into the room. A rhythmic beeping was the only noise. As he walked around the curtain, he saw his daughter for the first time in months. She looked so small and defenceless to John, her blonde hair mostly hidden under a bandage that was tightly wrapped around her skull. There were wires leading from her hands to machines next to the bed, but her heartbeat was steady, to John's relief.

"Oh, princess," he blurted, dropping to his knees next to her. He gently lifted her hand into his, kissing it with dry lips and prickly whiskers. "What have they done to you?" He pulled a chair up, seating himself before resting his head on the bed next to his daughter. He held her hand once more, rubbing his thumb gently over Lottie's palm, something he used to do when she was a baby to help her sleep after her milk.

He heard footsteps behind him as his family filed into the small room. "Oh, Lottie," Margaret cried, walking around the other side of the bed. She leaned against the window frame, resolve ebbing away from her as she sobbed openly. Derek held her tightly as Judy stood next to John, placing a comforting hand on his shoulder.

"Mr Wilson?" a voice said from the doorway. They all looked towards the exit as a young Asian doctor entered the room.

John stood up, walking over to the approaching man. He extended his hand and the doctor took it readily. "Hi."

"I'm Doctor Ahmed," the man stated, his kind expression putting John at ease somewhat.

"Is she going to be okay?" John asked, bracing himself for the answer.

"Yes. She sustained quite a nasty bump to the head. She also has mild hypothermia, but we are confident that she will make a full recovery. There is some swelling on the brain, which is common for this type of injury," he continued. "We'll keep her in for a few days to monitor her." The doctor walked towards the end of the bed, checking the notes on the metal clipboard that hung there. He pulled a pen from his breast pocket, making a few tuts and nods before placing it back on the metal frame.

"Please make her better," Margaret pleaded, as she clung to her husband.

The doctor nodded at her, turning back to John. "I am very sorry for what happened to your wife, Mr Wilson. I believe there is an officer outside who would like to speak to you. I will be back in a few hours. You look exhausted. You should ensure that you rest up, too, you've had a traumatic episode."

"Thank you, Doctor. I'll be okay."

The Asian man looked into John's eyes, seeing the desolation that emanated from them. He also saw the resolve that was holding the young soldier together. "I'll check back in a few hours," he replied, before leaving them with Lottie.

Margaret took a few paces forward, leaning over to kiss her granddaughter on the head. "Wake up, princess. We need you back."

"Who wants a coffee?" Derek said matter-of-factly.

John looked at him and smiled. His father had always been a steady ship, pragmatic in every situation. He knew that his father was hurting, the grief evident on his weathered face. But he also knew that his father was old school, believing that a cup of coffee and a sandwich were needed when times were tough. "Please, Dad. Could you grab me a sandwich, too? I've not eaten in about twenty-four hours."

"Okay. Love, do you want anything?"

Margaret shook her head. "I'm okay at the moment," she replied, her eyes focused on her granddaughter.

"Judy. Anything for you?"

"I'll come with you. I need to use the ladies and stretch my legs." The two of them walked out of the room, leaving John and his mother in silence save for the beeping of the machine above Lottie's bed. Margaret pulled up a chair at the end of the bed, resting her hand on the fitted sheets.

John plugged his mobile phone into his charger, finding a power point in the corner of the room before sitting back down. Mother and son sat there, lost in their own thoughts until a slight movement underneath the sheets made John look up.

"Daddy?" Lottie asked groggily.

John moved quickly up the bed, embracing his only child, fresh tears wetting the pillow next to his daughter's head. "Oh, princess," he choked. "I'm so glad you're awake." He buried his head into the pillow, inhaling his daughter's scent.

Margaret joined him, weeping openly. "Oh, Lottie," she cried. "We're all here with you."

"Where's Mummy?" the little girl asked. "Where am I, Daddy?"

John moved back slightly, sitting on the bed, holding his daughter's hand. "You're in the hospital, princess. Do you remember anything?"

Her expression clouded for a few moments, then her body started to shake as memories began flooding back. "Daddy, two nasty boys took me away. They hurt me, Daddy."

"I know, Lottie. The police have arrested them."

"Are they in jail?" she asked, her blue eyes focusing on her father.

"Yes, princess. They'll not be hurting anyone again."

"Where's Mummy?" she asked impatiently, looking beyond John around the room.

John looked at his mother, not really knowing what to say. She squeezed his hand, nodding slowly. "Lottie," he began his voice trembling. "The nasty boys who took you hurt Mummy as well. She was trying to protect you from them."

"So, where is she?" she asked, her eyes pleading.

"They hurt Mummy really badly, Lottie. Sometimes when a person gets hurt, they do not get better."

A stray tear fell from Lottie's eye, trickling down her cheek. "I want Mummy."

"I know you do. We all do. But Mummy has gone up to the stars. I'm so sorry, princess." The little girl's eyes filled with tears, breaking John completely. He leant forward and held her as her little hands snaked around his neck. Lottie squeezed her father with all her strength, her body shaking as she cried. Her breathing became ragged as John stroked the top of her head in a vain attempt to comfort her.

"I want Mummy," she sobbed.

"We all do, princess," he said, feeling utterly beaten.

A nurse appeared in the doorway, walking briskly over to the bed. "Hello, Lottie. I'm Angie. Nice to see you're awake." She turned to John, seeing the expression on his face. "I just need to check her over. You can stay if you want. There is a policewoman on the ward who I think would like to speak to you."

"Okay. I will leave you to it for a minute." He bent down, looking into his daughter's eyes. "Daddy just needs to speak to someone, princess. Nanny Margaret will stay here with you while the nurse makes sure that you're okay."

"Don't go, Daddy," she pleaded, her face streaked with tears, her arms outstretched.

"I'll just be outside the door. You'll still be able to see me."

The little girl nodded reluctantly as the nurse took her hand, checking her pulse. Nodding at his mother, John walked out into the main ward. The policewoman rose from her chair and walked over to him. She was roughly John's age, tall for a woman, with dark curly hair, tied into a ponytail.

"Mr Wilson?"

"Yes," he replied, peering back at his daughter.

"I'm Constable Walker. Are you okay to talk?"

"Yes. The nurse is just checking on Lottie. What happened?"

"We cannot discuss everything here, as I'm sure you can appreciate. Lottie was abducted by two youths, who led her away to a building site a few hundred yards away from the Fort shopping park. I have no information on the suspects, or their motives. Your wife managed to track them down, where some kind of altercation took place." The officer paused, aware of how the next few sentences would affect the man in army fatigues who stood in front of her. "Your wife was assaulted, before being set on fire by the youths. I'm very sorry, Mr Wilson. Truly I am. My colleague, Detective Inspector Blaney, would like to speak to you as soon as possible."

John let out a sigh. "Okay. Where?"

Constable Walker was about to reply when Judy and Derek returned from the café. Realising that their granddaughter was awake, they bustled past, placing coffee cups and sandwiches on the windowsill before crowding around the bed. John could hear them crying, ramping his own emotions back up a notch.

The officer smiled, letting him have a moment. "We could either do it at the station, or Inspector Blaney could come to you. Do you live far?"

"Longbridge, just by the Rover plant."

"Could you write your details out for me, please?" she asked, handing him a pen and pad. He did so, then handed the items back. A few seconds later, voices drifted out from Lottie's room. "Thank you. Inspector Blaney will be in touch at some point today, Mr Wilson. And I'm very sorry for your loss."

"Thank you," John replied, wanting to be back next to his daughter. He turned and walked back towards the bed just as the nurse was finishing up her brief examination.

"Her sight is a little blurry, which is common with head injuries. The doctor will be back shortly to assess Lottie," she stated, her tone neutral.

"Thank you," John replied, looking over at his daughter who was now seated on her grandad's lap. "Hey, princess," he said. She opened her arms towards him as John walked around the bed to swap places with his father.

"Daddy, where is my Iggle Piggle and Upsy Daisy? We had them at the shops."

"I don't know, princess. Mummy may have put them in the car." He looked at Judy. "Where are Lucy's things?"

The mere mention of his wife's name brought tears to his and Judy's eyes. "I don't know, love. I would imagine that the police will have them."

John turned, noticing that the policewoman had left the ward. "Shit. I guess I'll have to wait until they contact me."

"There's no rush, Son," Derek whispered. "It will all work itself out."

"I just don't know how it will, Dad," John responded, visions of his wife flooding his mind. He needed answers. And fast.

9

Detective Inspector Martin Blaney stopped the tape, placing his pen on the desk. He rubbed his eyes, suddenly feeling all of his fifty-one years. He'd been a police officer for thirty years, working his way up through the ranks of the West Midlands Police Force. For the last fifteen years, he'd worked his way up from pounding the beat as a local bobby before being drafted into the CID branch of the force. His reputation was steady, if not spectacular, solving a few high-profile cases in his early years as a detective, before attaining the rank of Detective Inspector a few years later. Now, as he'd recently crested the half-century milestone, he was starting to feel the miles on the clock. He was on his second marriage, two children from his first still eating into his pockets even though they were now adults. His second marriage had yielded two more children, now in secondary education. His wife, a former police constable, now stayed at home to look after domestic matters. It worked for them, even if things were now simply ticking over, the initial fireworks of romance now extinguished amid school runs and long hours.

He looked into his coffee cup, sighing when he saw the white porcelain bottom staring back at him. "I'll get you a refill," Detective Sergeant Jenn Shaw said, scooping the mug from the table.

"Make it a strong one," he replied. "I'm running on empty."

"I know the feeling," she agreed, exiting the office. He looked out of the office window, looking at the dreary expanse of Birmingham's city centre. Lloyd House was the headquarters of the force, sitting at the end of Colmore Row. Half a mile to the north, the famous Jewellery Quarter lay, its many outlets offering gold, diamonds and hope. He knew it well, having bought two lots of rings over the past twenty years, much to the annoyance of his bank balance. He looked at the two mugshots on the wall, still unable to comprehend the crime that had just been committed just a few miles to the north.

"Jesus," he breathed. *Such a waste of life*. He walked over to the board, the staring eyes of the two brothers following his every move. He stood, looking at them, trying to glean something – anything – from the expressions looking back at him. The younger brother offered no clues. *He looks shit scared,* Blaney thought, as he picked at a piece of loose skin from his thumb. His eyes fell on Sean and the detective nodded to himself. The youth's file was on his desk, with enough content to tell the detective that he was looking at a bad apple. The teenager's expression was neutral, with just a hint of something that Blaney had seen over the years from various perps. Defiance. *You're in a world of trouble, young man,* he thought as Shaw walked back into the office, handing her superior a steaming mug of black coffee. "Thanks," he said, enjoying the heady aroma that wafted upwards.

"When will we contact the husband?" Shaw asked, standing shoulder to shoulder with Blaney, almost matching his height.

"In the next hour. He's just arrived at the hospital, so I will give him a bit of time to take everything in. Poor guy. Fighting the Taliban should be enough hell for anyone's lifetime. Now he has to deal with the loss of his wife and the attack on his little girl."

Shaw blew out a breath. In her mid-thirties, Jenn had a young daughter of her own. The thought of anyone trying to harm her made her stomach churn. "He looks like a right piece of work," she stated, indicating Sean.

"Yes, he does," Blaney replied. "I spoke to Bob Jones at Erdington station. Sean Terry is a real little shit, with a fairly lengthy record. Luke has never been in trouble, and I'm guessing that he'd tagged along for the ride. We need to speak to their mother, Mandy. But we'll give it a few hours. You saw the commotion she caused when they dragged her in. The amount of Class A drugs found at the house should put her away for a fairly decent stretch." He took a sip of his coffee, his shoulders sagging. "What kind of mother leaves skunk lying around the house? That would have undoubtedly contributed to the brothers acting the way they did, especially as it was mixed with vodka. Fuck! What a mess."

Jenn nodded before taking a sip of her coffee. "So, when do we speak to them again, guv?"

"Probably in the morning. You saw the shitstorm that we walked into yesterday. Lawyers and psychiatrists were already assembled before we even got there. This is going to get messy, especially as the youngest is so young. His identity will have to be kept from the public eye, Sean's too, as the link will be made in no time if we name him."

Jenn nodded, her eyes resting on a photograph of the crime scene. "Poor woman. Not exactly the way I would want to go."

"Tell me about it. I'm not looking forward to speaking to the husband."

"What did you think of the interview tapes?" Shaw asked, her tone sombre.

Blaney leaned back in his chair, looking at the ceiling while he tried to sum up the past hour's recording. They had both sat in silence, listening to the sequence of events as told by both brothers. "In truth, Jenn, harrowing. I've seen some pretty awful things in my time, but nothing comes close to that. The way that Luke broke down, the realisation of what they'd done. That will stay with me for life."

"I know, guv. It's an open and shut case. Even though Sean tried to state that he was defending himself, Luke was pretty black and white. His version of events was clear enough, despite the emotions."

"Yes. They snatched the girl, then killed the mother when she intervened. It's pretty conclusive, but people will want to know why they did it. Throw in a broken home, a prostitute for a mother and a large helping of cannabis and vodka and you have your answer."

Jenn took a sip of her coffee, her eyes never leaving the incident board. "Why didn't Social Services flag this up? Surely the Terry family was on their radar?"

"Probably not," Blaney replied, placing his mug on the table. "I'm sure that both brothers attend school regularly. Apart from Mandy and Sean's records, they have pretty much stayed off the grid. It's a bit like when some crazed kid in the States walks into a school and guns down their classmates. No previous convictions, no history of mental illness or troubles at school. It just happens. And it's harder to spot than a young Muslim chap who's been radicalised at the local mosque, who suddenly drops onto our desk. You can plan for that. This." He paused. "This is almost impossible to detect or stop."

"Jesus," Jenn replied. "Poor guy. I have no idea what he's going through right now."

"Well, we need to find out. Come on. Let's get some fresh air," Blaney urged, reaching for his jacket.

They climbed into the unmarked police car, pulling out of the car park, joining the traffic. The sun was almost on the horizon as they threaded their way from the city centre towards Bordesley Green, Blaney flicking on the car's headlights as they saw the hospital a half a mile ahead. They found a place to park on a busy road behind Heartlands hospital, walking briskly as the first drops of rain began falling from the leaden sky above. They knew their way around the hospital, subconsciously walking towards the children wards. Blaney stopped at the reception desk, flashing his warrant card at the nurse on duty. After a brief exchange, they were given directions to Lottie Wilson's room. They plodded along the ward, making a few turns before they came to the end of a short corridor. There were two rooms, one on the right that was in darkness and one on the left that was full of people. Blaney and Shaw stood for a moment, watching as four adults crowded around the bed next to the window.

Blaney knocked on the door as a tall man in army fatigues turned around. "Mr Wilson?"

"Yes," John replied, walking towards them.

"I'm DI Blaney. This is DS Shaw. We're from West Midlands Police."

"Oh. Hi," John replied.

"I know this is a very difficult time for you, but could you spare us a few minutes?"

"I guess so," John said, looking back at his family. They looked over, unsure of what to do. "They're police officers. Are you okay to stay with Lottie for a bit?"

"Of course, Son," Derek replied. "Take as long as you need."

John nodded, turning towards Blaney and Shaw. "Shall we get a coffee and sit down?"

"That works for us," Blaney replied, turning towards the corridor.

They walked in silence, the few hundred yards to the café seeming to take forever. As they arrived, Jenn took the order, signalling for the two men to find a table. They did so, in a quiet corner away from anxious relatives and grieving loved ones. The two men sat there people-watching until Shaw arrived back with three large coffees. She placed them in front of the men, both of whom nodded their thanks as she pulled a small pad and pen out of her inside pocket.

"I just want to offer our condolences, Mr Wilson. We are truly sorry for what has happened to your wife and daughter."

John played with the handle on his mug, unsure of what to say. He blew out a breath, looking at both officers in turn. "So, what happens now?"

Blaney took control, Shaw letting her superior paint a picture of the next few days and weeks. "Both brothers have been arrested and charged with murder. They are local boys who live in Erdington with their mother. When we brought them in, both were under the influence of drugs and alcohol, which we were informed came from the mother, although not with her consent. She, too, has been arrested after we raided her house a few hours later. We discovered significant amounts of Class A and Class B drugs inside the property, which is enough to send the mother down for a considerable stretch."

"What are their names?" Wilson asked, his face reddening.

"I'm afraid we cannot name them, Mr Wilson. They are minors, aged below sixteen. Their identity will have to be protected during any trial that they face."

"That's bollocks!" John retorted, drawing a few glances from nearby patrons.

"I'm sorry, Mr Wilson, but that is the law. Their mother's identity can be shared, however it will not be linked to the murder, for obvious reasons."

John looked into his coffee cup, a tumult of thoughts washing over him. "When was the last time you spoke to your wife and daughter?" Shaw asked.

"A few days ago. I've been in Afghanistan for a few months. I spoke to them on Skype. I was due to call them again tonight."

"Did everything seem okay?" Shaw asked.

"Yes. Perfectly normal. They were going shopping at The Fort."

Both detectives nodded. Shaw made notes in her pad.

"We'll need you to formally identify your wife's body, Mr Wilson. I know that will be the most difficult thing you have ever done. But it has to be done, sooner rather than later."

John nodded. "When?"

"Today, if possible. Your wife's body is here."

Tears formed at the corners of his eyes. He swallowed hard, nodding once more. "Okay. I guess it has to be done. I cannot believe this is happening. My Lucy. Dead!"

"We're really sorry. We will do everything we can to ensure that her killers are convicted."

"Is that really justice?" John countered, his knuckles whitening as he gripped his mug.

"We understand that no sentence, however long, can assuage the pain that you and your family are feeling," Blaney soothed. "We can arrange for some counselling, Mr Wilson. It will help you come to terms with what has just taken place."

"Call me John. And I don't need counselling. I need to get through this. Somehow?"

"Well, the offer is there, John," Shaw replied before taking another sip of her coffee.

"How could this happen?"

"Truth is, John, we just don't know. Violent crimes are rare, especially ones like this. It's not something that you can plan to stop."

John finished his coffee, taking a deep breath. "Okay. I think I need to identify Lucy's body now."

"Are you sure you're ready for this?" Shaw asked tentatively.

"No. But I'd rather get it done and out of the way."

"Okay," Blaney said, draining his coffee. "Let's go."

They stood up, heading out of the café. Blaney led the way, his footsteps echoing off the walls. Shaw and John walked a few paces behind him. *You can do this,* John thought. *You have to do this.* Try as he might to convince himself that he could handle what was about to happen, his hands began shaking the closer they got to their destination. *Hold it together,* he told himself, before visions of Lucy flooded his mind, the ashes of his resolve blowing away on the wind.

10

John sat down in a bland room outside the hospital mortuary. DS Shaw sat next to him as Blaney walked into the room beyond the double doors to speak to the mortician. The soldier's breathing was shallow, his brow and hands clammy, despite the cool temperature. He thought back to his last conversation with Lucy, remembering that she was talking about booking a holiday for the three of them. He imagined Lottie splashing around in the pool as his wife lay sprawled on a sun lounger, a happy expression on her tanned face. He blew out a breath, staring at the tiled floor.

"Are you sure you're able to do this?" Shaw asked.

"I have to. As hard as it's going to be, at least I can finally believe it. At the moment, it all seems like some twisted nightmare that I'm hoping to wake up from."

Shaw placed a hand on his shoulder. "We'll be right with you. Unless you'd rather be alone?"

"I'd rather you were with me. I cannot do this on my own."

"Okay," she replied calmly as the door opened. Blaney walked towards them, his face sombre. They stood, John's legs feeling rubbery.

"I've spoken to the mortician. We're ready when you are. Once you have confirmed your wife's identity, the coroner will perform an autopsy to confirm the cause of death. Do you understand what I've just told you, John?"

"Yes."

"Okay. If you'd rather not do this now, we can come back later, or tomorrow?"

"I'll be okay."

"All right. Let's go," Blaney replied. They walked through the doors, Shaw's hand on John's shoulder. A tall man with sloping shoulders stood next to a rectangular metal table in the centre of the room. The rest of the enclosed space was dim, a single light above the table casting its glow across the morgue.

"Mr Wilson," the man stated. "You may find this distressing. Because of the nature of the injuries your wife sustained, you will not be able to identify her, due to the extensive burns that cover her head and upper body. However, there is a small tattoo on the body's left ankle. Did your wife have a tattoo on her ankle?"

"Yes," John replied, his voice quivering. "A seahorse." The man nodded, removing the sheet over Lucy's lower body. John looked down, his breath catching in his throat. On the pale ankle, a blue seahorse was clearly visible on the grey-coloured skin.

"*Nooooo*," he cried, grabbing the table with both hands. He wept, the noise harsh in the low-slung room. John's arms shook, his knuckles whitening as he squeezed the chromium ledge, his head bowed. "Lucy!" he croaked. "I'm so sorry, babe." He took a step towards his wife's head, placing a kiss on top of the sheet. "I love you, Lucy," he whispered as more tears fell.

The mortician placed the cover back over the lower body, nodding to Blaney. "Thank you, Mr Wilson. I am very sorry for your loss."

They led John back out into the ante-room, guiding him over to the chairs. He sat down heavily, sobbing uncontrollably. The officers sat with him, letting his grief and pain pour out. After a few minutes, John stood up, pacing the room. "So, what happens now?"

Blaney remained seated as he addressed him. "The coroner will perform his autopsy and after that, you will need to make arrangements for your wife's funeral. The funeral directors will contact the hospital to arrange the transfer of the body."

"And the suspects?" John asked, the mention of the word *body* forming a knot in his stomach.

"They will appear in court in a few days' time for an initial hearing. The court case could drag on for a few months, due to the nature of the crime. Even though we believe that we have the perpetrators, there will be a case for the defence which could get messy as the suspects are minors. It will be all over the news, John. You'll need to prepare for that. There will be examination and cross-examination. It will be in the papers and on local radio. It will be tough."

"So, what do I do?"

Blaney looked at him, feeling the younger man's pain. In all the years he'd been dealing with crimes of this nature, it never got easier. It was wearing him down. "Be with your family. They will need you, and you'll need them. Hopefully, your daughter will be out of hospital in a few days, John."

John blew out a long breath, leaning against the white wall behind him. "I killed two men a few days ago." Shaw and Blaney exchanged glances before focusing back on the soldier. "We'd just gotten the call to return to base. We were a few miles from Camp Bastion when we were ambushed inside a tight ravine. One of our team was hit, high up in the thigh. We managed to exit the Jackal, returning fire. If we'd not acted quickly, Gittus would have probably bled out. I managed to enter a series of walkways, finding the two combatants perched above our position. I threw a grenade into their hideout, killing them both. They looked like they could be father and son, and yet I killed them without thought. It was us or them. But that is different, right? We're at war."

"But it doesn't make it any easier when the dust settles," Blaney replied.

"No. Those was my first confirmed kills and it will stay with me for life. I wonder if my wife's killers will feel the same? I'm guessing they won't, as they won't see the pain and suffering that we'll all endure."

"Probably best not to think about it," DS Shaw replied. "I know that's easier said than done, John."

"How can I not think about it? My wife is dead! She never hurt anyone. She was kind and loving, a wonderful mother. Now I'll have to bring up our daughter without her, all because two psychotic bastards decided to murder her." He slid down the wall, burying his face in his hands as he wept. The police officers looked at him, unable to give comfort. They both knew that the soldier was in his darkest hour. And that the hour could well last a lifetime.

They walked back, Shaw and Blaney a few steps behind John, whose feet seemed to drag along the blue flooring. After a few minutes, they entered the ward, the officers waiting outside as the man in army fatigues collapsed into his father's arms. "Son? What's happened?"

John wept, clinging onto his dad as his legs began failing him. Derek walked him towards the bed, seating him next to his daughter. "Lucy," he croaked. "I've just identified her."

Judy and Margaret, gasped, tears spilling as they began wailing, the realisation hitting them both like a killing blow. Judy grasped the windowsill, doubling over as she called her daughter's name. "Lucy!" she sobbed. Margaret pulled her upright and embraced her. Blaney and Shaw looked on, seemingly detached from the scene. Inside, though, they were both screaming at the injustice of it all.

"Daddy," Lottie started. "Is Mummy not coming home?"

John went to her, lifting his daughter into his arms. "I'm sorry, princess. Mummy is not coming home."

"But... but I want Mummy home, Daddy. It's nearly Christmas and Mummy said I could decorate the tree with her. We made a fairy to go on top of it." The little girl looked at her grandparents, seeing the pain yet not fully understanding the gravity of what had happened.

"Daddy will help you with the tree, Lottie. I promise."

"I want Mummy, Daddy," she cried, sniffing back the tears.

John held her, feeling totally empty. He looked across at the police officers, noticing that Shaw was wiping tears from her eyes. The older officer turned to her, pointing to a set of plastic chairs. John watched as they both sat down heavily. He closed his eyes tightly, inhaling his daughter's smell, hoping that when he opened them, he'd wake from this twisted nightmare.

11

Twenty-four hours later, Blaney and Shaw sat down in an interview room with Mandy Terry. A duty solicitor sat next to her, peering at the two officers through her steel-rimmed glasses. The young woman had a defiant expression on her face, letting the two detectives know that they were not in for an easy encounter.

"Interview started at fourteen-thirty hours on Tuesday 8th December 2005. Present in the room are DI Blaney, DS Shaw, Mandy Terry and duty solicitor Karen Martin." Blaney looked at Terry, who stared back at him, her eyes red-rimmed. He wondered whether it was due to lack of sleep or tears.

"So, Miss Terry. You're aware of the charges that your two sons are facing. When interviewed, they stated that they had taken a bottle of vodka, along with two roll-ups that we have confirmed contained cannabis. After your sons were arrested, we gained access to your property where we found a large consignment of Class A and Class B drugs."

Mandy looked at Blaney, her eyes boring into his. She let the seconds tick away, trying to hold her composure. "No comment."

"A large amount of controlled drugs were recovered from your property, Miss Terry. Whether you say 'no comment' or not, it does not detract from the fact that you were in possession of them."

Mandy stared at the desk; her mind overloaded with possible outcomes. She knew she was banged-to-rights. After a few seconds, she raised her eyes to Blaney. "Never had any drugs in my house. Someone must have planted them there." Mandy looked sideways at her solicitor, who stared blankly back at her.

"I see," replied Shaw. "Someone just so happened to plant them in a black suitcase, in a wardrobe inside your bedroom. How could someone have done that without you knowing about it?"

"No idea, love," she sneered. "Maybe one of my boys put them there when I was not looking?"

"Why would they place them in your room?" Blaney asked. "Surely, if one of your sons had a large amount of drugs, would they not want to keep them hidden from you? Placing them inside your room does not strike me as a good place to hide them."

Silence descended over the interview room, as the woman stared at the drab ceiling. "No comment," was the brief reply.

"Both your sons stated that before they left the house, you had a visitor. Could you confirm that?"

"No comment," she replied, looking towards the solicitor, who remained silent.

"Sean told us that the visitor's name was Jerome. Could this perhaps be Jerome Marshall?"

Mandy stiffened in her chair, the mention of her visitor's name appearing to unsettle her. *Shit, Sean! You fucking blabber mouth.* "No comment."

The senior detective let the words sink in, watching the woman across the table as the seconds ticked away. "We know of Mr Marshall, Miss Terry. He's been in and out of prison over the past few years, mainly drug offences and ABH. Were the drugs we found his?"

"No comment," she replied, scratching the back of her neck.

She looks scared, Blaney thought, decided to press his advantage. "Miss Terry. You're looking at several years in prison for possession of Class A drugs. The amount found could suggest that you were supplying them, which can carry a life sentence."

The words hit home. *Life in prison.* She felt a sinking feeling in her stomach as her emotions started to simmer. "I don't know anything about them," Mandy hissed, becoming more agitated as she chewed her thumbnail.

"Well, here's the thing," Shaw countered. "We've found two sets of identifiable prints on the packaging. One belonging to you, the other to Jerome Marshall." The duty solicitor looked at Terry, unable to come to her client's defence. She'd been called in at short notice and was more used to domestic violence cases. This was a whole new level.

Mandy started crying, her sobs loud in the small room. The detectives looked on, knowing it was only a matter of time. After a minute, red-rimmed eyes stared back at them. "I was just holding them for Jerome. Honestly, I didn't know that they were Class A. He told me that it was just skunk."

Both officers wrote down notes in their respective pads. They both knew that the packaging was brown paper, which had been unopened. *She could be telling the truth on that score,* Blaney thought, deciding to try a different tack. "Well, the ball's in your court, Mandy. If you could confirm that you were merely holding them for Mr Marshall, your sentence could be reduced, especially if you were unaware of the exact contents. You might get three years, out in two. Sounds a lot better than fifteen, doesn't it?"

She pondered his words for a moment. Two years. Prison for two years. Or life. Think, Mandy. Think. "Okay. I was holding them for Jerome."

"Thank you, Miss Terry," Blaney replied. "Interview terminated at," he checked the clock on the wall, "fourteen forty-one." He stopped the tape, looking at Mandy. "You'll be remanded into custody, before your court appearance."

"What about my boys?" she asked, her voice wavering.

"They have been charged with murder, Miss Terry. They will appear at Birmingham Magistrates Court in three days, where they will have their charges read out to them. From there, it will go to Crown Court for trial."

"They're just kids!"

"Kids who attacked a small child and murdered her mother."

"So the pigs say!" The solicitor placed her hand on Mandy's arm in an attempt to stop an escalation.

"Your sons were seen leaving the Fort shopping park with the little girl. CCTV has confirmed that. They were also seen by the security guard who found Mrs Wilson. And we have fingerprint matches for both Luke and Sean at the scene, along with prints on the girl's clothing."

"So, what will happen to them?"

"That's for the courts to decide, Miss Terry."

"But what do *you* think will happen?"

"Well," Blaney started, raking his fingers through his hair, "if found guilty, they are both looking at life. Even though they are below sixteen, they can expect to remain behind bars for at least twenty years."

"They can't do that! They are just kids, for fuck's sake!"

"Believe me, they can. The court may even impose At Her Majesty's Pleasure, which could mean a whole-life term handed down to them, Miss Terry."

"Jesus!" she exclaimed, placing her head in her hands. She sat there, trembling at the thought of never seeing her boys again. She began crying again, her hands shaking as tears landed on the table-top.

Blaney stood up, Shaw following suit as they both looked at the young woman. "Your court appearance will be in a few days' time. I suggest you talk things through with your duty solicitor before you appear at the Magistrates Court. Good day, Miss Terry."

They exited the interview room, walking down a long corridor towards a coffee machine. "Well, at least it looks like we can pin the drugs on Marshall," Shaw stated.

"Hopefully. Getting that scumbag off the streets for a stretch will do no harm." They arrived at the vending machine, Blaney fishing around in his pocket for some change. Thirty seconds later, he handed Shaw a limp cardboard cup of watery cappuccino before selecting one for himself. "Jesus," he retorted as he took a sip. "Shall we get some fresh air, and fresher coffee?"

"Sounds good to me," Shaw replied, as she poured the milky concoction back into the drip tray. They left the station, climbing into Blaney's unmarked saloon. He gunned the engine and wove his way out of the city centre towards the northern suburbs of Birmingham. They stopped on the Tyburn Road and ordered two coffees from a roadside snack bar before driving the two miles to the crime scene. A uniformed police officer waved them through as the saloon bounced over the rutted ground, Shaw deftly ensuring that all the coffee remained in the Styrofoam cups. Blaney killed the engine and accepted the steaming coffee from Shaw. They sat there for a few minutes in silence, the windscreen gradually misting over before Blaney turned on the fan. It cleared the screen quickly as both officers peered through the glass at the taped-off area in front of the car.

"Poor woman," Blaney said sombrely. "She died protecting her own. Something that you or I would do without thinking."

"You're not wrong, guv. She went out fighting. That's bugger all comfort for her family, though."

"No," he replied. "What makes people commit crimes like this? I'd expect it from seasoned perps. But two kids, one barely out of First School?"

"It boggles the mind," Shaw replied, before sipping at her coffee. "We both know that they'll never serve whole-life terms, either."

"No. There will be a raft of lefties trying to get them released as soon as they are behind bars. My best guess is that they'll be out in less than ten years."

"By which time there will probably be no turning back for either of them?"

"Probably not. They'll be in and out of nick on a regular basis. Or, they may be given new identities."

"Hmm. I'd not considered that," Shaw added.

"Well, it's a high-profile case which is already drawing huge media attention, both here and abroad. Witness Protection may step in, if and when they're released. You know what will probably happen? New identities, relocation. They will be set up pretty good."

"So unfair, guv."

"I know. We do our best to keep filth off the streets, only for the

Justice System to support them and give them decent lives once they set them free. They pay no heed to the grieving families."

"I suppose there is one good reason why the brothers might be relocated."

"What's that?"

"The father. Would you want an ex-Royal Marine knowing your name and where you lived?"

Blaney considered the question for a moment. "You're right. A grieving father is one thing. A grieving ex-soldier with his skills is something else. They may need to move them to the dark side of the Moon."

Shaw looked through the windscreen at the crime scene in front of them. "I have a feeling, guv, that the dark side of the Moon might not be far enough."

12

Luke sat in his room, looking out at the yard area of the young offenders' centre. He wiped his eyes, sniffing as he tried to piece together what had happened to him and his brother. *I want Mum,* he thought. *Why did we have to take the little girl?* Visions of the burning woman flooded his mind.

His thoughts were interrupted as three youths sauntered into the room. "Look what we've got here," a dark-skinned teenager stated. "It's the baby-snatcher." The two lads with him sniggered, advancing a few steps into the room.

Luke stood up from the bunk, moving towards the window. "Leave me alone," he snivelled, a trickle of urine leaking into his underwear.

"Look," the ringleader laughed. "He's pissed his pants!" The others laughed, too, making Luke shrink further towards the bunk, trying to find a means of escape. "Now you know how the little girl felt, you fucking nonce!" the dark-skinned boy hissed as he moved forward a few more paces. "Do you know what happens to nonces in here?" Luke shook his head, trying to slide further away. "They get fucked up!" the ringleader spat. "Fucked, then fucked up. And that's what's gonna happen to you, you little faggot!"

Luke started crying, grabbing hold of the bunk bed ladder. In two quick movements, he vaulted onto the upper-level, pulling his legs away from the goading youths. "Get away from me, or my brother will come and sort you out!"

"And how is he going to do that, stupid?" another youth asked. "He's not even in here. You're all alone, Lukey boy!" Luke got up on his hands and knees, shaking his head as the three teenagers began rocking the bunk bed. It came up against its securing brackets, only moving a few inches. The gang renewed their efforts, tugging and heaving on the metal-framed bed until the brackets holding it against the wall snapped.

Luke cried out as he felt the bed jolt against the wall, his grey joggers becoming soaked as he tried to cling on. "This is what happens to baby-snatchers," the ringleader taunted as he pulled harder on the end of the bunk, causing the whole structure to tip over further. Luke screamed as he felt the bed begin to lurch towards the other side of the room. He tried to grip the metal rails, the bed frame gaining momentum as it started dropping towards an inbuilt wardrobe on the opposite wall.

"The nonce is going for a ride," a boy laughed, his laughter ringing in Luke's ears as the bed fell further.

"*NOOO*!" Luke screamed as he felt himself falling towards the opposite side of the room. He looked left and right before leaping from the bed in an attempt to save himself. As he pushed off from the metal frame, his foot slipped on the rail, his leap stalling before it had even begun. He fell head-on towards the corner of the wardrobe, his skull striking the corner of the stout structure with a sickening crunch before he fell to the carpeted floor.

"What the hell is going on in here!" a man yelled from the doorway. The three youths barged past him, running down the corridor as the man hurried towards the prone figure underneath the bunk bed. He hefted it from the floor, pushing it back into place before turning to check on Luke.

"You okay?" the man asked, gently turning the boy over on the floor. "Oh no!" he exclaimed, noticing the blank stare that peered past him towards the ceiling. "Call an ambulance!" he hollered as footsteps converged on the room.

The room above Luke became dark, blinking out as he slipped into unconsciousness. An eternal blackness awaiting him.

~

Blaney sat in his favourite armchair, a large crystal tumbler in his hand. The television was on, but the man was not watching it. He stared past the set, his eyes peering out through the French doors onto his patio. It was dark outside, the back garden illuminated somewhat from the kitchen window next to the lounge. He could hear his wife washing up before she headed upstairs for a night in front of *QVC*. Their routine had become that predictable. He took a sip of his whisky, enjoying the mellow burn that hit the back of his throat as he swirled the amber liquid in its glass. He glanced at the opposite wall, smiling at the photograph of their wedding day. They'd looked so happy, so in love. And they were. Children and busy lives had intervened, taking over their lives, turning them into the people that they now were. Ticking along, almost on autopilot.

Suddenly, his garden was bathed in light as the security light picked up a prowling cat as it padded across his garden before becoming lost in a line of conifers. He took a swig of his Scotch, draining the glass before walking over to the cabinet in the corner of the room. He pulled out the stopper on the bottle, pouring three fingers of the fiery liquid before slumping back down in his armchair. As the security light was extinguished, his phone screen lit up, gently vibrating on the soft leather arm of his chair.

"Shaw," he answered, taking another sip.

"Guv. We've got a situation."

"What's up? Shouldn't you be putting the kids to bed?"

"Leon's doing that," she replied. "We've had a call from the young offenders' centre where Luke Terry is being held. There's been an incident."

Blaney sat up, placing his tumbler on a small table next to his chair. "Go on."

CCTV footage is being examined now. It appears that two or three youths got into Luke's room. They tipped his bunk over, with him on top of it. He fell and hit his head. He's dead, guv."

"Fucking hell!" Blaney groaned. He looked at his glass. "I'd drive down there, but I'm over the limit, Jenn."

"I understand. I could pick you up, if that helps?"

"How long?" he replied, trying to factor in her drive from the small town of Bromsgrove to his house in Sutton Coldfield.

"Forty-five minutes if I leave now."

"Okay. As long as you're sure?"

"It's no bother, guv. I'm guessing that we should attend the scene whilst it's still fresh."

"Yes, we should. I'll tell Tracey that I have to work. She won't miss me."

"Okay. See you in a bit."

Blaney ended the call, downing the Scotch in one swig, letting the burn warm his throat and chest. "What a mess," he reflected, before heading upstairs to give his wife the good news.

The ride across the city to the young offenders' centre took less than thirty minutes as a cold winter rain pelted Birmingham. "We'll need to notify Mandy Terry in the morning. Shit! She's going to go ballistic. I thought things were bad. It's about to get much worse."

"I know. This is turning into a right circus," Shaw replied.

"We'll need to take a look at the CCTV. Any news on the boys responsible?"

"They have been identified and are currently locked in their rooms. It's probably too late to speak to them tonight," Shaw replied.

Blaney nodded as the car left the main road, heading down a quiet driveway on the outskirts of the city. "We'll round them up in the morning, at the station. Hopefully, that will get the little bastards talking."

"It's a shame though."

"How do you mean?" Blaney replied.

"From what I can see, Luke was just tagging along for the ride. And because of that, he's dead."

"I agree, Jenn. He wasn't a bad lad. He was barely out of short trousers. And now he's gone. Sean will go down for sure. Not only will he have to live with what he's done, but he'll also have to live with the fact that his brother is dead because of him."

The car pulled up outside a large single-storey complex and both officers climbed out stiffly. "Right," Shaw began. "Let's go and wade through the shit."

13

Blaney looked across the interview room at Mandy Terry. She was dressed in a grey tracksuit, her dark hair tied up in a bun. Blaney noticed dark smudges under her eyes as the woman across the desk glared at him. "Mandy. It seems there was an altercation where Luke was staying. Some of the boys decided to tease him, which ended with them tipping his bunk over. He fell and hit his head."

"What? You're shitting me. Is he okay?" she exclaimed anxiously.

"I'm really sorry to tell you this, but he was confirmed dead at the scene."

"What? No!" she cried, tears brimming in her eyes. "Please tell me this is not happening?"

"We're really sorry," Jenn replied.

"*Nooooo*," she wailed, "not my Luke!" She began shaking her head, drawing her hands over her face. The police detectives sat there, unable to say anything as the young woman was torn apart from the inside-out. The chair skittered behind her as Luke's mum shot to her feet, pacing the room. "I can't believe this is happening!" she cried, sliding down the wall into a crumpled heap on the floor. She lay there, legs drawn up to her chest, a high-pitched keening sound coming from her contorted mouth.

Shaw got to her feet and knelt next to the woman. "We're really sorry, Mandy."

"This cannot be happening. You must have made a mistake. You've got the wrong boy. I want to see Luke. I want you to take me to him, now."

"We can take you to him, Mandy," Blaney said from his seated position. "You need to formally identify the body."

"*Body?*" she cried, before wailing uncontrollably on the floor. The detectives were used to this. They let her pain come out. They both knew that it was just the beginning, knowing that the pain would last a lifetime. They'd witnessed this event too many times for their liking. As recently as a few days before, when an innocent husband was on the receiving end.

"I want answers," she snapped, wiping her nose with the back of her hand. "I want to know who killed my boy."

"We cannot tell you that, Miss Terry. The suspects are minors. Surely, you must understand, especially in light of recent events."

"Got a fucking answer for everything, pig!" she spat. "Well, I'll find them. Even if it takes me the rest of my fucking life. I'll find them and kill them!"

"We can understand how distressing this must be for you," Shaw replied evenly. "But issuing threats is not going to do you any good, Mandy."

"What do you expect me to say?" she spat back, tears streaming down her cheeks. "Luke! Oh baby, not my Luke." The woman collapsed onto the table, her cries echoing around the small room.

The detectives sat in silence, waiting patiently until the sobs subsided. "Are you sure you're ready for this?" Blaney asked.

She rose from the table, wiping a hand under her nose. "Take me to him," she ordered.

Five minutes later, Blaney, Shaw and Mandy Terry walked across the police station car park, both officers flanking the woman whose wrists were encased in steel cuffs. Blaney helped her into the car and walked around to the drivers' side before pulling out onto the busy city streets. They headed east, towards the suburbs of Small Heath and Bordesley Green as cars and humanity went about their daily routine. The interior of the car was devoid of conversation for the fifteen-minute journey, each occupant consumed by their own thoughts. Blaney indicated left, pulling into a large car park, hunting for a space close to the hospital's entrance.

They filed out of the saloon, Blaney helping Mandy out of the rear seat.

"Any chance you can remove these?" she asked, holding her hands up in front of the detective's face.

"Only when we're in there. Sorry. Police rules."

"Whatever," she mumbled, turning towards the hospital with the two detectives flanking her again. People glanced at them as they made their way along busy corridors. Mandy was trying not to make eye contact with any passers-by as they headed for the mortuary. She could feel a rising anxiety in her chest at the thought of seeing her dead son laid out on a metal slab in front of her.

Blaney led them into the mortuary ante-room, telling the two women to wait there whilst he spoke to the Mortician. Mandy's heart was thudding. After a few moments, the detective came out of the double doors, motioning for her and Shaw to come forward. "Are you sure you're ready for this, Mandy?" Blaney enquired calmly.

"Not really. But I need to see him." She could feel tears threatening as her chest started to constrict.

"Very well," he replied, removing her cuffs which he then slipped into his coat pocket. He led her through the double doors into a muted, low-slung room with a single light shining in the centre above a raised platform. A white sheet covered the table, the unmistakable shape of a small figure underneath it.

Mandy started to shake, tears spilling down her cheeks as her feet dragged across the tiled floor. "Oh, Luke," she wailed. "My poor baby."

A tall, middle-aged man approached the trio from the edge of the room, his thinning pate shining underneath the lamp's glare. "Are you ready, Miss Terry?" he asked quietly.

She nodded, wiping a hand under her nose "Yes." He pulled back the sheet, folding it gently before stepping back a few paces.

Mandy cried out, the noise reverberating around the stark room. "Luke! My baby," she whimpered, burying her face into the crook of his neck. "I'm so sorry, Luke. Really, I am."

She stayed there for a minute, brushing his hair with her fingers before placing a kiss on his cold lips. She stood up, taking two steps backwards with her head bowed. She nodded at the mortician who gently replaced the white sheet over the body before excusing himself. She felt distant, removed from the scene, as if she were in an alternative reality.

"We're very sorry, Mandy," Shaw said.

"Take me back to the station. I want to be alone."

"We understand," Blaney responded, guiding her towards the door.

"Do you want a cup of tea before we go?" Shaw asked.

Mandy looked at the female detective, realising that she'd not drunk anything for hours. "Coffee, please."

"Okay. Let's stop off at McDonalds on the way back and grab some drinks," she offered.

Fifteen minutes later, they were back inside Blaney's saloon as winter sunshine bathed the land in light. Mandy sat on the back seat, sipping at a large cappuccino while Blaney and Shaw looked out of the windscreen at the file of cars, waiting for their Big Macs. "Can I ask you a question?" Mandy asked.

"Of course," Blaney replied, placing his coffee on the dashboard.

"The woman who died, what was her name?"

Shaw and Blaney exchanged glances, the older detective nodding. "Her name was Lucy Wilson."

"Lucy," Mandy replied. "Nice name. Can you tell me a bit about her? I know I shouldn't ask, but I need to know."

Blaney turned around in his seat, trying to get comfortable. "She was in her early thirties. She had one daughter, Lottie, who is four. Her husband, John was serving with the Royal Marines in Afghanistan. As you can imagine, he's been allowed home to look after his daughter. Hopefully, she will be out of hospital in a few days."

"I am so sorry for what happened. I know Luke would never do anything like that. I'm shocked that even Sean could do what he did. Yes, he's a little bastard sometimes, but killing someone, that's not Sean. I know that the drugs did it. They twisted his mind. Luke's, too."

"Well, the trial will bring all that out, Mandy," Blaney replied gravely.

"I want to help you. Jerome gave me stuff to hold. The skunk was also from him. I want him to suffer, like the others who are now suffering!"

"Good. Let's drop you back to the station. Then we can talk."

"I know I'll go down for this. And I'm okay with that. But Jerome needs to go down, too. I have lots more to tell you. Lots more."

The door burst open as several black-clad officers entered the house. "Armed police!" the leader shouted. The six officers bustled through the house, Blaney and Shaw readying themselves at the front door. A few seconds after two armed officers had headed upstairs, the detectives heard shouts and banging.

"Come on," Blaney urged. "I think they've got him." They hurried down the hallway, taking the stairs two at a time. The noises came from their left as Blaney strode down the short landing until he entered the bedroom, where two officers were standing, weapons aimed at a figure on the bed.

"You got the wrong guy," Jerome insisted, his naked body barely covered by a stained duvet.

Blaney walked forward a few paces. "Jerome Marshall, I'm arresting you on the suspicion of possession of a controlled drug with intent to supply. You do not have to say anything, but it may harm your defence if you do not mention when questioned something which you later rely on in court. Anything you say may be given in evidence."

"What!" Jerome exclaimed, as two armed officers hefted him from the bed. He stood there naked, his face twisting in anger. "That bitch! She dropped me in it. Didn't she?"

"Get dressed, Jerome. You're in for a long day," Blaney advised. He exited the room with Shaw as Marshall began clothing himself, guns levelled at his chest. They walked down the staircase, the smell of grease suddenly apparent as it wafted up the stairs towards them.

"Jesus!" Shaw exclaimed, wrinkling her nose. "Remind me never to come around here for dinner."

"I think he's not going to be cooking for anyone for a very long time."

They walked out onto the stubbly-grassed lawn where a waiting officer advanced towards them.

"I want a top-to-tail search of the premises, Sergeant. Call me, and me only, when you have completed the search. Take him to Steelhouse Lane and book him in. We'll be along shortly."

"Yes, guv," the officer replied, his tone clipped and professional.

They walked from the garden onto the pavement, walking past police vans until they reached Blaney's car. Once seated inside, the older detective turned to Shaw. "I think a celebration is in order. Coffees are on me."

14

Four days after touching down, John was walking up his garden path, Lottie wrapped around him tightly. He opened the front door and walked through the hallway with his daughter in his arms. "Let me put you on the settee, princess. I'll get you some juice and a packet of crisps. Okay?"

"Okay, Daddy."

He placed his daughter gently on the sofa, draping a soft blanket over her. John bent down, kissing Lottie on the forehead. "Love you, princess."

The girl reached up, wrapping her arms around John's neck. "I love you too, Daddy. Are the nasty boys far away?"

Tears stung John's eyes. "Yes, princess. No one will ever try and hurt you again." She nodded, looking over at the television. "I'll put something on for you while I make your juice."

He walked into the kitchen, flicking the kettle on then rifling through the cupboards to find a plastic bottle. Eventually finding it, he made his daughter a drink and grabbed a bag of crisps from the pantry as the kettle started to boil. Just then, the doorbell rang. John looked down the hallway as Lottie started screaming. He strode towards the front door as his daughter came barrelling out of the lounge.

"Daddy! The nasty people are back!" she cried, jumping into his embrace.

"It's okay, Lottie. I think it's just the postman. No one is going to hurt you. I promise."

He took a step forward, opening the door. Smiling back at him was his regular postman. "Hello. Got something here for your wife."

"Oh, thanks," John replied awkwardly.

"Mummy is up in the stars," Lottie stated.

The postman looked at John, a quizzical expression on his face.

"It's okay, princess," he replied, as the postman offered John the small cardboard box. "Thank you," he said. The man on the doorstep nodded before walking down the path to continue his round.

John closed the door, placing the parcel on the telephone table that sat at the foot of the stairs. "It's okay, princess. It was just the postman."

"Sorry, Daddy. I thought the nasty boys were here."

"They are in jail, princess."

"What's jail, Daddy? I've seen it on the television."

John smiled, walking back into the kitchen. He picked up the juice and crisps with his free hand and headed back into the lounge. "It's where they send nasty boys. The boys who hurt you will never hurt anyone again. They will stay in jail for a very long time."

He placed her on the settee, walked back into the kitchen and re-boiled the kettle. Five minutes later, he sat down next to his daughter, finding a suitable channel for her as he sipped at his tea.

"What shall we do today, Daddy?"

"I don't know. What would you like to do?"

"Could we go to the adventure playground? Mummy took me there a few weeks ago."

"Sounds like a good idea," John agreed, sipping his tea.

"Can have a Happy Meal on the way home too?"

"For you, anything," he replied, as he placed his mug on the coffee table. He scooped Lottie into his arms, holding her tightly against him. His daughter snuggled in closely, burying her face in his chest. They sat there in silence, John feeling the rhythmic beating of the little girl's heart.

"Daddy…" she began.

"Yes, princess?"

"What happens now?"

"How do you mean?"

"Will you be looking after me now?"

John looked at his daughter, his heart straining as he looked at her forlorn expression. "Yes, princess. Daddy will take care of you now." A thought suddenly occurred to him. *I've got so much shit to sort out.*

"I really miss Mummy. But as long as I've got you, Daddy, I'll be okay."

John burst into tears, falling backwards against the cushions. He pressed his fists into his eyes, trying to shut out the world. His body shook as uncontrollable sobs escaped him, until he felt two soft hands gently pulling his fists away from his face.

"Don't cry, Daddy. Please. I will take care of you."

John laughed, the sound cracked and strained. He pulled Lottie towards him as tears streaked his bearded face. "I love you, princess. Forever."

"I love you too, Daddy. You're the best daddy ever."

"Thanks, sweetheart," he replied, wiping his eyes. "Right. I'll go and grab a quick shower, then we'll go up the Lickeys."

The red Vauxhall bumped over the rutted roadway as John navigated potholes and huge speed bumps before parking a few yards away from the visitors' centre. He climbed out of the car, opening the rear door for his daughter. He slid her out of her child seat, zipping up her pink jacket as the bobble on her woolly hat bobbed about in the cool breeze. They walked hand-in-hand down a steep slope, towards the impressive adventure playground that lay further down the hill.

John had spent his childhood playing in and around the Lickey Hills. Lottie let go of her father's hand, scooting happily towards the swings. "Careful now, princess," he called. "Don't fall over."

"Daddy, can you put me in the swing, please?"

"Of course, I can," he replied, the strain and heartbreak of the past few days melting away slightly. He placed her in the swing, placing her gloved hands on the cold metal chains. "Hold on tight," he said as he pulled the swing towards him. He let it go, sending Lottie swinging backwards happily. He pushed her for a few minutes, drawing smiles from a couple of young mothers a few yards away.

"Daddy, I want to get off," Lottie exclaimed, as the sun suddenly dipped behind the clouds, subduing the country park somewhat.

"Come here, princess," John comforted, lifting her out gently. She ran off, skipping towards a large climbing frame, complete with ladders, rope bridges and slides. He ambled after her, resting against a wooden fence as he watched his daughter begin a measured ascent towards the top of the structure. He stood there, watching Lottie as she carefully navigated the rope bridge.

"She's having fun," a female voice said. John turned around as a woman stopped a few feet away from him and sat down on a wooden bench.

"Yes, she certainly is," he replied, as his daughter appeared from a tubular slide. Lottie landed clumsily before skipping back towards another ladder.

"How old is she?" the woman asked.

"Four," John replied, turning to look at the woman. She looked roughly his age, with a kind face and black-rimmed glasses. She wore dark jeans, boots and a purple padded jacket. Her dark hair was partially hidden underneath a pink woolly hat, similar to his daughter's. "Where's yours?"

"Over there," the woman replied. "On the roundabout with her cousin. She's five, going on sixteen."

John smiled, the feeling somewhat strange under the circumstances. "I suppose I've got all that to look forward to."

"Believe me, it is a challenge," she replied, eyeing his wedding band. "Does she have any brothers or sisters?"

John's smile faded slightly. "No. It's just Lottie."

"Are you having any more?"

John suddenly felt weary. He walked a few paces, sitting down next to the woman. "No. We had planned to. But Lottie's mum died recently."

"Oh," the woman exclaimed. "I'm so sorry."

"It's okay," John replied. "I guess I'll have to get used to telling people that Lucy has passed away."

"Was she sick?"

"No," John began, his emotions starting to surface. "She was murdered last week. You may have seen it on the news."

The woman's hand came up to her mouth in shock. "Oh no! You poor thing. I did see it on the news," she gasped, tears forming at the corners of her eyes.

John looked over at the playground, checking to see if his daughter was okay. "I'm John, by the way."

"Ruth," the woman replied, extending her gloved hand. John took it, squeezing it briefly. "I really am so sorry."

"It's okay, Ruth. It's been a surreal week. A few days ago, I was on manoeuvres in Afghanistan. Now, I'm watching my daughter play happily while my wife lies in a morgue. Not quite what I was expecting. Merry Christmas, eh?"

"I really don't know what to say. I just hope that you both get through it."

"Thanks, Ruth," John replied. He looked over at his daughter as she finished scaling a rope with large knots in it. She looked past him, stiffening, her expression changing in a split-second.

"Daddy!" she cried out, running over the footbridge before appearing at the bottom of the slide a few seconds later. She bounded over to him, diving onto his lap, her whole body trembling.

"What's wrong, princess?" John asked, concern edging his voice.

"Look!" the girl cried out, pointing behind him. "The nasty boys are back."

John turned around on the bench and spotted a pair of teenagers who were standing next to a huge boulder-like structure, smoking and laughing. "It's okay, sweetheart. They are not nasty boys. They are just boys." He looked at Ruth, who tried to smile reassuringly.

"I want to go home, Daddy. I don't want the nasty boys to come and hurt me again. Please, Daddy," she pleaded, as tears rolled down her cheeks.

"Okay, princess. Let's go home and have some lunch." He looked at the woman seated next to him. "Nice to meet you, Ruth."

"You too, John," she said, her eyes drawn to the trembling girl in his lap. "Take care of yourselves."

"You too," he replied, rising from the bench with Lottie in his arms. He carried her back to the car, kissing the top of her head after he'd clipped her into the car seat. "Okay. Let's go."

"Okay, Daddy," she murmured, seeming calmer now that she was inside the car. A few moments later, the red Vauxhall was trundling back up the uneven road.

As he drove, John's mind was a tumult of thoughts. *She may need some help.*

15

Mandy Terry returned to her cell, her grey jogging bottoms dragging across the floor as she walked over to her single bed. She lay down, the conversation with the two detectives still fresh in her mind. She zipped her tracksuit top up, the cell feeling as though it was barely above freezing as her breath clouded in front of her. She reached over to a stainless-steel table, dragging a packet of cigarettes from the polished surface. As she lit the cigarette, the words kept spinning around her head, as if on an endless carousel. Mandy blew a stream of smoke into the air, watching as it dissipated into the dark cell.

Fuck, she thought. *Seven years in prison. I'll be almost forty by the time I get out. And then what? A dead son, the other in prison for who knows how long?* She started crying, curling up on the bed as cigarette ash dropped onto the thin duvet. *Poor Luke. He was just a baby. He didn't deserve this.* Her thoughts drifted to Jerome. *I'll make you fucking pay, Jez. You'll be sorry you ever laid eyes on me.*

"What did you think?" Shaw suggested, as she carefully lifted her coffee from the machine.

"I think we have a strong enough case for the CPS to prosecute. I do feel sorry for her, though. Yes, she's a bit rough around the edges, but she never meant for her sons to steal her stash and kill someone. Added to the fact that her youngest has recently passed away, and her cooperation in bringing Marshall in, I'd say the judge will be lenient. She may get four, out in two if she behaves herself. Her life will probably be pretty shitty after that, though. And Marshall is connected. She may need to start afresh, possibly with a new identity."

"I agree," Shaw replied, as they walked over to a pair of fake-leather chairs. They sat down next to each other, looking out through the window at the darkening evening.

"What plans have you got for Christmas?" Blaney asked, taking a tentative sip of his frothy cappuccino.

"Quiet one, guv. My folks are coming over on Christmas Day. They will spend the day spoiling Erin before we all fill our faces. That's about it. To be honest, I've not really thought about it. And you?"

"No idea. It's only two weeks away and I've not bought a single present. Tracey will probably make a complete hash of the dinner as usual. The kids will probably drag themselves downstairs for an hour, before locking themselves away in their rooms for the evening. I'll just immerse myself in a few bottles of wine and fall asleep in my chair. Tracey will do what Tracey does best."

"*QVC*?" Shaw stated matter-of-factly.

"You got it. While I'm dozing, she'll be spending my money. Sorry, I forgot. *Our* money."

Shaw smiled, placing a hand on his knee. "It's not that bad, is it?"

"It's just life, Jenn. We're just plodding along, almost like two flatmates cohabiting under the same roof. Don't ever end up like us."

"Hmm," Shaw wondered. "It's the job, isn't it?"

"Yes. If any of my kids wanted to be a copper, I'd steer them well clear. It's a worthy profession, but our loved ones suffer."

"I know, guv. It's not easy juggling work and family life."

"Do you want my advice?"

"Always," she replied.

"Don't do this forever. I've seen so many marriages go down the pan. Police divorce is more prevalent than in almost any other career."

"I'm not sure what else I could do?"

"You're young, Jenn. With a great career behind you already. You could do whatever you wanted. An officer I know from the south side of the city, his brother-in-law has just left the force. Apparently, he's going to be a Private Investigator. I've known a few retired officers who have made the switch and they are doing well for themselves."

"Maybe one day, guv. I can't quit now and leave you all alone."

"Don't worry about me, Jenn. My time will come soon, and you know what?" he paused. "I'm looking forward to it."

"Let's change the subject, guv. All this talk of leaving and retirement is making me feel old."

Blaney smiled. "Fair enough. Let's finish these and get ourselves home. What's for tea tonight?"

"I think Leon's cooking a chilli. Erin will probably have pasta. You fancy some?"

"Believe me, it probably will taste amazing compared to whatever Tracey rustles up. But I'll pass. I just want a hot bath, a glass of whisky and an early night."

"Okay, guv," Jenn replied as she finished her coffee. "I'm ready when you are."

They deposited their plastic cups in a green recycling bin, heading through the station towards the front entrance. A few fairy lights could be seen inside the offices, but Blaney and Shaw kept walking, eyes facing forward. Five minutes later, they were both heading home in opposite directions across the busy city.

John sat on the settee with Lottie, the local news on the TV in front of them. She snuggled into him as he read her a story, the first flakes of snow began to fall outside. After a few minutes, he placed the book on the coffee table before scooping his sleepy daughter into his arms. "Come on, princess. Let's get you showered and into bed."

"Okay, Daddy," she replied. "Will you sit with me after?"

"Yes, Lottie. I will sit with you while you have your milk."

"Thank you, Daddy," she whispered as John crested the staircase. "I like you sitting with me. I feel safe, Daddy."

His heart swelled in his chest, his throat constricting as he walked into the bathroom. He pulled the cord and the bathroom sprang to light around them. "Do you want me to help you with your clothes?"

"I can do it, Daddy," she replied as John switched the shower on. He looked down at his daughter as she struggled with her pink socks, her tongue sticking out as she concentrated on the task ahead. Steam started billowing around the bathroom, the warm water pulsating into the large bath.

"Come here, princess," John offered, lifting Lottie into the bath.

She walked underneath the cascading water, giggling as it drenched her. "It tickles, Daddy."

"You're funny," John laughed, squeezing a dollop of shampoo onto his palm. "Come here, princess," he said. Lottie took a few steps forward and John gently lathered her hair. He scraped it all up away from her eyes as a few stray suds dripped onto her face. "Get under the water, while I get the shower gel," he instructed, as his daughter tottered back to the falling water. He opened a cupboard, retrieving a bottle of own-brand shower gel, before sitting on the edge of the bath. "Open your hands," he said, as the last vestiges of shampoo fell into the bath at his daughter's feet.

"Okay," she replied, letting John deposit a generous blob of pink gel into her upturned palm.

"Rub that all over you while I go and get you some milk." He padded downstairs, the tinkling of water diminishing as he walked into the kitchen. He pulled a small plastic bottle out of the fridge, placing it in the microwave. He warmed the milk for a minute before heading back up to the bathroom, his daughter's giggles filling his ears. He smiled as he walked into the bathroom and his daughter returned the smile. *She looks like her mum,* he thought, feeling his throat constrict.

"Finished, Daddy," she exclaimed.

John shut off the shower and lifted her onto a floor mat, wrapping a large bath sheet around her. "Stand still," he said as she wriggled in his grip. He towelled her hair vigorously as she dutifully complied with her father's orders. "Right, let's get you into bed."

"Okay, Daddy," she replied happily, running naked out of the bathroom.

He followed her, milk in hand, making his way along the landing to the bedroom a few feet away. Lottie was already on the bed, pulling her pyjamas on as John entered the room. John turned off the main light and placed her milk on top of the wooden headboard before flicking on her nightlight. He sat down in a red upholstered chair, getting comfortable.

"Okay," he began. "Lie down, princess and drink your milk." She did so, flapping her pink comforter up and down as she began gulping down the warm liquid. He watched her, smiling in the darkened room as Lottie's eyes suddenly grew heavy.

A minute later, she held the bottle out across the gap. "Finished, Daddy," she whispered sleepily as John gently pulled the bottle from her grip. He placed it on a chest-of-drawers and knelt next to the bed. He placed a tender kiss on her forehead. "Night-night, princess. Sweet dreams."

"Night night, Daddy. Love you," she replied hugging John tightly.

"Love you too," John murmured.

He walked out of the room, leaving the door ajar a few inches and quietly descended the stairs, heading into the kitchen once more, where he opened the fridge and pulled out a can of lager before walking into the lounge. He cracked the seal on the can, taking a swig before carrying his laptop over to the settee. Opening the black case, he moved his finger across the mouse pad, making a few clicks before the last picture of his wife appeared on the screen.

"Hi, babe," he whispered. He drank in her smile, loving how one side of her mouth was always higher than the other. Her dark eyes met his, John's pain and despair growing with each heartbeat. "Why did this have to happen?" He took another swig of lager, wiping a hand across his mouth without taking his eyes of Lucy. She smiled back at him, frozen forever in time. He began crying. Gently at first, as his wife's image shone back at him. He placed the laptop on the table as his sobs intensified. "*Noooo*," he uttered, his vision blurry with tears. Then he fell sideways, curling up on the settee as his emotions boiled over.

"Daddy?" a voice said behind him. He shot up, seeing Lottie in the doorway, her comforter dangling from her fist. She ran to him, diving on top of him as her own tears began falling. "Don't cry, Daddy. I will take care of you."

"Oh, princess," John blurted. "I know you will." He squeezed the little girl, burying his face in her blonde curls. "I'm sorry. I just really miss Mummy."

"I know, Daddy. I miss her too. She was kind and funny."

John laughed. "Yes, she was," he replied, kissing Lottie on the cheek. "She was very kind and funny. Loving, too. She loved you, Lottie. You were the apple of her eye."

"What does that mean?"

"It means that she loved you more than anything else."

"Did she love me to the Moon and back?" she asked. Her matter-of-fact question made John smile.

He wiped his eyes. "Yes, princess. She loved you to the stars and beyond."

"Well, maybe she is up in the stars with Grandad Brian."

"I'm sure she is," John replied. He thought of his father-in-law, who had suddenly passed away a few months before. John had liked him. The older man had accepted him into the fold from the word go. He missed Brian, knowing that it had hit Lucy hard, her mother too.

"Come on, let's get comfy," John soothed.

Lottie melded into him, father and daughter becoming one in the dark lounge. He lay there, listening to her breathing slow down until her snores drifted to his ears. With one arm holding his daughter and the other tucked behind his head, he realised that he could not reach his lager unless he woke her. So instead, he closed his eyes, letting sleep overcome him quickly. Cloudy images invaded his dreams. Two young boys, standing next to a burning pyre as his wife's screams echoed through his mind.

16

CHRISTMAS DAY – 2005

"Thanks, John," Judy said, as she dumped her bag on the single bed.

"You can swap with me, Judy. I don't mind sleeping in here."

"I'll be just fine. You need a double," she insisted as Lottie walked into the single bedroom and climbed onto the bed, her pink dress and woolly tights drawing a smile from her grandmother. "You look like a proper princess, Lottie."

"I am Princess Lottie," the little girl exclaimed.

John and Judy looked at each other, smiling as the little girl bounced up and down on the bed. "Well, do you want me to do your hair for you?"

"Yes please, Nanny," Lottie replied happily.

"Come on then. We can leave Daddy to sort a few things out." She extended her hand, Lottie taking it readily as John left the room.

He walked down the stairs, heading into the lounge to begin the clean-up of discarded wrapping paper and cardboard boxes. A few minutes later, he deposited a large black bag into the recycling bin at the side of the house and nipped back inside out of the cold. As he wiped his slippers on the hall mat, a phone began to ring. He walked into the lounge, heading over to the hearth where a large Christmas tree took pride of place. He grabbed the cordless phone, answering it on the eighth chime.

"Hello?"

"Merry Christmas, Son."

"Merry Christmas, Dad," John replied, a feeling of guilt washing over him. *It doesn't feel very merry.*

"Your mum's in the kitchen, just getting everything ready to bring over. Is Judy there?"

"Yes. I picked her up at ten. She's upstairs with Lottie, doing her hair."

"Women, eh?" his father replied. "Look, I won't stay on the phone gassing all day. We'll be over in about forty-five minutes or so."

"Okay, Dad. See you both then. 'Bye for now."

"'Bye, Son."

John ended the call and walked into the kitchen. On the countertop, a large turkey sat in an oven tin. John had dressed it just after breakfast, streaky bacon adorning the carcass. To add a bit more flavour, he'd stuffed the bird with a large red onion and a few cloves of garlic. Despite being a soldier, John loved to cook. When he was home, he had regularly taken over the reins in the kitchen, leaving the girls to potter about the house or play in the garden.

There were various cookery books on the shelf opposite the oven, Rick Stein, Jamie Oliver and Nigella Lawson amongst the collection. He didn't need their help today, though. He knew how to cook a roast dinner. His problem was that he didn't feel the inclination to do so. It was Christmas Day. A time when families come together. His family was now fractured, Lucy's death a massive void in their once happy tribe. He felt lost, unsure of the future without his wife to love and guide him.

He checked the time, turning the oven on as it was just after midday and the turkey would need to be put into the oven soon. Laughter drifted down the stairs, making John stop in his tracks. He leaned against the doorjamb, the rest of the world forgotten for a moment as Lottie's giggles echoed around the house. A single tear ran down his cheek as footsteps could be heard from above.

"Daddy, look!" Lottie exclaimed as she bounded down the stairs. "Nanny Judy has made my hair pretty."

He looked down at his daughter, smiling at the proud expression on her face. Her blonde hair had been arranged with matching pigtails that bounced in time with Lottie's movements. "Very pretty, princess. Nanny has done a fabulous job," he agreed as Judy came walking down the stairs.

"I'd have done it quicker if madam had not spent so much time wriggling. Ants in your pants you have, young lady," she chided as she bent down to kiss Lottie's curls.

"Mummy would be very pleased, princess," John said. The word was out, like a lightning bolt. Judy reacted immediately, choking sobs coming from the older woman as she sat down heavily on the second step of the staircase. John and Lottie both went to her, the little girl wrapping her arms around Judy's neck.

"Don't cry, Nanny."

Judy sniffed loudly, taking a tissue from her sleeve. She wiped her nose, scrunching the tissue up in her hand. "Oh, I'm sorry, poppet. I just miss your mummy. So very much."

John pulled his mother-in-law towards him, his own tears falling freely. "It's okay, Judy. We'll be okay. Today is just going to magnify everything. There will be tears and sadness. But we will get through this."

She squeezed him tightly before pulling back. "Thank you, John," she blurted, kissing him on the cheek. "You're a wonderful man."

"Stop it. You'll make me cry like a baby," he replied, pulling the woman to her feet.

"Well, it's true. Lucy loved you. Lottie too. You were a wonderful husband and an equally wonderful father. I'm so proud of you, John. And yes, we'll all get through this. Together. Now, I don't know about you, but I could do with a glass of wine. Care to join me?"

"Sounds like a plan," John agreed as he ruffled his daughter's hair. "I'll grab a bottle out of the fridge. Lottie, would you like some juice?"

"Please, Daddy."

"Okay, sweetheart. If you go and play in the lounge, I will bring one in for you." Lottie took her cue, heading out of the hallway to play with her new presents. John and Judy walked into the kitchen as rain started falling outside.

"I'll get some glasses," Judy suggested, walking over to a glass-fronted cupboard. She placed them on the countertop as John cracked the seal on the wine. He filled the two glasses with crisp white wine then clinked glasses with his mother-in-law.

"Cheers," he said.

"Cheers, John. To Lucy. I know she's smiling down on us."

No more tears emerged. John took the statement in his stride. "Yes. I know she is. If she were here now, she'd be fussing around the kitchen, tidying up after me."

"Well, that's Lucy for you. She was never one for mess. Bless her."

John took a long sip of his wine, leaning against the wall. "So, I suppose I'd better start thinking about getting a job soon."

"Yes, I suppose you need to consider your options. What are you thinking?"

"Not sure yet. Lottie will be going to school soon. So, I'll have to think about school runs and flexible working, which is not great."

"I can help out."

John looked at her, smiling. "I know you would. But you live the other side of the city. And you don't drive."

"That's true. Brian did all the driving. But I was talking to Lucy about the possibility of moving over this way."

"Really?" John replied, mildly surprised.

"Yes. I'm rattling around that house on my own. The buses are no good and the road is not as nice as it once was. Over the past year or so, lots of Polish families have moved in. Not that I mind that. But there are cars everywhere and lots of comings and goings. When we bought the house in Eighty-two, we knew everyone in the street. Most of them are either dead or have moved onto pastures new. I think a change of scenery will do me good."

"Well, it sounds like you've given this some thought," John replied.

"It's been on my mind for a while now. The house is paid for and

Brian's company paid me a lump sum as he died in service. Plus, I'll have his pension one day. So, I'm not hard up. Well, not yet, anyway."

"Okay. Well, I will help you with anything you need. It would be great to have you close by. Lottie would like that. I would, too."

"Well, let's get the New Year out of the way, then I'll pop into my local agents to get the ball rolling."

"I'll drink to that," John stated, raising his glass.

"Then you won't have to worry so much about school runs. I'm sure I can help out."

"Thank you. I'm sure Mum and Dad would, too."

"Well, there you go then. You've got a support network, right on your doorstep. Like I said earlier, we'll get through this, together."

John finished his wine and made Lottie a bottle of juice. He kissed Judy on the top of the head as he walked out of the kitchen, returning a moment later to refill the glasses. They sat chatting once the turkey was in the oven, recounting precious memories as a few well-placed tears fell between them.

A shrill sound rang down the hallway, signalling the arrival of John's parents. He opened the front door, smiling down at them. "Hi, guys. Come in," he urged, gratefully accepting an armful of food from his mother.

"Merry Christmas, Son," she said, kissing him on the cheek.

"You too, Mum."

"Merry Christmas Son," Derek Wilson repeated.

"Hi, Dad," John replied hugging his father. "What have you got there?" he said, looking down at the hessian carrier bag in his father's hand.

"Booze. Your mother is driving back later, so I thought I'd bring a few cheeky beers with me. And a drop of sherry for your mother of course."

"She'll only have one, knowing Mum." He moved to one side, letting his father past before closing the door. As they made their way into the kitchen, Judy rose from her chair.

"Hello," she began. "Merry Christmas." It was spoken tentatively and accompanied by a wry twist of the mouth.

They deposited bags and trays on the kitchen table, then Margaret hugged the other woman. "Merry Christmas, love."

The two of them held onto each other as their emotions surfaced. John and Derek stood by as the women cried in each other's arms. Both mothers. Both grieving.

After a minute, they parted, letting Derek move forward.

"Hello, Judy," he said, embracing Lucy's mother warmly.

"Hi, love," she replied, kissing him on the cheek.

"So," Margaret began. "What do you want me to do?"

John knew his mother well enough to know that she would not sit idly by as he cooked the dinner. She would simply not hear of it. "Well, the turkey has had about half an hour, so I'll take it out in a minute and baste it. All the veg is prepared. It just needs cooking, in probably an hour or so."

"Okay. Well, I'll do that." She turned to her husband. "Love, would you unpack the pigs-in-blankets and the stuffing balls, please?"

"Sure," he responded. "Thirsty work though," he stated, looking at his son.

"I'll pour you both a drink. Dad, beer?" His father nodding readily. "Mum?"

"I'll just have a coffee for now. Oh gosh. I nearly forgot. Where's Lottie?" she asked, suddenly feeling guilty.

"Lottie!" John called. The lounge door opened.

"Nanny, Grandad," she chirped, skipping down the hallway into the kitchen. She ran into Derek's embrace, laughing as he hefted her onto his hip.

"Hello, poppet," he gushed, planting a kiss on his cheek.

"Hello, Grandad," she replied, squeezing his nose playfully.

"Hello, sweetheart," Margaret added, sniffing back the tears. She walked over, kissing her granddaughter.

"Hello, Nanny," Lottie beamed, holding her arms out. Margaret eased her away from her husband, twirling the girl around. "Do you like my hair? It's pretty. Nanny Judy did it for me."

"Oh, it looks wonderful, Lottie. You are a proper little princess," she beamed, noticing the similarity between her granddaughter and daughter-in-law. A cloud passed over her horizon, emotions rising once more.

"Come with me, Nanny. I want to show you my Lil Miss Makeup."

"Lead on, princess," she replied smiling at the others.

"I'll bring the coffee in, Mum," John said, flicking the kettle on.

"Thanks, love," she replied, as Lottie began dragging her down the hallway.

John busied himself with the coffee. "Right, who wants what?"

"I'll have a small wine," Judy replied. "Or else I'll be asleep before the Queen's Speech," she stated, a half-smile tugging at her lips.

"I'll have a beer please, Son. They should still be pretty cold," Derek added.

"Coming right up," John said, trying his hardest to sound cheerful. A minute later, the three of them raised their glasses, each lost in their own thoughts as Lottie's voice filtered in from the lounge.

"John tells me that you're about to retire?" Judy enquired as she placed her wine glass on the table.

"Yes. I'm finishing in a few weeks' time. And I'm ready for it."

"I don't blame you, Derek."

"And you? How's work?"

Judy took a sip of her wine, telling herself to slow down. "It's okay. Keeps me ticking over. I may look for something else, especially if I move over this way."

"Oh!" Derek exclaimed, a surprised look on his face. "You're moving?"

"Yes. I spoke," she paused, controlling her emotions, "to Lucy about it. It's been on my mind since Brian passed away. And now, with everything that's happened, it makes sense to move closer to John and Lottie."

"Yes. I suppose it does," Derek replied, taking a pull on his beer.

"We were talking earlier. John will need to think about a job soon. Won't you, love?"

John nodded. "Yeah."

"So, if he gets a regular job, he'll need help with Lottie. School runs and so on."

"Yes. I suppose he will. We'll both help out, too. After all, I'm retiring. It's only fair that we all do our bit."

Judy rose from her chair, walked over to Derek and planted a kiss on his cheek. "Thank you. John and Lottie really do have a wonderful family around them."

Derek tried to speak, his throat tightening with emotion. He simply nodded, fighting back the tears as he grabbed his beer glass. "Derek," Margaret called as she walked from the lounge, "Lottie wants to show you her dolly."

"Okay. Here goes," he replied, getting up and heading for the lounge.

Margaret placed her empty mug in the sink and turned to John. "Right. Shall we get cracking?"

Sean returned to his cell, his makeshift Christmas dinner sitting uncomfortably in his gut. He sat down heavily, slipping off his trainers before stretching out on the bunk. *Luke.* He'd received the worst news in his short life. His younger brother was dead. He'd had to be restrained after staff at the detention centre had given him the news, as he'd tipped over furniture and smashed a cabinet. He'd been led to a holding room, placed in isolation to cool down. An hour later, he'd been let out for dinner, led to the canteen by two orderlies. He wiped his eyes, wincing out loud. He gingerly touched the swelling on his cheek. *Fuck,* he cursed as his finger played over the inflamed flesh that had turned an angry scarlet colour. He'd received a sucker punch the day before, whilst queueing for dinner. He'd gone down hard, coming to in a side office, away from the main canteen. Word had gotten around. He was a child snatcher and a murderer. Many had given him a wide berth, his petulant scowl enough to make some think twice. However, a few of the inmates had seen it as a challenge.

And as he lay on the bed, his next thought came to him. *When's the next helping?* The guv'nor, as everyone called him, had quickly moved Sean to a single room, away from the others. For the first time in his life, Sean felt scared. Scared that he'd not make it out alive. Scared that he'd never see his brother and maybe never see his mother again. His tough exterior was cracking at the seams. He felt small and fragile, not the confident boy at school who ruled the roost. Sean turned onto his side as tears began flowing down his cheeks. He wept quietly, not wanting anyone to hear his sobs. His weakness.

John flopped down heavily on the settee, barely managing to keep his wine from spilling. His parents had departed an hour before, John having to walk his rather drunk father to the waiting car as his mother tutted in a half-playful way. They'd waved them off before John got Lottie ready for bed. He'd lain next to her, stroking her hair, watching her eyelids grow heavy before the oblivion of sleep took her. John tidied a few things away in the kitchen while Judy showered. Then, as soon as the bathroom was free, he immersed himself in an almost unbearably hot shower. It did the trick, revitalising him somewhat as he changed his clothes and headed downstairs in grey joggers and a T-shirt.

Judy was sitting on the opposite settee, in light-blue pyjamas, holding a glass of wine. "Lovely dinner, John," she said, raising her glass to him.

"Thanks. It wasn't bad at all." He looked at his mother-in-law, noticing how tired she now looked. He'd always regarded her as an attractive woman, who wore her age well. Now, as he studied her, he noticed that the recent events had taken their toll.

"It was nice not to have to cook on Christmas Day. I may be here next year," she ventured, taking a sip of her wine.

"You're on." John looked at the TV, his mind a tumult of thoughts. "I still can't believe it, Judy. I just can't accept that she's gone. It kinda hits me in waves. I keep expecting her to walk through the door as if nothing has happened."

"I know, love. I think Lottie is handling it better than all of us. Kids are resilient. I lost my dad when I was seven. Mum was in bits, but me and my brother just got on with it. We're all going to go through the mill, John. But as long as Lottie is okay, that's the main thing. God, I never thought I'd be burying my own daughter. You hear people talk about it, thinking that it must be an awful thing to do. Now that I'm actually about to do it, I've no idea if I'll get through it in one piece. Especially after losing Brian a few months ago."

"You'll get through it, Judy. I know you will. When Brian died, Lucy commented about how strong you were. She said that you can handle anything that life throws at you. I know, this is probably worse than losing a partner. But we'll all get through it. And we'll make sure that Lottie is loved and raised just how Lucy would have wanted."

The older woman nodded, quickly wiping away a tear that had fallen onto her cheek. "Thank you, John. I couldn't do this without you."

"Well, I'm always going to be here."

She nodded, then another thought came to her. "Have you heard any more from the police?"

"Not for a few days. I suppose they are taking a few days off over Christmas. The detective did tell me that the trial might not happen straight away. It could take a while."

"I'd love to know their identities. Bastards!"

"Me too. But the police said that their identities will be protected due to their age."

"I think that is a pile of shit! Killers are killers, whether they are eight or eighty. I don't care how long they go down for. Knowing our lot, they'll probably be out in ten years or so."

John nodded. "Probably."

"And if they are, John, they'll need to pay. A prison sentence with Playstations and ping-pong is not justice."

"What are you saying?" John asked, placing his wine glass on the table.

"I'm saying that if I ever find out who they are, I'll stick a knife in them myself. I don't care how long I have to wait. One day, they'll get what's coming to them."

The drinks continued to flow as John and Judy sat on the settee. Empty glasses were re-filled as the evening wore on. Halfway through the conversation, John broke down, falling forward onto the carpet. "I miss her, Judy. I'm not strong enough to get through this. How can I carry on without Lucy?"

Judy pulled him back against the settee, holding his face in her hands. "Now listen, John. I don't wanna hear such nonsense. You have to get through this. You have a little girl who is scared and in pain. You need to be strong, for her. The rest of us will be strong too, despite the pain that we're all feeling. You hear what I'm saying?"

"Sorry," he replied, attempting to sniff back the tears. "I just feel lost. One minute everything seems like normal, the next, I feel like the world is about to swallow me up. I don't know what to do."

"You'll be okay. We all have to forget our own heartbreak. It's Lottie who needs us. You've seen what can happen to kids these days when their parents break up. Some go off the rails, because it affects them so badly. And it's the same for Lottie. She needs twice the love that she's already been given, John. Lucy gave her so much. And now," she paused, her emotions threatening to boil over. "And now she's gone. So, we're all going to have to fill in for her. Give Lottie the love that Lucy would have given. Does that make sense?"

John nodded, wiping his red-rimmed eyes. "I guess so. Thank you, Judy," he replied, giving her a hug.

"No need to thank me. We're family. That's what families do. Now, come on. Let's get you off the floor and into bed. Or else we'll both be suffering tomorrow."

John nodded, rising unsteadily to his feet. They switched off the lights, John making sure that the back and front doors were both locked before he trudged upstairs after Judy, wondering just how much suffering he was still to endure.

17

JANUARY – 2006

John stood next to Judy, his arm around her. They looked straight ahead at the wooden coffin on the raised dais in front of them. A few moments before, they'd walked along dark flagstones, down the centre of the crematorium, family and friends of Lucy filing in behind them. "My baby," Judy croaked, sagging slightly.

John steadied her, squeezing her shoulders. "I know, Judy." Outside, dark clouds hung over the town of Redditch, a few miles to the south of Birmingham. He glanced to his right, at his parents, watching as they clung to each other for succour. John looked away as he caught sight of his father's tears, wanting to hold it together as much as he possibly could. *Ludovico Einaudi* played gently in the background. John had chosen the track which was one of Lucy's favourites.

The Celebrant walked past John and Judy, stopping to greet them both. "Good morning," she began, her soft Welsh accent barely audible over the pipe-music. "Are you both okay?"

"Not really," Judy replied tearfully. "But we'll get through this."

"It will be a lovely service," she soothed, her kind face settling Judy somewhat. "John has given me so many wonderful memories of Lucy. I will speak to you in a short while," she said, excusing herself as she walked up to a wooden podium. The music ended, gently fading out as the Celebrant addressed the packed crematorium. "Please, be seated." Everyone took their cue, the sound of creaking benches filling the stark interior.

John placed his hand on Judy's giving it a brief squeeze. "Love you, Judy."

She looked at him, her eyes red-rimmed. "Love you too, John."

The Celebrant placed her hands on the podium, looking over towards the coffin that lay in front of large glass windows. "Well, thank you all for coming. There are many family and loved ones here today, a true testament to Lucy. We are here this morning to pay our last respects and bid farewell to her. We are here to honour and pay tribute to her life, and in our own way, to express our love and admiration for her.

"I know that everyone, myself including, is deeply saddened and shocked by Lucy's death, and though she was taken from the bosom of her family and friends far too early, we will try in the short time we have here this morning to make this occasion a celebration of her life, and to express our thanks for having known, and loved her.

"I sincerely hope that at the end of this farewell ceremony for her, you will also feel glad that you took the opportunity to do some of your grieving in the presence of others who have known and loved Lucy.

"Lucy was not religious. She did not want a service in the eyes of God. Therefore, you have my company this morning, as Lucy would have wished."

John wiped his eyes, his hands shaking slightly as he stared at the coffin. Lucy's name was spelled out in white flowers on one side of the coffin. On the other side, the word 'Mummy' was displayed. A lump formed in the soldier's throat.

The Celebrant continued. "All of you seated here today, at one point or another, and to some degree or other, have had your lives enriched by Lucy's presence. That is why we are all here. Because Lucy made our lives better, in many different ways.

"I'd like to read that great message of hope and comfort that was written by Henry Scott Holland for his wife just before he died. I feel quite sure that Lucy would have shared the sentiments expressed in the words." She stepped back a few paces, her back resting against the wall.

"All is well.
Death is nothing at all.
I have only slipped away into the next room.
Whatever we were to each other, we still are.
Please, call me by my old familiar name.
Speak of me in the same easy way you always did.
Laugh, as we always laughed, at the little jokes we shared together.
Think of me and smile.
Let my name be the household name it always was,
Spoken without the shadow of a ghost in it.
Life means all it ever meant.
It is the same as it ever was.
Death is inevitable, so why should I be out of mind because I am out of sight?
I am but waiting for you, for an interval very near.
Nothing is past or lost.
One brief moment and all will be as it was before.
Only better and happier.
Together forever.
All is well."

Judy let out a sob that echoed around the crematorium. Margaret put her arm around the woman's shoulder. "It's okay, love. We're all here." Judy nodded, looking down at her lap.

The Celebrant waited a moment until the service was ready to continue. "A popular Buddhist saying is, 'What the caterpillar perceives as the end, to the butterfly is just the beginning.' Know that all that has life has its beginning and its end.

"Life exists in the time-span between birth and death, and life's significance lies in the experiences and satisfaction we achieve in that lifespan, and though we know that Lucy's departure was shocking and sudden, this morning I would like to leave that to one side and focus on her earlier life and also her more recent past, as well as the other more positive aspects of Lucy's life and her personality.

"She was born Lucy Marie Rogers at the Queen Elizabeth Hospital on May 30th, 1975, to Judy and Brian. And so began the life of the woman that the people gathered here today were proud, honoured and privileged to call their wife, their daughter and their friend. And there is someone else who is not with us here today, who was proud to call her, Mummy." The Celebrant paused, letting a few tears fall amongst loved ones.

"She was an only child, but never let that solitude affect her. She was an outgoing girl, a constant stream of her friends turning up at Judy and Brian's house. Sleepovers and parties were commonplace, with Brian regularly putting up with such timeless classics as *Rhythm is a Dancer* and *Saturday Night*. I'm sure you can remember, Judy, wondering if a pack of teenagers were about to join you and your beloved Brian on the settee from above." Judy smiled, tears running down her cheeks as she thought of her husband.

"Lucy was very sporty at school, excelling in anything she put her mind to," the Celebrant continued. "She was captain of the hockey team, along with being a very proficient swimmer. She was always involved in something, never becoming bored or disenfranchised with life. She was, in essence, a very happy person.

"Lucy was a lot like her father in many respects, always willing to help others. She was clever, funny and kind. And, as John has shared with me, sometimes a bit scatty. She would often say things to John in conversation, suddenly realising that she had made a terrible faux pas. Comments like, 'you're not going to use me as an escape goat'. Or when she thought that Juan Pablo Angel was the name of the statue on Sugarloaf Mountain, when in fact, he played for *Aston Villa*." The Celebrant smiled when she saw a few people amongst the throng exchange warm glances with loved ones.

"She was very social, having a few close friends who she enjoyed a night out with on a regular basis. If she was not out socialising, Lucy enjoyed having friends and family over at the family home, enjoying spending quality time with Gemma, Vicky and Michelle in particular.

Friends that she had grown up with, whose friendships had strengthened as they approached adult life.

"When she left college, Lucy began working for a property management company in Birmingham. She enjoyed the job, making new friends and impressing her peers. Around this time, she met John, at a nightclub. She was out with friends, celebrating her birthday when she got chatting to a young soldier, who was home on leave. They exchanged numbers and agreed to meet the following evening. And the rest, as they say, is history. They were married on July 1st, 2001. They had already settled in their new home when Lucy discovered that she was expecting their first child.

She looked at John, who was struggling to keep it together. "When Lottie arrived, it changed their lives. John was the loving father and husband, Lucy the attentive mother who nurtured and loved Lottie with a strength that she never knew she had."

John broke down, Judy and his mother holding his hands as their own tears fell freely. "It's okay, Son," Margaret soothed. "We're here."

The Celebrant continued, her voice steady and calm. "Lucy felt complete, being a loving wife and mother in equal measure. Even when John was overseas, which was a lot, Lucy had the support of her parents, Judy and Brian, along with John's parents, Margaret and Derek. It was a close family. And a loving one, too.

"Lucy had a very gentle easy-going nature and she very rarely lost her cool. John can only recall one such incident, when he'd left their passports in the hotel safe, only realising when they'd arrived at the Palma Airport. And, like all women seated in this room, she never let him live it down." John smiled, remembering the simmering red-faced woman, decked out in sandals and a summer dress, cursing at him in front of the check-in staff. "But I'm sure wherever she is, she is smiling down, enjoying the memory.

"Sadly, Lucy lost her father last year. Something that deeply affected her. She struggled to come to terms with Brian's untimely departure, spending time with her mother to share the grief. It was Lottie who helped her mother and grandmother get through the pain. Her love and energy focused Lucy and Judy's efforts, bringing them even closer together."

The Celebrant continued, highlighting specific moments in Lucy's life, drawing more smiles and even more tears from family and friends. As the sun broke through the low-slung clouds, the Celebrant walked over to the wooden coffin, now bathed in light. "Let's now spend a few moments in silence, so we can each remember Lucy in our own special way. For those of you that hold a religious faith, you might want to say a silent prayer for Lucy's family, which may offer you some form of comfort and strength in the coming days, weeks and months ahead."

A few moments later, the Celebrant stood back as music wafted across the crematorium. *Arrival*, by Abba, played out clearly as John, his parents and Judy walked over to the coffin, the others who were seated behind them looking on sadly. John held onto Judy as the four of them stood there, unable to speak as emotions took hold of them.

Finally, John stepped forward, bending to kiss the coffin's lid. "Goodbye, babe. I love you so much. And I always will." He stayed there for a few moments, his hands feeling the texture of the wood as the others looked on.

"Farewell, Lucy," Derek whispered, placing his hand on the coffin, stroking it gently. He wept silently, holding onto his wife who stood trembling next to him.

"Goodbye, sweet Lucy. We all love you," Margaret whimpered, her voice thick with emotion.

John looked up suddenly as the coffin shifted. He gathered Judy in his arms as she began to sob, the noise echoing for all to hear. "No. I can't do it, John. I can't leave her."

"It's okay, Judy," John comforted, his own voice trembling.

"But it's not. She cannot leave us. She's my baby!"

Derek and Margaret moved away, giving Judy her space. "We need to say goodbye, Judy," John soothed. "I know it's the worst thing we'll ever have to do. But we must do it. Take my arm." She did so, nodding as she wiped the tears from her eyes.

"Sweet dreams, my love," she croaked, before John led her past the Celebrant and the other mourners. He led her past floral tributes, laid out on the flagstone floor. He averted his eyes, wanting to feel fresh air on his skin. They both walked down a small flight of stone steps, stopping next to a gravel pathway.

"Let's just stand here for a minute or two," John suggested.

Judy nodded, pulling a packet of cigarettes out of her handbag. She lit one, inhaling deeply before blowing smoke into the air. "It was a lovely service. But no mother should have to see that."

"I know, Judy. Yes, it was a nice service and there was a great turnout. She was a popular girl." He leaned against the wall next to his mother-in-law, his tears running down his cheeks. "I just don't know what I'm going to do. She was my world. I never thought this would happen. If anything, I thought it would be me lying in a coffin, with Lucy saying goodbye to me."

"She did worry about you, John. She dreaded watching the news, thinking that bad news would filter through to her. She was counting the days to when you came home."

John nodded as his parents appeared through the doorway. Derek walked up to his son, embracing him. Margaret hugged Judy, the two women bound in grief. "It's alright, Son," Derek said. "We've laid her to rest. I know this is probably one of your darkest days, but every day from now on, it will get that little bit easier."

"Thanks, Dad. I don't know what I'd do without you all."

His father looked into John's eyes, seeing the pain etched there. He was reminded of a younger version of himself, short dark hair and dark eyes. A son to be proud of, in many ways. Now, Derek was proud of his son's strength. He knew the soldier would get through this nightmare. And they would all be there to help rebuild both his, and Lottie's life. Brick by brick.

18

John opened the front door, to be greeted by DI Blaney and DS Shaw. "Hi," he said neutrally.

"Good morning, John," Blaney replied. "Can we come in?"

"Sure. I've just brewed some coffee."

"Great timing," Blaney stated, holding his hand out so Shaw could enter the house.

"Come through," John began, ushering them into the long kitchen. "Who wants what?"

"Coffee, please," Shaw replied politely. "White with one."

"Same for me, please, John," Blaney added as he leaned against the kitchen worktop.

John busied himself for a moment, before handing steaming mugs to the detectives. They nodded their thanks, nodding again in appreciation of the heady brew. "That's really good stuff," Shaw proclaimed.

"Thanks. One of my few indulgences. You can't scrimp on coffee and toothpaste. My dad taught me that."

"Wise man," Blaney countered dryly. "We thought we'd give you some space to adjust and get Christmas and the funeral out of the way, John. However, we have an update for you."

"Go on," John said, placing his mug on the table.

"The younger brother involved in your wife's murder is dead."

"What?" the ex-soldier blurted.

"It seems a couple of young scrotes at the detention centre tried to scare him. They tipped his bunk over, with him on top of it. He fell and hit his head. He pretty much died instantly."

"Jesus," John whispered. "I don't know what to say."

"We'll never really know his involvement in your wife's death, John," Shaw continued. "But it does look like he was pulled along for the ride by his older brother. Added to that, he was under the influence of alcohol and cannabis. He was just a little boy. In the wrong place at the wrong time."

"And the older brother?" John asked, as he picked up his mug.

"His trial begins in four weeks at Birmingham Crown Court. It will be pretty drawn-out, but we're confident of a conviction. And the mother has been convicted for possession of Class A drugs. We can't tell you her name, John, for obvious reasons."

"I understand," John muttered.

"However, after she found out about the death of her son, she's pretty much complied with everything we asked. She's helped us get a notorious drug dealer off the streets, which has been reflected in her sentencing. Yes, she's done wrong. But I think she knows that. Her life is pretty much over, John," Blaney stated. "She'll be out in a few years' time with one son in prison, the other in the ground." The detective took a swig of his coffee as the younger man digested the information.

"And the drug dealer?" John asked.

Shaw placed her coffee on the countertop. "He'll be inside for a good stretch. We've had our eye on him for a few years, but were unable to pin anything substantial on him until the mother offered us an olive branch."

"I'm glad he's off the streets. If it were not for him, Lucy might still be alive."

"Maybe, John," Blaney replied. "But try not to dwell on that. Lots of things all happened at once, which led to your wife's death. By the way, how is your daughter?"

"She's doing okay. Kids are resilient. She's had a couple of episodes, where she thought that someone wanted to hurt her. But other than that, she's doing as well as can be expected."

"And how about you?" Shaw asked.

"I don't know, I guess I'm just trying to get on with things. It's finally sunk in. The first few weeks I was on autopilot, reacting to stuff. Now, I've had time to accept the fact that Lucy is not coming back. I've applied for a few jobs, too. I can't sit around all day moping. I need to get back into the swing of things, which would be hard enough for an ex-soldier to do in normal circumstances."

"I know, John," Blaney agreed. "I know many ex-coppers, who struggle with life once they leave the Force. But you're young. You'll adapt well."

"I hope so. Lucy's mum is moving in next week. She's sold her house in Tamworth and is looking to buy something close by. She's offered to help out with Lottie, who'll be going to school in September. And my parents are only a few miles away and have also offered to chip in. I am grateful for that, at least."

"It looks like you've got a nice little support network," Shaw said.

"I know. They've been brilliant. I honestly don't know what I'd do without them."

Shaw reached forward and squeezed John's hand. He gave her a brief smile before looking down at the floor. "Well, you keep them close, John. You'll all get through it together."

Sensing a change in the dynamic of the conversation, Blaney intervened. "We'll give you an update when the trial reaches its conclusion, John. I know you said that you didn't want to attend court?"

"No. I'd rather not. One, because it would be too upsetting. And two, because I'd probably try and get at the suspect. It's better that I'm well away from it all."

"Okay. Be advised, though, there is a chance that the identity of the suspect will be released during the trial. I just want to pre-warn you. Have you had any people knocking on your door, or asking you questions?"

"No. Not that I'm aware of. Don't worry, if I get any attention, I will just say nothing."

"Good to know," Blaney replied, draining his mug. "Right. I guess we'd better be on our way. Thanks for the coffee and we'll be in touch, John."

"Thank you." He walked down the hallway, opening the door as a gust of cool wind invaded the warm house. John shook their hands, watching from the doorway as they walked down the street towards a dark saloon car.

"He seems to be doing okay," Jenn offered, as they stared out of the windscreen.

"He does. He's a soldier. They are tougher than most."

"I know. But he's still human. You can see that he's not out of the woods just yet. Shame. He seems like a really nice guy."

"He does. It's always the nice ones that get put through the mill. Come on, let's get back to the station. That was probably the best coffee that we'll get today."

Shaw smiled thinly as the car pulled away from the kerb. Her eyes lingered on the semi-detached house as they rolled past. *Hang in there, John,* she thought as Blaney depressed the accelerator, propelling them towards the junction at the end of the road.

John watched the car turn right, vanishing from sight. He turned from the bay window, walking back through the lounge and into the kitchen. He picked up his phone from the table, checking the home screen for messages. Finding nothing of interest, he placed the mugs in the sink, before heading upstairs. He'd been in the middle of something when the detectives had arrived at his house. He now stood in his bedroom, a large white plastic bag in his hand as he looked at the contents of his wife's wardrobe.

"Let's get this over with," he murmured to himself as he laid all Lucy's clothing out on the bed. He took a dark coat off its hanger, checking the pockets before folding it and placing it at the bottom of the bag. A small leather jacket was next as John rooted through the numerous pockets. His fingers found something, pulling out a paper poppy. He twirled it in his fingers, smiling briefly. He knew that Lucy wore her poppy with pride, as the slogan stated. He placed it on the dresser in front of him and folded the jacket carefully. He worked his way through the garments, nipping downstairs to fetch two more bags. Half an hour later, he'd filled three large refuse sacks. He stood there, looking at the empty space inside the wardrobe, his heart aching. A tear ran down his cheek as he closed the doors slowly. He sighed heavily before taking the sacks downstairs and deposited them at the front door.

A noise in the kitchen made him turn around. His mobile phone was gently vibrating on the kitchen table. He picked it up, pressing the green button on the handset.

"Hi, Judy," he began.

"Hello, love. How's things?"

"Not too bad. Just had the police here. They've given me an update on the case."

"Oh? What did they say?"

"Well, the younger brother was killed, not long after he was detained. Some of the other kids tipped his bunk bed over in some kind of prank. He hit his head and died at the scene."

"Bloody hell!" his mother-in-law exclaimed.

"The older brother's trial starts very soon. And the mother has already been sent down. It looks like she helped them with the investigation, putting the dealer that gave her the drugs behind bars."

"Oh well, that's something, I suppose."

"Yes. The detectives think that the younger brother was probably not the instigator, more likely that he was dragged along for the ride. It's a shame. After all, he was just a little boy, only a few years older than Lottie."

"I suppose you're right. At least the older brother will face justice. Well, if you can call it that. He'll be well looked after. Too many do-gooders around these days. That's Labour for you."

"Hmm," John replied, not wanting to get drawn into a political debate. "I probably won't hear back from them until the trial is over. And they've warned me to keep an eye out for roving reporters."

"That's the last thing we need. Snooping so-and-sos!"

John smiled, liking his mother-in-law's turn-of-phrase. "Anyway, I've bagged up all Lucy's clothing, like you said. I've got three sacks that I will take to the charity shop in Northfield. I'll leave all the jewellery for you to sort out. Is that okay?"

"That's fine, love. The next time I'm over, I'll take a look. Anyway, it looks like I've got a moving date," she replied, trying to sound positive about things. "The couple buying my house have exchanged contracts and they want to move in two weeks on Friday. So, I've started boxing stuff up. Say thanks to your dad for all the boxes. They've been a godsend."

"Okay. We need to look at hiring a van then. You leave that with me, Judy. I'll make a few calls."

"Thanks, John. And the storage?"

"There's a local company that will take all your stuff. The costs are reasonable, and I'm hoping that you won't have your stuff there for long."

"Me too. That's the other reason I'm calling. I'm going to look at a house tomorrow in Rednal. I found it on the internet the other day, so I called the agents to arrange a viewing."

"Sounds good. How are you getting over?"

"On the train."

"I can pick you up, Judy. It's no trouble."

"It's fine, love. I tell you what, if you're free, perhaps you can come with me?"

"Yes. I'll come along. What time is the viewing?"

"Eleven. I'll get off at Longbridge."

"Okay. I'll be waiting outside. We can grab a bit of lunch afterwards if you fancy?"

"Sounds like a plan," she replied. "The house looks nice. Two bedrooms, which is enough for me."

"Great. It will be nice having you close by."

"I know. It will be nice to think that you're both just down the road."

"Okay. Well, I suppose I'd better get my arse in gear and drop this stuff off at the charity shop. I'll be outside the station in the morning."

"Thanks, John. I'll see you then. Love you."

"Love you too, Judy," John replied before ending the call. He headed upstairs, not looking at his wife's belongings next to the doorway. Three measly bags, waiting for a new owner.

19

JUNE - 2006

Sean sat in the dock, his face impassive; only the tapping of his feet gave away his nerves. The trial had dragged on, with examination and cross-examination. The youth, who'd just turned sixteen, had been relieved that no family members had been present at the trial, in which he'd been grilled by the prosecution. The jury had retired the previous evening to consider the case and decide on a verdict. Sean looked across the courtroom, seeing the two detectives who were leading the case. *Wankers,* he thought, locking eyes with the middle-aged man. The detective held his gaze, forcing Sean to look away. He heard the judge begin proceedings, the words not quite registering as Sean thought once more of his brother. *I'm so sorry, Lukey.* He sighed as a member of the jury stood up.

"Lady foreperson, have you reached a verdict in this case?" the Judge asked.

"Yes, your Honour," a woman close to the Judge replied.

"In regard to the first crime, that of murder, how do you find the defendant?"

"Guilty." Sean flinched in his chair, his vision starting to swim as a low murmur spread across the court.

"In regard to the second crime of attempted murder, how do you find the defendant?"

"Guilty." More murmuring. Sean looked up to see the detectives looking at him, their faces impassive.

"In regard to the third and final charge of abduction, how do you find the defendant?"

"Guilty."

"Thank you, Jury, for your service today. Court is adjourned for one hour."

Sean was led from the gallery by two police officers. They walked him below, ushering him into a holding cell, closing the door behind him. "Fuck," he uttered. He paced the room, his suit feeling unnaturally snug, the tie constricting his throat. He loosened it, feeling sweat trickle down his back as he tried to get his thoughts under control. *Why did I plead not guilty*? he thought. *He's gonna throw the fucking book at me!* He slumped onto the bed, tears dripping onto the concrete floor as he let his emotions escape him. Sean lay on the lumpy mattress and sobbed, his whole body shaking, his mind wondering what would become of his life.

"Sean Terry, on 10th December 2005, you and your younger brother knowingly abducted a young girl. You both led her away from her mother with intent to commit harm, whether physical or psychological. The fact that the victim of this crime intervened, led to an escalation with the direst consequences. I have taken into account the fact that both of you were under the influence of alcohol and cannabis. However, you were fifteen years old at that time and knew right from wrong. You led the young girl to an empty construction site, where you attempted to conceal your crime by hiding the body of the girl underneath burning pallets. However, when the girl's mother attempted to stop her, you struck her.

"The coroner has stated that the injury sustained when Lucy Wilson landed on the ground would not have killed her, but that she would have received a significant brain injury. You heinously tried to cover this up by setting fire to the victim, then leaving the scene of the crime with your brother, Luke. It is my belief that you did not leave the house that morning with the intention of killing anyone. In mitigation, I have also taken into account the fact that your younger brother has recently lost his life, and that your mother has been imprisoned for drug-related offences. However, I cannot lose sight of the fact that you knowingly abducted a young girl and killed her mother when she tried to intervene."

Sean stood in the dock, his legs quivering as the judge continued. A trickle of sweat slipped from his forehead, running down his jawline.

"Mother and daughter were enjoying a day out at the shops, buying items of clothing for John Wilson, who was serving in Afghanistan with the Royal Marines. He received the tragic news of the attack on his family whilst serving his country with distinction. Now, he has to rebuild his family's life without his wife. A young girl will grow up without her mother, all because of your heinous actions."

Sean bowed his head, not able to look the judge as he continued.

"I also have to consider the seven convictions you have already accumulated as a minor. Because you are only sixteen, the sentence I shall impose aims not only to punish you for your crimes, it also will serve to protect the public. The sentencing exercise involves a number of distinct steps. For the three charges, of which you have been found guilty, I could impose three separate sentences, which would run concurrently. However, with all the factors involved in the case, it is my judgement that I impose upon you the maximum sentence of Her Majesty's Pleasure. You will be detained at a young offenders' facility until you reach eighteen. From there, you will be sent to a prison for young men, where you will remain until you reach twenty-five. From there, you will be detained indefinitely at one of Her Majesty's prisons."

Sean wilted into his chair, the judge's words becoming indistinct, before two uniformed guards led him from the court. His eyes played across the gallery, coming to rest on a middle-aged woman with steely-grey hair. Her eyes locked onto his and Sean felt a burning hatred emanate from the woman as he passed by her. He was led along a dimly-lit corridor then hustled down two flights of concrete stairs. They approached a double door which one of the guards unlocked with his swipe card. As daylight flooded in, Sean stared at the white van in front of him, its door hanging open.

"Take one last look at the outside world, prick," the guard spat. "It'll be a fucking long time until you see it again." He was bundled inside, shuffling towards a grey bench against the panelled wall of the van. He bowed his head and began sobbing.

Judy waited until Sean Terry was out of view before she crumpled to the bench, sobbing uncontrollably. Margaret placed a comforting arm around her shoulders. "Let's go home, love," she said soothingly. "It's over."

"It's over, John," Margaret stated into her phone as she stood outside the court. Judy was a few paces away, puffing on a cigarette as light rain blanketed central Birmingham.

"Okay. What was the verdict?"

"Guilty. He's being detained at Her Majesty's Pleasure."

"Good. At least the little bastard will be off the streets for a long time," John replied.

"Not long enough. He'll be out one day. Free to carry on his life. Whilst we have to live with his actions. He killed our Lucy."

"I know. And if it were up to me, they'd hang him."

"I agree. Judy's not doing too good. We're going to jump on the bus in a few minutes. It's bedlam here. There are reporters, TV vans and hundreds of people jostling for position."

"Do you want me to come and fetch you both?"

"No, love. You stay there with Lottie. We'll be home in a bit."

"I'll bring her over to yours in about an hour. Is that okay?"

"Of course, it is, Son. I think we all need to be together today."

"Okay, Mum. I'll see you in a bit. Love you."

"Love you too, John," Margaret replied, ending the call. She linked arms with Judy as they walked steadily towards Corporation Street, with its numerous shoppers and endless bus stops.

An hour later, Sean stood in a small room, looking out at greying skies. He'd been given a pair of dark joggers and a grey pullover to wear, along with a cheap pair of pumps. He'd felt hundreds of sets of eyes follow his slow progress through the main canteen and had tried to avert his gaze as sniggering and laughter had drifted towards him. His few belongings had been taken away from him by a uniformed officer as Sean had stood at a serving hatch, flanked by two burly men. Then, he'd been led to his room, the door locking behind him. A man had stood watching for a few minutes, for what reason, Sean did not know. He'd turned his back, walking over to the barred window that looked out onto a small grassed area, with tall conifers beyond. He played the incident over in his head. His mind focused on the dead woman's hands, how her fingers had twitched as she'd lain there. How her eyes had rolled back in her skull as Sean had stood over her, wondering what to do next.

He was snapped out of his daydream as the door behind him opened. Sean turned, looking into the eyes of something he didn't expect to see. A woman, wearing a flowery dress which finished just above the knee. He guessed her age to be around the early forties mark. She was petite, with dark curly hair. Her kind face and appealing smile put Sean at ease slightly. As he'd grown into adolescence, Sean had developed a thing for older women. When he did attend school, he spent certain lessons staring at certain teachers. One in particular had been the focus of his daydreams and night-time fantasies. Looking at the woman in front of him, Sean felt a similar stirring, despite his grave situation.

"I'm Julia Sutton," the woman said. "You could say that I'm the guv'nor. Some people call me that. All you need to know, Sean, is that I'm in charge."

"Okay," Sean muttered.

"Someone will bring you your dinner in a few minutes. You're a high-profile case, people in here will latch onto that. Better to keep you out of circulation for a few days. Are you okay with that?"

"I guess so," he responded, head slightly bowed. "So, everyone knows what I did?"

"Some do. But don't let that concern you," she countered, her light Black Country accent steadying the youth's nerves some more.

"I just wanna stay out of trouble."

"Well, that's a good start. You'll be with us for the next two years, Sean. I know it feels very strange right now, but in time, you'll adjust." She looked at her watch, blowing her hair out of her face. "I will speak to you soon, Sean."

"Okay," he murmured as the woman turned and left the room, the door locking behind her.

Sean returned to the window, trying to figure out exactly where he was. He'd forgotten the name of the facility as he'd walked in through the entrance. He'd been watching everything else. Wondering what to expect. Hoping that he'd make it to his room in one piece. A plane appeared on the horizon, climbing steadily towards low-slung clouds. *I must be close to the airport,* he thought, absently picking at a loose piece of skin on his thumb. He tore the skin off with his teeth, swallowing it as he watched the airliner heading from right to left across his limited horizon. *I'd give anything to be on that plane. Anywhere but here.*

He leaned against the window sill as the plane disappeared from view. *One day,* he thought. *I'll be on a plane like that. Heading far away from this shithole. From this nightmare.*

20

AUGUST - 2006

"Come here, princess," John offered as he held out his arms. Lottie walked towards him, letting her father lift her gently from the grass, her slender legs wrapping around his waist.

"What, Daddy?" she exclaimed.

"Just stay here for a moment with me."

"What for?" she replied inquisitively, looking over his shoulder towards the open kitchen door.

"Happy birthday to you, happy birthday to you, happy birthday, dear Lottie. Happy birthday to you," her grandparents sang, as they advanced from the kitchen across the patio towards her. Judy was holding a cake in both hands. A white cake, square in shape with a mermaid figurine nestled between white and blue iced waves. She placed it reverently on the garden table, turning to smile at the little girl.

John placed Lottie on the ground, noticing that her bare feet were lightly tanned. "I hope you like it, princess. I know you like *The Little Mermaid*."

"Let me light the candles," Derek said, carefully lighting the five pink candles that were spaced evenly at the one end of the cake, away from the mermaid.

Lottie stood there, unsure of what to do as the candles burned evenly in the afternoon sun. She took a step forward, whilst taking a deep breath. In one motion, she leaned over the cake, blowing all the candles out in one go. "Hip, hip, hooray," they all proclaimed, their words sounding ever-so-slightly hollow.

"Have you made a wish?" Margaret asked.

"Yes. But it won't come true," the five-year-old replied.

"What did you wish for?" Derek enquired, realising his mistake as soon as the words left his lips.

"I wished for Mummy." The mood was extinguished, like the candles that now stood smoking in the sunlight.

"I know, princess," John whispered as he hefted his daughter into his arms. She whimpered in his embrace as John felt her emotions rise to the surface. Her tears began dampening his T-shirt as Lottie's whimpers turned into sobs. Her grandparents stood there, unable to speak or move. They just watched them, their hearts breaking for the pain the little girl was still enduring.

"Give us a minute," John said. With Lottie still in his arms, he walked into the kitchen and through to the lounge, where he sat down on the settee, cradling his daughter on his lap. "Come on, princess. Don't be sad. Mummy would not want you to be upset, especially on your birthday."

"I miss Mummy, Daddy. I am so sad that I will never see her again," she cried, her face streaked with tears.

"I know, princess," John replied, his own tears dripping down his cheeks. "I am very sad, too. And I think of Mummy every day. But do you know what?" Lottie shook her head. "If we're both together, we'll be less sad. And Nanny Margaret, Grandad Derek and Nanny Judy will be here, too. They are also sad about Mummy. But we'll all stick together and make each other happy again. Do you understand?"

"Yes, Daddy," she replied, wiping her face. John looked towards the rear garden where three faces were looking back at him, their expressions grim. He nodded his head, signalling that things were okay. The threesome turned away, letting father and daughter have a moment of privacy. John watched as Derek started pointed at plants against the fence, a silent conversation with Judy ensuing as Margaret listened selectively. "Come on, princess. Let's go back outside. Is that okay?"

"Yes, Daddy. Will you cut the cake?"

"Do you want me to?"

"Please. Can I have a big slice, Daddy?"

John's heart melted as he stared into his daughter's blue eyes. "Of course, you can," he agreed, standing up with his daughter in his arms. "As long as Daddy can have a big slice, too."

The afternoon passed into evening, the atmosphere somewhat subdued. Lottie sat in the shade of an apple tree with her grandad, chattering about nothing in particular. Derek didn't mind, though. He drank in the moment, letting his son bring him refills of ale and lemonade for Lottie.

John, Judy and Margaret sat on garden chairs, enjoying the coolness of evening after the sweltering afternoon. "How's the new job going?" Judy asked as she placed her beer on the table in front of her.

"Not bad," her son-in-law replied. "It's not particularly taxing. And it's a set routine. One drop to Stoke, down to Milton Keynes, then back up to Brum," he replied. He'd been working for two weeks, after an old school friend had found him a job as a delivery driver for a local haulage company. "It'll pay the bills and give me plenty of quality time with Lottie."

"Well, that's the main thing," Judy replied softly.

"And thank you, both of you, for helping out. I wouldn't be able to do this without your help."

"Think nothing of it," Judy countered. "It's what families do. Right, Margaret?"

"Exactly," the other woman responded. "Whatever you need, Son. We're all here."

John levered himself out of his chair, walking over to hug his mother. She returned the embrace, her eyes closing as she squeezed her only child. After the brief contact, he did the same to his mother-in-law, who reciprocating willingly. "Thanks, guys. I love you both to bits."

The women looked at each other, smiling. "The feeling is mutual, Son," Margaret replied, tears welling up in her eyes.

John sat back down, looking up the garden towards his father and daughter. "Shall I set up camp for them?"

"Might be a good idea," Judy agreed. "They look inseparable."

"He loves Lottie to bits," Margaret stated as she lifted her glass from the table. She took a sip of wine, smiling at the scene at the bottom of the garden. "Funny, how both John and Lucy had no siblings. And now we have Lottie, who's in the same boat."

"True," John replied. "We both talked about that. How Lottie would never have cousins. That's why we'd hoped to add to the litter someday."

"You have time, John," Judy replied. "You're still young enough to start again."

John looked at his mother-in-law, shaking his head. "No, Judy. I was married once. Lucy was the love of my life. I can't even imagine being with someone else."

"I know, love. But in time, that may change. God, you're a good-looking bloke. They'll be queuing up for a guy like you. If I were twenty years younger, I'd be in that queue."

John almost choked on his beer, placing it back on the table. He laughed, drawing smiles from the women. "Bloody hell! You can't say something like that. You're my mother-in-law!"

"I think Judy is right, Son. You may not think it now, but one day, you'll meet someone else. No one will ever replace Lucy. But Lottie will need a mother-type figure in her life. You're a wonderful father. But you're tough, and you like man things. Lottie will need someone softer. Lucy gave her that softness. She was so attentive and caring. And one day, someone else will be that person."

"I can't think about that yet, Mum. Lottie needs me more than I need another woman."

Judy looked at her son-in-law, her heart swelling with pride for the young man sitting next to her. "I know, John. But in time you may. I didn't tell you, but one of my new neighbours has asked me out to dinner."

John and Margaret looked at her, surprised expressions spreading across their faces. "Really?" Margaret replied. "And have you said yes?"

"I have. No one will ever replace Brian. But I'm not quite drawing my pension yet. I need to live a little. You're a long time dead, as my Mum used to say."

"So, who is he?" the other woman enquired, becoming increasingly interested in the potential for a bit of good old gossip.

"He's called Bob. He lives a few doors down from me. We've been chatting off and on since I moved in. I've even been to his place for a coffee."

"Bloody hell!" John exclaimed. "You've kept that quiet."

"It's only coffee," she smirked. "But a few days ago, he asked me if I'd like to go for something to eat at the Hare and Hounds. So, I said yes. He's a widower, so we have a few things in common, I guess."

"Is he dishy?" Margaret probed, trying to sound neutral, even though she was now perched on the edge of her seat.

"He is actually. He's a few years older than me. Mid-fifties. But he's got all his own teeth and is quite sporty. He plays squash twice a week."

"What does he do?" John asked, noticing that his mother was now perched on the edge of her chair. He smiled. *Nosy bugger.*

"He's a builder, with his own business. So, even if we don't hit it off, he's a useful guy to have around."

"I like your train of thought," Margaret agreed. "I hope it goes well."

"I'll let you know," Judy replied, also noticing the other woman's sudden interest. "It's been over thirty years since I went on a date. I've no idea what to do."

"Just be yourself," John suggested. "You're a very attractive woman, with a lovely personality. Just go for it."

"Thanks, love," Judy gushed, her eyes brimming with fresh tears. "Now, I need a drink before the waterworks start. I've already redone my make up once today!"

~

Sean never saw the first punch coming. It was a glancing blow that sent him to his knees as the youths crowded around him. The ringleader stood over him, aiming a well-placed kick that caught Sean just under the jaw, snapping his head back. His vision burst into a million stars as his skull bounced off the concrete.

"Come on, white boy," the leader commanded, delivering a kick to Sean's groin. He rolled over, curling up into a ball as fists as trainers rained down on him. "Pick him up," the ringleader commanded.

"What for, Leroy?" the boy next to him asked.

"Just do it," he spat back.

Sean let himself be hefted from the ground as the afternoon sun touched the rooftops of the detention centre. "Stop it," he pleaded as he faced the mob. He counted six of them. Most of the youths were either his size or slightly smaller. It was the ringleader that stood out. He was a good few inches taller than Sean, with wiry, muscled arms and a dark, pock-marked face. As he smiled at Sean, a gold incisor glinted in the fading sunlight.

"Think I'm a pussy now, white boy?" he hissed.

"I never said that," Sean replied half-heartedly as a fist was driven into his ribs. He heard something give, one of his ribs cracking under the impact. He wilted, the boys straining to keep hold of his dead weight.

"Fucking liar. Jay told me, didn't you, Jay?"

"Damn right," another boy agreed, sneering at Sean. "He said you were a black pussy."

"Let him go," Leroy urged, looking around him to make sure they were out of sight. He didn't want to be disturbed. The boys did so. Sean leant against a pebble-dashed wall as his foe towered over him. "Come on then. Let's see how much of a pussy I am."

The boys melted away, giving their leader enough space to do this thing. Time seemed to slow down to Sean. He appraised his attacker, looking for any weakness. He watched as the boy came up on the balls of his feet, preparing to attack. Although Sean was smaller in stature, he was a natural fighter, constantly testing himself inside and outside of school. He'd never been bested and knew that if he was to get through prison life, he'd have to fight.

"Come on then, wanker!" His rebuke had the desired effect as he saw Leroy's face darken with anger. He fired out a jab, Sean feigning away from it, moving to his left. Leroy followed him, his fists floating in front of him as he advanced on his quarry.

"Fuck him up, Leroy," one boy shouted, goading his friend on.

"Come on, white-bwai," Leroy taunted, his accent switching from deep Brummie to Jamaican. He set himself for another punch, telegraphing it as Sean stepped forward a step, the fist sailing past his left ear. He fired off his own punch, catching Leroy in the solar plexus. The goading fell silent as the ringleader crumpled to his knees.

"Fucking black pussy," Sean hissed, before cupping the dark-skinned boy's skull in his hands. In one fluid motion, he yanked the skull downwards, driving his knee into Leroy's face. The snap of bone was audible to the gang members as they looked on in disbelief at the sight of their leader falling backwards onto the ground, bright blood oozing from his nostrils. He lay there immobile, as Sean faced the others. "Anyone else feeling brave?" he asked, a red mist descending over him.

They all took a collective step backwards as uniformed guards came running around the corner. "Oi!" one man bellowed, pinning Sean against the pebble-dashed wall. Another man went to the fallen youth, giving him the once-over.

"Call an ambulance," he shouted, as a female guard joined them in the courtyard. "He's in a bad way."

"You're in deep shit, Terry," the one guard stated.

"They started it. I was just defending myself."

"Tell that to the guv'nor," he replied as he yanked the young man towards the building.

Sean took one last look at his fallen adversary as the red mist dissipated. He looked down at him and smiled as he was led away. *Well, at least they'll not fuck with me anymore,* he thought, as he was frogmarched to Julia Sutton's office.

. . .

"I want everyone back in their room," Sutton ordered to the uniformed guard.

"Yes, guv," he replied, closing the door.

"Martin?" she called.

The man opened the door. "Guv?"

"I want all the CCTV from the courtyard. Have it ready for me as soon as you can."

"Will do," he replied, closing the door after him.

She looked at Sean, her face stern. "I told you to stay out of trouble."

"And I have been. They started this."

"How?"

"One of the inmates, called Tyler, told Leroy that I called him a pussy."

"And did you?"

"No way!" Sean retorted. "He's the kingpin in here. No one messes with him. Even the guards keep well clear."

"I know all about Leroy McLaren. He's been with us a while and, if I'm honest, he'll be in and out of prison for most of his adult life. However, it looks like he'll be spending some time in hospital."

"Well, he shouldn't have messed with me. I was just minding my own business."

"Can I give you some advice, Sean?" Julia asked, her face and tone softening.

"Okay."

"You've just taken down the big dog. People will give you a wide berth for a while. But it won't last long. And when you move to the next prison, things like this will escalate far quicker, with far more serious consequences. I used to work at Winson Green prison, which is where you may find yourself in a few years. Inmates murdering fellow inmates was a regular thing. No matter how tough you think you are, there is always someone tougher. And even if they are not tougher, they will think nothing of sticking a knife in you. Just be mindful of that. If you truly want to stay out of trouble, you need to walk away. Even if you can't, trying to be the top dog will bring danger. Remember that."

"Okay. Thank you," Sean replied. He shifted in his seat, a stabbing pain in his side making him wince. "I think he broke one of my ribs."

"Well, we'd better get you checked out. I'll arrange for you to be taken to Heartlands Hospital. And just to warn you, this incident will have to be reported. You may face charges."

"I understand."

"Now, go and wait in your room. Someone will be along shortly to take you to hospital."

"Thanks, guv," Sean mumbled as he gingerly rose to his feet. He shuffled over to the door, his body aching.

"And Sean."

"Yes, guv?"

"No more trouble. I mean it."

"Loud and clear," he replied, attempting to smile.

Julia made a quick call, asking for Sean to be taken to the local hospital. A minute later, she was staring out of her window, reflecting on the conversation with the young man. *He's beyond hope,* she thought grimly, knowing that more trouble would be heading his way. *Maybe not today, but soon.*

21

Rain pelted the cab as John pulled in at the truck stop. He killed the engine, removing the Tachograph from the dashboard, placing it in the glovebox. He rubbed his chin, reminding himself to shave at some point. John looked out at the lorry park, noticing a building in the far corner. *Doesn't look too inviting,* he thought. *It certainly is grim up north.* He pulled his smartphone from the plastic holder on the dashboard, dialling a number. "Hi. How's things there?"

"Hi John," Judy replied. "Things are okay. Lottie's been in the spare room since she got in from school."

"Why?"

"The usual, John. Someone trying to wind her up about Lucy. Someone put a burnt doll in her desk."

"You're bloody kidding me! Jesus Christ! How can someone be so fucking nasty?"

"I know, love. She said it's the same girl that's been bothering her for a while. I think you need to speak to the Headmaster."

"Yes. I think I do. This is becoming a joke and it's going to affect her schooling."

"I know. Senior school has not been kind to her so far. She's becoming more closed-off, even to her family."

"Well, I'll be back tomorrow afternoon. I'll speak to her and I'll pop down the school on Monday and see if anyone will speak to me. I'm not having this, Judy."

"Don't let them fob you off. You know what these bloody do-gooding teachers are like."

"Don't worry, I'll get some answers."

"Where are you?" Judy asked, changing the subject.

"Just pulled into the truck stop. I'm about five miles outside Doncaster. It's pissing down."

"Same here. Bob's on his way over. I'm just in the middle of preparing his tea."

"Sounds good. I'll see what northern delicacies await me inside the truck stop."

"Okay, love. I'll see you tomorrow. Take care."

"Will do. You too, Judy."

He ended the call, grabbing his backpack off the bed at the back of the cab. A few minutes later, John was dodging puddles, his pack over his shoulder as he hustled towards the reception. He checked himself in, heading for the shower area. *Not exactly the Ritz,* he thought as he opened his bag on a tired-looking bench. Two fluorescent strip-lights, one flickering, barely illuminated the shower area. The walls were white, flaking paint chips gathering in corners of the square changing room. He grabbed his wash bag and towel, wrapping it around his naked waist as a large truck driver walked towards him, dripping wet. John nodded, walking past the man into the shower. *At least the water is hot,* he thought as water bombarded his head and upper body. *Need to sort Lottie out.*

He squirted a blob of shower gel into his palm, rubbing it vigorously into his hair then over his body. His mind returned to his daughter as images and memories flashed through the former soldier's mind. Tantrums and screaming fits were now commonplace, with John having to calm his daughter down on a regular basis. He'd hoped that the pain of losing Lucy would diminish over time. However, the opposite was true. John still missed his wife. Still woke up sad when he saw one side of the bed empty. But he was getting on with it, as Lucy would have done if he'd been killed whilst serving his country. Lottie, however, seemed angrier. The girl had transformed from a sad little girl into a bitter, insular teenager. Conversation was stilted and forced, John trying his best to coax information about school and friends out of his daughter. He knew that she may need to see someone, but she resisted every time the subject was brought to the table. Her hate was being directed towards his wife's killer. Lottie was frustrated and embittered that prison was the only option. She wanted retribution.

So did John, but he knew how things worked and trying to convince a twelve-year-old about the laws of the land always ended with screaming and tears, from both of them. He turned off the shower, walking back into the changing room as he towelled himself dry. Minutes later, he was hanging a damp towel over his steering wheel, setting the heating inside the cab before he headed back out for a beer and some food.

John opened the swing door, letting it close behind him as he walked over to the bar. Two staff members stood chatting. Two young women, a few years younger than him.

"Hiya, love. What can I get you?" one of them asked.

"Pint please," he said, pointing towards a lager pump. "And are you still serving food?"

"We are, love. Until nine."

John scanned the menu as his glass was filled, opting for a burger and chips. "Thanks," he replied, taking the head off the pint. "Bit dead in here," he said, looking around at the scant number of patrons.

"Half-term," the barmaid stated, smiling at John. She had a pretty face, long dark hair and tattooed arms that John's eyes rested on for a few seconds.

"Okay," he responded before taking another sip of his pint. A television was playing above the bar, *BBC News* spewing out the latest headlines. He couldn't hear the commentary, but John could see images of a young Pakistani girl, who'd been shot by the Taliban. He'd seen the same headlines a few hours before, and turned away from the television to take another sip of his drink.

"Not seen you in here before," the barmaid enquired.

"No. I'm on a new run. Not been to Doncaster before."

"Oh, right," she replied, appraising him. "Can get a bit lonely, life on t'road." Her Yorkshire accent easy on the ear.

"I guess so. Not really thought about it."

"You married, love?"

"I used to be. She died," John said, his voice even, his pulse quickening.

"Oh. Sorry to hear that, love," she replied solemnly. "I'll go and check on yer burger."

He nodded as she headed to a corner of the bar, disappearing from sight. The other woman barely looked up from her smartphone, which suited John. He wasn't looking for conversation. He had more than enough to occupy his mind on a rainy Friday night in Doncaster.

Twenty minutes later, his plate cleared away, John took the first sip of his third pint as the door in the corner of the bar opened, swinging closed as a dark-haired woman approached the bar. She pulled up a stool a few feet away from the ex-soldier, ordering half a lager from the barmaid. He looked at her, giving a brief smile before turning back towards the television as the weather forecast was being shown. Much of the United Kingdom was swathed in cloud, a young presenter pointing at various locations across the map.

"Gonna rain all weekend," the woman stated.

John turned his head away from the forecast. "Looks like it," he replied.

"You staying here for the night?"

"Yes," John replied, feeling slightly awkward. In the six years since Lucy's death, he'd had little conversation with the opposite sex. He'd never dated, focusing on Lottie and his family.

"I'm Amanda," the woman stated, extending her hand.

"John," he replied, reciprocating. Despite the awkwardness, John could see that the woman was attractive. She had minimal makeup, her face naturally pretty. She wore a short black leather jacket, with an even shorter black dress and dark nylons. As his eyes ventured south, his pulse quickened when he noticed her legs were slightly apart, giving him an eyeful. He tore his gaze away, picking up his pint.

"Shouldn't you be at home with your wife and kids?" she enquired, testing the water.

John's shoulders slumped slightly. He placed his pint down, turning towards his new acquaintance. "My daughter is staying with my mother-in-law tonight. I'm not married. I was. She died a few years ago," he said, his words stilted.

"Oh. I'm sorry to hear that, John. She can't have been old. Was she sick? Sorry to pry."

John was lonely. His daily conversation centred around Lottie, his parents, Judy and work colleagues. He couldn't remember the last time he'd struck up a conversation with someone. "No, she wasn't sick. She was murdered."

Amanda's face changed from mildly inquisitive to shock, in the blink of an eye. "Oh, my God! I'm so sorry."

"That's okay, Amanda. You're not the first person to say that. Over the years, I've become used to it." He paused, taking a sip of his semi-cold lager. "You may have heard about it on the news back in 2005. My wife was out shopping with our daughter. Two brothers abducted Lottie. Lucy tracked them down, where the older brother attacked her. It looks like they panicked and tried to conceal their crime. So, they burned her body." He breathed out as if his words had released something deep within him.

"I vaguely remember something about it. Weren't you a soldier at the time? God! How awful for you. I don't know what else to say." She reached over, gripping his hand. The contact was fleeting, John almost flinching at the woman's touch.

"Yes. I was serving in Afghanistan. It seems like a lifetime ago now, but not a day goes by that I don't think about Lucy, or what happened to her." He looked at his pint, then back to Amanda. "Fancy a beer?"

"Go on then, you've twisted my arm," she replied.

. . .

They waited whilst the beer was served, John peering at the television, Amanda following suit, her eyes drifting back to the man who sat next to her. She liked what she saw, the grizzled good looks, the stubbly chin. *Not many like him in these parts,* she thought, noticing how his dark sweater clung to the contours of his arms and shoulders.

"Cheers," John said, clinking glasses with the woman.

"Cheers," she replied, taking a measured sip.

"So, what do you do?" John asked, suddenly curious.

She placed her pint on the counter, locking eyes with the ex-soldier. "I don't have a proper job. I do a bit of this and that."

John chuckled. "That sounds a bit vague. But, that's your business, I guess."

What can I tell him? I'm a prostitute, who sleeps with truckers to keep a roof over my head? "I sell a few things, mainly car-boot sales and on the internet."

"Okay. Well, if it works for you and keeps you busy, happy days." He smiled at her, his face transforming for a few seconds, as if dark clouds suddenly shifted, allowing a shaft of sunlight to appear.

"It's not forever, just until I can get myself sorted."

"Are you married, any kids, etcetera etcetera?"

"No kids. I was married. It ended badly. He left me with bruises and debt that I've spent five years trying to get out of."

"Oh no. Sorry to hear that, Amanda."

"It's okay. Like you, I'm used to telling people about it. He was Turkish. I met him back in 2007, whilst on a girly holiday to Marmaris. He was working at a local bar. He was charming, good-looking and we hit it off. It was all very whirlwind, him moving to the UK a few months later. And for a while, it was good. Then, the fighting happened. He was a gambler and fritted away thousands. I had loan sharks turning up at the door every week. When I challenged him about it he lost his shit. I ended up at Leeds General Hospital. The police never found him. Vanished into thin air, the bastard!"

"He sounds a real piece of work. Why do men do that? It's the lowest of the low."

"Anyway, enough about my miserable past. When do you head home?"

"First thing. My delivery slot is at nine. If I'm lucky, I'll be home early afternoon. And you? How far do you live from here?" Before John realised what was happening, he was hoping that his new companion would not be heading home just yet. He felt something. Something that he'd not felt in a while.

"About a mile away. Although I'll wait until the rain stops before I head home."

"How can you tell from here? All the curtains are drawn."

Amanda looked at him, her incisors gently pinching her bottom lip. "How far is your truck? We could chat there until the rain stops."

He felt it again. A stirring deep inside. He knew what it meant. Part of his soul was fighting the sensation that was coursing through his body. He decided to go with his gut. "Okay. We'll finish these off then make a dash for my truck," he replied, feeling like a giddy adolescent.

They lay, clinging to each other as the rain beat down on the roof of the cab. Despite the coldness outside, the inside of the cab was warm. Sweat-covered limbs entwined in haphazard fashion. Amanda lay under him, her breathing ragged, her body still feeling the aftershocks. She ran over the last few minutes in her head. The kiss. How it had escalated from there. *He was like a fucking caveman,* she thought, knowing that she'd be sore in the morning.

She could not remember an encounter like this one. Most customers simply handed over the money and pulled trousers up over expanding waistlines before scuttling away. Even Mehmet had never hit the heights that she'd just reached. She knew, though, that John was not a customer. She needed that as much as the man on top of her did. Amanda felt his body gradually tensing. She looked up in the darkness, trying to make out his features. Something wet hit her cheek. A tear. Another one fell, landing on her forehead. "John. Are you okay?"

Her voice was the trigger for the release of emotions that the man had kept pent up for so long. He collapsed on top of her, rolling to the side, his back striking the rear of the cab. Amanda held him, feeling his body shaking in her embrace. "I'm sorry," he blurted. "I just feel so guilty. That's the first time in years. Since Lucy."

"It's okay, John. Let it all out." She continued to hold him until his racking sobs gradually subsided to whimpers. He lay still for a few minutes while she stroked his hair gently.

"I'll be okay. Just suddenly felt very guilty."

"That's understandable. But it's been years, John. It's not like you hopped into bed with another woman a few months after your wife passed. I think you needed that."

John snuggled into her, his head resting on Amanda's chest. "Maybe you're right. Putting the guilt aside, it felt pretty good."

"You're not wrong there. I'll be walking like John Wayne for a few days!"

The ex-soldier chuckled, then lay silent for a moment as his thoughts drifted towards his daughter. "God! My life is such a mess. I never expected it to turn out like this. Driving wagons up and down the motorway. Plus, my daughter is becoming more bitter every day. I thought she would be okay. But she's getting worse."

"How old is she?"

"Twelve," John replied, an image of a young Lottie appearing in his mind. He smiled briefly.

"Well, she's about to become a teenager. Most teenage girls become moody. Plus, their hormones are all over the place. Lottie will also go through that. It's just a shame that she's also dealing with the loss of her mother. That's gotta be tough, poor thing."

"I know. She was such a happy little girl. When Lucy died, she started changing. She was always on edge, thinking someone was going to snatch her. As she went through school, she was teased about her mum dying, which really upset her. I held off taking her to see someone, until recently when I broached the subject. I got a flat 'no' from her. Conversation is forced and she spends much of her time locked in her room."

"I'd say, give her time. But she's already had years. Maybe a holiday would do you both good?"

"Funnily enough, my mother-in-law said the same thing a few months ago. Maybe you're right. A holiday may bring her out of her shell a bit."

"It's worth a try," she replied. "Anyway, it looks like the rain's finally died down."

"I'd forgotten all about that," John responded, smiling.

"You should smile more often. You're a gorgeous-looking guy."

"Erm, thanks," he mumbled, feeling awkward.

"Right. I'd better get myself home." John turned onto his side, watching as the woman tried to dress herself inside the confines of the cab. After a few minutes, she was zipping up her boots on the passenger seat as John climbed into the front of the truck. She handed him a piece of paper from her purse.

"Here. If you're ever up this way again, give me a call."

He took the slip of paper, placing it in a cup holder next to the gear-stick. "I will. And thank you, Amanda. Tonight, was, well, unexpected, but great," he said, his words stilted.

"Likewise," she replied climbing over the centre console to kiss him. "And remember what I told you. Keep smiling. It's not all doom and gloom y'know."

"I'll remember that. Take care of yourself. I can drop you back home if you like?"

"It's fine, John. I need a fag and it's only a five-minute walk." She blew him a kiss, climbing carefully out of the cab before slamming the door shut. He watched her walk across the parking area, a plume of smoke following her.

"I'm sorry, Lucy. I hope you understand," he whispered, as thoughts of his wife flooded back towards him.

22

"Hello," John said as he swiped the green icon on his phone.

"Mr Wilson?"

"Speaking."

"It's Mr Shawcross, Lottie's Headmaster. We've had an incident at school involving your daughter."

"Incident. What kind of incident?"

"Are you able to come to the school and discuss it? I would rather do this face-to-face than over the phone."

"Sure. Give me twenty minutes."

"All right."

"Thank you, Mr Wilson." John ended the call, heading out of the kitchen to grab his boots and jacket.

"Yes. Can I help you?" the school receptionist enquired.

"John Wilson. I'm here to see Mr Shawcross."

"Okay. I will give him a call. If you would like to take a seat, he will be down to see you in a minute."

"Thank you," John replied, walking across the well-lit reception area to a row of chairs. He sat down, his eyes resting on a series of photographs on the wall. He could make out the Headmaster, his picture at the top of the improvised hierarchical tree. He checked his watch, a sudden hunger pang signalling that it must be nearly lunchtime.

"Mr Wilson?" a male voice asked. He stood up as a middle-aged man approached. He was tall, a good few inches taller than John who stood an inch over six foot. The Headmaster had wispy red hair, shoots of grey showing above his sizeable ears.

"Mr Shawcross," John replied, extending his hand.

The man took it; a brief but bone-crunching grip told John that the man was reedy, yet powerful. "If you'd like to follow me, please."

John tagged along as the older man ascended two flights of stairs in rapid succession, the ex-soldier trying his best to keep up with him. They came out on a long corridor. A row of chairs stood next to a wall where the Headmaster's office was located. On one of the chairs, Lottie sat, her face streaked with tears, her left eye puffy and swollen.

"Hey," John began, his daughter turning towards him. "God! What happened to you?"

"I got into a fight, Dad."

"If you'll come with me, Mr Wilson, we can discuss this morning's incident. Lottie, you can wait here until I call you in. Okay?"

"Fine!" she replied, her eyes never leaving the floor.

As John walked past, he stooped and kissed his daughter's head. Lottie flinched slightly. "It'll be okay. Just wait here, princess."

"I wish you'd stop calling me that!" she exclaimed, as the Headmaster held the door open.

John walked in, seating himself at one of the chairs in front of him. The older man walked around the desk that was flanked on two sides by large windows, giving him a good view of the school grounds. "Okay, I won't go around the houses, Mr Wilson. I'll get right to it."

"Fine by me," John replied, liking the man's directness.

"Lottie was involved in a fracas this morning with a girl in her class, Alicia Teale. According to some of the other children, Lottie punched Alicia in the face after a heated disagreement."

"Okay. What was the disagreement about?"

"I'm aware of what happened to your wife, Mr Wilson. And for what it's worth, I am very sorry for your loss. It appears that Alicia made a comment about your wife. Lottie reacted, striking the other girl."

"Did the girl strike her back? She has a mark on her face and her clothing looks a little dishevelled."

"According to witnesses, Lottie banged her face during a scuffle. It only lasted a few seconds, then their teacher arrived and separated them."

"So, where is this Alicia?"

"She left about half-an-hour ago. Her mother is taking her to the doctor to get her checked over."

"Doctor? Exactly what injury did she sustain?"

"A suspected broken nose," the Headmaster replied gravely.

John smiled, holding in the laugh that was trying to explode from his chest. "I never knew she had it in her."

"This is no laughing matter, Mr Wilson. Your daughter could be suspended, possibly even expelled. Violence will not be tolerated at my school."

"What! That's bollocks. She was defending herself and her mother's honour."

"That's no reason for violence, Mr Wilson."

"Can I ask you a question?"

"Of course," the Headmaster replied.

"Do you know why the *Titanic* sank?"

The older man looked at the former soldier, his brow knitting. "I'm not sure I follow?"

"The *Titanic*. Do you know why it sank?"

"Yes. It hit an iceberg in the North Atlantic."

"Yes and no. Yes, it hit an iceberg and sank. But there were a series of steps that led to it hitting the iceberg. It's called root cause analysis. You start at the event and work backwards to find the cause. This applies to what happened this morning. Do you seriously think that she punched a girl in the face because she made one hurtful remark?"

"Well," the Headmaster began, his words trailing off.

"We both know that this has been going on for a while. I've seen it at home when she gets in from school. She's becoming withdrawn. Then, last Friday, someone placed a burnt doll in Lottie's desk. Were you aware of this?"

"No, I was not."

"So, tell me, Mr Shawcross, if Lottie was your daughter and someone placed a burnt doll in her desk, referencing the tragic death of her mother, what would you think? What would you do?"

"I cannot answer that question, Mr Wilson. Placing burnt dolls in a pupil's desk, whether it relates to the death of a family member or not, is wholly unacceptable. If it does relate to your wife's death, then I want to know who was responsible and they would be dealt with accordingly."

"What does that translate to? A slap on the wrist? A detention? And yet, you're thinking of expelling my daughter for defending herself?" John let out a deep sigh, his shoulder sagging. "I take it you know what happened to Lucy?"

"Yes, Mr Wilson. It was a terrible crime that shocked the whole city."

"I was serving in Afghanistan when Lucy was murdered by those bastards. It broke Lottie's heart and my familys too. She was incredibly close to her mother. A happy little girl. She's had her childhood taken away from her, Mr Shawcross. She has lost her mother, who was the most important person in Lottie's world. I was overseas, only seeing her every few months. When I came home, I was virtually a stranger to her. It was Lucy that was her mother and father all rolled into one. And all of a sudden, she's gone, and I have to pick up the pieces, trying to raise a little girl when all I really knew about was serving my country."

"It must have been terribly difficult."

"It was. And it still is. Lottie has changed. She's become closed-off. We never talk like we used to. I'm just worried that permanent damage has been done to her, and that I'll never get my daughter back."

"I could refer her to the school psychologist."

"Okay. I didn't know that schools had such things?"

"Many do nowadays. I think that expelling Lottie, especially after our conversation, would not benefit her. If she is willing, I will arrange for her to sit down with Angela."

"Angela?"

"Yes. Angela Rhodes. She's worked here for a few years now. I will speak to her, once Lottie is in agreement."

"Okay. Great. How long would this kind of thing go on for?"

"Hard to say, Mr Wilson. But if I was a betting man, I'd say that Lottie will need several sessions."

"Okay. Let's give it a try."

Shawcross rose from his chair, skirting the table on his way to the door. John remained facing forward, hearing muted words from the corridor before his daughter's footsteps approached. She sat down next to her father, exhaling. "Lottie," Shawcross began. "Have there been any hurtful remarks made about your mother whilst you've been at this school?"

"Yes," Lottie murmured.

"From Alicia? Or are there others?"

"Alicia. Her friends egg her on. But she's the only one that has actually said anything."

"Okay. Your father tells me that someone placed a burnt doll in your desk a few days ago. Is that correct?"

John looked at his daughter, reaching over to hold her hand as her eyes filled with tears. "Yes. Last Friday."

"Did you report it?" the Headmaster asked.

"No, sir."

"Why not?"

"Because Alicia said that if I grassed on her she'd get me after school."

"No one's going to be getting anyone after school, Lottie! I will not stand for bullying. Tell me, what happened this morning?"

Lottie looked at John, her eyes brimming with tears. "It's okay, sweetheart. Tell Mr Shawcross what happened."

"She said..." Lottie paused, composing herself, "that my mother was a slag, and that's why she was burned to death."

"*What*!" John exclaimed, his seat skittering across the office behind him. Shawcross rose from his chair, holding his hands up to the former soldier in a vain attempt to placate him. "The fucking little bitch!"

"Don't shout, Dad," Lottie pleaded, tears falling from her eyes. "She's not worth it."

John was about to say something when he caught sight of his daughter's expression. He wilted to the floor, sobbing uncontrollably. Lottie went to him, kneeling on the wooden floor, her arms around his shoulders. "I'm sorry, Lottie. I just miss her so much."

Shawcross looked on in stunned silence. He wanted to remonstrate with the man, telling him that his language was entirely inappropriate. But, how could he? How could the Headmaster scold the man before him when he agreed with him, understood him, empathised with him?

"Mr Wilson, I think it would be best if I sent Lottie home for the day. Emotions are running high and I think that putting Lottie back into her classes would not be beneficial to her. Take her home, Mr Wilson. She can return to school on Monday as normal and in the meantime, I will speak to Mrs Rhodes."

"Thank you," John replied, climbing to his feet. "Come on, Lottie. Let's go home." They exited the office, walking hand-in-hand across the school grounds towards the car park.

"I'm a bit hungry, Dad."

"Me too. Fancy fish and chips?"

"Yes, please," Lottie replied, almost happily.

"Come on then. Let's go and fill our bellies."

They parked the car a few hundred yards from the chip shop, fresh autumnal sunlight bathing the village of Rubery in a warm glow. "What do you fancy?" John asked.

"Fish, chips and curry sauce, Dad," his daughter replied.

"Sounds good to me. I think we can eat inside at this chippy."

"Oi!" a female voice called out behind them. They both turned as a young woman approached, her strides purposeful. A young girl trailed behind her, a twisted scowl on her face. John noticed bruising around the girl's eyes, her nose slightly swollen, the skin reddening.

"Can I help you?" John asked, his tone friendly.

"Have you seen what your fucking daughter has done to Alicia?"

John looked around himself, an in-built mechanism he'd retained from his time in the forces. This was not Afghanistan, but John sensed danger, his pulse quickening. "So, this is the girl that's been bullying Lottie?"

"What the fuck you talking about? She's bullied no one."

"Well, that's not what Lottie says."

"I couldn't give two fucks what that little bitch says. Look at my daughter's nose. I'm taking this further."

John felt the skin reddening around his neck, anger building inside him at the woman's words. "Don't use language like that around my daughter. It might be acceptable for you, but not for me. And if you want to take it further, be my guest. Planting burnt dolls in my daughter's desk is sick. What kind of person does that?"

The woman took a step forward, a few feet from John. He noticed passing shoppers slow down to see the spectacle. This was not what he wanted. *Wrong place, wrong time,* he thought.

"Alicia didn't do that, did you?" she asked, turning to her daughter.

"No, Mum. She's a liar."

"Yes, you did, Alicia," Lottie responded angrily. "Spencer and Claire both saw you put it in my desk."

"They're lying," she replied, sneering at Lottie.

John entwined his fingers around his daughter's, pulling her closer to him, sensing something was about to happen. "Come on, Lottie. Let's get some chips," he urged.

"What's going on, sis?" a male voice called out to John's right. The former soldier turned as a large man crossed over the road towards them.

"Alicia got punched in the face by this little bitch at school. I'm just giving them a piece of my mind," she replied, as her brother approached.

"What?" the man blurted, his hands coming out of his joggers.

John looked at the approaching figure. He was taller than John, a good fifty pounds heavier, although it was largely bulk, not muscle. A few gold rings adorned his large fingers, a thick gold chain around his neck with a Birmingham City emblem dangling from it. The man's head was shaved, a tattoo of a swallow on the left side of his neck. John's heartbeat increased, his body tensing, ready for whatever was about to happen. "Is this true?" he demanded.

"My daughter did punch your niece, but only after she was provoked," John replied calmly.

"No one fucks with my family," the man hissed, advancing on John. The ex-soldier shepherded Lottie towards a shop doorway, noticing Alicia taking a few steps towards her, dropping her school bag onto the pavement.

Shit! John thought, readying himself for an attack. "She started it, mate. If she'd left Lottie alone, none of this would have happened."

"Who you calling mate? I ain't your fucking mate," the man spat.

"You tell him, Deano," the woman urged, stirring the pot. "They think they can mess with us and get away with it."

"GET OFF ME!" Lottie screamed.

John spun around, watching in horror as his daughter was dragged to the pavement by her hair. He tried to advance on her but the woman blocked his path as Alicia's first kick connected with Lottie's ribs. She cried out in pain as more shoppers looked on in stunned silence.

"Get off her!" John bellowed, just as a meaty arm wrapped itself around his neck from behind, cutting off his air. He was pulled backward, a glancing blow connecting with his temple as his daughter's screams echoed through his head. He watched as the woman advanced on him, her left leg swinging viciously towards his groin.

All voices and noises seemed to fade away as his eyes locked on the approaching boot. He relaxed, letting the man think he had the upper hand as another blow caught him on the cheek. Before either could react, John pivoted his feet, sending the blow bouncing off his upper thigh, deadening the muscle. The man behind John didn't expect the manoeuvre and was sent slightly off balance. During his time in the Royal Marines, John had been trained in hand-to-hand combat. He'd considered himself a proficient student, not the best in the class but certainly not the worst. He knew enough to get by. And now, he needed to get by. And quick. He pushed his backside into the man, dropping down a few inches as a female voice called out nearby. In a blur of movement, John violently twisted his body down and to the left, his attacker going with his motion. His legs came off the ground as the ex-soldier used the man's momentum against him. The back of the man's head hit the pavement, stunning him as his flailing legs caught his sister full in the face, knocking her sideways.

John was on his feet a split-second later, watching as two female police officers pulled Alicia off his daughter. He decided on caution, though he wanted nothing more than to drive his fist into the man's face, over and over again. He resisted, standing over his fallen assailant, gently touching the side of his face.

"You fucking wanker!" the woman spat, groggily climbing to her feet. "Did you see that? He assaulted us. I want him arrested," she hollered as the entranced shoppers held their ground, stunned expressions etched on their faces. John noticed many shaking their heads and hushed whispers being exchanged by elderly villagers who never expected a show quite like this to take place in broad daylight.

"Lottie," John said as he went to his daughter, lifting her into his arms. "Are you okay?"

"I'm fine, Dad," she replied, wincing slightly as her father hugged her.

John looked at the two police officers, one of whom was holding the young girl by the arm. "Did you see all this? They attacked us."

"Yes, we did," the one stated. "We were coming out of the station when we heard the commotion."

"My daughter and that girl had been involved in an altercation in school this morning. We were just about to go to the chip shop when we were approached and then attacked by them."

"He's right," an elderly man began. "I saw the whole thing. We all did."

"You're a fucking dead man," John's attacker growled, stumbling to his feet.

"Dean Teale," one of the officers said. "You up to your old tricks again? You're already in enough bother. Don't make it worse. Just stay there and calm down, or I'll nick you!"

The other stepped forward, pulling out a small pad. "I think we need to continue this over at the station. All of us."

John pulled Lottie towards him, wrapping a protective arm around her. "It's okay, sweetheart. It's over."

"It ain't over," the woman countered. "You've no idea who you've just messed with."

"Shut it, Tracey Teal," the one officer commanded. "Like your brother, you're already in enough trouble. Now. The station. All of you," she ordered. "Could you get some statements from the witnesses?" she asked her fellow officer.

"Yes, Sarge," the younger woman replied dutifully.

"So much for a quiet lunch of fish and chips," John whispered into his daughter's ear.

"You lot. Go over and wait for me at the front desk. Don't go anywhere else. Understood?" The trio slouched off, crossing the busy road before walking the few hundred yards to the station. The police officer turned to John and Lottie. "Are you both okay?"

"We'll be alright," John replied. "He got a few cheeky punches in, but no damage has been done. Lottie, are you okay?"

"Yes, Dad. She caught me a couple of times. But I don't think anything is broken. I'll live."

John smiled at his daughter, kissing her on the top of the head. "Brave girl," he soothed.

"We'll have to do this by the book, Mr?"

"Wilson. John Wilson."

"Mr Wilson. I'm sure you'll appreciate that we need to follow procedures, regardless of who is at fault."

"I understand," John responded, his stomach rumbling.

"And by the way, nice move. You took them both down in pretty quick fashion. Ex-forces?"

"Yes, Royal Marines."

"Me too. I'd have executed the same move if I'd been in that situation."

"Thanks," he replied, half-smiling at the officer. "Come on, then. Let's get this over with," he huffed, as he took his daughter's hand and began walking over towards the police station.

23

"Here you go," John offered, placing the fish and chips in front of Lottie.

"Thanks, Dad," she replied, tucking into her meal with vigour. They sat in silence, each lost in their own thoughts before a noise from the hall made them both turn around.

Judy walked into the lounge, placing her handbag on the settee. "Come here," she said to Lottie, hugging her granddaughter. "Are you both okay?"

"We're fine, Nan," Lottie replied, her mouth half-full of cod.

The older woman kissed her son-in-law on the cheek. "Is that where he smacked you?"

"Yes. It's fine. Just a graze," John replied, his tone neutral. "Do you want a chip?"

"No thanks, love. I've not long eaten. Bob's taking me out for a Chinese later. You two enjoy your grub," she responded as she pulled out a chair. Seating herself, she looked at John. "So, what's the outcome?"

"Nothing. I said that if the mother and uncle were not going to press charges, then I wouldn't, either. I will have to report the incident to the school on Monday, just to put them in the picture. Once it had all calmed down, I spoke to the one police officer. It seems that this Alicia's family are known to the police, which does not surprise me. They looked like trouble. Let's hope that today's events are the end of it."

"Swines," Judy cursed. "Fancy starting a fight like that. Especially when it's the other girl's fault."

"I know, Judy. They're just scum."

"You should have seen Dad," Lottie proclaimed. "He did some crazy karate move on them. Flattened them both."

Judy looked at John, who was blushing slightly. "Good. At least you gave them what for? They'll think twice about doing that again."

"Oh, I don't know," John replied gravely. "People like that love trouble. To them, it's all a big game. The guy who attacked me looks like a right piece of work. The officers knew him by name, which makes me think he's a small-time criminal, possibly the local drug dealer. Let's hope I never bump into him again."

"Let's hope so. And if you do, make sure he doesn't get a chance. Knock his block off, John."

"Anyway, I spoke to the Headmaster. This Alicia said some pretty hurtful things to Lottie. Things that I'm not going to share with you, Judy. When I heard what she'd been saying, I went ballistic."

"He did, Nan," Lottie confirmed. "I've never seen Dad like that before."

"So, what happens now?" Judy asked, pinching a chip from her granddaughter. She pulled her tongue out at the girl, drawing a big grin from Lottie.

"She's going back to school on Monday. I'll go down with her, just to let the Headmaster know what has happened. He also wants Lottie to see a psychologist."

"Why?"

"Because, he thinks it will help. And Lottie has agreed to it."

Judy reached across, squeezing her granddaughter's hand. "Are you okay with that?"

"Yes, Nan. If Mr Shawcross and Dad think it's a good idea, then I'll do it."

"I'm sure it can't hurt, love. Go in with an open mind, okay?"

"Okay, I will."

"Changing the subject," John began. "I've been looking at holidays, Judy."

"Oh! That's nice. Where are you thinking about going?"

"Majorca."

"Really, Dad?"

"Yes, sweetheart. You've never been abroad. I think that a few weeks in the sun will do us good."

Lottie smiled, liking the idea of escaping. "When would we go?"

"I was thinking the Easter holidays," John suggested as he lifted a lump of curry sauce-covered cod to his lips.

"Well, I think it's a brilliant idea," Judy replied happily. "You both need this."

"You could come with us, Judy."

"Really?" she exclaimed. "I guess I could. I could even ask Bob?"

"Why not? Would you like that, Lottie?"

"Yes. I like Bob. He's a nice guy."

"Well, I never expected the conversation to turn out like this. One minute we're talking about the school bully, the next, we're discussing holidays!"

"Well, think it over," John suggested. "It would be nice to have you both there."

"What about your folks?" Judy asked.

"They are going away at Easter. Mediterranean cruise, I think. So, they are already sorted."

"Okay. Well, I'll run it by Bob tonight. I'm sure he'd be up for it."

"Great! Now, who wants a cuppa?"

Judy stood up, pinching another chip from her granddaughter. "You both finish your chips. I'll put the kettle on."

"Come in," Tracey urged as her younger brother went slouching past her into the dimly-lit hallway. "Go into the lounge, I'll get you a lager," she said and walked through into the kitchen.

Dean Teale flopped down onto the settee, trying to get comfortable on the lumpy cushions. Crooked Venetian blinds filtered light through the front window, the autumn sun about to hit the rooftops across the road. He pulled out a packet of cigarettes, lighting one before slumping back onto the settee. "Here," his older sister offered, handing him a can of lager. "I'll get you an ashtray."

"Thanks, sis," he replied, taking a swig of his beer. "Where's Alicia?"

"In her room. Alicia?" she called. "Come here."

Tracey sat opposite, on a black fake-leather chair. She'd changed her clothes, sporting a grey pair of joggers, hooded top and matching slippers. She took a drag on her own cigarette, blowing a long plume into the stuffy confines of the lounge. On one wall, a flat-screen television sat on top of a stand. Further along the wall towards the rear French doors, a large bookcase stood next to a round dining table. The walls were devoid of pictures, the odd framed photograph collecting dust on the bookcase.

"What?" Alicia huffed indignantly.

"Your uncle Deano is here to see you," Tracey responded.

She turned to the man on the settee. "Hiya," she mumbled.

"Hi," her uncle replied.

"Tell your uncle what you've told me about the girl at school?"

Alicia looked at her uncle. "Her mother was murdered a few years ago. By two brothers."

Deano's face changed from one of indifference to shock. "The murder at the Fort?"

"Yes," Tracey replied. "I went on the internet this afternoon. Looks like the little girl was out shopping with her mother, when two brothers abducted her. Do you remember the story?"

"Some of it. Was years ago?" Deano replied, taking a drag on his cigarette.

"The murderers were only kids at the time, their identity kept private. However, it was the same time that Jerome was sent down for dealing."

Deano suddenly looked up. "Do you think it's connected?"

"It could be, bruv. Do you remember the name of the woman who was holding his gear?"

Deano's brow knitted, trying to dig the name out of his memory. "Mandy, I think. Why?"

"It just seems a bit of a coincidence. This Mandy lived a few hundred yards from Jerome. He was her pimp, yet she dropped him in the shit. Why were the police in her house?"

"Dunno," he replied, not completely understanding where the conversation was heading.

"Okay. Here's a theory. What if Mandy's kids were the ones who killed that little bitch's mother? The police raid the house and find a shit-load of gear. From what I've read about the case, the two brothers were stoned when they took the girl. Think about it, bruv."

"They were high on Jerome's gear?"

"Exactly. Maybe that's why this Mandy dropped him in it? Maybe they reduced her sentence for cooperating with the Old Bill?"

"All I care about it setting the record straight with the girl's dad. I'm gonna fuck him up."

"Well, you need to be careful, bruv."

"Why?" Deano replied, shifting in his seat.

"Because I found a few things out. He's an ex-Royal Marine. He was serving in Afghanistan when his wife was murdered. So, if you wanna piece of him, you'd better be prepared. Or, get help."

"Like who?" Deano asked.

"When's Jerome due out?"

Deano wiped his nose on his sleeve. "In about twelve months, if he keeps his nose clean. Which to be fair, he has so far. You're not thinking that I need him to help me sort this wanker out, are you?"

"I'm not saying that you need to involve him. But he knows people. They may be able to help you."

"But I know a few people who are local. They could have my back if needed."

"Okay. I'm just saying that Jerome may be interested, especially as the guy is linked to why he was sent down in the first place. Plus, he owes you."

Deano nodded, remembering how he'd saved Jerome from a rival drug dealer a few years before. He knew that if he hadn't intervened, the competitor could have killed Jerome, or at least taken him out of business for a long time. "Okay. It's been a few months since I've visited. Maybe I need to go and see him."

24

Deano slouched on the plastic chair, scrolling through his phone as a door opened at the far side of the room. Several prisoners filed in, making their way over to family and friends. Deano looked up as a dark-skinned male approached. "All right, bruv."

"Deano," Jerome replied, embracing him quickly, aware that the prison guards would be watching out for contraband. "How's things?"

"Not bad. You're looking well," Deano stated, as he appraised his older half-brother. His once long dreadlocks were gone, his salt and pepper hair kept closely-cropped. The older man had a few days' growth on his face, making him look a few years older.

"Can't complain," he began. "I'm keeping my head down and doing some training. Hopefully, when I get out, I'll have a few more strings to my bow."

"Nice one. You gonna go straight?"

"Yes, bruv. I've not seen my kids for six years. I need to keep on the straight and narrow, for their sakes. Anyway, why the visit?"

"I need your help with something, bruv."

"Go on, I'm listening," Jerome replied, moving closer to his younger sibling.

"I got into a dust-up the other day. You remember Alicia?" Jerome nodded. "She got into a fight at school with another girl, who gave her a dig. Anyway, a few hours later, this girl was up Rubery with her dad. Tracey was having a barney with him, so I got involved. I got a few digs in, before he did some Bruce Lee shit on me."

"Okay. Someone made a mug out of you?"

"I didn't expect it. The police turned up and carted us all off to the station. No arrests were made. The dad didn't want to take it further."

"Wise move."

"Maybe. But no one has ever done that to me. I want to settle the score."

"How?" Jerome enquired, becoming more interested.

"That's why I'm here. Do you know anyone who could help me out?"

"I know a few people. What are we talking about?" Jerome asked, his voice dropping in volume. He knew the guards picked certain things up during visiting time.

"Nothing too serious. I just wanna teach this cunt a lesson. One he'll never forget. And there's more."

"Go on."

Deano looked around, satisfied that no one was listening in. "It just so happens that the dad's wife was murdered a few years ago. At the Fort." He saw his half-brother stiffen. "Tracey reckons that the mother was murdered by someone you know."

"Luke and Sean Terry. Mandy's kids!" Jerome spat.

"Right," Deano agreed, pleased that his sister had been on the mark. "What else can you tell me?"

Jerome leaned even closer, Deano doing the same. "The brothers killed that woman. Then Mandy's house was searched. They found a load of gear. My gear. I thought she'd take the hit. I was wrong. I reckon it was revenge because the brothers stole some of my skunk, which they were smoking just before they killed the woman. That's probably why she dropped me in it."

"I see," Deano replied as he digested the information. "Why didn't you tell me any of this before?"

"I've told no one. Kept it under wraps for years. No point in telling anyone, I was banged-to-rights. Anyway, I've heard a few things on the inside. It looks like the younger brother, Luke, died before he could stand trial. Some kind of accident at the detention centre. Sean is still in prison. Not this one, though. He could be anywhere. And that bitch Mandy is probably out by now. I've asked a few people to look for her. No one has heard anything, which makes me think that she's done one. She could be living anywhere."

"Would you wanna settle the score?"

"Not me. I'd get someone else to pay her a visit."

"Could that someone help me pay the dad a visit?"

"You really sure that you wanna do this, bruv? You could end up in here with me."

"That won't happen. Not if I'm careful."

"You'll need to be. I seem to remember that the dad is ex-forces. Tangling with him might be difficult."

"That's why I need your help. Because you know people that could handle him."

"Leave it with me. Come back and see me next month. I may have a name for you."

"Cheers, bruv. I appreciate it."

"Anything for my little brother," Jerome stated, a half-smile tugging at his lips. "There is something that you could do for me in return. I know that I owe you one, but this is just a little thing."

"Name it," Deano replied eagerly.

"Do a bit of digging. See if you can find Mandy Terry?"

"How do I do that?"

"Well, I've already asked a few people to look on Facebook, but she's not on there, or she's hidden herself pretty good. I've been thinking about it recently, trying to find someone that would be connected with her. Nothing. None of her mates know where she is. But a few weeks ago, I got chatting with another inmate, from Leicester. Turns out his sister-in-law is called Gabrielle. Gabrielle Phillips. That's Mandy's cousin. I've been racking my brain, trying to remember what her name was. She's got four kids, all mixed-race. I think the eldest is called Jodie. I only know that because Mandy mentioned years ago that she was going to her niece's christening. Jodie. Find her and you may find a link to Mandy."

"Bruv, I don't even know what this Mandy looks like," Deano stated, as he massaged his neck.

"Well, she's probably changed since I last saw her. She had long brown hair, kinda good-looking. I know that's not much to go on. But there is one distinct thing about her."

"I'm listening."

"She has a mole on her face. By her top lip. She may have gone to lengths to change her name or appearance, but I don't think she'd remove the mole. Plus, she liked it. Thought it made her stand out a bit."

"Okay, I'll see what I can do." The men sat talking for a few more minutes, discussing their football teams, Aston Villa and Birmingham City, along with general chit-chat. A buzzer on the wall sounded, signalling the end of visiting. The brothers stood up, shaking hands. Deano turned away from the guards and slipped a small plastic sealable bag into his brother's palm.

"Good to see you, bruv," he said.

"Likewise," Jerome replied, closing his fist around the bag, which he then slipped into his prison uniform.

Deano watched as his half-brother filed out of the visiting area, other prisoners following suit. *Okay, soldier boy. I'm coming for you,* he thought, a smile spreading across his face as he made his way back towards the visitors' waiting room.

A few hours later, Deano knocked on his sister's door as street lights began illuminating the darkening street. He waited for a minute until the door was opened by his niece, who stood looking at him expectantly. "Hello, Deano," she murmured.

"Uncle Deano to you. Where's your mum?"

"In the kitchen, cooking dinner."

"Sounds good. What you having?"

"Pizza," Alicia said.

"Save a slice for me. I'm starving!"

"Come in," she offered, moving to one side.

The man flounced past her, walking down the carpet-less hallway to the kitchen beyond. "All right, sis?"

"Deano," she replied, mildly surprised by his visit. "You fancy a pizza?"

"Go on then," he replied readily. "Been sat on buses for two hours. I'm bloody starving."

"Okay. Take that into Alicia and I'll put you one in."

He took the chipped dinner plate off the worktop and carried it into the lounge. His niece was on the settee with a handheld console a few inches from her nose. "Here you go," he said happily. "Looks like double pepperoni."

"Thanks," she replied, pulling her brown hair back before securing it with a rubber band.

He walked back into the kitchen just as his sister closed the oven door, dropping an oven glove on the table. "Should be about fifteen minutes. You wanna beer?"

"I'll get it. You want one?"

"Sure," she agreed, lighting a cigarette. She opened the back door that led out onto a paved area. The garden was almost devoid of life, a stubbly patch of grass offering little colour. Tracey blew a stream of air into the darkening evening then turned to face her brother, who had a can of lager in his meaty palm. "Ta," she said, cracking the seal on the can with one hand.

Deano stepped past her, taking a swig of his own beer as he leant against the fence. "I spoke to Jerome. He's gonna help me get even with that prick."

"How?" Tracey asked.

"He knows lots of people, does our Jerome. Asked me to go back next month and he'll give me a name."

"Then what?"

"Then we fuck that guy up. Proper."

"Be careful, Deano," Tracey cautioned, touching the tender skin of her cheekbone. "I know things got out of hand before, and that little bitch will get what's coming to her. But I don't want you to get in trouble. Going after this guy may end up with you in prison."

"Relax, sis. Nothing's gonna happen. And I won't go mad on him. Just a few digs and a reminder not to fuck with the wrong people."

"Just make sure that you're careful. If he IDs you, he'll go straight to the Old Bill. Remember that."

"Chill. It's under control. And anyway, Jerome gave me some more info."

"Oh? I'm listening," she replied, flicking the ash from her cigarette onto the cracked slabs.

"Turns out, he knows who killed that girl's mother. Some kids called Luke and Sean Terry. Their mother, Mandy, dropped Jez in the shit. That's why he got sent down. You know about the drugs that were found?" The woman nodded. "Well, she was holding them for him. He reckons that she grassed him up to save herself, and because the kids that killed that woman were high on weed. Jez's weed. Of course, when the Old Bill raided his gaff, they found a load more gear, which fucked him up big time. He wants to settle the score with this Mandy. And he wants us to help him find her."

"Fucking hell!" Tracey exclaimed. "So, it is linked to the murder. Where is this Mandy now?"

"No idea. But he wants us to try and find her on Facebook."

"That won't be easy. If she's out of prison, chances are she's changed her name or moved away, especially with Jerome's connections."

"True," Deano responded. "But he wants us to try. I'm not on Facebook, but you are, sis. You can find her, I'm sure of it."

"There must be hundreds of Mandy Terrys about. Finding her ain't gonna be a walk in the park!"

"I know. She's got a cousin, Gabrielle Phillips, who lives in Leicester. There can't be too many of them knocking around?"

Tracey pulled a smartphone out of her joggers and swiped the screen as smoke billowed from her nostrils. She tapped the phone's screen a few times, using her thumb to scroll through the results on the screen. After a few tuts and shakes of her head, she looked up at her brother. "Found her," she proclaimed triumphantly.

Deano walked over, taking the proffered handset. He looked at the picture on the screen, a young woman with four children positioned around her, all smiling. "That must be her," he agreed, his pulse quickening. "Tasty, too. I'd do her."

"You'd do anything," his sister replied, a smile spreading across her face. "Let me take a look through her profile. Keep an eye on the pizza, bruv, it'll be ready in a minute."

Deano walked back into the kitchen, placing his beer on the table. Donning the oven glove, he opened the oven door, stooping to look inside. "Another five minutes, I think."

"Okay. Check on Alicia. She's probably finished hers by now. You can use her plate. Save me some extra washing-up."

Deano did as he was asked, checking on his niece. Sure enough, her plate was next to her on the settee, a few burnt crusts littering the plate. He picked up the plate. The young girl didn't take her eyes away from her console as Deano walked back into the kitchen. Dropping the crusts into the bin, he selected a large carving knife from the top drawer next to the sink. He flipped the knife in his hand, catching it deftly a few times as he headed back towards the oven.

"Bruv," his sister urged from outside. "Come here!"

Deano bustled outside and saw his sister smiling at him. "Here you go." He peered at the screen. Gabrielle Phillips gazed back at him in a Halloween costume. He looked her up and down, liking the shape of her legs and the ample cleavage that was on show. "What am I looking at?"

"Click on the 'likes' at the bottom of the screen."

Deano saw a small blue thumb next to a heart icon with the number 105 next to them. He pressed the icons twice and it revealed a list of friends who had either liked or loved the photograph. "What am I looking for?"

"Look at the fourth name on the list," his sister replied.

His eyes dropped down the list, coming to rest on a name and a small picture. "MJ Kerr," he whispered, looking at the dark-haired woman on the screen.

"M could be for Mandy. This Gabrielle only has a few pictures that I can see, and no one called Mandy has liked or commented on her pictures. That could be the one?"

Deano looked at the woman, studying her face. "Bingo!"

"What?" his sister replied, slightly confused.

"Jez said she had a mole on her face. By her top lip. Look at her face!"

"You're right. This could be the woman we're looking for."

"How old do you reckon she is? She looks about forty. Not bad looking though, although I'd rather bang her cousin."

"Try and keep your mind off shagging for a few minutes, bruv." Tracey studied the picture before looking through her profile. "Bollocks. No info at all. No age, no location, fuck all except one picture," she huffed, as she selected the photograph on the profile page. The image filled the screen, a dark-haired woman staring back at her, a half-smile on her face. Tracey zoomed in, something in the picture catching her eye. "Bruv, look at her necklace?"

Deano peered at the picture, a smile appearing on his face. "That's her," he said, noticing the Birmingham City pendant that lay against her black top. "The mole, the necklace. It's gotta be her. I bet my house on it."

"You don't have a house," his sister replied, nudging him on the shoulder. She zoomed out, trying to find more clues. "Doesn't look familiar," she continued, her brow creasing. "Hang on."

"What?" Deano replied eagerly.

"The name of the pub behind her."

Deano squinted at the screen. The picture had been taken on a sunny day and the lettering of the pub was clear enough to read. Behind the pub, blue sea stretched all the way to the horizon. "The Weigh Inn. Never heard of it?"

"Me neither. But I bet Google has," she replied excitedly, punching a few commands onto the phone's screen. After a few seconds, she smiled at her brother once more. "Ta-da!" she exclaimed proudly. "The Weigh Inn is in Scotland. A place called Caithness."

"Never heard of it," her brother replied.

"Nor have I. Hang on," Tracey countered, selecting another screen. "It's right up in the north, by John o' Groats. Bloody hell! That'll be a fair old drive for Jerome."

"She could be in Timbuktu," Deano replied. "If he knows where she is, I'm sure he'll find her. And then, he'll even things up."

25

Snow had arrived early, large flakes sticking themselves to John's windscreen. He lay there, watching as the outside world was slowly covered. The parking lot lights gave the scene an orange hue, but the world seeming muted to the ex-soldier.

"So, any special plans for Christmas?" Amanda asked from behind him. He turned over, pulling the sleeping bag over them. It was only body heat that kept the cab at an ambient temperature, the side windows misted over.

"Not really thought about it. And you?"

"Christmas is just another day to me. I rarely do anything special. I don't even bother with a tree. If I had kids, I'd probably make more of an effort."

"Fair enough," John replied, his fingers tracing a line across Amanda's naked shoulder. His finger found a ridge in the skin as he traced a line that ran a few inches towards her collarbone. "What's this?"

"Oh, that. An old war wound. Someone picked a fight with me a few years ago. I thought I had the upper hand, until the bitch pulled a knife and slashed me."

"Jesus," John uttered, not really knowing what else to say.

"Look, John. We don't know each other. There are things about me that would shock you."

"Not much shocks me anymore, Amanda," he replied quietly. "Try me."

"You really wanna know?"

"Why not? There's nothing on the telly. May as well talk," he replied, smiling in the darkness.

She smiled, too, before drawing in a breath. "Okay. I'm a prostitute," she stated matter-of-factly, studying his expression, expecting anger or disgust.

"Oh, right!" he replied, not sure how to react.

"Thing is, when you turned up a few weeks ago, my mate who works inside gave me a call. Told me there was a gorgeous trucker sat on his own, who may need some company."

"And is that what you thought when you saw me?" he enquired, testing the water.

"On both counts. I was hoping to make a few quid. But then we got talking and I realised that I didn't want that."

"I'm not sure what to say. Yes, I'm a bit surprised, but who am I to judge?"

"Thank you, John," she replied, kissing him. "And I'm clean, by the way, in case you're wondering? I give blood every few months, just to make sure that I've not caught anything. And you are the only guy in a long while that I've slept with without protection."

"It's fine, Amanda. Really. Maybe we just needed a smile and a bit of company?"

She smiled at him, wondering what the man in front of her had endured over the past few years. She snuggled into John. The front of the cab was cooling rapidly as goose-bumps appeared on her flesh. "I think you may be right. Get you! Gorgeous and wise." She pushed her face into his chest, rubbing her chin against the coarse dark hair. "So, tell me something nice?"

"Like what?"

"Anything."

He tried to think of something, but the cupboard of good news appeared bare. Then, something came to him. "We've booked to go on holiday."

"Lovely. Where are you off to?"

"Majorca. In April. We've not had a holiday for years. I think it will do Lottie good to get a change of scenery."

"I think you're right. A few weeks in the sun can't hurt. Is it just the two of you going?" she asked, wanting to find out a little more about the man who was wrapped around her.

"My mother-in-law and her fella as well."

"The dreaded mother-in-law, eh? Rather you than me."

He chuckled. "She's the exception to the rule. She's great. Since Lucy died, Judy's been the glue holding us all together. I could not have gotten through all this shit without her."

"That's nice, John," Amanda whispered. "It's good that you've got a nice family around you. I never knew my mum. She left when I was a little girl. Dad raised me, but he died a few years ago."

"I'm sorry to hear that," John replied sincerely. "Any brothers or sisters?"

"Nah. Only me. Dad told me that Mum couldn't even cope with one. Two or three and she'd have topped herself." John kissed the top of her head, pulling her closer. She welcomed the embrace, not used to feeling safe. It almost felt alien to her, such was her life. "What about you? What's your life story, apart from the stuff that I already know."

John looked out of the windscreen as a fox padded through the fresh snow. It paused for a moment before hustling out of sight at the sound of an approaching vehicle. "I had a normal childhood. Mum and Dad are great. No brothers or sisters, either. The Marines were my extended family. I joined up a few years after school and I never looked back. I'd only been there for a few years when 9/11 happened. That's when the world changed. Then, I met Lucy."

"What was she like?"

John closed his eyes, drawing on his memory. "She was beautiful. Dark hair, a lovely smile. And she was a great mum. She loved Lottie so much. We were a happy little family. I was only a few months from returning home when she was killed. I've thought so much about what might have been... Leaving the forces and getting a regular job... Holidays and family events. Lucy would have loved that. She was a real home bird, happiest with her family around her."

"She sounds lovely," Amanda stated, looking at the man next to her. "But, it's been six years, John. Don't you think it's time to move on with your life? I'm sure your wife would have wanted that. And I'm also sure that you'd have wanted that for her?"

John sighed, tears welling up in his eyes. "You're not the first person to say that. Even my mother-in-law has mentioned it. My parents, too. I just don't know? Maybe you're right, but I'm approaching forty, with a young daughter. I don't think I'm exactly top of many women's shopping lists."

"Are you kidding me," she replied, raising herself onto an elbow. "You're a gorgeous-looking bloke. You've got a lovely body, too. Women would be queuing up for a piece of that. And not just that, either. You're a lovely guy, John. I've only known you for a short time, but I can see that you're kind and decent. Believe me, many women want that, I should know!"

"Hmm," he replied. "Maybe one day. I just never thought my life would turn out like this. I assumed we'd grow old together. I never guessed I'd be raising Lottie on my own."

"You've had years to dwell on this. Get out there and start living, John. Life's too short, as well you know."

"Okay. I'll think about it," he replied, wanting to change the conversation quickly.

"Look. I've gotta go in a bit," Amanda said, pulling him towards her. "So, come and give me something to keep me warm before I head out into the snow."

"Yes, ma'am," he replied, climbing on top of her in the dark confines of the cab.

"Come on then, bruv," Jerome asked impatiently. "Did you find out anything?"

Deano looked at the prison guards, happy that they were either too far away, or concentrating on other conversations. "I think we've found her," he said, leaning close to his half-brother. "Her name is now MJ Kerr and we think she lives in Scotland."

"Think?"

"Yes. We found her cousin, and Tracey noticed that someone called MJ Kerr had liked one of her pictures on Facebook. So, Tracey looked at her profile. Not much info," he replied pulling a phone out of his jacket pocket. He brought up the picture, turning the phone towards Jerome.

He leaned close, analysing the picture. "That's her," he murmured, his heartbeat increasing. "The mole."

"We thought so, too," Deano replied, a satisfied air exuding from him. "There's a pub behind her in the picture. Tracey zoomed in and then Googled the name. It's in a place called Caithness, which is in Scotland."

"She's certainly put some distance between us. But that's okay. I'll find her. Thanks, bruv. I owe you one."

"It's fine. Happy to help. Are you really going straight when you get out?"

"Yeah. But I need to pay that bitch a visit first."

"To get even?"

"Partly, bruv. But not just that. She's got something of mine. Something that I asked her to hold onto before we were both arrested."

"What?" his half-brother asked inquisitively.

"Cash. A lot of cash. I knew that I needed to keep it separate from my gear, just in case. She must still have it, as she didn't keep it at home."

"So where did she put it? And how much did you give her?"

"Hundred grand," he whispered. "And I've no idea where it is. I told her not to tell me, which I thought was a good idea back then. But I'll find it and set the record straight. Once I've done that, I can carry on with my life, with a nice little retirement fund tucked away somewhere safe."

"So, when will you do this? As soon as you get out?"

"Probably," he replied, rubbing his beard. "But I'll be on parole, which means they'll be watching me. So, I may not be able to just drive up there and sort things out. I may need help?"

"Well, you can count on me, bruv. Whatever you need."

"Cheers," he replied. "And while we're talking about getting even, I have someone who can help you sort that guy out."

"Who?" Deano replied eagerly.

"His name is Rafal. Lives in Erdington, near the Villa ground. I don't have his number, but you'll find him in the Yew Tree most Saturday afternoons."

"Okay," Deano replied. "What does he look like?"

"He's big. About six-two, with a shaven head and a tattooed neck. You'll find him easily enough. Tell him I sent you, then outline what help you'll need from him."

"Cheers, Jez. I'll try and get over there this weekend, if possible."

"You need a car. What kind of dealer gets the bus and train everywhere?"

"I know. And I will. Just need to get a few more quid together."

Jerome nodded. "So, what else is going on out there?"

"Not much. Business is steady. Tracey is still the same. Different bloke every month."

"Jesus! Such a waste, bruv. She was smart at school. I thought she'd make something of herself?"

"So did she. Then she got up the duff and that was the end of that! How about you? How's things in here?"

"Good. No one messes with me. I've been doing plastering and carpentry classes. Do you know how much a good plasterer makes a week?"

"No idea."

"A lot. They've promised to sort me out once I'm released. I'll keep my head down for a few years, then try and go it alone. You should think about it, too. You can't carry on like this forever. Sooner or later, you'll need a proper job."

"I know," Deano replied, shifting in his seat. "But not yet. Maybe when I'm thirty."

"Okay, bruv. Well, don't leave it too long. And don't end up in here with me. If you're gonna get even with that guy, make sure you're careful."

"Don't worry," Deano replied. "That cunt won't know what hit him. Or who hit him."

26

"Hi, Dad," Lottie called as she walked out of the school gates.

John smiled, watching his daughter saying goodbye to her school friends before striding over towards him, her curly blonde hair buffeted by the brisk winter wind. "Hi, love," he replied happily, giving her a one-armed hug. "How was school?"

"Fine," she stated neutrally. "Although, I'm glad to be breaking up for a few weeks."

"I'm sure you are," he agreed. They chatted as they made their way towards the car which was parked in a side street. The rest of the world was shut off to them as they talked about Christmas.

Across the road, two men walked in the same direction, keeping a close eye on the father and daughter. One of the men zipped up their black puffer jacket, covering the tattooed flesh around his neck as a biting gale buffeted him.

"Dad. Can I go to Sharon's later? She's asked me to go for dinner."

"Okay," John replied. "I was going to get fish and chips, though."

"Well, why don't we stop off on the way home? You get something to eat, then I'll eat later."

"Okay. Seems like you've got it all worked out!" he responded, as they turned into the quiet cul-de-sac where John's red Vauxhall was parked.

"Just being prepared," she replied. She smiled at her father, then walked around the car to the passenger door.

He smiled back, placing an arm on the car's roof. "Just like your mother," John declared, before climbing in.

The black Mazda pulled across the junction of the dual-carriageway, briskly pulling into traffic as it accelerated to keep pace with the cars around it. Two cars ahead, the red Vauxhall drove sedately, keeping to the speed limit.

"Okay," Deano started. "Hang back a bit. I don't think they noticed us."

"Relax," Rafal replied. "I've done this before." His thick Polish accent made his words sound stilted and blunt.

Deano had relayed his plan to the bigger man next to him, so both men understood what was to follow. "What do you think of him?"

"He's big," the other man replied. "No fat on him. He'll know how to handle himself."

"Well, we're not going to tangle with him today, especially if his daughter's with him. I just wanna know where this wanker lives."

"Well, just sit back and relax. I'll keep close enough to him." The two men lapsed into silence, keeping their eyes trained on the red car a few hundred yards ahead. It pulled off the dual-carriageway, heading along another busy road. It passed Longbridge train station, then accelerated up a small hill towards a mini roundabout.

"Keep with them," Deano urged, fidgeting in his seat.

"Stop stress. I will not lose them," the Polish man replied curtly. They continued to follow the red car, slowing down as it pulled up outside a chip shop.

"Looks like he's getting them some dinner. I could murder a kebab!"

"That'll have to wait," Rafal stated.

He pulled up a few hundred yards behind the red Vauxhall. A few minutes later, they both watched intently as the man hurried across the wide pavement towards the car as a light rain started falling from the darkening skies above. The car pulled away from the kerb as the black Mazda followed steadily, blending into the early dusk that was falling over south Birmingham. After a few left and right turns, the Vauxhall pulled onto a driveway as the Mazda sped past.

"There's a place to turn around just up ahead," Deano urged.

"Hang on," Rafal replied, deftly performing a three-point turn on the quiet side street. They drove past the semi-detached house just as the man and girl exited the car, and watched the man unlocking the front door as his daughter stood behind him.

"Number twenty-nine," Deano confirmed, spotting the numbered plaque next to the front door. "Right. We know where they live. Good work, mate."

"Told you. Easy-peezy, lemon queazy."

Deano smiled at the bigger man's turn of phrase, not feeling the need to correct him. "Right. I don't know about you, but I could do with that kebab now. Fancy one?"

"Only if you're buying?" Rafal replied, smiling as he turned left out of the road.

John turned off the television as the news finished its daily update. He walked past the Christmas tree and into the kitchen, pulling a can of lager from the fridge. Opening a glass-fronted cupboard, John pulled his favourite glass from within. His wife had brought it back from Germany years before and it was the only glass that the ex-soldier now used. It was a pint glass, the gold-plated rim giving it a premium look. Pouring himself a drink, he walked back into the lounge, sinking into his settee as the Christmas trees lights pulsed gently. He looked across at the opposite wall, smiling at the framed photograph that hung there. It had been taken the year before Lucy had passed away. A professional shot of the three of them. All smiling. All happy, before life had turned upside-down.

"I miss you, sweetheart," he whispered, before taking the head off his pint. His phone buzzed on the settee beside him. Placing his glass on a side table, he activated the handset, seeing a text message from Amanda.

When are you up here next? X

John looked at the picture on the wall, averting his gaze from Lucy's eternal eyes. He tapped a brief message on the keypad.

"Monday. That's my last trip before I break up for Xmas. X

He waited for a minute, taking another healthy gulp of his pint. His phone buzzed again and John picked it up expectantly.

Fancy meeting up? X

Sure. I'll be up there at around 6 pm. X

Great. I'll buy you the best burger in the north. Lol x

John smiled. Despite her being a prostitute, John liked her. He knew it would never go anywhere, but he enjoyed her company. He also enjoyed their intimacy, although it was tinged with feelings of guilt. He kept his eyes locked onto the black handset as a shadow passed by his bay window.

Looking forward to it already. See you then. X

A noise from the back of the house made John look away from his phone. He sat stock-still, listening. *What was that?* he thought as a clattering sound wafted in from the kitchen. The ex-soldier rose to his feet, slipping on his old trainers on before heading into the dark kitchen. He pressed himself to the wall as a shape passed by the kitchen window. *Shit,* his stomach tightening. *Burglars.*

As John took a step forward, his phone buzzed from the lounge. He ignored it, his mind on alert. He watched as the figure moved to his left, testing the conservatory doors. As quietly as he could, the ex-soldier lifted the kitchen door key off the hook above the microwave, his fingers starting to tremble as he neared the door. The garden was in total darkness, no clues presenting themselves as John silently opened the door. Stepping out into the darkness, his arms broke out in goosebumps as the frosty night draped itself over him. He edged forward and saw the shadowy figure flinching as the stranger noticed his approach. In a blur of speed, the unknown person barrelled into him, knocking John into the brick wall behind him. The air was expelled from his lungs as the figure loomed over him, throwing an arching punch towards his face. He barely managed to deflect it, his assailant's knuckles grazing the rough brickwork behind him.

John focused, trying to get a look at his attacker's identity. A black mask peered back at him underneath a hooded top, giving the unknown assailant a macabre appearance. Time seemed to slow down for John as the man's rasping breath blew clouds into his face. Another blow was thrown, hitting John in the ribs. He winced, almost tripping over the drain that ran from his kitchen sink, his attacker following him, methodically. In the darkness, John tried to size the man up, noting that he was large, a few inches taller than himself. Heavy-set shoulders seemed to blot out the fairy lights from his neighbour's house as strong hands grabbed his T-shirt, yanking him into his shed wall.

At that moment, something stirred inside him. An animal instinct that he'd not felt for years. It told him one thing. *Survive.* He feigned injury, shrinking away as the man advanced. A noise in the darkness made John flinch – the sound of a flick-knife springing open in the man's hand. *Fuck this,* he thought, firing out a fast jab into the face of his attacker. It connected, setting the man grunting in pain, sending the knife clattering to the floor.

"You picked the wrong house, mate," John stated, aiming a kick at the man's knee. It connected firmly, though his own leg was jarred from the impact.

Another grunt, the man slowing down as his breathing became distorted and muffled. He tried to advance once more, his left leg dragging his foot across the slabs. "Fuck you!" the injured man hollered, barging past John, knocking him to one side as he made his way clumsily towards the side gate. Flinging it open, the man slammed it hard just as John charged, propelling the ex-soldier backwards onto the ground. He scrambled groggily to his feet as a car's engine revved and he heard tyres screech along the quiet suburban road as he staggered out onto his driveway. He caught sight of a black car as it sped past, towards the junction a few hundred yards away. Taillights lit up, before the vehicle turned right and disappeared from view, leaving John panting on the pavement. As the noise of the rasping engine and protesting tyres died away, John's pulse slowed slightly, the throbbing in his ears lessening as he gingerly walked back towards the house.

Sliding the bolt on the gate, he made his way back inside and flopped down on the settee. His mind was a tumult of thoughts. *That was no burglar. He was tooled-up!* Grabbing his beer, John downed half the pint in one go, quenching his throat after his exertions. Resting his head on the settee, he tried to take stock of the situation. *Should I call the police?* He decided against it as his phone began vibrating next to him.

"Hello?"

"Hello, is that John?"

"Speaking," he replied.

"Hiya. It's Zoe, Sharon's mum. Just to let you know that we'll be setting off in about half-an-hour or so?"

"Okay," he agreed, the rigours of the previous minutes forgotten momentarily. "Has she been well behaved?"

The woman chuckled on the other end of the line. "She's been golden. No trouble at all. Have you enjoyed a peaceful house?"

John touched his ribs, sucking in his breath. *You've no idea,* he thought. "Yes, he replied tentatively. "Just watched a bit of telly. Rock and roll, eh?"

"Well, I'll be doing that as soon as Sharon's in bed. With a large glass of wine!"

John smiled, the tension in his body ebbing away. "Sounds like you deserve it, Zoe."

"It's in the fridge, just waiting to be uncorked. Anyway, we'll see you in a bit."

"Okay. I'll keep an eye out. 'Bye for now."

"'Bye," the woman replied as John ended the call.

He placed the phone on the dark settee, gingerly lifting himself to a standing position. *Not broken, just bruised,* he thought as his fingers gently prodded his ribs. A minute later, John was out on his rear patio, looking around for anything of interest. Finding nothing, he walked around the side of the house, until his foot caught against something on the cold slabs that gave a metallic clink. *Jesus!* he thought, as he held the flick knife in his palm. His thumb tested the blade, the skin almost breaking when he applied slight pressure. *Thank fuck he never got to use this.* With shaking fingers, he closed the blade, clicking it back into the black handle. John walked back into the house, padding upstairs to his bedroom. Opening the wardrobe next to the window, he slid the knife to the rear of the top compartment, happy that it was hidden away from prying eyes and wandering fingers. He drew the curtains, shutting out the glow from the street lights, then headed back downstairs, to finish that beer.

"Pull over," Rafal urged as the Mazda sped along a quiet side street.

"Okay," Deano replied, sending the car grinding to an abrupt stop close to the junction with the busy road beyond. "You all right?" he asked, watching as Rafal tenderly manipulated his nose.

"I'll live. He caught me with a good shot. You were right. He knows how to handle himself. We've been impatient. We should have waited."

"I know. But I just want a piece of him so badly. Next time, we'll plan it better."

"Next time?" Rafal replied, wincing as he tried to flex his knee.

"Damn right! I'm not gonna let this lie. I want to settle the score. And I need you to help me."

"Fine. But not now. Let's wait until after Christmas. He will have family all around him. Better wait until he's alone again. And not in the house. If you want this to work, you need to follow this man. Maybe when he's at work?"

"Fair point," Deano replied. "Thanks. I appreciate your help, mate."

"It's nothing. Jerome has helped me plenty over the years. This is least I can do. Fuck!" he rasped. "My knee is fucking killing me!"

"Here, have some of this," he said, passing over the joint he was smoking. "It might help take the edge off."

The Polish man obliged, taking a long drag, the interior of the car glowing orange as he drew the concoction deep into his lungs. "*Dziękuję*," he replied in his native language.

"What?" Deano countered, his brow creasing.

"Sorry. It means thanks."

"No probs. Knock yourself out."

Rafal buzzed down the window, blowing a stream of smoke into the cold night air. "We also have to be careful of police. He may report this."

Deano thought about their potential dilemma, shaking his head after a few seconds. "I don't think he'll tell the police. When we had our dust-up, he didn't want to take it further. You could tell that he wanted to get out of the station as quick as possible. Chill! We'll be okay. The police won't get involved. Well, at least not yet."

"Meaning?"

"When I knock that prick out, I'm gonna make sure he doesn't get up. Then the police will probably get involved if he winds up in hospital. But they won't know who did it."

"Well, that is your lookout. I cannot be involved in what happens next. I have wife and kids. I'm not going back to prison."

"That won't happen. All I need from you is transport. I will do the deed myself."

"Okay. Now, I'll drop you back home. I need to get back to Erdington. My wife is going out later and I babysit."

Deano smiled. "Fair enough. Just drop me at the top of the road. I can get the bus back home. Via the pub."

"Then let's switch seats. And one more thing."

"What?"

"When he's on the ground. Break the fucker's legs. For me."

"Whatever you say, mate," Deano replied, before opening the driver's door.

27

"Come in," John said happily to the trio on the doorstep.

"Hi, Dad." Lottie gave him a hug before slipping off her black leather shoes at the bottom of the stairs.

He turned towards the woman and girl standing on the doorstep. "Thanks for bringing her back. Would you like a quick coffee before you get started on the wine?"

"Why not?" Zoe replied, ushering her daughter into the hallway. The ginger-haired girl kicked off her shoes, joining her friend next to the stairs.

"Dad, can I have some juice?" Lottie asked.

"Sure. Help yourself to whatever you want." The girls ran down the hallway into the kitchen, giggling.

"Nice to see her happy," John said to the woman.

"She's a lovely girl. Very polite, too."

"When she wants to be. Here, let me take your coat."

"Oh. Thanks," Zoe replied, shouldering her way out of the leather jacket. She leaned against the front door, starting to unzip her leather boots.

John's eyes drifted towards the floor as a flash of nylon-covered calf presented itself to him. He looked away, feeling a twinge of guilt and embarrassment. "That's fine. You don't have to take your boots off. No one else does."

"It's force of habit," Zoe replied as she placed her footwear next to the telephone table.

"Okay," he conceded, smiling. She smiled back as the air was suddenly charged with an awkward silence. "Right. Coffee," John confirmed a little too quickly. He extended a hand, ushering the woman down the hallway.

"Thank you."

He followed her into the kitchen, his eyes drawn to her shapely figure. *Knock it off*, he thought, in an attempt to banish the images that were flashing through his mind. "How do you take it?"

"Milk, one sugar, please, John," she replied evenly.

He filled the kettle, feeling her eyes on him as he took two mugs out of the cupboard. Time seemed to slow down as John waited for the kettle to boil as he occupied himself with taking milk from the fridge and generally fussing around the kitchen. "Here you go," he said at last, placing a large mug of coffee in front of her.

"Thanks," she replied. She took a sip and nodded her approval.

"Sit yourself down," John said, nodding towards the kitchen table and chairs.

"I'm okay. If I sit down, I won't wanna get back up again."

He smiled, appraising her. She was a full head shorter than John, with a full figure and wavy dark hair. She had a kind face, a sprinkling of freckles adorning a slender nose. Deep brown eyes stared back at him. She had a girl-next-door look that appealed to John. The attack earlier in the evening was forgotten as he stood awkwardly, trying to think of something to say to the attractive woman across the kitchen. "So, what's your plan for Christmas Day?"

She placed her coffee on the countertop. "The usual. We're going to my parents for dinner. Not terribly exciting. I usually end up having a bust-up with my mum. Families, eh!"

"Are you married?" It was out before John realised what he'd asked. He tried not to blush, feeling awkwardness rising to the surface once more.

She smiled, liking his direct question, even if he now looked a bit embarrassed. "Not anymore. Long story. It's just me and Sharon now. Has been for years."

"Oh, okay," he replied, surprised that he was standing there talking to a single mum. An attractive single mum. *Play it cool, John. Don't make a prat of yourself.* "Probably best. Men are pretty shit!"

She laughed, flicking a lock of hair from her face. "The ones I meet usually are." Her expression suddenly changed, becoming serious. "Sharon told me what happened to your wife. For what it's worth, I'm very sorry."

A dark cloud appeared on John's horizon, his face dropping slightly. "Thank you."

"I'm sure you're sick of people telling you that?"

"It's fine. It happened a long time ago now. So, I guess I've become used to it."

"I suppose you would, John. It must be tough, being mum and dad all in one?"

"It's not that bad," he replied, half-smiling. "The next few years might be a bit tricky. Teenagers, hormones, etcetera, etcetera."

"Don't I know it! Sharon is already in full teenage mode. Hissy fits and slammed doors are a regular occurrence in our house."

"That's where the wine comes in."

"Has there been anyone else, after your wife?" It was Zoe's turn to be direct, a tension wafting into the kitchen.

John blew out a breath, not really knowing what to say. *What can I say? That I've been sleeping with a prostitute in the back of my cab?* "No. Kinda sad, isn't it? I've never bothered. Lottie and work take up most of my time. Is that the lamest excuse you've ever heard?"

"Pretty much," she replied, a warm smile spreading across her face. "You should get back out there one day. You're a long time dead." She flinched at her own words. "Sorry, that came out wrong."

He laughed, the tension in the room dissipating. "I know what you meant. Maybe one day."

"Well, we have a Facebook group for mums and dads, that meets at the Stone every month. It's not as bad as you think. It's not a singles night or anything like that, just a get-together. Are you on Facebook?"

John shook his head. "I've never bothered with it. I'm a bit of a dinosaur about that kind of stuff."

Zoe smiled. "I'm on it, for my sins. It can kinda take over your life if you let it. And I've tried the whole online dating thing, too, with no success. Too many weirdos sending you dick pics."

John almost choked on his coffee, followed by a mini coughing fit. She watched, mildly amused as the ex-soldier tried to regain his composure. "You're really selling it to me! The online dating, I mean. I've never even thought of trying that. And now, I probably never will. Not a fan of dick pics!"

"You're funny," she replied, liking the unexpected turn of events that the evening had presented to her. "Come along. You may enjoy it."

John knew the Stone public house as it was only a few hundred yards from where they lived. It was one of the oldest pubs in Birmingham, still retaining an olde-worlde charm that many local pubs had sadly lost. "Maybe I will. I'm a bit out of the loop and rusty. It's been nearly seven years."

"Don't worry about that. It's just a friendly get-together. No pressure."

"Okay. When is the next one?"

She smiled, hoping that he would turn up. "A week tomorrow. Maybe we'll see you there?" She drained her coffee, placing the mug on the kitchen table. "Anyway, I'd better get back. It was lovely meeting you, John."

"Likewise, Zoe," he replied, still feeling a bit awkward.

She walked into the hallway, with John a few paces behind her. "Sharon!" she called. "Come on, love. We're going." She zipped up her boots on the bottom step, John leaning against the wall as the two girls descended the stairs noisily.

"Dad? Can Sharon come over during the holidays?"

Both parents exchanged glances, a nod of recognition shared between them. "Sure. You're welcome anytime."

"Thank you, Mr Wilson," the ginger-haired girl replied happily as she slipped on her school shoes.

"That's okay. And call me John. Mr Wilson makes me sound old."

"How old are you?" Sharon asked inquisitively.

"He's thirty-seven," Lottie stated. "Which is ancient!" John rolled his eyes.

"That's not old," Zoe replied evenly. "I'll be there in a couple of years." Her words hung in the air, a message to John.

Similar age. Nice looking, too. Maybe it is time to get back out there? John looked across at his daughter, the rest of the world seeming to fall away. Lottie looked back at him, smiling. *She looks happy. That's what Lucy would have wanted. Surely?*

"Come on then, Mum," Sharon urged, moving towards the door. Both girls hugged as their parents smiled at each other before bidding their farewells.

A minute later, John and Lottie were standing on the doorstep as a cold wind whistled around their ankles. "Come on then. Go and get showered, young lady."

"She fancies you, Dad."

"Who?" John asked, fishing for information.

"Duh! Sharon's mum. I showed her a picture of you earlier. She said you were very handsome."

"Why did you do that?" John asked as he closed the front door.

"Because, Dad, it's time you started living. I still miss Mum terribly. And I always will. But you've been on your own for as long as I can remember. You need to smile again. And maybe someone like Zoe can help with that?"

He walked over to his daughter, lifting her into his arms. He kissed her on the forehead as she wrapped her legs around him. For a brief moment, she was his little girl again. "Since when did you become so old and wise, eh?"

"I must get it from Mum," she admonished, a crooked smile on her face. "Zoe's right, Dad. You are handsome. And there will be lots of women who would jump at the chance of being with you. Just think about it, okay?"

"Okay, princess," he replied. "Now, get upstairs and get showered. Put your clothes in the wash basket, not on the floor."

She jumped down, sticking her tongue out before running upstairs. "Love you, Dad," she called over her shoulder before disappearing from sight.

"Ditto," he replied, his chest tightening with emotion. "And your mum loves you, too," he whispered before heading back into the kitchen to grab another beer, thoughts of attackers and flick-knives long forgotten. For now.

28

Amanda climbed into the passenger seat, dragging her sleeping bag with her. "You seem quieter than normal," she said. "Is everything okay?"

John raised himself up on one elbow, his naked body slick with sweat. "I may have met someone."

Amanda took a drag of her cigarette, blowing smoke away from John. "You don't mind, do you?"

John shook his head, a bit of smoke the least of his worries.

"So, who's the lucky lady?"

"The mother of Lottie's school friend. We got chatting the other day. She's invited me to a singles night at the local pub."

"Well, good for you. It's long overdue, John."

"Not sure if it will go anywhere. But I thought I'd tell you about it."

"I take it, if it does go somewhere, this will have to end?"

He blew out a long sigh. "Yeah. It will. Sorry."

"Don't be sorry. This is just a bit of sex. I do like you though, John. I think you're a great guy. But we live hundreds of miles away. If you find someone special, you should go for it."

"Can we still be friends?" he asked. *Fuck, that sounded lame!*

"Of course," Amanda confirmed matter-of-factly. "I will miss the sex.

No one's lit my fire like that before! Whoever she is, she's in for one hell of a ride. Literally!"

"Thank you, Amanda. I wasn't really sure how to tell you this. I'm so out of the loop regarding women. I've had nothing for years, then all of a sudden, my life suddenly becomes more complicated."

"Well, that's why we're here. To keep you blokes on your toes." She threw her cigarette butt out of the window, wrapping the sleeping bag around her nakedness. "So, are you all set for Christmas?"

"Think so," he replied. "They're all coming to our house. So, dinner for six."

"Sounds great. Who's cooking?"

"Me, with a little help from Judy and Mum."

"Well, you enjoy it, John. I'm pleased for you," she replied, her words sounding hollow.

"And you? What are you up to?"

"As I said before, nothing much. Probably just get shit-faced on cheap vodka. But enough talk about that. This may be the last time that I see you naked," she murmured, climbing clumsily onto the mattress. "Give me a Christmas present to remember!"

"Here you go, Nan," the woman said. "I'll put it on the table next to you. Okay?"

"What?" the elderly woman replied, her rheumy eyes trying to focus on the younger woman in front of her.

"Cup of tea, Nan. On the table."

"Oh. Thank you, dear. I'm a bit parched."

"Well, get that down you and you'll feel right as rain." The woman opened the curtains slightly, peering out at the snowy evening, her breath clouding next to the glass. Walking back towards a small settee, she sat down, watching patiently as the old woman raised the cup to her thin lips, her hand trembling.

A few minutes later, the cup sat empty on the pine table, the old woman seeming drained from her exertions. "Thank you, my dear. Just what I needed."

"My pleasure. What shall we have for dinner? I was thinking about faggots and chips. Or I could get you a piece of roe from the chip shop?"

The old woman's brow wrinkled, her paper-thin skin almost translucent. "I am partial to a bit of roe. But only if it's no trouble?"

"Trouble? Of course not, Nan. You've done so much for me over the years. A bit of roe and chips is the least I can do."

"Thank you, dear. You're a good girl. I've always thought so," she replied, as her glasses slid down her thin nose. She pushed them back into place without thinking. "I can never repay you for letting me move in with you."

"Think nothing of it, Nan. I enjoy having you here. Life can get pretty lonely."

"Indeed. It's been thirty years since Stan passed away. Oh, I do miss him. And he doted on you when you were little."

"I remember. I always loved Grandad Stan. He was a lovely man."

"That he was. A real gentleman. Not many like him anymore."

"Tell me about it," she agreed, reflecting on her past partners. She cast the thought aside, not wanting to spend another second dwelling on a conveyor belt of losers and monsters. "Shall I pop to the chippy and get dinner now? Are you hungry?"

"I could definitely eat something. Not too much, mind. Just a few chips to go with the roe."

"Okay, Nan. I'll be back in a bit," she responded, bending down to kiss her grandmother on the forehead.

"Thank you, Mandy," the old woman replied happily.

"It's MJ, Nan, remember? Mandy's gone. You need to call me MJ now. Okay?"

"Sorry, dear. I'm getting a bit forgetful these days. Thank you, MJ."

The younger woman smiled thinly before leaving the dark lounge. She walked along a dimly-lit hallway into a small kitchen. "Where's my bag?" she asked herself. After a few seconds rooting around the kitchen, she found it under a free newspaper. Depositing the paper in the bin, she delved into her bag, retrieving her purse. "Shit," she cursed as she peered at a solitary five-pound note. *That won't cover it.* She walked back along the hallway, turning left into one of two bedrooms. Opening the wardrobe, MJ pulled a battered shoebox from the top compartment. She lifted the lid, peeling a twenty-pound note from a thick roll. "Thank you, Jerome," she whispered. "Dinner's on you, again."

Heading down the hall, MJ squeezed her fluffy-sock-covered feet into a pair of tan Ugg boots before donning a thick winter coat. The cul-de-sac was quiet, muted by the fresh snowfall. MJ trudged the few hundred yards along deserted roads before she came out on the main thoroughfare, where a few pubs and restaurants were dotted along its stretch. She zipped up her jacket with trembling hands as a biting wind blew in off the North Sea, peppering her with stinging snowflakes. The barrage was soon over, as MJ ducked into the local chip shop, where a Mediterranean-looking man greeted her.

"Hello, MJ. Nice weather?" he said, his mild Scottish accent betraying his olive-skinned complexion.

"Hi, Felipe. It's bloody horrible. Why did you move from Spain to live in this shithole?"

The man smiled, holding up his hand and rubbing his forefinger and thumb together. "The big bucks."

"If you insist," she replied, in her fading Brummie accent.

"What can I get you?" he asked as he dropped a towel on the countertop.

"Can I have tinned roe and a cone of chips, please?" She paused, looking at the options on the large, colourful display boards above rotating kebab spits. "I'll have cod and chips, with curry sauce over the top."

"Coming right up," he replied cheerfully, leaving MJ standing next to the battered sausages and various pies.

She rubbed her hands on the glass-fronted display, happy to feel warmth eke back into them slowly. "Busy today?" she asked, attempting small talk.

"Not really. So close to Christmas. And the weather is not good. It might pick up later when the pubs empty. How about you? How's the job going?"

MJ smiled, the question almost alien to her. "It's fine," she replied, trying to sound enthusiastic. "The work is steady, and the people are nice." She'd been visiting the chip shop for a while and was now on friendly terms with the owner. They had chatted about various topics since she'd arrived in town. She welcomed the conversation, as prison had been a lonely place, where she had kept herself to herself.

"Well, that's good," he replied cheerfully. "Although, I don't see you on the checkout much. You want salt and vinegar?"

"Yes, please," she replied. "And I've been moved to the stores. I prefer it there. Let the youngsters do all the face-to-face stuff. At my age, I'm happy to stick to the shadows."

"Pah!" he exclaimed. "You're not old. And you're a very pretty lady."

Something happened that had not happened for years. The woman once known as Mandy Terry, a tough single mother who was as street-wise as they come, suddenly blushed, not knowing what to do or say. She just stood there, a wide grin on her face. "Erm, thanks," she replied awkwardly. "Sorry, I'm not used to compliments."

"That's okay," Felipe replied, seeing the woman's uncomfortable stance. "But it's true. You're a fine woman. Remember that. Is that everything?" he asked.

She stood there for a moment, almost in a trance before she snapped back to attention. "Erm, yeah. That's everything thanks."

"That'll be nine pound fifty, please."

She handed Felipe the money, smiling warmly. "Just give me a tenner back."

"Thank you, MJ. Enjoy your tea."

"Will do. If I don't see you before, have a lovely Christmas."

"You too, MJ. I hope Santa sends you something nice."

She nodded. As she left the warmth of the chip shop, her body was once more assaulted by strong winds and sharp snowflakes. She hunkered down, pulling her chin inside the coat as she made her way back home. Despite the temperature and conditions, the woman was smiling under her coat. *He likes me,* she thought. *And I think I like him, too. Maybe I'll get a staff discount?* She chuckled as she rounded the corner of her street, a warm feeling spreading through her body.

29

John walked into the Stone public house, shaking the rain from his leather jacket. The cosy lounge area was filling up with Christmas revellers and the bar was three-deep with waiting customers. He shouldered his way past a group of young men, nodding his thanks as they let him through. John stepped down into another section of the pub, where he spotted Zoe in the midst of a throng of people.

She noticed him approach and waved happily. "Hiya," she beamed. "I didn't expect you to turn up. Who's looking after Lottie?"

"I wouldn't have missed it for the world. Plus, Lottie threatened never to speak to me again if I didn't come. She's staying at her nan's tonight."

"Good old Lottie, eh?" Zoe replied, her eyes drifting up and down the man in front of her. "You look nice."

"Erm, thanks. You do, too, Zoe. In fact, you look lovely."

She blushed, her eyes dropping to the floor. "Flattery will get you everywhere," she gushed happily. "Would you like a drink?"

"I'll get you one. What's your tipple?"

"Pinot Grigio, please. I'll come with you."

John nodded, turning towards the mahogany bar, trying to find a spot that he could jostle himself into. After a few minutes of small talk with Zoe, a young barmaid nodded towards him. "A large Pinot Grigio and a pint of lager, please."

"Sure," she replied, dodging past a colleague as she headed off to pour the wine.

"A large one! I'll be hammered by nine," Zoe proclaimed, looking up at him.

"Pace yourself and you'll be fine," he replied, as the barmaid handed him a large glass filled to the brim with cold white wine. He carefully handed it to the woman behind him, pulling a ten-pound note out of his wallet.

He waited another minute before walking back to the group with Zoe, feeling a rising tension spreading through his body. He was not used to socialising. It had been over ten years since he'd been in a similar situation to the one he now found himself in. He smiled at the group as Zoe introduced him. He counted eleven of them. Four men and seven women, including Zoe. He appraised the other females as they did the same to him, smiling evenly at them before they resumed their conversations.

The group split into two and John hovered on the periphery with Zoe as two of the men began talking about the plight of their respective football teams.

One, a nondescript man a few years his senior, with a bulging waistline and blond, thinning hair, turned to John. "Who's your team?" he asked in his thick Brummie accent.

"Villa. Although, I've not been down for years."

"Hear that, Brian?" the man said to his friend. "He's a wanky Villa fan, like you!"

"Take no notice of Ian," Brian huffed, his words slightly slurred. "He's a bitter Blue Nose."

"No offence taken," John replied, wondering where the conversation was heading. *I thought this was a friendly get together? They're already pissed and talking about football. Can't see them having any success with the ladies.*

"So," Zoe began, taking his arm. "Are you all set for Christmas?"

Glad of the intervention, John turned away from the two men, who continued their debate. "Yes. We're all set. And you? Didn't you say that you were going to your parents?"

"You remembered. I am impressed!" She took a sip of her wine, then placed the glass on a nearby table that the group had just acquired from departing customers. "Yes. Just the four of us. My sister usually comes over, but she's going through a messy divorce at the moment and wanted to stay at home with her kids. Men, eh!"

"Men!" he repeated. "So, what's your story? Sorry to pry, but you said that you were once married?"

"A lifetime ago," she replied, her face dropping slightly. "I met Darren when I started my first job, which was nearly twenty years ago now. Jesus! I'm getting old." He smiled as she reached for her wine. "Things were great at first. He was, and still is, a personal trainer. Believe it or not, I used to be quite fit back in the day. I was at the gym almost every day and jogged two or three times a week."

You're still fit now, he thought, noticing the cleavage that was on show in front of him. A silver chain hung there, nestled next to creamy-coloured flesh. He averted his eyes, aware that Zoe had noticed his appraisal of her.

"Anyway, after a year or so, we moved in together and it kinda went from there. We were really happy, enjoying holidays and socialising on a regular basis. Then, a few years after we were married, we had Sharon and it all changed."

"How so?" John asked, hanging onto the woman's every word.

"Putting it bluntly, he stopped fancying me, practically overnight. I put on quite a bit of weight with Sharon, which I've never really lost. I stopped going to the gym and stopped jogging, too. Like, when would I have time? He always promised to help out with Sharon, but never did. He worked funny shifts, so we had no set routine. Then, the affairs started."

"Oh no! Sorry to hear that."

"It's okay, John. It was years ago. Darren was really good-looking, in a pretty-boy kinda way. Even when we first met, he had the girls swooning over him. But it was okay back then because he only had eyes for me. Once I was a mum, I lost my sex appeal as far as he was concerned, and it was only a matter of time until he strayed. The first time, he begged for forgiveness, telling me that it was a stupid mistake. And stupidly, I did forgive him, and things got better for a while. But it happened again, with a woman that he was giving personal tuition to, and lots more besides. So, I kicked him out and have been single ever since."

"Sorry to hear all that, Zoe. Sounds like you've been through the wringer."

"It's okay. All forgotten about now. He still has regular contact with Sharon, and he's a pretty good dad, all things considered. And the funny thing is, the woman who he cheated with ended up cheating on him a few years ago."

"Karma's a bitch, eh!" he replied, smiling over his pint glass.

"Exactly," she agreed, clinking glasses with him. "Is it as bad as you thought?" Zoe asked, nodding towards the others.

"No, it's fine. I wasn't really sure what to expect, if I'm honest. But it's fine and the company's great." The words hung in the air as John smiled at her.

God! He's gorgeous. Need to slow down on the vino, she thought as the skin around her neck flushed. "It certainly is." Another table became free. Zoe nodded her head towards it. "Fancy taking the weight off your feet?"

"Great idea," he agreed.

They slid onto a leather bench seat next to a small window, the frame rattling as the weather outside worsened. Something occurred to Zoe as she was getting comfortable, as a conversation she'd had with her daughter suddenly surfaced. "I was meaning to ask you. What happened with Lottie and that girl at school? Sharon said that you got into a fight with the girl's family?"

An image flashed across John's mind. A large, angry man looming over him. Before he could speak, another image presented itself, another large man, barging past him in the darkness. *Fuck! Could they be related? I never thought of that?* He snapped back into the room, his pulse racing. "Erm. Yeah. There was a bit of a scuffle. Nothing too bad though.

The girl's mother and uncle tried it on. We ended up at the police station."

"Oh God! Were you hurt?"

"Not really. A few bruises. I think they came off worse, though. Anyway, it was all smoothed over and I'm hoping that's the end of it."

"How awful. Sharon told me about the girl. Said that she's a right little bleeder. Let's hope that nothing else happens, John. Lottie's been through enough, if you know what I mean?"

"I do. She's a good kid who doesn't need any extra hassle that the class bully can throw at her. Fingers crossed, eh?"

They sat chatting as pub-goers came and went. As the evening wore on, the two football fans slipped away, leaving the group scattered across the pub. John and Zoe didn't notice, though. They were focused on each other, much to the annoyance of a few females in the group who were hoping to have the handsome stranger to themselves. Drinks were replenished, John's more so than Zoe's, who was starting to feel the effects of the wine. The ex-soldier drained his glass, nodding towards Zoe. "Fancy another?"

"One more," she agreed. "I'm a bit squiffy, so I'll make this my last."

"Okay. I need to pop to the gents, too. Back in a minute," he replied, sliding his way out from behind the table, lightly brushing against her as he did so.

She watched him walk off as two women from the group sauntered over. "You're monopolising the hottie," one teased. "Have you claimed him?"

Zoe smiled up at the two women, who she'd never really warmed to over the past few months. They were older than her, both divorced, both on the prowl for another man. "Sorry. We just got chatting. I never meant to keep him shackled to the table."

The other woman smiled. "Don't worry. We're only jealous. Not exactly many fit guys in here tonight, are there? And as for Brian and Ian, forget it! Who wants to talk about football all night? No wonder they're both single!"

The other woman, who was still unimpressed with Zoe's commandeering of the mystery man, piped up. "So, what's going on with you two? You look very cosy?"

"Just chatting. He's a widower, Lottie's dad. You've probably seen him around the school?"

Both women shook their heads in unison. The scowler, who was called Tanya, placed her glass on the table, watching as John walked back to the bar. "Believe me, if I'd seen that at the school gates, I'd have remembered him."

"Easy, Tanya," the other woman countered. "You'll make Zoe jealous."

Zoe laughed. "Debbie, it's not like that. Yes, he's good-looking, but we're only chatting. If you fancy a crack at him, be my guest." Her statement was hollow, without conviction.

"We won't cramp your style," Debbie began. "He's coming back. Come on, Tanya, let's give the lovebirds some space." They stepped back a few paces, both women watching as John made his way back to the table.

"Here you go," he said, noticing the two sets of eyes that were trained on him.

"John, this is Debbie and Tanya," Zoe replied, regretting every word. She knew that either woman would love to get their hooks into her new drinking partner and hoped that the night was too far gone to start up a group conversation.

"Hello," they both chirped in unison, eyeing up the ex-soldier.

"Hi," John replied, shaking both their hands. "Nice to meet you." Tanya held his grip for a few seconds longer, her hand falling away as her nails trailed across John's palm.

"Come on, Tanya. It's your round," Debbie stated, knowing that the eligible man was all but taken, at least tonight. They headed over towards the bar, leaving John and Zoe alone.

"Sorry about that," she began. "They've been giving me a hard time while you were in the loo. Well, Tanya was at least. Said I had my hooks into you good and proper. I think they're a bit jealous, which is silly, right?"

"Oh, right?" he replied. "I had no idea. Have you got your hooks into me?" he teased, winking at her.

She took a sip of her wine as she started overheating once more, trying to remain unflustered. "I don't know. Do you want me to?"

He leaned forward, planting a light kiss on her lips. "Maybe," he replied, his eyes staring into hers.

It took Zoe by surprise. She was not expecting a kiss so quickly. It was not even on a date, more like a friendly get-together as she'd previously stated. After the initial shock, she smiled, placing her hand over his as the two women at the bar stared over. "God. I'm so out of practice, John. I have no idea what to do or say?"

He laughed, squeezing her hand. "Nor do I. I do like you though, Zoe. Let's just take it steady. As you said, we're both a bit rusty. I would like to see you again, though." The words were out and John knew that he'd taken his first steps into a new world.

The statement hung in the air and Zoe smiled warmly. She looked down at her watch, noticing that their knees were touching. She also noticed, to her dismay, that it was approaching closing time. "I'll need to go soon. Mum's with Sharon and she'll need to get a taxi home. I need to think about ordering a taxi, too."

"Okay," he agreed, also disappointed that the evening was drawing to a close. "We'll finish these and head off."

"Fine," she replied, pulling her phone out of her small handbag. She squeezed John's hand before heading out of the pub to call the taxi company.

John sat there, checking his own phone, pleased that there were no missed calls or messages. He looked over at the bar, noticing that Debbie and Tanya were both looking over, one smiling, the other frowning. John smiled at both before averting his eyes back to his phone, feeling two sets of eyes fixed on his position.

"All done," Zoe confirmed, sitting back down a minute later. "Should be about twenty minutes. So, no rush to neck our drinks."

"Great," he smiled, taking a swig of his beer. He looked towards the bar, pleased to see that the two women were in deep conversation, facing away from them. "So, what's their story?"

Zoe looked over towards the bar before turning towards John, their knees touching under the table. "Both divorced. Debbie is okay, she split up with her fella a few months ago. She caught him in bed with a work colleague. All very messy. Tanya's been divorced for years. But it was her that did the cheating. I know her ex. He's a lovely guy, but a bit too nice. I think our Tanya likes a bad boy."

"She looks like she can handle herself. Keeps looking over and scowling."

"She's just jealous. A woman knows these things, John. The moment she saw you, she was probably trying anything she could to strike up a conversation. Unfortunately, or fortunately, you ended up talking to me," she stated, winking over her wine glass.

"I'd definitely say fortunately – for me, anyway!"

"Thank you. You've really made this a great night. Call it a nice early Christmas present."

"I like your way of thinking," he replied. "Let's try and put a date in the diary between Christmas and New Year?"

"Oh, I'd like that," she beamed, a wide smile spreading across her face. "But no pressure, John. As you said, let's see how it goes."

"Deal," he agreed, pulling her towards him. Their lips met, the rest of the pub melting away as they both took another small step. Towards a new sunrise.

30

NOVEMBER - 2013

Jerome lay on his bed, looking up at his bedroom ceiling. Downstairs, his mother was cooking a celebratory meal, the smell of curried goat wafting up the stairs. His mouth began to salivate, the aroma was intoxicating. *Beats prison food,* he thought, glancing across at the mobile phone on the bedside table. His mother had brought it for him and Jerome had charged it up a few minutes after entering the room. He stared back at the white ceiling, the afternoon sun dropping away quickly as shadows lengthened across the small room. *I'll ring Deano in a bit, then head up to the Yew Tree.*

"Jerome?" a voice called up the stairs.

"Yes, Mum?"

"Dinner in ten minutes."

"Okay. I'll come down and set the table in a minute."

"Okay, Son," the female voice replied before silence resumed.

He switched on his new phone, taking a few minutes to set it up. Once that was completed, he entered a few key numbers from a scrap of paper in his pocket. *I'll sort the rest out as I go,* he thought, heading downstairs.

. . .

An hour later, his belly full, Jerome was walking along a busy road towards the Yew Tree pub. Street lights lit the way ahead, a stretch of motorway looming over him as he ambled towards his destination. He pulled his phone from his pocket, dialling one of his contacts. "Alright, bruv?" he said cheerily.

"Jerome?" Deano replied, from across Britain's second city.

"The one and only," he replied, zipping up his dark hooded top, aware of the biting cold that assailed him as he passed under the motorway.

"When did you get out?"

"About three hours ago. I'm staying at Mum's until I get myself sorted."

"You should have said, bruv. I'd have come over."

"It's cool. I will come and see you over the weekend. I'm off to the Yew Tree, to reacquaint myself with a few pints. Rafal will be there. He picked me up from the nick earlier and he tells me you've not yet settled the score with that guy?"

There was a pause on the line. "Not yet. Did Rafal tell you that he's been in Poland for most of the year?"

"He did. His mum was sick."

"I know. The last time I spoke to him was after New Year. He explained what he needed to do, and I said that was cool. The guy isn't going anywhere. What do they say? Revenge is a dish best served cold."

"Something like that, bruv. So, when are you going to pay him a visit?"

"Not sure. I guess I'll need to speak to Rafal."

"I'll mention it later," Jerome replied as he walked past the entrance to an industrial estate. "So, what else has been going on?"

"Business is good. I managed to buy a car, too."

"Wicked. What you got? Something sporty?"

"Nah," Deano replied neutrally. "Just an old Golf. It's okay though, and it doesn't draw attention from the Old Bill."

"Wise move. You're starting to use your head."

"Well, I had to start at some point," he chuckled down the phone. "It's really good to have you out, bruv."

"It's good to be out. Fresh air, beer and pussy. What more does a man need?"

"Exactly. I'm sure you'll have fresh air and beer tonight. Not sure about the pussy though, old man!"

"This old dog still knows how to attract the bitches. I'll see you tomorrow, bruv."

"Laters," Deano replied.

Jerome ended the call as the pub came into sight on his left-hand side. He quickened his pace slightly, the promise of a cold pint moistening his throat. A few minutes later, he walked through into the pub.

Rafal spotted him immediately. "Welcome home, brother. Claire, a pint for my good friend."

Jerome walked over to him as patrons across the bar eyed the dark-skinned man. Some nodded in his direction, a few raising their pint glasses. A few others eyed him warily before returning to their conversations. He embraced the larger man, lifting his pint of lager off the bar. "Cheers," he said, downing half the pint's contents in one go. "Fuck, I've missed that."

"Don't worry. Many more will come your way," Rafal stated, in his thick Polish accent.

"Then I'm happy." He looked at the bigger man, noticing the gold cross around his neck. "When are you going back home?"

"In two weeks," Rafal replied. "Mother is not so well. My sister is still looking after her, but she's going on holiday. I will look after her until Ana returns from Lanzarote."

"Okay," Jerome replied, ready for his next question. "You remember the woman I was involved with before I got sent down?" he said, his voice dropping a few decibels.

"Mary? No, wait... Mandy?"

"Yes. Mandy. Well, not only did she send me down, but she also kept a stash of money that I'd asked her to look after."

"How much?"

"Hundred," Jerome stated. He took a swig and finished his pint. The young barmaid nodded in his direction, pulling two glasses from beneath the bar. Jerome smiled, liking the look of the woman who was probably twenty years his junior.

"That's a lot of money. And it was a long time ago. She could have spent it by now?"

"Maybe. But I have to find her."

"Do you know where she's living? I could pay her a visit and even things up."

"I was hoping you'd say that, mate. From what Deano has told me, she's living somewhere in Scotland. He has all the details, which I'll get from him tomorrow."

"Scotland? That's one hell of a drive."

"I know. I'd go myself but, as you know, I need to remain in Brum."

Rafal nodded. "So, when do you want me to go up there?"

Jerome smiled as their drinks were replenished. He handed a note to the barmaid, saying, "Have one yourself, sweetheart," which drew a beaming smile from the blonde-haired woman.

He turned his attention back to Rafal. "Not sure. How are you fixed before you go away?"

Rafal considered the question as he took a swig of his beer. "I've got nothing on next weekend, does that help?"

"It does, mate. I'll talk to Deano. He can go with you as he knows what she looks like."

"Okay. Let us be clear, what do you need me to do when I find her?"

"Bring back the money. If she gives you any problems, give her a slap. I don't want her hurt badly, as it may come back to haunt us."

"Okay. I will not overdo it."

"Now, tell me what's happening with soldier boy?"

Rafal's brow knitted slightly. "Not much to tell. We pay him a visit last year and I tussle with the man."

"Tussle?"

"Yes. Not really a fight. He spot me at the back of house and we exchanged a few blows before I got the hell out of there."

"That's not like you, mate. I thought you'd have wiped the floor with him?"

“He was tough. That is all I can say. If Deano is going to try his luck with him, he’d better be prepared.”

Jerome took the information in, pondering for a few moments. “I’d say leave it be. The guy’s been through enough. But if Deano wants a piece of him, I’m not going to stand in his way.”

“How do you say? He has a real hard-on for that guy. Anyway, he’s grown man. It’s his choice. Now, let’s get pissed!”

“Amen to that,” Jerome replied, smiling once again at the passing barmaid. *I think I’m in for a good night,* he thought as the woman returned the smile, twirling her blonde hair between her fingers as the older man’s eyes feasted on her.

31

DECEMBER - 2013

"Fuck me, it's cold," Deano exclaimed, zipping his jacket up to his neck.

"Pussy! Back in Gdansk, this would almost be summer. You Brits are wimps!" he taunted, winking at the other man.

"Whatever, mate," Deano huffed, a half-smile etched on his face. "Not exactly the kind of place I'd want to live."

"You're right. It feels like edge of world. This place is not very big," he said, as a cold wind kicked up from the North Sea. "If she's here, we'll find her. We have until Sunday morning."

Deano nodded, stretching his back. They had taken it in turns on the drive up from Birmingham, the seventeen-hour journey sapping the strength of both men. Now, on a sleet-laden Friday afternoon, both men scanned the main street that ran through the town. "We need to find our digs before beginning the hunt for this woman."

"According to Google, the hotel is few hundred yards away," Rafal stated. He turned and pulled two pieces of A4 paper out of the car. He handed one to Deano, the wind almost tearing the papers out of his meaty hands. "Here you go."

Deano turned away from the wind, holding the sheets in both hands as he stared at the woman's face staring back at him. Before setting off,

Deano had asked his sister to print off two pictures of their target. "I'd still bang her, mate."

"Focus on job," Rafal chided. "And we need to be careful. We can't just walk around town asking people if they know this woman. She wants to stay hidden and someone may alert her that two men are looking for her."

"Fair enough," Deano replied, suitably rebuked. "Well, I'm starving. Why don't we find the nearest chippy before checking in?"

"Good idea. I could murder kebab. We can leave the car here," he replied, folding the paper twice over before placing it in his coat pocket. "Lock the car and let's go sightseeing."

"Okay," Deano replied, smiling at the other man's turn of phrase. He locked the car, lighting a cigarette as he surveyed the main street. Rafal did the same, blowing a billow of smoke into the air before setting off towards their lunch destination.

They walked in silence for a few minutes, their eyes scanning the sparse array of shops and roughcast-covered houses. Spotting a chip shop in the distance, the two men crossed over the road, stepping onto the opposite pavement in front of a Tesco supermarket. Deano scanned the interior through large plate-glass windows, no one of interest presenting themselves as he skulked past, large hands buried deep in his pockets. A minute later, they bustled inside the small chip shop, glad to be out of the increasing wind.

An olive-skinned man stood on the other side of the counter, a large pair of silver tongs in his hand. "Afternoon, gentlemen," he said, his Mediterranean looks in conflict with his Scottish accent. "What can I get you?"

"Large kebab meat and chips," Rafal stated matter-of-factly.

"Same for me," Deano replied, eyeing the man up across the counter.

"Coming right up," he agreed happily, selecting two large polystyrene containers from the far wall. He walked over to the two men, scooping a good portion of chips into each tray. "Salt and vinegar?" he asked.

They both nodded. "Cheers," Deano replied, his stomach rumbling.

The owner of the chip shop walked over to the two large kebab sticks, lifting two chrome-topped lids from the counter. "Both types of meat?"

"Yes," Rafal responded tersely.

Undeterred by the cool customer, the man lifted a generous helping of lamb and chicken meat into each tray. "Sauce and salad?"

"No salad for me," Deano replied. "Just some garlic mayo."

"No salad. Chilli sauce for me," Rafal added, his own stomach starting to growl.

A minute later, the shop owner was placing the change into Deano's upturned hand. "Here you go. I hope you enjoy." He handed two plastic forks to the smaller customer.

"Thanks," the Birmingham man replied, dropping the change into his jacket pocket.

"You're not from around here, are you?" the man asked, slightly inquisitively.

"No," Rafal replied, pulling Deano towards the doorway. They shouldered their way into the Arctic wind, looking for a suitable place to eat their lunch.

"Here you go." Deano offered the Polish man a plastic fork.

"*Dziękuję*," he replied, his fist folding around the piece of cutlery.

"Over there," Deano urged, as sleet began blowing in from the coast. "There's a covered bus stop. We can eat in there."

"Okay." They hustled across the road, heads bowed as the onslaught battered them. After shaking themselves down, the two men stood in the shelter, consuming their steaming kebab meat and chips with gusto.

"We should look for a decent pub later."

"I agree. But not until we've taken a good look around. We're not on holiday," Rafal countered, in between mouthfuls of kebab meat. "We need to find this woman. We only have a few days."

"I know, mate," Deano replied, closing the lid of his now-empty container. He dropped it in the corner of the bus stop, lighting a cigarette. "But we should try and blend in and ask a few questions. Where better than the local pub? Maybe even try the one in the picture?"

"Okay. Once we get to the hotel, I will call Jerome and tell him that we've arrived and what our plans are."

"Come on then. Let's go and get checked in. I'm busting for a shit."

"You're a real gentleman," Rafal declared, before they began the tortuous walk back to the car.

"Hi, MJ," Felipe said happily, as the woman shouldered herself through the glass door. "Have you been singing again?"

She smiled, shaking droplets of rain from her coat. "Something like that. How are you?"

"Fine. Quiet today," he replied, placing his tea towel on the countertop. "What can I get you?"

"Chicken and mushroom pie and chips and tinned roe and a cone of chips, please."

"Coming right up," Felipe replied. He started getting the order together. "Plans for tonight?"

"Nothing too exciting," MJ stated dryly. "Probably end up watching some god-awful movie on the telly whilst Nan snores on the settee next to me. How about you?"

"Not sure yet. Becky is coming in shortly to take over. I'm giving myself a well-deserved night off." He paused, readying himself for his next question. "Say, why don't we go out for a drink?"

She smiled nervously, shifting her feet as her awkwardness rose to the surface. "I'd like that, but not tonight, Felipe. I'm shattered. Plus, I think I'm coming down with something. Maybe next time?"

"But of course," he responded, slightly crestfallen. It had taken him a long time to build up the courage to ask her out. Now, he wondered if his chance was gone. "Just let me know when you're free?" He placed the food in front of her, smiling.

"I will, Felipe. You're a nice guy, one of the only people I get a chance to talk to. I promise, once I feel better, we can go for something to eat. It's been ages since I actually went out anywhere. How much?" she asked, reaching for her purse.

"It's on the house. You enjoy and I hope you're feeling better very soon."

"Don't be silly," she exclaimed, reaching for a crisp note. Jerome's note. "I can pay."

"I know you can. Tell you what, you buy the first drink when we go out. Deal?"

MJ smiled, flushing visibly at the neck. "Deal," she replied. "Have you got a pen and paper? I'll give you my number."

He reached under the counter, pulling out a stack of Post-it notes and a black biro. MJ jotted her number down, a fluttering sensation spreading through her body. "Here you go," she said, still feeling slightly awkward.

Felipe tore the paper in half, jotting his own number down. "And here's mine, even if you're just placing an order for roe and chips," he replied, winking at her.

"Enjoy your night off and I'll see you soon."

"Enjoy yours too. 'Bye."

She exited the chip shop, heading home as street lights began flickering to life along the street. MJ crossed a junction between two streets, a hotel taking up the corner plot. She pulled the hood over her head as fresh sleet began to fall. She spotted two large men who were standing outside the front of the hotel, puffing away on cigarettes. One of them looked vaguely familiar to her as MJ tried to recollect where she'd seen the shaven-headed man before. Unable to put a name to the face, she continued on, turning left onto a quieter street where her small terraced house was located. A minute later, she was laying a large brown paper bag out on the small kitchen table, unwrapping the contents as she enjoyed the warmth that radiated through the wrapping.

"Nan!" she called. "Dinner!" She set the table, placing salt and vinegar in the centre, along with a bottle of red sauce and some cutlery

"Sorry, dear," the older woman replied. "I was spending a penny upstairs. Hmm, that smells nice. You didn't have to get a takeout. I could have cooked. I've some faggots in the freezer that I've been meaning to cook."

"Never mind, Nan. I've saved you the bother. Plus, I've got your favourite. Tinned roe."

"Oh! Thank you, dear. You're a good girl, Mandy."

She was about to correct her for the umpteenth time, but chose not to. She smiled as she began her dinner, daydreaming about the olive-skinned man and his perfect smile.

32

"At least there are people here," Deano stated, as he walked with Rafal over to the bar. "Not like the last place. What a dead-end that turned out to be."

"I know. We'd have more chance of finding ghost in that place," Rafal replied, as he tried to get the barman's attention.

The youth spotted him and walked over briskly. "Evening, gents," he began, in a broad Scottish accent. "What can I get you?"

"Two lagers," Rafal replied, pulling a note out of his wallet.

The barman began pouring the drinks as the men surveyed the room. It was a little after eight and the large pub was filling up with weekend revellers. A big Christmas tree in the corner reminded the two men that the festivities were soon to begin. Rafal's thoughts drifted to his wife and daughter, a crooked smile appearing on his face. He handed the barman the money, waiting for his change as Deano leaned against the bar, his eyes firmly locked on a table filled with young females.

"Bit of crumpet in here tonight, mate. If we don't find her, we can always try our luck with the locals."

"You can. I have wife."

"Come on. She'll never know, mate. Have a bit of fun."

Rafal gave the younger man a stern look. "I have never cheated. That's one thing I would never do."

"Fair enough, more for me to get my teeth into."

"Good luck. But first, we should ask around, but discreetly. We don't want to ask the wrong person."

"Okay. Have you done this kind of thing before?" Deano asked, suddenly curious about the other man.

"A few times. Not for Jerome, though. Back in Poland."

"And did you find them?"

"Yes," he replied matter-of-factly.

"Okay. I will let you do the talking," Deano replied, eyeing the women across the bar. "And I'll do the stalking," he continued, smiling at the larger man.

They stood talking and drinking, observing everyone that came and went over the course of the evening. A little after ten, a Mediterranean man walked into the bar, heading over to the barman. Rafal and Deano watched the man from the chip shop order a drink and exchange pleasantries with the man behind the counter. They watched the barman placed two beers in front of him as another man joined him at the bar.

"Do you think they're queer?" Rafal asked.

"Dunno," Deano replied. "You never know these days. My best mate at school turned out to be a faggot. But you'd never know to look at him. He just looks like a normal guy."

"Well," Rafal began, "if anyone knows MJ, chances are this guy might. After all, the whole town probably goes in his shop. Let him get a few beers down his neck first. Then, he might be more, how do you say? Receptive to questioning."

"You sound like a copper," Deano replied.

"I like to watch your English television. Especially police drama." They stood chatting, casually watching the other two men, who were constantly ordering more drinks. After half an hour, Rafal turned to Deano, pulling the photograph out of his pocket. "Stay here. I will order drinks and get chatting with them."

"Okay, mate. I'll stay here."

"Keep eyes peeled. You never know what might happen."

Deano nodded as the bigger man took a few steps across the bar to get the barman's attention once more.

Felipe recognised the man next to him from earlier in the day. He smiled, mildly surprised when the surly-looking man smiled back. "Hi. You were in my shop earlier."

"Yes," Rafal replied amicably. "Very good kebabs."

"You're not from around here? Are you working, or on holiday?"

"I am looking for an old friend," the Polish man countered, unfolding a sheet of paper. He handed it to Felipe, who looked at the picture. Rafal noticed a slight flinch in the man's posture, a flash of recognition on his face that lasted a split-second. "Do you recognise her?"

Regaining his composure after the initial shock, Felipe showed the picture to his drinking partner. The other man shook his head, returning to his beer. The chip shop owner passed the picture back to Rafal, shaking his head. "No. I've not seen her around here," he confirmed, his voice slightly shaky, his heart hammering in his chest. "Why are you looking for her? Are you police?"

Rafal smiled, shaking his head. "No. Nothing like that. This woman is an old friend of mine, but we lost contact. Her mother is sick and wanted Mandy to get in touch before she dies. Cancer."

"Sorry to hear that," the smaller man replied, trying to appear indifferent. He knew that MJ lived with her nan. Over the past few months, they had briefly chatted about their respective families. He remembered clearly that she'd told him that her mother was dead. Someone was lying to him, and Felipe's instinct was telling him that it was the large man with the foreign accent. The alcohol seemed to evaporate from his system, a cold feeling spreading through his body.

"I know. It's very sad. Thanks anyway," Rafal said, before ordering two more drinks. He waited patiently, trying to keep an eye on the olive-skinned man next to him. After paying for the drinks, he walked back over to Deano, handing him a cold pint of lager.

"Any luck?"

"He knows her. I could tell by his reaction to the photo. But he claims he's never seen her before."

"So, what do we do know?" Deano asked.

"We watch him." Rafal half-turned away from Felipe, engaging in small talk with Deano as the other customers continued with their evening.

"He's whispering to his mate," Deano observed. "Don't look around though. Hang on. He's heading towards the bogs, mate and he's taking his phone out of his pocket."

"Stay here," Rafal replied, placing his pint on the bar. "Any trouble, we get the fuck out of here, quickly."

Felipe let the swing-door close behind him before he locked himself inside a cubicle. He'd inputted MJ's name into his phone earlier, partly out of hope, but also because he knew he'd lose the scrap of paper. He dialled the number. "Hi. MJ?"

"Yes," the female voice replied.

"It's Felipe. Just listen. I'm in the pub next to the front. Two men are asking after you. They have a photograph and told me that you're old friends."

"Shit! What do they look like?"

"Big. One sounds Polish, the other is English. Hang on," he said, as the main toilet door opened. He heard a cubicle door close to, the bolt being drawn across loudly. He heard a pair of trousers fall to the floor as the unseen male occupant got comfortable.

"Meet me at the side of the chip shop in two minutes," he whispered.

"Okay," MJ replied nervously.

"Okay, 'bye," he said, ending the call. Felipe walked out of the cubicle, his heart racing as he strode for the exit, leaving the toilet in total silence.

After a few seconds, a cubicle door opened and Rafal stepped out towards the sinks. *Right. Let's go hunting.* He headed back out into the bar, noticing that the two men had left. He walked quickly over to Deano, downing the rest of his drink in one go. "Come on. We've got to go."

"What happened?" the small man asked.

"He phoned her. Told her to meet him at the chip shop in two minutes. We need to follow him."

"Right," Deano replied, gulping down his lager. "Let's do it."

The sleet and rain had stopped and the streets were almost deserted as the two men strode towards their destination. After a minute, the neon lights of the town's chip shop came into view. Both men crossed the road quickly as a single-decker bus trundled towards them.

"Right. Follow my lead. If it kicks off, start swinging," the large Polish man instructed, taking his sovereign rings off his meaty fingers before dropping them into his pockets.

They stuck close to the shop fronts, trying to remain as inconspicuous as possible, which was difficult for Deano as he was beginning to feel the effects of the lager. At the side of the shop, a narrow alley presented itself. Rafal stopped Deano in his tracks. "Shh. Don't move. I think they are down there." He motioned with a tilt of his head.

"Okay."

"This will be piece of cake."

"You think?" Deano replied, suddenly feeling uncertain.

"Relax. A forty-year-old woman and a bent chip shop owner. What could go wrong?"

"Who are they?" Felipe asked the woman, who was skulking in the shadows. The alleyway was compact, tall dark brick edifices rising up over it. Black bin bags bulged at the seams next to a fire exit from the chip shop and the ground was littered with discarded cigarettes.

"I don't know. It could be something to do with someone I knew a few years ago."

"Are you in trouble?"

MJ looked past Felipe, checking that the alleyway was devoid of intruders. "Honestly, I'm not sure. There are lots of things that I've kept to myself since moving here. No one knows about my former life. Not even my nan."

"Well, I can help you. Whoever they are, they seem keen to talk to you. I just wanted to tell you in person, rather than by text."

"Thank you. But I think I need to get back home and lie low for a few days."

"Maybe we should all go back to your home," a male voice called from behind them. "So you can give me what you stole from Jerome."

MJ and Felipe flinched, turning around to see two large silhouettes approaching from the main road. "Who are you?" Felipe demanded, stepping in front of MJ.

"Fuck off, mate," Deano replied calmly, balling his hands into fists as he took a step forward.

"You can't threaten me," Felipe stated defiantly. "This is my home. I'm going to call the police." Before he could pull his phone from his pocket, a large fist connected with the side of his head, his vision exploding into a million stars. He dropped to one knee as Deano delivered a hard kick to his ribs.

"Felipe!" MJ cried in anguish.

"You ain't calling anyone, lover boy," Deano taunted, a large smile spreading across his face. He delivered one more well-placed kick, catching Felipe under the jaw, snapping his head back. He lay motionless as the two men turned their attention to MJ.

"So, Mandy. Long-time no see?"

"I saw you earlier, in the bus shelter," she replied, her voice faltering.

"Yes, you did. You probably don't remember me. I'm a good friend of Jerome. He asked me to pay you visit. You have something of his."

A trickle of urine escaped MJ and her legs began to feel rubbery underneath her. She clamped them together, a warm feeling spreading down her thighs. "I don't know what you're talking about," she countered, half-defiantly.

"Really?" Rafal replied. He took a step forward, firing out a swinging punch that caught MJ in the ribs. She went down hard, drawing her knees up to her chest, trying to reclaim the breath that had been driven from her lungs. She rolled over onto all fours, a hacking sound coming from her throat. A jet of vomit hit the tarmac, Deano wrinkling his nose up at the sight below him.

Rafal reached down, hefting MJ to a vertical position before slamming her into the wall behind her. "I will ask again. Where is Jerome's money?"

"I don't know what you're talking about," MJ replied, her voice scratchy, her breath ragged.

"Okay. We do this the hard way," the Polish man huffed, his shoulders slumping in resignation. He slapped her across the face, the noise echoing along the alleyway. MJ's eyes rolled back in her head as she sagged against the wall.

"Fuck her up," Deano encouraged.

A groaning sound came from ground-level. Rafal looked down, noticing Felipe trying to get up clumsily. "Keep him quiet, Deano" he ordered. "Don't..." His voice cut off mid-sentence.

"Don't what?" the other man asked, looking up at his partner. "What the..."

Rafal looked down at his chest, not quite comprehending what he was looking at. A long black handle was protruded from the opening in his jacket, gently quivering "Bitch!" he blurted, then fell to his knees, rolling over onto the wet floor.

"Rafal!" Deano shouted, dropping to the ground next to the larger man. He turned him over, a cold knot forming in his stomach when he saw the lifeless eyes staring back at him. He looked up at the others and was about to say something when a boot connected with his jaw. His head also snapped backwards as Deano fell against a collection of black bin bags before lying still.

"Jesus!" Felipe exclaimed. "He's dead."

"Yes, he is," MJ replied gravely. "They would have killed us, Felipe."

"Really?"

"Yes. There is a lot you don't know. But I think you need to hear the truth, especially after what's just happened. I'm not going back to prison. This was self-defence."

"Prison? You've been to prison?"

"A long time ago. But let's not go into that now. We need to do something. If anyone else sees Rafal, the police will be all over us."

"Shit," Felipe cursed. "I don't want the police sniffing around here. I've worked so hard to build what I have, MJ."

"Then, we need a plan. We need to get rid of the body."

33

Deano stirred, his eyes opening slowly. He looked up at the raindrops and wet brickwork before attempting to move. Gradually, he sat up, his head spinning. "Fuck," he muttered, his vision blurring for a few seconds before refocusing. His next thought was Rafal. It flooded back to him. The lifeless eyes. The knife handle sticking out of his chest. "Rafal," he croaked, looking around the alleyway. There was no sign of him or the others. Deano checked his watch, trying to figure out how long he'd been unconscious. He could feel his pulse, his heart hammering in his chest as he began to panic.

Think. Climbing to his feet, Deano walked the length of the alleyway on shaky legs, leaning on the wet brickwork for support. *Where the fuck has he gone? And where are the other two?* Walking back to the spot where he had come to, Deano noticed a black steel door set into the wall. He walked over, testing the cold metal handle. It turned, but the door remained firmly locked, despite a few forceful tugs by the groggy man. *She killed him. That bitch fucking killed Rafal.* Despite his anger, Deano was suddenly wary. *I need to get the fuck out of here,* he thought. *I need to get home.*

Dusting himself down, he set off for the hotel, a cold drizzle falling from the sky. After five minutes, he was back in his room, tossing his few belongings into a black holdall. Walking back down the corridor, he tried to remain as quiet as possible, the night shift receptionist not even glancing his way as he made his way back out onto the street. A minute later, Deano got behind the wheel of his Golf, typing a quick message to Jerome, who lay sleeping several hundred miles to the south. *I hope I don't run into the Old Bill,* he thought as he pulled away from the kerb, indicating left at the junction before gently making his way out of town. Heading back home, to regroup.

"Has he gone?" MJ asked, her heartbeat beginning to slow. Across the storeroom, Rafal lay on his side, his skin starting to pale.

"Yes. He turned right out of the alley," Felipe replied, closing the steel door and locking it. "If I were a betting man, I'd say we'll not see him again. At least not for a while."

"Why?"

"Because you said they were going to kill you. Or at least hurt you. They do not want any police involvement. So, I'm pretty sure the other guy will be lying low somewhere. Or maybe even heading home."

MJ considered his words, before walking over to him. "How are you? They really stuck the boot in."

"I'll be okay," the man replied, rubbing his jaw. "My jaw is pretty sore, but I've had worse. Don't worry."

"But I got you into this," she replied, hugging the man in front of her. He returned the embrace, the world around him melting away for a few moments. Despite the dire situation, Felipe smiled. He had daydreamed of this moment over and over whilst serving customers.

After a moment, they broke the embrace, a sudden awkwardness descending over them. "So, we need to figure this out somehow."

"Tell me about it." She sat down on a large sack of potatoes, preparing herself. "My two sons murdered a woman in Birmingham, many years ago." MJ looked over at the man and saw his expression changing from neutral to wide-eyed surprise. She had his attention. "They were high on drugs and alcohol and snatched a young girl who was out shopping with her mother. To this day, I don't know why they did it, or what they were going to do to her. Anyway, the mother followed them. There was a fight and the mother was killed by my eldest, Sean. The thing is, they took some of my skunk, which probably fuelled whatever crazy scheme they were going to carry out. They were arrested shortly afterwards. That's the last time I saw them."

She paused, tears filling her eyes. "Luke, my youngest, died in custody before he stood trial. Some freak accident with some of the youths at the detention centre. Sean is still in prison. I've had no contact with him since the morning he was arrested."

"Shit," Felipe replied sadly. "I'm so sorry, MJ."

"Don't be sorry. I was a right piece of work back then. I was a part-time prostitute and involved with a local drug dealer. He was paranoid that the police would one day catch up with him, so he gave me a hundred grand to keep safe for him. Which I did. I still have it – well, most of it. That's why these guys came looking for me. Jerome is probably out of prison and sent his muscle up here to take back what he thinks is his."

"We need to get rid of that," Felipe said, pointing towards the cooling body on the even cooler floor. "My cousin has a boat. He was with me in the pub tonight, before you called. He could dump it in the sea."

"Really?" MJ exclaimed. "I don't want you to risk getting in trouble."

"If the police find out, you'll go back to prison. I will also probably go to prison. Our lives could be ruined. He knew what he was getting himself into when he came here. And I'm pretty sure the other guy will not report this. We have to do this, MJ."

"Okay. When?"

"Now," he replied, striding across the storeroom. He turned the body over, rifling through the dead man's pockets. He placed a wallet, bulging with banknotes, along with a mobile phone on a metal shelf, then pulled his own phone out of his pocket. Felipe swiped the screen with his finger, dialling a number. He paced the room, his Spanish words lost on MJ, who just sat watching him. After a minute, he put his phone back into his pocket. "Okay. He's on his way."

"I hope you understand what you're about to do?"

"I do," Felipe replied, looking down at the first dead body he'd ever seen, not knowing what the future held, but hoping the woman across the room would be a part of it.

The small black van pulled away from the front of the chip shop, leaving Felipe and MJ standing close to the alleyway. He turned to her, placing a reassuring hand on her shoulder. "It will be okay. Raul will load the body onto his boat and set off early, before many of the other fishermen. He'll know what to do."

"I can't believe he was so calm!"

"He always is. Relax, he's very, how do you say? Resourceful. He said he'll text me when it's done."

"Where will he do it?"

"No idea. Probably right out at sea, where there is no danger that the body will return to the shore." He looked at his watch, realising that it was well after midnight. "Coffee?"

"Sure. Why not?" MJ replied, following the man back through the steel door.

Felipe led the way, walking down a small corridor that led to an alcove next to the kitchen. He busied himself, filling mugs with milk and sugar as the kettle boiled. He handed MJ her mug a minute later, seating himself on a plastic chair. MJ followed suit. She tested her coffee, nodding her thanks.

"Quite a night, eh?" he observed, half-smiling.

"Tell me about it," MJ replied. "I'm still trying to get my head around it. If Jerome sent two men up here to take his money and rough me up, he'll not rest until he gets revenge. He was friends with the man I killed. He'll want to settle the score on that point, along with taking the money. I'm a sitting duck."

"How do you think they found you?"

MJ considered the question for a moment as she took a sip of coffee. "I'm not sure. Maybe they…"

"What?" Felipe replied, watching as she pulled her phone out of her coat pocket.

"Facebook," she replied, logging into her account. There were no messages, notifications or friend requests, such was the inactivity on her account. "I'm gonna deactivate my account." She scrolled through a few menus, finding the option after a few seconds. "There. All done, I think. If they've used Facebook to find me, I need to think about moving on."

"Don't be too hasty," he replied. "You've created a life here. You have a job and friends."

"I have a job, but very few people I'd call friends."

"What about me?"

She looked at the man, liking his kind face and flawless complexion. "Yes, we're friends. Maybe one day, we could be more than that, if I've not scared you away?"

"It will take more than this to scare me away, MJ. You're a very nice woman and one day I would like to get to know you much better. But that may have to wait until the dust settles, if you know what I mean?"

"Perfectly. Anyway, how come you're not married? Good-looking bloke like you should have been snapped up years ago."

"I was married, a long time ago," he replied quietly. "She died, during childbirth. Our baby died, too."

"Oh God! I'm so sorry," she replied, placing a cool hand over his.

"It's okay. Many years have passed. I still think about them, but time heals, as they always say. That's why I left Valencia and came here. To start a new life. Raul came with me because he'd heard that there were opportunities for fishing. And here we are, a little older and a little greyer."

"Well, you're a good bloke, Felipe. You've been through plenty of shit but have come out the other side with a smile on your face."

"And so have you."

"Hardly. I've been in prison. My youngest son is dead and my eldest may spend the rest of his life behind bars. I live with my nan in a tiny house at the edge of the world, where it seems to rain almost every day."

"But you're here. You made it, MJ. You didn't fold your cards. You're a survivor."

"Thank you. You're very sweet. Whatever happens over the coming weeks and months, I want to be your friend, if you'll have me?"

He leaned across the gap, planting a soft kiss on her cheek. "Definitely. And I will help you with whatever you need."

"Thank you. You've no idea what that means to me." She placed her coffee on the counter, a faint glimmer of hope appearing on her horizon, shining brightly through the dark thunderheads.

34

"Deano?" Jerome quizzed. "What's wrong? You're back early?" He looked past his half-brother. "Where's Rafal?"

"Can I come in?"

"Sure. Mum's in town, doing a bit of shopping." He stepped to one side, letting the man walk into the hallway. "Go through to the kitchen." Jerome followed the younger man, flicking the overhead lights on. Outside, the afternoon was grey, low clouds clinging to the land as a fine drizzle fell from the sky. "Coffee?"

"Please," Deano replied, seating himself at the table.

A minute later, Jerome placed two mugs of coffee on the kitchen table, seating himself opposite the other man. "So, spill the beans."

"Rafal is dead."

Jerome almost spat his coffee across the table, wiping his lips with the back of his hand. "What the fuck you talking about?"

"We found her, mate. It's the same woman. Cut a long story short, we were at a pub by the front. We asked the local chippy owner if he'd seen Mandy. He said no but left in a hurry a few minutes later. We tailed him, eventually finding him behind the chip shop with Mandy."

"And?" Jerome asked, a cold knot forming in his gut.

"She said she's not got your money. Rafal roughed her up a bit and I twatted the guy she was with to keep him quiet. Then suddenly, she stuck a knife in his chest. We didn't expect her to do that, mate. Rafal pretty much died on the spot. Then, the chippy owner came from nowhere and knocked me the fuck out. When I woke up, they'd vanished."

"Jesus Christ!"

"I tried to get into the chip shop to see if they were hiding out, but it was locked. By that time, Rafal's body was gone, too. So, I got the fuck out of there and drove back to Brum. I'm sorry, bruv. I fucked up."

"It's not your fault, mate. I never would have thought she'd stick a fucking blade in him! This changes things. Rafal was married, with kids. People are going to be asking questions. Lots of them."

"Does anyone know where we were?"

"No one. Not even his wife, which, looking back now, is a good thing. Fuck!"

"What do you wanna do?"

"Slit the bitch's throat. Slowly. But we'll have to leave her be, for now at least. I can't go up there immediately and I'm not sending anyone else to do it. It could get even messier than it is now."

"So, what do we do?"

"I need to think. I'm on license for a long time, but I can travel within the UK. I can't leave it too long. This will have spooked her. She may fuck off with my money. I need to get up there soon and sort the bitch out. For stealing my dough and for killing Rafal."

"Fair enough. Next time I'll come with you. She may have more reinforcements and I know where the chip shop is and what the owner looks like."

"Okay, good." He raised his mug. "Here's to getting even."

"Amen, bruv."

A few miles to the south, John and Lottie walked along a tree-lined dual carriageway, towards the Lickey Hills. They hunkered down as the rain began to fall heavier, a cold wind buffeting their clothing. "It's freezing, Dad."

"I know, sweetheart. Just a few more minutes." A double-decker bus drove past them, heading down the hill towards Birmingham, a trail of cars following it slowly.

"I'm starving, too."

"You're always starving. Don't worry. They should all be there by now. We'll order as soon as we sit down. Okay?"

"Okay, Dad," she replied happily, linking her father's arm with her own.

John smiled, enjoying the contact and closeness that had blossomed over the past months. His little girl was returning. The carefree princess he remembered from years past.

They crossed the junction of two roads, striding the last few hundred yards as the rain began turning to sleet. Shaking themselves down inside the pub, John spotted a group of people standing by the bar. He smiled as Zoe walked over to him, wrapping her arms around his neck and planting a kiss on his lips.

"Hello, sexy," she breathed, slightly flushed.

"Hey, gorgeous. You look amazing," John replied, holding her at arm's-length.

"Flattery will get you everywhere, Mr Wilson," she gushed, as the others joined them. John hugged his parents, then Judy, who then planted her own kiss on her son-in-law's lips. Zoe bristled slightly, a pang of jealousy washing over her. She liked Judy and knew that John and Lottie thought the world of her. It was irrational, but Zoe couldn't help it. She had fallen for John and he was now *her* man.

"Hey, John, hey, Lottie," Bob said as he walked from the bar. Both men shook hands warmly, Bob putting his arm around the young girl, who reciprocated enthusiastically.

"So, we're all here," John declared happily. "Shall we grab a table? Lottie hasn't eaten for over an hour."

She stuck her tongue out at her father, as Sharon walked over and hugged her. "Hey."

"Hiya," Sharon replied. "I was in the loo," she said, blushing.

"Come on then," Judy began. "There's a large table at the back of the lounge. Let's go and grab it before the place fills up."

"Who wants a drink?" John asked. They all gave him their orders as John's father and Bob followed him to the bar.

"Congratulations," John said to Bob. "She's a great woman. One in a million."

"I know," the older man replied happily. "I never thought I'd ever meet anyone else after Elaine died. I've really come up trumps."

Their drinks were placed on the bar and the three men carried them carefully past groups of young pub-goers, who were getting ready for a Saturday night of revelry. The men walked past a large Christmas tree, its twinkling lights adding to the cosy atmosphere inside the pub. They seated themselves just as Judy was showing off her engagement ring to Lottie.

"Wow, Nan. It's beautiful," Lottie exclaimed.

"Isn't it just?" the older woman replied, a beaming smile etched on her face. "I had no idea he was going to propose."

"You sly old goat," John laughed, drawing a smile from the middle-aged man across the table. "So, when's the wedding?"

"Probably June or July," Judy replied. "We're looking at Cyprus. Not a big wedding. Nice and intimate."

"Sounds lovely," Margaret countered. "We went to Cyprus years ago. A lovely place, wasn't it, Derek?"

"Stunning. Bloody hot though. I burnt my legs and had to wrap them in a wet towel for a few days."

John smiled at his father's memory. "Well, I'm sure you won't get sunburnt. You'll either be in bed or in the bar."

"John!" Margaret admonished. "Really!"

"He's just having a laugh, love," Derek soothed, placing a hand over his wife's.

"He has a point, though," Judy replied, squeezing Bob's knee under the table. "And you're all invited. I know it's a long way to go for a wedding and we understand if you can't make it. But we'd love you all to be there. Bobs only got a sister, who lives in Devon. She probably won't come as she had a stroke a few months ago. So, it will be a quiet affair."

Lottie picked a menu from the centre of the table. "Right. Shall we order?" They all looked at her, smiling, as she brushed a lock of hair away from her face.

An hour later, the pub had filled up considerably, with revellers constantly passing by the large table in the corner. Dinner plates had been taken away and drinks replenished as the group sat chatting. Judy looked across at John, who had Zoe snuggled next to him, her hand on his. *Such a nice girl. He does look happy. Lucy would like that,* she thought, a pang of sadness drifting across her sunny disposition. She pushed it aside, concentrating on the here and now. "So, what plans do you have for Christmas?"

John looked at Zoe and smiled. "We're not sure yet," he replied diplomatically. "We were going to discuss it tonight. What is everyone else doing?"

Judy took the initiative. "We were thinking of having Christmas dinner here."

"Okay," John replied, slightly relieved. "And you guys?" he asked, looking over at his parents.

"Not sure, John," Derek responded. "But listen, we know that you'll probably want to spend it with Zoe and Sharon. So, if that's what you want to do, do it. Don't worry about us oldies, we'll be just fine."

John looked over at Judy, who nodded. "Okay. Well, we can chat about it later," he suggested to Zoe, who pinched his thigh under the table.

A woman walked past on her way to the toilets. She stopped, looking over at the table, watching the happy, chattering group who were completely oblivious to her presence. She took out her smartphone and snapped a picture covertly before tucking her phone away and carrying on to the ladies. A few minutes later, the woman was standing outside, next to a newly-erected smoking shelter. She leaned against the stout structure, examining the photograph. "I thought it was you," she whispered to herself, before dialling a number from her contacts list.

"Deano. It's me. I'm up The Hounds. Guess who's here?" She listened to his reply, shaking her head. "No, dummy. Soldier boy." A brief response had her shaking her head in frustration. "What do you mean you're not coming up? He's here, ready for a kicking."

Another reply from the other end of the line made Tracey blow out a sigh. "Okay. Fill me in later. I may just make my presence felt, if you know what I mean. Catch ya later." She ended the call and stubbed out her cigarette before walking back inside, where her drinking partners were getting into the Christmas spirit.

"Where've you been?" a dark-haired woman asked, as she poured a glass of Prosecco for the three other women.

"Just to the loo and for a fag. Is that okay, Mum?"

They all laughed, liking the forked tongue Tracey often displayed. "Well, we've been scouting the place out whilst you've been away," the dark-haired woman replied. "There is a table of lads over there, but they look a bit young. Probably just out of college."

"I don't wanna marry them," Tracey declared. "I just want some cock!"

The dark-haired woman, called Tina, prodded the blonde sat next to her. "How about him, Lorna?" All four sets of eyes drifted over to the bar, where a tall, dark-haired man leaned casually against the counter.

"I'd do him," Tina observed. "Nice body, too."

Tracey looked at John Wilson, seeing him for the first time as a man, not an adversary. "Not bad looking, for an old 'un."

The redhead next to Tracey piped up. "He's not old. Probably mid to late-thirties. I'd love a piece of him."

"You're married, Charlotte!" Tracey reminded her.

"Have you seen Chris lately? He's probably at home, jerking off to ladyboys. That's if he can find it underneath his gut!"

The women collectively burst out laughing, drawing a few glances from the patrons around them. Tracey regained her composure first, taking a sip of her crisp wine. "Anyway, he's taken. I saw him earlier. He's sat over in the corner with his missus."

"Shame," Tina replied. "I'd bang that all night like a Salvation Army drum!"

Tracey spat Prosecco across the table, causing the other women to howl with laughter. The man at the bar looked over at the commotion, his eyes lingering on the group of women for a few seconds. He locked eyes with Tracey. The recognition was immediate. Her smile vanished, replaced with a scornful look that the man absorbed. He kept his expression neutral, turning back to the bar to pay one of the bar staff for his drinks.

"Damn," Charlotte groaned. "The eye candy is walking away."

"Relax," Tina countered enthusiastically. "A group of guys have just walked in. Over there," she observed, nodding her head towards the bar.

"Great," Charlotte exclaimed. "I'm going to the loo to touch up my make-up."

"Hurry up," Tina urged. "I may have shagged them by the time you get back. And get some more fizz. We're running low."

"Everything okay?" Zoe asked as John sat back down. He handed her a gin and tonic, smiling.

"Fine, love," he lied. He'd instantly recognised the woman across the pub, knowing that she and her brother wanted to settle the score with him. He put the thought to the back of his mind, concentrating on the chatter around the table. His phone started buzzing in his pocket and John took it out.

"Who is it?" Zoe asked, mildly interested.

"Colin from work," he replied, wondering why his boss was calling him at the weekend. He answered the call. "Hello?"

"John. It's Colin."

"Hiya," John replied. "Everything okay?"

"Fine, but there is a change of plan for Monday that I thought I'd give you the heads-up on. Are you okay to talk for a minute?"

"Sure, but the signal is crap in here. Hang on. I'll step outside. Bear with me." He excused himself, walking across the pub towards a side entrance. Once outside, John walked a few paces past a smoking shelter, putting the phone back to his ear. "Okay. Shoot."

"Is there any chance that you could come in earlier? Sorry to put this on you, mate, but Trevor's rung in sick, bad back and I need someone to do the Glasgow drop. I'll make it worth your while."

"What time do I need to be there?" John asked, aware that the double doors had opened behind him.

"Five? Is that okay?"

"It's fine. I'll ask Judy if she can have Lottie tomorrow night. Shouldn't be an issue."

"Cheers, mate. You're a lifesaver. I'll see you Monday morning. Sorry to call you at the weekend."

"No problem. I'm just at the pub having a bite to eat."

"Well, you enjoy, mate. See you Monday."

"Cheers, Colin. 'Bye," he replied, ending the call. John turned around to walk back into the pub but found his progress blocked by a familiar face.

"I thought it was you," Tracey said evenly.

"Just enjoying a family celebration," John replied calmly, even though his heart had ramped-up a few notches.

"Well, I won't do anything to spoil it. But remember, me and Deano have a score to settle and he's itching to have a piece of you."

"I don't want trouble," John countered, as a few smokers looked over from the shelter. "And nor should you."

"What the fuck's that supposed to mean?" she spat.

"We've already tangled once. Let's not do it again. We have kids to think about."

"You're wrong," Tracey hissed. "You have a bitch daughter to consider. It won't be a fight. This will be a beating. Watch your back, soldier boy. We're coming for you." She turned and walked back inside the pub, leaving John rooted to the spot.

35

JANUARY - 2014

MJ tapped her fingers on the seat in front of her as the single-decker bus wound its way around the streets of Castletown. A few minutes later, it was trundling along an empty stretch of road that led to Thurso. On her right, the North Sea hammered itself against the green Scottish coastline. She stared out of the window, watching as seagulls and other birds battled against the oncoming storm. She smiled, liking the isolated stretch of land to her left and an endless ocean to her right as the bus carried on its journey towards home. She'd been to see a ground floor maisonette after she had applied to be re-housed. Her explanation was both simple and plausible. Her nan was struggling with the stairs, which, in truth, she was. It just so happened to fit in with her plan. She wanted to put some distance between herself and the town. The town where they had come for her.

Now, she felt happier, knowing that if it all worked out, they would be in a new home in a few short months. She knew he could come before that. But MJ doubted it, especially after weeks of inactivity. She could sleep better in her bed, knowing that soon, she would be a few miles away. *Maybe I can change jobs?* She smiled at the idea, as she didn't really like the supermarket. It was fine, it was an income, but MJ wanted to try something else. Something that maybe tested her brain a little more. In truth, the pay didn't matter. She still had over £80,000 of Jerome's money. Money that she'd earned. Blood money for her two sons. Their faces were now a distant memory, Luke's in particular. His image had become fuzzy around the edges whenever she thought about him. She still had her photos, but she seldom pulled the box down from the top of the wardrobe to take a trip down memory lane.

Once she was settled in her new place, MJ had a whole host of plans, that had been formulating for the past few weeks. Her thoughts strayed to Felipe and she smiled at the mental image inside her head. *He's a good bloke. Maybe I will let him take me out soon?* They had spoken a few times since the night of the fracas. He assured her that Raul had disposed of the large Polish man, his body hopefully picked to bits by the creatures that inhabit the ocean floor. A pang of nerves hit her as the bus passed by the first few buildings of Thurso. *Relax. He's long gone,* she thought as an old-age pensioner climbed up the step onto the bus, showing her pass to the driver. The elderly lady shuffled past MJ, smiling down at her before continuing towards the rear. They passed the chip shop as MJ climbed out of her seat as the bus approached the stop. She caught a glimpse of Felipe through the shop frontage as he served a group of teenagers.

MJ smiled again as the bus came to a jerky stop. "Thanks," she said to the driver before stepping down onto a wet pavement.

"See you again," he replied, before the doors slammed shut as the bus carried on its route along the north coast of Scotland.

She was about to head home when a strong impulse turned her heels in the opposite direction. She walked the few hundred yards back to the chip shop, noticing that it was now in darkness, the closed sign gently swaying against the glass door. "Shit," she cursed, her shoulders sagging slightly before a metallic sound to her right made MJ flinch. She hurried around the side of the building, smiling when the sight of Felipe taking the rubbish out presented itself to her.

"Hi," she called, the man turning around. He was wearing grey joggers, trainers and a tight woollen jumper that clung to his athletic frame. *God! You look hot,* she thought, blushing slightly.

After a moment's hesitation, Felipe returned the smile. "*Buenas tardes,*" he replied, his accent shifting back to his native Iberia. "You okay?"

"Yeah. Just been to Castletown to look at a flat."

"So, you've found a place?" he asked, his smile fading slightly.

"Think so. It's only down the road, though. I'll still come here for my dinner."

"Promise?"

"You can count on it. It's the best chip shop around here."

"How many others have you tried?" he asked, mocking her gently.

"Well, in truth, none. But I'm sure yours is the best."

"I'll let you off," Felipe teased, rubbing his hands against his apron. "Fancy a coffee?" he asked, more out of hope than anything. "I've just finished up for the afternoon."

"Sure. As long as it's no bother?"

"You're no bother. I'm glad you popped by. I've missed you." There. It was out. Now, Felipe stood there, like a schoolboy waiting to be remonstrated with.

"Well, I've missed you too," she replied, blushing even more. She watched him as he regained a degree of confidence.

"Come on in then. It's about to pour down."

She followed him into the back of the chip shop. The smell was intoxicating. "God! I didn't realise how hungry I was until I stepped inside."

"I can throw a few chips on a plate, MJ? I think I have a chicken and mushroom pie, too. You fancy it?"

"Go on then," she replied, removing her coat and hanging it on a hook in the corridor. "You've twisted my arm."

He led her through to the small kitchen, pulling out a chair next to a stainless-steel worktop. "I'll be back in a minute."

As he walked past, his arm brushed her shoulder, sending a crackle of static through the now-seated MJ. She shivered, not fully understanding the dynamic between them. She was gazing around the kitchen, not really focusing on anything in particular, when he returned, sliding a plate in front of her.

"Here you go," Felipe offered. "Still fresh."

"How much do I owe you?"

He bent down and kissed the top of her head. "On the house."

She smiled again, the muscles in her face not accustomed to the new movement. It almost felt alien to her as she watched him brew two mugs of coffee. A whiff of vinegar invaded her nostrils as MJ picked up her fork and began munching away happily. "Just what I needed," she declared a few minutes later, placing the cutlery on the plate before resting her elbows on the table. "You sure know how to treat a woman."

"Believe me. It gets much better than that."

"So, when are you going to take me out for dinner?" Suddenly, MJ's heart rate increased as she became unsure of the answer that was hanging in the air.

"I thought you'd never ask," he beamed, a wide smile transforming his face. "What are you doing Saturday night?"

"Going out for dinner."

"Oh! Okay," he replied, crestfallen.

She smiled. "With you, silly." MJ took in his features, loving how a single smile could alter his face.

He looked back at her, grinning. "Oh. I thought you meant someone else?"

"You're funny. So, where shall we go?"

"Don't mind. Where do you fancy?"

"We're not exactly blessed with good food around here, present company excluded. There is a nice-looking pub in Castletown. How about that?"

"Sounds good to me. Meet me here at seven?"

"Deal," she agreed happily. Another thought came to MJ, fading her smile somewhat. "Have you thought much about that night?"

His expression changed too as the atmosphere in the room suddenly became charged. "Yes. Every day."

"And how are you feeling about it all?"

Felipe rested his forearms on the table, blowing out a breath. "He came here to do you harm. They both did. They made a choice to come here, MJ. I'm sorry that the man is dead. But if you hadn't done what you did, maybe you would be dead. Maybe both of us? It was him or you."

"When you put it like that, I think you have a point. I've not slept well lately. I think it's the worry of either having the police turn up at my door, or Jerome finding me." The words hung in the air, both of them knowing the consequences that could arrive any day. Either officially, or shadowy.

"There is no chance that the body will wash up. Raul was very thorough. I have thought about the man. If he was married, or if he had children. But if he did, what was he doing up here, wanting to hurt people?"

"He didn't think too deeply about our families, did he?"

"No. He didn't. What's done is done. Hopefully, there will be no comeback."

"Not from the police. But Jerome will never let this lie. Sooner or later, he'll show his face."

Felipe folded his arms, his expression suddenly grave. "Then if he does, he'd better be prepared. Or he'll end up as fish food like his friend."

~

"You need to be careful," Gabrielle warned, her voice edged with concern.

"I am being careful," MJ replied.

"But they've already found you once. This Jerome is not going to let it lie."

"I know he won't." MJ sat on the settee, the lounge in almost total darkness save for a shaft of illumination from the streetlight outside. She was cold and had a woollen blanket draped over her shoulders to ward off the chill that threatened to seep into her bones.

"Then you need to get the hell out of there!"

"I can't, Gabe. I've made some sort of life for myself here. But I want to take some precautions."

"Like what?"

She shifted in her seat. "You know about the money I took from him?"

"Yes. A hundred grand. How much do you have left?"

"About eighty. I've been careful since I got out. Anyway, I don't want him getting his hands on it. So, I'm going to put it somewhere safe. Then I'm going to send you a letter, addressed to Sean."

"Sean?"

"Yes. I'm hoping that one day he will get out. I'll write to him in prison over the next few days, telling him to look you up. Once he finds you, give him the letter. That will tell him where the money is hidden. If something happens to me, at least Sean will have some kind of a chance in life. You just need to promise me to keep the letter safe, no matter what."

"Of course. I'll put it up in the loft, in my old school box. No one will ever find it."

"Thanks, Gabe. I knew I could rely on you."

"Just be careful. You're family and I love you."

Tears stung MJ's eyes. "I love you too, Gabe. You're my favourite person in the whole world."

36

FEBRUARY - 2014

"She won't be as easy tet motorway. Darkness shrouded the landscape, offering little to look at. To the east, the sky was beginning to brighten, smokestacks on the horizon barely visible to Jerome as they drove by.

"I know. That's why we're gonna spend a few extra days up there. Plus, we're gonna be careful. No getting into a ruckus with the locals. We will find her. And the bitch will pay!" Silence descended inside the car for a few minutes until Jerome broke it. "I need a piss and a coffee. Where are we?"

"Just north of Stoke. There are services a few miles away. We can stop there."

"Rafal's wife phoned me a few weeks ago."

"Really? What did you say?"

"What could I say? I had to lie. Said I'd not seen him for a while. Apparently, he does this every now and again. Goes AWOL for a couple of weeks, before turning up as if nothing has happened. I know he wasn't playing away. For all Rafal's faults, cheating on his missus wasn't one of them."

"So, what happens now?"

"No idea, mate. I guess she'll keep asking about, probably phoning home to see if he's turned up there. It happens. My uncle Cyril vanished one day when I was a lad. His wife and kids had no idea what happened to him. It was only years later that they found out what happened."

"What did happen?" Deano asked.

"He'd shacked up with another woman in Coventry. Even had another couple of kids. Crazy, eh!"

"Sure is." They drove on, the grey expanse of road ahead a long-drawn-out ribbon that led ever northwards.

They made two more stops, in Carlisle and Glasgow, before ploughing on ahead towards the northern Scottish coast. As the sun began to set, the surrounding countryside became rugged and mountainous, purple-covered slopes rising up over the plucky Golf as it sped towards their destination. At a little after 6pm, they pulled into the same stretch of road where Deano had parked weeks before. They sat there, the car's interior filled with cigarette smoke. "That's the chip shop over there," Deano stated.

Jerome nodded. The bright lights of the shop's frontage were the only illumination on the dark street. "I'm fucking starving. But let's find somewhere else to eat. It might ring alarm bells with Mandy's fella if we walk in there."

"Fair enough. Let's go food-hunting," Deano replied, his voice edged with excitement. They trolled the streets of the small town, not finding anything of interest, save for a few pubs and an Indian restaurant. The car headed out of town, heading east towards another small settlement, nestled next to the rough sea.

"There we go, bruv," Jerome declared. "Chippy dead-ahead."

"Great," Deano replied, his stomach rumbling. They pulled in a few yards away as rain began to fall over the grey town. "What do you fancy?"

"Just get me fish and chips."

"Okay. Back in a minute."

Jerome surveyed the street ahead, finding nothing of interest. The odd car passed by before disappearing around a bend in the road. From his sitting position, he could almost see the coast, the sound of seagulls carrying to his ears. "What a fucking dump," he whispered to himself, lighting another cigarette. He buzzed down the window a few inches, blowing smoke out into the dark skies above.

The door opened and Jerome flinched as Deano piled into the car. "Here you go."

Jerome accepted the warm paper bundle. "Cheers," he replied, his taste buds beginning to moisten. "What have you got?"

"The usual. Kebab and chips." Deano handed Jerome a plastic fork which Jerome accepted with a nod.

They sat in relative silence as they ate, the windscreen of the car becoming misted over from the inside. After discarding their empty containers and papers, the men sat waiting for the screen to de-mist. "So, let's go and get checked in. We can grab some cans from an off-license and stay in the room tonight."

"Good plan, bruv. I'm knackered."

"Then tomorrow, we can have a scout about the place. If Mandy's up here, she's got to show her face at some point. It's not a big place."

"Might be an idea to keep an eye on that chip shop, too. After all, she knows the owner."

"Okay. We'll do that while we're out and about. Now, come on. Let's go and grab a few cans and get settled in." The car pulled away from the kerb, performing a U-turn on the wide street before heading out of Castletown.

MJ lay slouched on the sofa, the television on in front of her. She was not watching it as she sat there alone. Her fingers were tapping away on the screen of her phone, a serene smile spreading across her face. Backing out of the message to Felipe, she clicked onto the Facebook icon, reactivating her account. She'd been sent a text earlier in the day from Gabrielle, who gave her some happy news. She was expecting, and had posted a picture of the baby scan on her profile. MJ sat there smiling, looking at the grainy image, her thumb hovering over the tiny face, then the phone suddenly buzzed in her hand, causing MJ to flinch as the screen lit up.

She swiped the green icon, smiling. "You scared the shit out of me!"

"Sorry," Felipe replied. "I'm having a quick break and I thought I'd call you."

"Well, it's nice to hear from you. I miss not walking past your shop every day and seeing that gorgeous smile." She could almost see his expression change, imagining a huge smile on his tanned face.

"I was just wondering, what are you doing Saturday night?"

"No plans. Why? Do you fancy doing something?"

"I fancy doing you, again."

MJ sighed, clenching her thighs together. "I fancy that, too. I'm still smiling from the last time."

"Really?" he replied, fishing for a compliment.

"God, yeah! It was wonderful. The whole night was too, but you know what I mean?"

There was a brief pause, Felipe unsure of what to say next. "Well, how about we go to the movies and have some food afterwards? I'm sure there'll be something decent to watch at the cinema?"

"Okay. Sounds like a plan. What time?"

"Six-ish?"

"Perfect. I'll sort Nan out with her tea, then make my way over."

"Looking forward to it already," he replied, his voice tinged with a huskiness that she picked up on, rubbing her thighs together once more.

"See you then, hun. 'Bye for now."

"'Bye MJ."

She ended the call, placing the smartphone on the settee next to her, forgetting to deactivate her Facebook account. A random thought came to her. *It's Sean's birthday.* An image of her son came to her. *Fuck! How could I have forgotten that? Twenty-three. What a waste of a life.* She sat there in the darkness, wondering how her eldest son was. Where he was and when or if she would ever see him again. She still loved her son, but she had never been able to visit him once she'd been released. Partly due to her own relocation, but mainly because he was a murderer. He'd taken a life. An innocent life that was now just ashes and dust.

But I'm a murderer too. I killed that man, even if it was self-defence. The courts would find me guilty. Like mother, like son. She stretched out on the settee, suddenly feeling weary. As sleep took hold, the last image that floated before her was of a young, carefree boy with a cheeky smile and bright ginger hair.

37

Friday came and went without any real significant moments. MJ spent a shift at the supermarket before heading back to Castletown on the trundling bus. She sat with her nan, watching forgettable television before heading off to bed. On Saturday morning, she was cooking bacon and egg sandwiches, humming away to Neil Diamond on the radio while her nan sat at the kitchen table, attempting her latest word search.

"What are your plans for the weekend?" the older woman asked.

"Going to the movies tonight with Felipe. I'm not working today, so I thought I'd stretch my legs and walk along the coast. The weather looks okay out there."

"Lovely. What I would give to be able to walk along the beach. Or go to the movies, for that matter." She paused, drawing on a distant memory. "The last movie I went to see was *Carmen*. Back in '84, I think. Your grandfather was not one for movie theatres. He preferred the working men's club on a Friday and Saturday night. Not that I'm complaining. We had some wonderful nights there."

"I'm sure you did, Nan. I do miss Grandad. He was a lovely bloke."

"That he was, MJ. A real gentleman. Not many of them around today. Although, this Felipe sounds nice."

"Yes, he is. He's got an old head on his shoulders. And he knows how to treat a woman. I've never had that before and I'm kinda getting used to it."

"Well, you enjoy yourself, love. You're a long time dead."

The words hung in the air, MJ standing there in silence as she moved the bacon and fried egg around in the pan before placing them on a slice of crusty white bread. Placing another piece on top, she cut the sandwich into four equal pieces then put the plate on the table in front of her nan. "Here you go. I'll brew some tea."

"Thank you, dear. You're a good un'."

Am I? Yes. I think I probably am now, she thought, before placing two more rashers in the hot pan. "I won't be home late tonight."

"You're a grown woman. You come home when you want to. Maybe you'll stay out all night, if you know what I mean?"

MJ looked at her nan, seeing a twinkle in her rheumy blue eyes. "Okay," she replied, awkwardly. "We'll see how the night pans out."

Twenty minutes later, MJ boarded the bus towards Thurso, seating herself just behind the driver. She was the only passenger, rocking left and right on the bench seat as the bus navigated its way through the potholes that littered the quiet stretch of road. Her eyes scanned the Scottish scrubland, not really focused on anything as the bus carried on its short journey to Thurso. She alighted a few minutes later, walking along the main street towards the sea. She looked left and right before crossing another road, spotting the tired-looking hotel on the corner. MJ carried on walking, seeing the sign for the Spar store a few hundred yards ahead.

Above the town, small clouds scooted across the sky from east to west, the weak sun offering little warmth as it bathed the northern tip of Scotland in watery sunlight. She reached the Spar as the shop's door opened before she had the chance to push it. A large man, his face obscured by his hood, had opened it for her, letting her pass by. "Thanks," she said as the man stood to one side before walking out of the shop.

She walked down the first aisle, looking for a few snacks to keep her going during her trek along the coastline, not noticing the set of eyes that followed her progress towards the far end of the store. MJ walked along the next aisle, not finding anything of interest as she came out next to the tills. Heading down the third aisle, she picked up two flapjack bars before returning back towards the tills to pay for her goods, completely unaware of who was circling in to greet her.

"It's her, bruv," Deano stated as he crossed over the road.

"Are you sure?" Jerome replied from his hotel room.

"Hundred percent. She's still inside the shop."

"Okay. I just need to get dressed. Follow her, mate and keep your phone handy."

"Will do. Hang on, she's just left the shop and is heading for the front."

"Hang back a few hundred yards. I'll be out in ten minutes. Call me back in nine."

"Okay, bruv," Deano replied, ending the call. He waited a minute until the woman was a few hundred yards ahead before he crossed the road in pursuit. He gripped his phone inside the pocket of his grey hooded top, checking the time every minute. Eight minutes later, he dialled Jerome's number.

"And?" he asked impatiently.

"She's walking along a coast path, away from the town."

"Which way is she heading?"

"Towards the place where we bought chips. I'd say it's about two miles or so."

"Okay. I'll take the car and drive over there. Then, I'll approach from the opposite side."

"Like a pincer movement? Like in the movies?"

"Something like that, mate. Whatever it's called, she'll have nowhere to go. Is there anyone else out walking?"

"No, bruv. It's very quiet out here," Deano observed as he passed through a metal gate. The ground underneath was uneven, puddles and large stones adorning the narrow coastal path. "I'll ring off and keep her in sight."

"Okay," Jerome replied breathlessly. "I've just got to your car. See you in a few minutes."

Deano ended the call, sliding the phone into his joggers as one of his trainers splashed through a large puddle. "Bollocks," he swore, as the frigid water seeped into his sock. He looked ahead and noticed the woman glancing back his way before quickening her pace slightly. To his right, the buildings thinned out, giving way to scrubland, dotted with purple heather. On the left, the path dipped down towards the sea a few hundred yards ahead, before climbing towards a small headland between the two towns. Deano stopped to light a cigarette, trying to act casual, even though his heart was hammering in his chest, partly due to lack of exercise, and partly due to anticipating what may happen in the next few minutes. He set off again, his left foot squelching with every heavy footfall.

MJ upped her pace, aware of the man from the front of the shop who was a few hundred yards behind her. Something didn't feel right, even though her rational side was telling herself that everything was fine. *I need to get inside,* she thought as she looked along the coastal path towards Castletown. The ground rose up, MJ's thighs protesting as she headed towards the sea at a brisk pace. She could make out the church in the distance, gauging the distance to be a little over a mile. Seagulls flew over the sea, their wing-tips almost touching the surf as it crashed onto the rocks. She looked behind her, noticing that the man had closed the gap slightly. *Shit!* Ahead, the path was lost to sight as it neared its summit before winding its way towards the small settlement along the coast. *Shall I run?* she thought as she passed a wooden bench next to the path. On impulse, she sat down, opening her bottle in an attempt to appear unruffled. She sat there, one eye on the sea, the other on the approaching man. He closed to within fifty feet, pulling his phone out of his pocket, slowing down to a stop. *Fuck! This feels wrong.*

"Hello, Mandy," a voice called to her right. She flinched, rising to her feet as a familiar figure approached her.

"Jerome," she blurted.

"The very same. I knew I'd find you, one day."

MJ looked behind her, a knot forming in her stomach when she saw the other man approach, removing his hood. "Shit," she exclaimed. "You're that guy."

"Yeah. The one you left for dead in an alleyway," Deano replied, moving ever closer.

She half-turned towards Jerome, feeling small and vulnerable as he closed to within a few feet of her. "What do you want?"

"Stupid cow!" he hissed. "My money."

"It's gone," MJ replied, trying to think on her feet. "Spent it."

"On what? Not much to buy up here."

"A house," she lied, trying to form a story in her head.

"Bullshit," he replied, pulling a knife from his coat.

She backed away, her hands held up in front of her. "Please, Jerome. We can figure something out."

"It's too late for that, Mandy. I want my fucking money. If you hand it over, I may let you live."

"I haven't got it. It's all tied up in the house. I'd need to sell it."

"Do you think I was born yesterday?" he spat, taking a step forward. MJ took a step backwards, bumping into Deano, who smiled down at her menacingly.

"Okay," she relented, her shoulders slumping in resignation. MJ scanned the ground to her left, seeing that it was fairly even as it approached the cliff edge. Taking the men by surprise, she darted away from them, covering the ground quickly. A few yards from the drop, she cut right, sprinting towards Castletown, not looking back. A small fence lay a few hundred yards ahead, blocking her escape. She sized it up, time slowing down as she closed the gap. Suddenly, she was sprawling into the scrub, her ankle twisting as it went down a rabbit hole.

"Not a wise move," Jerome chided, as he turned her over a few seconds later.

She looked up at the men who were both breathing heavily, and tried in vain to scramble backwards towards the fence. Her vision exploded as Jerome's fist connected with her face, splitting her lip. MJ's head hit the ground, a salty tang filling her mouth as blood trickled between her lips. "Please," she pleaded, noticing that the cliff edge was only a few feet away

"Game's up." In a blur of speed, Jerome slashed her across the cheek, the skin parting with ease.

She cried out in anguish as the blade sliced through her flesh. Warm blood seeped down her face and inside her clothes as Jerome pulled her easily to her feet. "Okay, you win. I'll give you the money," she pleaded, her voice distorted due to the large gash in her face. She could feel cool air wafting in through her wound and knew that the game was indeed up. *He'll kill me whatever I do,* she thought. *But if I take him home, he'll kill Nan, too.*

"Good girl," he replied softly as he put the knife back in his pocket. "Let's go and get it."

She raked her nails across his face, making Jerome curse in pain, then ran towards the cliff edge, turning around to face the advancing men. "Fuck you, Jerome," she spat. "You're the reason that Luke is dead. You're the reason that Sean is in prison. You've ruined our lives." She took a step backwards, keeping her eyes trained on the dark-skinned man.

"Fucking bitch!" he cursed, blood dripping from his face. "Give me my money." The other man kept pace with Jerome and was barely more than six feet away from her as she took another step towards the edge of the cliff. *I love you, Luke. I Love you, Sean.*

"*Noooo!*" Jerome shouted.

MJ heard his cries as the rush of wind around her assailed her senses. An image flashed in her mind. Two happy little boys, with chocolate-smeared faces. Then, nothing.

Deano and Jerome peered over the cliff-edge, looking down at the body fifty feet below them. "She's gone," Jerome stated. "And so's my money."

"We'd better get the fuck out of here, bruv. Money or not, the Old Bill will be swarming all over this."

"Shit!" he cursed, as he looked down at the body on the rocks below him. "And here's me trying to go straight. I'll never make that money back now."

"You will, just not in the way you thought, bruv."

Jerome pointed a finger at the body below him. "Fuck you, Mandy. And fuck your family, too. This ain't over."

They headed away from the cliff-edge, striding towards Castletown as rain began to fall. Jerome looked out to sea, watching as storm clouds headed towards them, his own storm of emotions building within him as his life's journey altered once more.

38

John turned off the television, thinking that the news seemed more and more depressing every day. He'd been watching the TV whilst eating toast and drinking his first coffee of the morning. *There seems to be murders every day,* he'd thought, watching a reporter on a remote Scottish beach relaying what had happened to a woman a few hours before. *What a way to go. Slashed across the face then thrown off a cliff. The world's going to shit!*

He walked into the kitchen, placing his mug and plate in the sink. "Lottie?" he called up the stairs.

"Yes, Dad?" she replied from the confines of her room.

"What do you want for breakfast?"

"I'll sort something out in a bit," was the clipped response.

"What are you doing?"

"I'm on the phone to Sharon, Dad. I'll be down in a bit!"

Taking the hint, John walked back into the kitchen, flicking the kettle back on as his phone buzzed on the countertop. "Hello?" he said answering the call.

"Hey, handsome," Zoe replied. "I was going to call you on the land-line, but Sharon and Lottie are hogging the phone."

He smiled, leaning against the fridge. "Tell me about it. I'll have to get a lock for the phone, like we had when I was a kid."

Zoe laughed. "Oh God!" she laughed. "We had one, too. Then my folks brought a new phone with buttons instead of the dial, then realised that they couldn't lock it."

It was John's turn to laugh. "I miss the Eighties. Such a different world from today."

"Tell me about it. It's all social media. I can barely get a response out of Sharon sometimes. She's always on her iPad."

"Kids, eh? Anyway, to what do I owe the pleasure of your voice?"

"Smooth talker," she replied. "I was wondering if you fancied doing something today? I've missed seeing you this week, babe."

"I've missed you too," John replied, meaning it. His week had been busier than usual, working long hours until he'd literally collapsed into bed on Friday night. "What are you thinking?"

"How about a walk up the Lickey Hills followed by lunch at the Barnt Green?"

"Sold," John agreed. He'd not visited the Barnt Green Inn for many years, but could remember spending many a happy night there in his younger days. "What time shall I pick you up?"

"This is my treat. I'll pick you guys up."

"You're wonderful," John declared, a beaming smile etched on his face. He could hear the woman on the other end of the line exhale slowly.

"You're pretty amazing yourself. Oh, and before I forget, some of my work friends are meeting up at Hollywood Bowl next weekend. I wondered if you fancied it? Would be nice to show you off."

A mile away from John's house, the newly-created suburb of Great Park sat. Once the site of a mental institution and wasteland, it had fast become a hive of activity, with a cinema, bars and restaurants littering its roads. He'd only visited on a handful of occasions and couldn't quite remember when he'd been there last. "Sure. What day?"

"Saturday night. We can talk about it over lunch. Do you think Judy would look after Lottie?"

"I'm sure she would."

"Hope so. You can stay over. I really need you inside me!"

John released his own sigh, a familiar sensation taking hold of him. *Down, boy!* he thought, as he headed into the lounge to sit down and hide his arousal. "I've had to sit down. I've come over all hot and bothered."

A throaty chuckle came down the line. "Good. I bet you look sexy as fuck."

John liked how Zoe spoke to him when they were intimate. Lucy had never liked to talk dirty, their lovemaking being mostly tender and loving. It was Lucy all over. And he loved it, never feeling the need for more. Zoe was different. She was vocal, to the point of alerting the neighbours. She enjoyed dressing up for John, which he'd grown to love after the initial tentativeness. He would never dream of comparing the two women. They were just different, in their own unique way. But time had moved on and Zoe was showing him that he could love again after such a great loss. Despite being a cliché, time really did heal.

"Hardly. I've not showered and I'm wearing joggers and a scruffy T-shirt that I normally wear to cut the grass."

"Wow. I wish I was there right now. Those joggers would hit the floor in no time."

He pushed his head into the settee cushions behind him, growing more aroused. He was about to reply when the lounge door swung open and he had to sit up straight to hide the obvious.

"Dad," Lottie began. "We're going for lunch with Sharon and Zoe."

"You hear that, babe?" John said. "Apparently, we're going for lunch today?"

Zoe chuckled. "Is she in the room with you?"

"Yes," he replied, his voice slightly louder than normal. "She's right here." He could feel himself blushing slightly as his daughter regarded him quizzically.

"So, you can't say anything naughty to me?" she teased.

"Twelve-thirty. Sounds great," he replied, beads of sweat forming in his hairline.

"I want you in my mouth," Zoe replied huskily.

John groaned inside, placing a cushion on his lap. "Sounds wonderful. Really looking forward to it."

Lottie stood there, unmoved. John wanted her out of the room, upstairs where she could not hear what his girlfriend was telling him. She didn't take the hint, though and plonked herself down next to him on the settee.

"Okay. I'll lay off, for now," she replied, her voice still husky. "It'll keep until next weekend. And you'll not know what hit you, Captain Wilson."

"Okay, babe. We'll go and get ready and see you in a bit. Can't wait," he replied, slightly over-enthusiastically.

"See you soon, sexy."

"'Bye, babe," John replied, ending the call, relief washing over him.

"Are you okay, Dad? You look a bit flushed. Are you coming down with something?"

"I'm fine, sweetheart. It's just a bit warm in here."

"It's not. The heating isn't even on," she replied as she climbed off the settee. "I'll go and get ready."

She left the lounge, leaving John alone, his heartbeat gradually returning to normal. "Roll on next Saturday," he whispered to himself as he levered himself to a standing position, wondering just what was in store for him.

A Week Later

"All sorted?" Jerome asked impatiently, as Deano pulled two cans of lager out of the fridge.

"Relax, bruv. I took the car to the breakers' yard like you said. I even watched as they removed the plates and crushed the fucking thing."

Jerome breathed out, accepting the cold can of lager. He cracked the seal, taking a swig as Deano sat down at the kitchen table. "And the new car?"

"Sweet, bruv. Always wanted a Merc."

Jerome had walked past his half-brother's new car as he'd walked along the cul-de-sac to his flat. He knew it was like his old car, in as much as it was not registered to Deano. No paper-trail. This made Jerome feel easier as no one knew that they'd travelled to Scotland. Even the hotel was paid for in cash, the owners not requesting any identification or asking them to write down their particulars.

"You'll have to take me out for a spin."

"Okay. We'll have a few cans first, though. I need to drop off some gear in about an hour."

"Where?" Jerome asked as he picked up his beer.

"Hollywood Bowl," the younger half-sibling replied.

"Okay. And how are you after last week?"

Deano looked at him, shrugging his shoulders. "Fine. She had it coming. Plus, she killed Rafal. We never pushed her. She did it all by herself."

"True. Although, the Old Bill would still nail us for it. After all, I slashed her face. For that alone, I'm looking at a long stretch, if they ever find out that we were there."

"But they won't. It's a pisser about the money. But at least you've taken some kind of revenge."

"I know, bruv. The thing about revenge is, you don't really feel better afterwards. What's done is done. I always wondered how I would settle the score with Mandy. I never imagined it would play out like that, though."

"Oh well, let's put it behind us. If the Old Bill come sniffing around, we'll just play dumb."

"We need to be smarter than that, bruv. The car cannot be traced. But there will be CCTV footage of us walking about the place. At some point, the pigs are going be sifting through it. We may need to lie low. Or relocate."

"Relocate? Where?" Deano asked, a frown appearing across his face.

"Spain? Hadn't really thought too much about it. I have friends down there, though. I could do with some sun."

"Do you really think they will find us?"

"Anything is possible," Jerome replied gravely.

"Fuck!" the younger man cursed, his chair scraping against the tiled floor. "Well, if you're gonna do one, I may come with you."

"Relax, Deano. Let me make a few calls over the next few days. Let's enjoy our Saturday night and not worry about the Old Bill."

"Okay," he replied, stopping his pacing of the small kitchen. He took a swig of his beer, regarding the older man. "Any more news on Rafal?"

"Nothing. It's all gone quiet. Let's hope his wife thinks he's fucked off with another woman."

"Hope so. God! So much has happened over the past few weeks, bruv. My head is spinning."

"Have you told our sister about any of this?"

"Fuck no! Only you and I know about this."

"Good. Let's keep it that way. If we need to shoot off, no one can know about it. Now, come on. Let's get a spliff on the go and open some more cans."

John kissed his daughter and mother-in-law and stepped out into the dark February evening. Cars passed by on the busy dual-carriageway as he walked toward Zoe's house. He enjoyed stretching his legs as the cool evening air invigorated his lungs. At his daughter's demands, John dressed up for the evening out, wearing a dark pair of jeans, leather boots and a navy jumper that was covered by his brown leather jacket. After a few minutes, he unzipped it a few inches, letting the cool air hit his exposed neckline. He crossed over the road, his stride loping and carefree as he headed for his girlfriend's house a mile away. He walked past darkened shops and the occasional pub, then turned onto a long, tree-lined road. His phone beeped in his pocket. John pulled it out and swiped the screen.

The door's open. Let yourself in. Xx

He smiled and dropped the phone back in his pocket. Two minutes later, John entered Zoe's modest three bedroomed semi-detached house. He closed the front door and stood in the dimly lit hallway where a table lamp tried its best to illuminate the ground floor of the house. "Hi, babe," he called, sitting on the stairs to unlace his boots.

"Hi," Zoe answered from upstairs. "I'm just getting ready. Come up."

"Okay. Is Sharon at your parents'?" he asked, as one boot landed on the hall floor.

"Yeah. I dropped her off an hour ago. Is Lottie at Judy's?" was the muffled response.

"Yeah," he replied, as the other boot landed on the carpet. Placing them side by side on the mat, John straightened his socks. An image flashed in his memory of Lucy playfully scolding him due to the unruly appearance of his socks. He cast the memory aside as he walked up the stairs, the odd creak following his ascent. John turned left onto the landing and pushed Zoe's bedroom door open. He stepped inside. "I'm picking her up..." He froze, his mouth falling open at the sight before him.

"What's the matter," Zoe purred. "Cat got your tongue?" She stood in front of him, straightening her stocking tops, a feline-like smile on her face.

"Oh!"

"Oh?" she replied deliberately, tutting at him. She moved over towards the bed, crawling across the dark velvet cover on hands and knees before stretching herself out in front of him.

John's eyes took in her dark lingerie and black sheer bra, her breasts seeming to be at odds with the silky see-through material. "I thought you were getting ready?"

"I was. Ready for you."

"Huh?" John replied dumbly.

Her smile vanished, replaced by a stern look that John was not used to seeing. "Take off all your clothes. Now."

He did as he was asked, removing all his clothing. He stood in front of her, wearing nothing but a faraway smile.

"Have you eaten, John?" she asked quietly, her voice throaty.

"This afternoon," he replied, not picking up on her line of enquiry.

She slipped her underwear off, one stocking-clad foot flicking the lacy garment towards him. "Well, do you fancy an appetizer, before the main course?" She opened her legs slowly.

"Jesus," he groaned, his voice barely audible.

"Here," she demanded, holding out one hand toward him.

He rose over the bed, his knees sinking into the mattress as he inched towards her mouth.

She shook her head. "No."

"I just want to kiss you," he replied breathlessly.

"You can kiss me all you want. But not on my mouth. At least, not yet," she countered, as red manicured nails dug into the flesh at the back of his neck.

She guided him down her body until he was between her legs, looking up at her. "Now, Captain Wilson. You may kiss me," she cooed, gently pulling his head towards her body. Zoe's eyes closed as his warm breath caressed her skin, as delicate white teeth gently pinched at her bottom lip, the world around them melting away.

Sometime later, John lay on the bed, propped on an elbow as he watched her dress. The stockings had been discarded on a chair and Zoe was pulling on a pair of opaque tights before stepping into a chocolate brown dress. "Can you zip me up, babe?" she asked.

"Sure," he replied, moving off the bed. He gently kissed the bare flesh of her back, Zoe's eyes closing as she pushed herself backwards into her man.

"Are you enjoying your evening?" she teased.

"You could say that. You're incredible."

The woman turned around, kissing John, her arms wrapping around his neck. She felt his arousal as a horn sounded outside. "Damn. The bloody taxi's here. And I was just about to give you a treat."

His shoulders slumped dramatically as John pulled a sad face which made her giggle. "I've already been given plenty of treats. Any more can wait until later."

"Hold that thought, babe," she purred, reaching for a pair of black leather boots. "Now. Get dressed and get in the taxi. I'll be two minutes."

"Yes ma'am," he replied, giving her a mock salute before hastily throwing on his own discarded clothes. He padded down the stairs, tying his boots quickly before heading out towards the waiting saloon car. The driver seemed oblivious to the approaching man, his eyes fully-trained on his phone. As John opened the passenger door, the taxi driver placed his phone under the centre console.

"Alright, mate," the man said. "Where to?"

"Hiya. Hollywood Bowl please, mate. She'll just be a minute."

"No worries," the middle-aged man replied, pressing a few buttons on his meter.

A few minutes later, the lights went off inside the house as Zoe appeared, wrapped up in a large black coat. She climbed into the rear of the car, smiling at the driver in the rear-view mirror. "Sorry about the wait," she said breathlessly.

"Don't worry about it. Part of the job." He pulled away from the kerb, heading steadily down the road.

"Let the fun begin," Zoe declared from the back seat of the car, her slender fingers reaching through the headrest to stroke John's neck as they headed towards their destination.

39

The Mercedes-Benz A-Class carrying Jerome and Deano pulled up outside the bowling alley. "What time is the guy getting here?" Jerome asked.

"Any minute now," replied Deano, buzzing down his window. A plume of smoke left the car, lost on the strengthening wind. They sat there, Radio 1 playing on the stereo system.

"Turn that shit down," Jerome complained. "Fucking rubbish."

"Okay, old man." Deano turning the volume right down until only the passing traffic could be heard.

"This old dog could teach the pup a thing or two," Jerome replied, playfully digging the younger man with his elbow.

Deano sat up in the driver's seat as a shadowy figure emerged from the night, a hooded top obscuring the man's features. He stooped his considerable frame, peering in at the two men. "Chris," Deano began. "How's things?"

"Okay, man," the tall figure replied, handing over a bundle of notes. Deano placed the money inside his coat pocket, holding his closed fist outside the car window. The exchange took a split-second, then the man stood up slowly. "Sweet. Be seein' ya," he mumbled, walking off before becoming lost to the shadows.

"Strange-looking dude," Jerome observed.

"He's harmless. Bit of a weirdo really. Lives on his own above the launderette in the village. He's one of those gamers."

"Gamers?" Jerome replied, a look of confusion on his face.

"Yeah, y'know. They sit around all day playing PlayStation games and shit. He even gets paid to do it."

"The world is a fucked-up place, bruv."

"You're not wrong. Now come on, shall we have a few drinks? There might be some pussy in there," Deano suggested, tilting his head towards the bowling alley.

"Go on then," the older man replied. "Let the old man show you how it's done."

They climbed out of the car, Deano pulling his baseball cap low over his head before walking stride for stride with his half-brother towards the bright lights of Hollywood Bowl.

John was losing. Losing badly. Try as he might, he'd never mastered the art of ten-pin bowling, missing more skittles than he hit. Added to his shame, Zoe had already won two games, hitting three strikes in the current game, wiggling her bum in his face. That was the highlight of the evening, save for the other type of wiggling that had taken place a few hours before.

"Come on, John," Zoe beamed. "Your turn. Come on, babe, you can do it," she encouraged playfully.

"God help me!" he muttered, selecting a size ten ball, not that it mattered. *I'd stand more chance with a golf ball than this bloody thing,* he thought soberly. He walked past Zoe, planting a kiss on her forehead which drew smiles from her female colleagues and indifference from their other halves. *You can do this,* he told himself, as he approached the taped line on the floor. Throwing it with only half his strength, John stood and watched as the ball headed down the lane, his mouth falling open when the red ball smashed all the pins into a skittering pile. "Jesus!" he exclaimed, turning around to face the others.

"Woohoo!" Zoe hollered, racing over to John to hug him.

He caught her mid-leap, spinning her around a full circle before placing her gently on the wooden floor. "It was just a fluke," he said sheepishly, smiling at the others who were standing by the control panel, clapping and drinking in equal measure.

"There you go. You got your aim just right. A bit like earlier," she blushed, slapping his rear end playfully.

John laughed out loud, waving his finger in the woman's face. "Keep it down. Your mates will find out what a harlot you are."

"Well, this harlot needs a drink. My round."

"I'll come up with you, babe."

"Okay. Does anyone else want one?" she asked the group.

"It's okay," one woman replied. "We'll send the guys up in a minute."

Zoe and John walked arm in arm across the top of the bowling alleys, a large arcade to their left where children and adults hovered around various machines. They walked over to the bar, Zoe snuggling into her man. He looked to his left, noticing a dark-skinned man next to him, a crumpled note in his hand.

"Yes, love?" a young barmaid said as she walked over to him.

"Erm, I think this guy's first," John replied, motioning towards his left.

"Thanks, man," Jerome said before addressing the young woman. "Two lagers, please."

The woman pulled two glasses from under the bar, looking away from Jerome, who in turn looked to his left at his younger drinking partner. His face creased in confusion as he looked at Deano, who was gesturing with his finger, pointing behind Jerome. "What?" he mouthed, noticing the younger man fidgeting in his seat. He paid the barmaid, walked over to the far corner of the bar and placed the drinks on the table. "What was all that about?"

"That guy next to you at the bar?"

"What about him?" Jerome replied, looking back at the couple who were now being served.

"That's soldier boy. The guy I tangled with."

~

"So, what do you wanna do?" Jerome asked, taking a sip of his fourth pint.

"Get even," Deano replied, as he took a swig of his frothy pint.

"But he's with his missus. Leave him be."

"Can't, bruv," the younger man insisted. "Help me out here?"

"Fuck!" Jerome cursed, putting his pint on the table. "He seemed okay. Maybe you two just off on the wrong foot? He let me get served first. At least the man has manners."

Deano leaned forward, his face solemn. "I helped you out in Scotland. Now, return the favour."

Jerome nodded, his pulse beginning to race. "Okay. So, how you wanna do this? Not in here?"

"Nah," his half-brother replied. "Outside, when they leave. They're probably bowling. Give them an hour and they'll be over here. We can keep an eye on them."

"Okay. But he's all yours. If you wanna settle the score, do it one-on-one."

"Fair enough, bruv," Deano replied, taking another pull on his pint.

The group moved away from the bowling alley and headed over to the bar for more drinks. John mingled, chatting to a few of Zoe's work colleagues. She watched him, a warm smile on her face as her man chatted, his self-deprecating manner winning over the women around him. As he excused himself, Zoe did the same, politely moving away from Janice and Bethany, wanting to exchange notes with her closest co-workers.

"He's lovely," one of them gushed encouragingly.

"I know," Zoe responded, a huge smile on her face.

"Has he got a twin brother?" the woman added, making Zoe giggle.

"Sandra," she scolded. "You're married!"

"Yes," the older woman replied sombrely. "But not to that!" The other two women with Sandra also giggled, making Zoe smile even more.

"He's a lovely bloke. A real catch. Sometimes, I can't believe we're together."

"Why not?" another woman called Paula asked, her face curious.

"Because he's gorgeous. Plus, he really knows how to treat a woman. I'm not used to that."

"Well, you enjoy," Sandra replied happily. "And I bet he knows how to treat a woman, too, if you know what I mean?"

More giggles from the four women, the alcohol and the atmosphere loosening them up. "Oh, believe me, he does. He gave me a real treat before we came out."

"Come on," Paula quipped. "We wanna know the details. Tell us jealous bitches what we're missing out on?"

"I can't," Zoe replied, beginning to blush.

"Come on," Sandra urged, agreeing with Paula. "What did he do for you?"

Zoe took a large gulp of her drink, trying to compose herself. "He went south."

"Oh God!" Paula gasped. "Was it good?"

"Amazing," Zoe replied proudly. "And he stayed south until I'd practically screamed the house down. God knows what the neighbours thought!"

"Well, lucky you," Sandra declared, patting Zoe on the shoulder. "Tony's not been south since about 1996. And if he tried it now, he'd need a bloody instruction manual!"

The women howled with laughter as John appeared next to Zoe. Seeing him appear, they attempted to stifle their laughs, with little success. "You girls okay?" he asked, wondering what was so funny.

"We're fine, lovely," Sandra replied heartily. "Just talking about work and stuff. Anyway, it's my round. Who wants one?"

"I'll come with you," Zoe replied. She walked off towards the bar with her colleague, leaving John with two grinning females.

~

"She's at the bar, bruv. With another bird."

"And?" Jerome replied, putting his phone on the table for a moment.

"You wanna pint?"

"Okay," Jerome replied warily.

Deano walked to the bar, placing his elbows on the countertop a few inches away from Zoe. He could hear them giggling as a young barman nodded his way. "Two lagers, please." The barman nodded again, walking towards the end of the bar with two glasses. Deano watched them as the other woman put her purse into her handbag before they both picked up their drinks. He lurched to his right, bumping into Zoe, who almost dropped her two drinks on the polished wooden floor.

She turned around, the front of her dress soaked with wine and cider. Looking up at the large man, she placed the half-empty glasses on the bar. "Sorry," she exclaimed automatically.

"You should be more fucking careful," Deano spat. "You pissed or something?"

"Erm, excuse me!" Sandra retorted. "You bumped into her. It's you that should be apologising."

"It's okay, Sandra," Zoe replied, her body beginning to tremble. "My mistake." She looked at the man in the baseball cap who loomed over her, feeling very small vulnerable. "Sorry for bumping into you."

"You'd fucking better be. Do it again and I'll knock you the fuck out!"

The line had been crossed, Deano knew that as the other woman's face changed utterly. He knew he was in the wrong and that he'd never normally speak to a woman like that. However, he needed a reaction to start the ball rolling.

"What the fuck?" Sandra exclaimed. "How dare you talk to her like that, you prick!"

Deano smiled, took the half-empty drink from the bar and tossed it in Sandra's face. "Don't forget your drink, bitch!"

The young barman returned with Deano's drinks, having witnessed the exchange of words as he'd poured the pints. As the drink hit the woman's face, the young man poured the beers down the sink. "You're barred," he declared, trying to sound authoritative.

He looked at the empty glasses in the barman's hands, shaking his head. "Pour me two more, or I'll smash those glasses in your fucking face."

The man stepped back, his face paling before heading away from the bar quickly.

"Come on, Sandra," Zoe urged, her voice faltering as she reached for the other woman's arm.

"Scumbag," Sandra tossed back at the man, throwing her handbag over her shoulder.

"Go fuck yourselves," Deano replied as the women walked away. He leaned against the bar, looking over at Jerome who sat there watching on, his expression grave.

Raised voices to his left made Deano turn towards the bowling alley, where he noticed the women he'd just spoken to relaying the events to their friends. *Bingo,* he thought as he caught sight of his target, who looked clearly pissed. *Come on, soldier boy.* The woman he'd purposefully bumped into was trying to restrain him, blocking his path. The other woman was standing with two other women, who were staring over in his direction.

His target moved to the woman's left and came walking over. Deano took his baseball cap off and placed it on the bar before smiling at John. "Remember me?"

John processed the new development in a heartbeat, knowing why the altercation had taken place. "Was that a ploy to get me to come over?"

"You gotta admit, it was a good ploy."

"It was. If you wanted a piece of me, you should have come to me. You don't take it out on my girlfriend."

"Oooh!" Deano teased, as the bar manager came through a side door. "Girlfriend, eh? Moved on from your dead wife now, have ya?"

"Fuck off," John countered. "You know nothing about me."

The bar manager, a large middle-aged man, stepped between the two men. He looked at Deano. "You, out!" he ordered, folding his thickly muscled arms over his barrel chest.

"Outside, soldier boy," Deano taunted, inching closer to John, stepping around the man-made barrier in front of him.

John felt a tug on his arm and turned to see Zoe. "Leave it, John. It's not worth it," she insisted.

"Hiding behind your missus?" Deano spat. "You wanna settle this, come outside. If not, I'll find ya, maybe when your bitch of a daughter is with ya."

John turned to Zoe, his face calm. "It'll be okay. This is the guy from the school that I told you about. I'm going to sort this out. I promise I'll be okay."

"Then we're coming with you," Zoe countered, her determined expression telling John that arguing was pointless.

He turned towards the bar manager. "If it gets out of hand, call the police."

"I'm calling them anyway," the larger man replied. "Don't do this, mate."

John looked at Deano, "After you."

His adversary turned, heading towards the exit, a dark-skinned man following close behind. John took up the rear, Zoe and Sandra at his side, not knowing what was about to unfold.

40

They stepped out into the cool night air. Deano took his cap and jacket off, handing them to Jerome, who stood a few paces away. "You sure you wanna do this?" he asked.

"Damn right. I'm gonna enjoy it, too."

John inched the sleeves of his jumper up until they were just below the elbow. Jerome cast his eyes over his half-brother's opponent, noticing the defined muscles on his forearms, along with the contours of his upper body. *Shit. He's gonna have his hands full with this one,* he thought ominously. "Get it over with, bruv."

Deano nodded towards his half-brother before squaring up to John. "Come on then, ya cunt."

"Don't do this, John," Zoe pleaded, trying to pull him backwards by his jumper.

He looked behind, shaking his head at his girlfriend. "Step back." As she did so, John heard footsteps and, sensing the punch heading his way, he brought his right arm up, deflecting the shot, the shock and power of the blow knocking him back a step. He sized up the younger man, focusing on his eyes. John knew there and then that he would win, seeing the glassy expression on the younger man's face. It would be messy, not like in the movies. But John would finish it.

Deano moved in, his footwork sloppy as an arcing haymaker sailed through the air towards John. Time seemed to slow down as John heard the whoosh of air from the flailing arm. He dodged right, the punch falling over his left shoulder. Both men were inches apart, Deano's face flushed from the exertion. The ex-solider could see his opponent readying himself for an attack. To counter it, he brought his right boot back a step, planting it firmly. In a blur of speed, John grabbed the front of the man's top, yanking him forwards. At the same time, the ex-soldier snapped his head forward, butting Deano across the bridge of the nose. The sickening crack of bone was clear to all of them, except Deano. He fell backwards, landing on the paved slabs, his nose ruined.

John stepped back, vision fuzzy, legs rubbery as he tried to regain his composure, readying himself for the dark-skinned man's advances. It never came. Instead, Jerome moved over towards the fallen Deano. "Roll onto your side, bruv. Don't choke on your own blood," he urged, pulling the slack body towards him.

"Ugh," Deano grunted, letting Jerome pull him into a sitting position.

"Is he okay?" John asked, concern edging his voice.

"He'll live," Jerome replied, not looking at the ex-soldier. "Come on, bruv, it's over. Let's get out of here."

Deano climbed to his feet, swaying like a sapling in the breeze. He touched the bridge of his nose, wincing. "Fuck! You've busted my nose!" he shouted, his words slurred. He lunged for John, falling to the ground as the ex-Marine side-stepped easily.

Zoe grabbed John's arm. "Let's go, John. I want to go home."

"Okay," he replied, turning towards the two men. "It's over. You wanted this, mate. I didn't. Let that be the end of it."

"You're a fucking dead man!" Deano shouted, trying in vain to scramble to his feet. He lunged once more for John, but Jerome stopped his advances.

"Leave it, bruv. It's over," he stated firmly.

"Not over," Deano replied. "I'll fucking say when it's over. When I've fucked him up properly."

Jerome turned to John. "I'd get out of here. He won't stop until you're in the hospital."

"We're going," John replied, stepping backwards.

"Come on, Deano," Jerome said. "Let's go."

"Get the fuck off me," the younger man replied. "You're just gonna let him go after what he did?"

"You're drunk and you're making a prat out of yourself," his half-brother said sternly.

"Bollocks," Deano retorted. He looked at John. "You know who this is?" he said, trying to refuel the fire as he pointed at Jerome.

"What are you talking about?" John replied, turning to face his adversary.

"Come on, John," Zoe pleaded, tears running down her face. "Just leave it, please."

Deano was regaining some composure. He laughed at John. "He's the guy who gave drugs to the boys that killed your wife. Ain't that right, bruv?"

"Shut your mouth!" Jerome shouted. "He's been through enough."

John's face changed, his mouth trying to form the words that would not come. He looked at Jerome, who stood planted firmly, hands coming out of his pockets, ready for the attack. "You!" the ex-soldier blurted. "You gave them the drugs? And then they killed Lucy." He moved forward a step, his fists clenching as Zoe held onto him.

"It was a long time ago, mate. I never gave them the drugs, they took them from their mother. I ain't got no quarrel with you. Don't make this worse than it already is."

"John!" Zoe shouted. "Leave it. He's goading you, can't you see that?"

He turned to her, his eyes filled with tears. "They killed Lucy and he had a hand in it."

"I'm going home. Stay if you like, but I'm not." She walked over to Sandra and the others, who were with a large group of onlookers who had gathered outside the entrance to the bowling alley.

John looked at the two men, pointing at Jerome. "This isn't over," he declared, tears spilling down his face. "I'll find you."

Jerome nodded, knowing that he'd made a mortal enemy. One that would track him down. One that would want revenge. He turned to his half-brother as the ex-soldier walked away, head bowed. "You fucking idiot! Don't you think he's been through enough pain? Now he knows that I'm involved in his wife's death. You've really fucked things up."

"Then let's end this," Deano replied, pulling his car keys out of his pocket.

"What are you talking about?" Jerome replied, a feeling of dread settling over him.

"You'll see," Deano replied, bolting forward towards the car park. Jerome stood there, not comprehending what was about to happen as the younger man ran towards the far side of the bowling alley.

What the fuck's he doing? he thought, the realisation hitting him as the car's headlights came on as the Mercedes pulled out of the car park.

"Wait!" John called out as Zoe headed away from Great Park, walking quickly but unsteadily towards a petrol station on her left-hand-side. "Babe, wait," he repeated as Zoe slowed to a standstill.

He caught up with her a few seconds later, wrapping his arms around her protectively. "I've got you."

"I hate fighting, John. Why did you have to do that?"

"I don't know," he replied, letting go of her. He leant against a low wall, his emotions coming to the surface as he began to cry. "That man was involved in Lucy's death."

"I know, John. I heard what he said. But what can you do? You have to think about Lottie now. And me."

He looked up, his red-rimmed eyes showing that he understood what she meant. He was a father. He had responsibilities. Responsibilities that were more important than male pride and macho bullshit. His shoulders sagged.

Zoe wrapped her arms around him. "Let's go home, babe," she soothed.

John closed his eyes. He did not see the pavement suddenly becoming illuminated by oncoming headlights. His eyes flicked open as the sound of a revving engine reached his ears and the crunch of a car mounting a pavement made him flinch. He blinked, blinded by the twin beams. A scream filled the night. Then, darkness.

Jerome heard the scream, followed by the dull thud of the car hitting bodies, as he sprinted along the pavement. He came around the corner and his stomach turned to lead as the scene unfolded before him. The car's rear lights gave the street a red hue as he approached, every step becoming more difficult than the last. Deano spilled from the vehicle. Jerome walked past him towards the front of the car. He looked down, sucking in his breath when he saw two bodies, sandwiched between the vehicle and the wall.

"Fuck," he exclaimed, turning to Deano. "What have you done?"

Deano walked to where he was standing, looking down. "He had it coming, bruv."

He was about to continue when a stinging slap knocked him into the car.

"I think they're dead. Bruv, they're dead. Do you hear me?"

Deano looked down, sobering up as his actions hit home. The man lay underneath, barely visible. The woman was sprawled on top of him, haphazard limbs stuck out at strange angles. "What do we do?" he asked quietly.

"We get the fuck out of here. *Now*. The police are already on their way. They'll be here any minute. Then, we're both looking at life in prison. Move! In the back of the car. I'll drive."

Deano complied, staggering towards the rear door before flinging himself across the backseat. Jerome started the engine, reversing back a few feet before putting the car in gear. Before he pulled off, he looked at the bodies on the ground, feeling sick to his stomach as the car's rear motion unpinned them from the wall, leaving the man and woman lying still on the pavement.

He mashed the accelerator, the car clunking down onto the tarmac as he sped towards the main road a few hundred yards away. *Spain it is then,* he thought gravely. *But first, we need to lie low.*

41

John's eyelids opened slowly. The world above him was bright and blurry so he shut them again, his closed lids feeling like they were burning a hole in his head. Images flashed before him. A bright light, then darkness. Zoe's scream and the scraping of metal flooded his mind. He opened his mouth, his tongue feeling dry, devoid of moisture.

"John?" a familiar voice said.

"Judy?" he replied, opening his eyes once more. After a few seconds, the room came into focus somewhat and a figure seated to his left took hold of his hand.

"It's okay, John. I'm with you."

"Where am I?"

"Queen Elizabeth Hospital," she replied, her voice shaking with emotion.

"Hospital? What happened?"

"Do you not remember?"

He tried to recollect. *The fight. The car.* "Zoe. Where's Zoe?" John moved his head from left to right, seeing no one else in the small room. He tried to sit up but a dull pain in his side stopped him in his tracks. Another memory flashed before him. Zoe lying above him, her eyes closed.

"Let's get you some water, love, then I'll call the nurse."

John felt two arms slide themselves under his armpits as his mother-in-law shifted him into a slightly more vertical position. "Ugh," he grunted, his body protesting at the sudden movement.

"Sorry, John. Here, have some water," she offered, placing a straw between his dry lips. He sucked weakly on the straw as cool water trickled into his mouth, offering some relief.

He focused on her, noting the red-rimmed eyes and lack of make-up. "Judy, where's Zoe?"

She gripped his hand, tears rolling down her cheeks. "I'm so sorry, John. She didn't make it. The doctors tried to save her, but I'm afraid she passed away."

"What?" he cried, trying to sit up, wincing in pain. "No. Please no," he blurted, shaking his head. "Not Zoe. Please God, not Zoe." He began sobbing and Judy took him in her arms as his pain boiled over. She held him there as a nurse appeared from the outer corridor.

"I'll call for the doctor," the nurse said, walking over to John. "Mr Wilson, I'm Rachel. Let me just check you over."

Judy let go of him, walking shakily over towards the window to give the nurse some space. "I'll call Lottie. She's at home with Bob. Be back in a minute."

"How long have I been in here?" John asked, as the nurse checked him over. She had shoulder-length hair, with streaks of red that shimmered under the harsh lighting.

"Well, it's Monday morning, so about thirty-six hours or so."

John looked down at his legs, baulking at the sight before him. His left leg was encased in a pink brace, a series of straps holding it in place. He wiggled his toes, relieved to find there was movement in them, meaning his legs weren't paralysed. "And where's Zoe?" *Judy must have got it wrong. This same nightmare can't be happening to me again.*

"I'm not sure, Mr Wilson," she replied, her face dropping slightly. "Wait until your mother-in-law returns. She may know. I'm very sorry I can't be of more help. I'll let the doctor know that you've come round." She patted his hand gently and walked out of the private ward, leaving John alone with his thoughts.

Oh God! Zoe. Why did I get involved? I should have walked away.

His thoughts were disturbed as Judy walked back into the room with a cup of coffee. "I've let them know that you're awake. Lottie's very upset, John. It's brought it all back for her."

"Jesus. I'm sorry, princess," he whispered.

"Your parents were here, too. I'll let them know you're awake. Do you want me to get you anything? There's a shop downstairs."

He shook his head. "No. What happened to Zoe?"

Judy leaned against the wall, pulling an electronic cigarette out of her bag. She held the slim device in her fist, taking a sneaky drag, her eyes on the door. She turned to the window, blowing a tiny trail of vapour against the glass before walking over to her son-in-law. "Not sure, love. I think they brought you both in together. But from there, all I know is that she'd passed away. Her parents and daughter were here yesterday. They're distraught, John. And I should warn you, they want to know what happened."

"Jesus," he replied. "This is all my fault."

"What did happen? There was something on the news about it. Apparently, the police are looking for two men, but have not caught up with them yet."

John reached over, taking another sip of water from the plastic beaker. "You remember the altercation I was involved in at the school?"

"Yes. With the mother and uncle."

John nodded. "Well, I saw the mother a few weeks ago at the Hare and Hounds. She warned me that I was in for a kicking. Then, while we were at the bowling alley, the brother had a go at Zoe and her friend. It all went downhill from there. The brother was with a black guy, his half-brother, I think. Anyway, it came to blows outside."

"Oh God, John."

"I know. I took care of the brother, who was already pissed. But then he told me something that has changed everything."

"What?"

"The half-brother is the same guy who gave drugs to the brothers that killed Lucy."

Judy's mouth fell open, her eyes widening as she gripped the side of the bed. "What!" she exclaimed, dropping into the plastic chair next to the bed. She buried her face in her hands, racking sobs shaking her body. "No. Please, God no," she cried, her face streaked with tears.

"I'm so sorry, Judy." He lay there, unable to say anymore as his own grief took over. He wept with her, his ribs aching with every sob. John embraced the pain, letting it fuel something else that was building inside him. Rage.

An hour later, John was sitting up in bed as the doctor informed him that he had a fractured tibia, along with four broken ribs and mild concussion. He was going nowhere for a while and this was making him feel hopeless and frustrated. *I'm going to find you,* he thought. *You're going to fucking pay for this.* A half-eaten sandwich lay on a paper plate in front of him. John pushed it away as a middle-aged couple entered the room. His heart sank as he recognised Zoe's parents, Sheila and Gordon, staring down at him.

Judy stood up from the chair and walked around the end of the bed. "He's been awake for about an hour," she said, unsure of what else to say.

Sheila looked at John, her face stricken with pain. "What happened to my daughter?"

"I'm so sorry," John replied quietly.

"I'm sure you are. But, she's dead," the woman stated flatly. "I want to know why." Her husband came to her side, wrapping a supporting arm around her. He looked older, his face drawn.

"Okay," John replied, trying to compose himself. He relayed the entire story, from the altercation between his daughter and the girl in her class, right up to the point where they were mown down by the shaven-headed man.

"I hope you're proud of yourself," Gordon spat. "Our daughter is dead. Sharon has lost her mother. And for what? Because you dragged her into a fight that had nothing to do with her. You should be fucking ashamed of yourself. You've killed our daughter!"

"Now hang on," Judy countered, her face reddening. "John wasn't to know that this would happen. You heard what he said. The one guy verbally abused her and threw a drink in her friend's face. What would you do if that was your wife?" She placed her hands on her hips, ready for the fight.

"I would have walked away," Gordon replied, his shoulders slumping. "Fighting solves nothing."

"I know, Gordon," John replied. "I'm not the kind of guy who fights outside pubs. But he pushed my buttons. Not only did he have a go at Zoe, but he also brought my wife into it. I saw red and knew that it had to be settled there and then. I know now that I should have walked away."

"Well, it's done now," Sheila hissed, her body shaking. "And you'll have to live with what you've done. Stay away from my family and you're not welcome at our Zoe's funeral." They shuffled out of the room, leaving John and Judy staring after them.

"They're just upset, love," Judy said. "And who can blame them? We both know how they feel."

"I've fucked things up," John replied. "First Lucy, now Zoe. It feels like I'm cursed."

"Now, don't get all maudlin," Judy countered walking over to him. "Yes, maybe you should have walked away. But you weren't to know that the guy would try and kill you both."

He was about to reply when two more figures appeared in the doorway. It took John a second to recognise the pair, whom he'd not seen for many years. The man looked older, greyer. The woman's hair was longer, her face unchanged since he'd last seen her. "Hello, John," Detective Inspector Blaney said. "Long time no see."

42

"I'll go outside for a smoke," Judy said, taking her cue. "I'll be back in a bit, love." She left them as the room fell silent for a few seconds, until Blaney drew up another chair for Jenn to sit on.

"How are you feeling? Stupid question, I know," the detective asked.

"Not sure," John replied. "They killed Zoe."

"I know," Jenn responded. "We're really sorry, John. Believe me, you're the last person that we ever thought we'd be speaking to again. Nor did we want to. You've been through enough already."

"Thank you," he replied. "What's happened to the two guys that did this?"

Blaney took over, his expression neutral. "We're still looking for them, John. But they've probably gone to ground. Dean Teale is known to us, as is Jerome Marshall. Marshall had recently been released on license and looked to have been keeping his nose clean. Or so we'd thought…"

"Meaning?" John countered, suddenly curious.

"Okay. Another investigation is ongoing, so I cannot say too much. But what I will share with you, off the record, is that Marshall and Teale are being sought by the Northern Constabulary in Scotland, relating to the murder of an MJ Kerr, formally Mandy Terry."

John tried to compute the information, his brain not quite keeping up. "And who's she?"

Blaney sighed as he looked over at his partner. Jenn nodded, her expression taut. "Okay. If the Chief finds out I've told you this, I'll be off the Force by the end of the week. Can we keep this between the three of us?" The ex-soldier's nod was enough for Blaney to carry on. "Mandy Terry was the mother of the two boys that killed your wife." He looked at the younger man, expecting a more surprised reaction.

John nodded, shifting uncomfortably in bed, his face impassive. "I'm just trying to piece this together in my head. Just after the fight, this Deano character told me that the black guy with him supplied the drugs that the brothers took before they killed Lucy."

Shaw and Blaney looked at John. Jenn shook her head and moved forward in her seat. "Sorry, John," she said. "You have to understand, we could not give you all the details back then."

"I do understand," John replied, nodding his head. "So, Jerome Marshall is the name of the guy who supplied the drugs." It was a statement rather than a question. John burnt the name into his memory, a dark-skinned face appearing in his mind's eye.

Blaney took over brusquely. "We're unsure of their motives. Could be revenge, or there could be something else at play here. All we know is that Mandy was found on a beach near Thurso a few weeks ago. It looks like she'd either been pushed or had fallen to her death. She'd been slashed across the face with a sharp implement just before she died. Probably a knife of some sort. CCTV footage confirms Teale and Marshall were in the area at the time she was killed, and we were working in conjunction with our Scottish colleagues to apprehend them. Unfortunately, this information only came to light a few days ago, John. I'm sorry."

"It's not your fault," was all he could say in reply.

"Well, we'll find them, John. Even though Marshall was not involved in Miss Palmer's death or your injuries. It looks like he fled the scene with the perpetrator. He's looking at several charges, many of which carry a custodial sentence. And with his record, he's looking at another considerable stretch inside."

"It won't bring Zoe back, though," John countered, tears rolling down his stubbly cheeks.

"No," Jenn replied. "But we'll get them. Both of them will soon be in custody, John. You can count on that."

Blaney looked at his partner. *Steady. We've not got them yet,* the detective thought bleakly. "We'll do all we can," he added, attempting to sound positive. "You just rest up, John."

"So, Mandy Terry was released from prison. What about her son?"

Blaney shifted in his seat, his expression pinched. "He's still inside, John. Try not to think about him. There is every chance that he'll never be released."

"What's his name?" he probed.

"I've already told you enough. I'm sorry, but I cannot give you that information. And even if I could, it would not do you any good."

"Why not?" John replied, his voice slightly raised.

"Because, it would eat you up inside. His mother and brother are dead and he's off the grid. You've just been through another major trauma. You need to heal, both physically and mentally. Do you understand what I'm telling you?"

John slapped his hands down on the bed in surrender. "Okay. Sorry. I shouldn't have asked that. Just find the bastards. Before I do."

"No sign of them," Shaw stated as she placed a coffee on Blaney's desk. "No one's seen them since Saturday afternoon."

Blaney sat back in his chair, the mechanism squeaking loudly. "My guess is that they're long gone. We can reach out to other forces, but I bet they come up with bugger all."

"What are you thinking, guv?" she asked, sitting down across the desk from her boss.

"Another part of the country, maybe even Europe."

"Do they have any connections over there?"

"Teale won't. He's small-time. But I'm guessing that Marshall will have contacts on the continent."

Shaw blew out a breath, running her fingers through her dark hair. "Finding them will be near impossible."

"Probably. What a bloody mess! One thing is for sure, though."

"What's that?"

"It would be far cleaner if we found them. I saw the look in John's eyes. I think they've messed with the wrong man."

"He's certainly been through the mill. Poor bloke."

"Oh, I think it's more than that. I think he would happily kill them if he got the chance."

"And who could blame him?" she replied. "I know I shouldn't say that. But still..."

"You remember that guy from Erdington? Griffiths?"

Shaw nodded. "Hard to forget."

Blaney cast his mind back ten years, remembering the scene of carnage that had greeted both of them when they'd been called to a terraced house near the city centre. Flashes of blood-splattered walls appeared in his mind's-eye as he recalled how the man had walked past him with his arms covered in blood as he was led away. They'd thought him a monster, until it all came out in the trial. A cheating, abusive wife who'd regularly abused their children, until the mild-mannered husband had set about her with a carving knife.

"How any mother can do that to their own kids is beyond me. Yes, he murdered her, but I sympathise with him. Women, eh!" Their eyes met, the younger officer smiling at her partner as a mischievous grin appeared on his face.

"Just remember that when you're working me to the bone," she countered, winking at him.

His face suddenly dropped slightly. "How are things at home? Any better?"

"Not really," Jenn replied, the atmosphere in the room cooling somewhat. "He's still moaning about the hours. Telling me what a bad mother I've been for missing out on seeing Erin grow up. And he's right. She's close to leaving school and I've not really been there for her."

"I know it's hard, Jenn. And I'd understand if you wanted to take a step back. You're a fine detective, the best I've ever worked with, but family should come first. Unfortunately, we tend to put the job first, myself included."

"How are things at your end?" Shaw asked, knowing that Blaney was also having problems.

"Still the same. We're like strangers. I know she's seeing someone, but I just don't have the fight any more, Jenn. She could walk out tomorrow and I'd be fine."

"God! What are we like? A right pair of losers."

"We've still got each other though," he countered, smiling again. His face was transformed, years seeming to fall from the aging detective.

"Still as strong as ever," she replied, taking a sip of her coffee.

"Seriously, though. If you want to call it a day, do it. Think of Leon and Erin first. I've been thinking the same thing lately, as well you know. Maybe it's time for some new blood in this department."

"We'll see, guv. There's one thing we need to do first, though."

"What's that?" he asked.

"Find those bastards and throw the bloody book at them. The last thing we want is for a decent man to go to prison."

"Amen to that," Blaney agreed, swivelling to look at the bulletin board where two undesirable faces stared back at him.

43

AUGUST - 2014

A banging at the front door eventually shook John from his unconscious state. His bleary eyes opened, trying to focus on the empty whisky bottle on the carpet below him. The banging continued, until the ex-soldier rolled off the settee onto the floor, his head woozy. Walking shakily to the door, John unlocked it, pulling it towards him.

Judy stood there with his daughter, Lottie, hanging back a few steps. "Look at the state of you," Judy admonished. She looked at her granddaughter. "Put the kettle on, love," she asked, before turning back towards her son-in-law. "Go and grab a shower, John. You look like death warmed up."

"Okay," he replied, padding up the stairs as his mother-in-law closed the front door. A few minutes later, he walked into the lounge, sitting down heavily on the settee.

"Drinking yourself to death isn't the answer," Judy stated bluntly. "I know you're still hurting, love, but this has to stop."

He hung his head, wiping away a stray tear. "I know, Judy. But it's harder than I thought. When Lucy died, I don't think I ever grieved properly. That was mainly down to Lottie. She was just a kid and needed me twenty-four-seven. Now, she's independent."

"She still needs you, John," Judy replied calmly. "You've seen how she's been since Zoe died. She's told me about Sharon. How she misses her mum and hates living with her dad. I think Lottie is soaking up her friend's pain. She hardly said a word to me or Bob last night. Just finished her tea and went up to her room. That's not Lottie. We need to watch her, John. Or else she'll go off the rails."

"She won't," John replied. "She's a good kid."

"I know she is. But she's at that age now where she could go either way. My sister was the same. When Mum and Dad broke up, Mel went off the rails. She was fourteen at the time, a few years older than me. She started smoking, taking drugs and having sex. And this was nearly forty years ago. There weren't the pressures on kids that we have today. All I'm saying is that we need to make sure that Lottie stays on the right path."

"So, what do we do?"

"How about the school psychologist? She had a few sessions with her before. She might need her again?"

"Maybe you're right. I'll phone the school on Monday and see if there's anything they can do to help."

"But that's only half of the help she needs, John. You need to lay off the heavy stuff. We all like a drink but downing a whole bottle of whisky and passing out on the settee is not the answer. You're nearly forty. If you keep this up, you'll not reach fifty."

"Just miss her," John croaked as tears began forming. "I miss them both. I think Zoe's death has opened up old wounds. It feels like I'm grieving for both of them."

Judy shuffled across the settee, pulling the man towards her. John went to her, burying his head in the crook of her neck, shuddering sobs racking his body. "Get it out, John. Don't hold onto it. Bottling it up is bad for you." Judy rubbed his back like she'd often done for her granddaughter over the years.

After a few minutes, John pulled away gently, wiping his tears away with his sleeve. "Thanks."

"We're all here for you. Me, Lottie and your parents. A problem shared is a problem halved. Remember that. And no more spirits. If you're going to have a drink, stick to lager. Okay?"

"Okay," he agreed, leaning forward to kiss her on the cheek. "Thanks, Judy. I don't know what I'd do without you."

"Don't worry about that. I'm always here. But the same applies, John. I don't know what I'd do without you. And Lottie certainly wouldn't. Remember that."

~

"What do you want to do for your birthday?" John asked Lottie as they stood on top of the Lickey Hills.

"Dunno, Dad," Lottie replied quietly. "I don't really feel like celebrating."

"But you'll be thirteen. It's a milestone, sweetheart. You're about to become a teenager."

"It's just another birthday, Dad. But I'll try and think of something."

"We could go bowling?"

"No thanks," she replied. John realised what he'd said, the tension in the air almost palpable.

"Sorry. Bad idea. How about you ask a few mates round for a party?"

"I don't have many friends. Only Sharon really, and she's in a bad place at the moment."

"I know she is. I wish Zoe were still here. This has hit us all badly."

"I can't really remember Mum. But I really liked Zoe, Dad. I had hoped that one day you'd marry her. Then, Sharon and I would be sisters. That'll never happen now."

"But you'll always be friends with Sharon," he replied, realising how hollow the response sounded.

"I guess so. It's just really hard for her right now. She doesn't like her dad. She says he's a bit of a dickhead."

"Lottie!" John exclaimed, trying not to laugh.

"Sorry, Dad. But he is. I've only met him once and he hardly spoke to me. He's really up himself. Not like you."

"Hmm," John replied, turning around. "Come on. Let's walk back to the car."

They traversed a steep hill, a series of crisscrossed pathways dropping them down onto a wide path that skirted a golf course. The sun shone through the trees above, rays of sunlight shining like beacons along the forested pathway. They came out at the end of the golf course, turning right towards a duck pond and a tired-looking café. "Fancy a drink?" he asked.

"Nah. I've got some juice in the car. I can wait."

"Fair enough," he replied as they walked next to the park's tennis court, climbing steadily towards the Beacon Hill. "Come on, race you to the top," he suggested.

"Isn't that Claire from school?" Lottie said, pointing back towards the duck pond.

"Where?" John replied, the scuffing of feet on loose stones telling him that he'd been had. He turned around, smiling at the sight of his daughter sprinting up the gravelly slopes towards the summit. He took off after her, gradually gaining ground on Lottie, laughing as she screamed in delight at the thrill of the chase. "Gonna get ya," he panted, drawing another squeal from Lottie as he gained on her.

"You're too fast, Dad," she conceded, slowing down as her lungs screamed for oxygen. They fell on a patch of dry grass, a few hundred yards before the top of the hill, gasping for breath and laughing.

"I never knew you were so fast," John panted, his breathing gradually returning to normal.

"Nor you, Dad. You're quite fit, for an old man."

"Cheeky sod!" he admonished playfully, pulling his daughter into his embrace as passers-by looked on, smiling.

Lottie climbed on top of her father, squeezing him. "Love you, Dad."

"Love you too, princess," he replied as tears stung his eyes. They lay there for a few minutes, staring up at the clear sky as birds of prey floated on the warm thermals high above them. "Fancy an ice cream?"

"Go on then," Lottie replied happily, a far cry from the sullen preteenager of the last few weeks.

"Come on then," John urged, climbing to his feet.

"There is one thing I would like to do, Dad. Not for my birthday. Just something I need to do."

"What's that?" John asked, noticing the change in his daughter's expression.

"I want to visit the Fort, Dad. I want to go to the place where Mum died."

Two hours later, John parked his silver Volvo on the outskirts of the Fort shopping park, switching off the engine. They sat there in silence for a minute, each lost to their own thoughts before John turned to his daughter. "Are you sure you want to do this?"

"Yes, Dad," she replied. "I need to do this. I want to retrace the steps if I can."

"Okay. Let's do it."

They exited the car, skirting the various outlets inside the horse-shoe-shaped retail park. "Over there, Dad," Lottie began. "That's the coffee shop where we were sitting before I was taken."

"Shall we go inside and get a drink?"

"Okay," Lottie replied, linking hands with her father.

They walked past various outlets, sports stores and clothes shops, finally stopping outside the coffee shop that lay nestled in the corner between two larger units. As John opened the door for his daughter, a trickle of sweat ran down his back, making him shiver. He'd never been back to the Fort, except to retrieve Lucy's car shortly after she'd died. In all the years that had followed, John had never thought about returning to the place where his wife's existence had been so cruelly snuffed out.

He followed Lottie over to the counter, smiling at the barista on the other side of the counter. "Hi," he said politely.

"Hello," the young woman replied, a piercing on the side of her nose glinting under the spotlights above. "What would you like?"

Lottie was busy looking at the array of goodies adorning the counter as John nudged her gently. "Could I have a caramel flapjack and a Coke, please?"

"And a large latte as well, please," John added.

"Sure," the woman replied, busying herself at the counter.

"I'll go and grab a table, Dad," Lottie suggested, leaving John to pay for their items.

A minute later, he walked across the small coffee shop, trying not to spill the coffee that balanced precariously on a plastic tray. Setting the tray on the table, he looked at Lottie. "Are you okay?"

"This is where we sat, Dad. I'm sure of it."

John pulled out his chair and sat down before adding sugar to his milky coffee. He looked around the small space, noticing a door in the corner. "Is that where Mum got locked in?"

"Yes," Lottie replied quietly. "Then I was taken outside by a woman, I think."

They sat in silence, John feeling a sense of dread seeping through his body. *She must have been terrified,* he thought, trying to picture a frantic Lucy trying in vain to locate her daughter amongst a sea of people. He could feel his pulse quickening, his throat drying out as he imagined her last moments. He took a swig of his coffee, barely appreciating the heady aroma. He looked over at Lottie, who had finished her snack and half of her drink. "How do you feel?"

"Not sure, Dad. Okay, I guess. Let's go and look in there," she suggested, pointing at the door in the corner of the shop.

John finished his coffee, sliding it into the middle of the round table. "Come on then," he agreed, rising to his feet. They walked through the wooden door, finding themselves in a short corridor with three doors opposite them.

"That's where Mum was," Lottie stated, pointing towards the furthest door. She took a few steps, standing next to the wall. "She told me to stand here."

"Okay," John replied, trying to get a sense of what it would have been like all those years before. "Come on, it smells in here. Let's get some fresh air."

Lottie nodded, pushing the door into the coffee shop open. She held it open for John, who then followed her outside. They stood on a wide pavement, shoppers bustling past them, paying no heed to the father and daughter as they stood rooted to the spot next to the road. "This is where I was taken," Lottie stated confidently.

"Which way did they take you?" John asked, starting to feel uneasy once more.

Lottie looked away from the shops, noticing a footbridge a few hundred yards away. "That way, Dad. Come on." They linked hands once more, dodging and weaving around slow-moving cars until they reached the footbridge. They both relinquished their grip on each other's hands as they climbed the steps, walking over the traffic underneath as incoming clouds from the north blotted out the warm sun.

Dropping down the other side of the bridge, they stopped next to a line of tall hedges.

"I remembered that there was tall fencing along this stretch of road. When I picked your mum's car up, I drove past this part. There was police tape along here. Jesus! It seems like a lifetime ago."

A smaller hand linked his, Lottie squeezing his fingers tightly. "I think it was just up there," she replied, pulling him along with her. After a hundred yards, the hedge parted, a tall steel fence barring the way. They peered through, seeing abandoned train tracks and waste ground. "There. That's where Mum died."

John's eyes took in the patch of ground, tall grass swaying in the wind the only movement on the other side of the metal fence. Lucy's image flashed before his eyes as the ex-soldier gripped the fence, his knuckles turning white. "I love you, Lucy," he whispered.

Lottie snuggled into him. "I love you, Mummy," she added, using the name he'd not heard for many years. "Do you ever think about the boys that did this?"

"I used to. The younger one died shortly afterwards. The older brother must be in his mid-twenties by now."

"What would you do, Dad, if you ever saw him?"

"Honestly, I don't know. For years, I thought about getting my hands on the guy that did this and beating him to death. But I don't know, now. Things have changed recently."

"What do you mean?" Lottie asked, looking up at her father.

He blew out a breath, turning away from the fence. "There is something that I've not told you. I found it out the night Zoe was killed."

"What, Dad?"

"The guy that ran us over was with another man. After the fight, Deano told me that this other guy was involved in your mum's death."

"What!" Lottie exclaimed, her voice elevated. She looked at him, an incredulous expression on her young face. "How?"

He looked at her, seeing the pain resurface. *She's been through too much already,* he thought. *But she needs to know.* "His name is Jerome Marshall. The two brothers took his drugs before they killed your Mum. He was sent down shortly after and was only released recently. It looks like Jerome and Deano found the boys' mother and killed her. She was found a few weeks ago in Scotland. She'd been thrown off a cliff."

"Why did they kill her?"

"The police are unsure. Probably revenge for his prison sentence. She would have cut a deal back then, getting a reduced sentence. If he's only just been released, then this Jerome would have been inside for several years."

"And where are they now, Dad?"

"No idea. And the police don't know, either. But they'll find them."

"They deserve to die."

John looked at Lottie, seeing the hatred in her eyes. "Best not to think about that, sweetheart," he replied, hugging her. "The police will sort this out."

"But they won't, Dad. They'll be sent to prison for a few years. Then, they'll be back out. Mum's dead. Zoe's dead and this Jerome was involved in both. I'll kill him myself!"

"Sweetie, I know you're upset. But you're just a kid. These are dangerous criminals. They would hurt you, too. And I need you." He kissed her head, closing his eyes. "I've lost too many people already. I can't lose you, princess."

She looked up at him, her tear-streaked face making his heart constrict. "Then, if the police don't find them, you need to get them, Daddy. And make them pay for what they've done."

44

MAY - 2017

"You've done so well, Lottie." Angie Rhodes beamed from across the desk. "You should be proud."

"Thank you, Mrs Rhodes," Lottie replied, brushing her hair away from her face.

"Call me Angie. You've finished school now, unless you head into Sixth Form, which I hope you will?"

Lottie smiled, liking the kind, calming face of the school psychologist, whose dark hair framed delicate, elfin features. She had immediately put the teenager at ease. "Okay, Angie," Lottie replied happily.

"We've come a long way since you first stepped in here a few years ago. Now you can relax for a few weeks until your results are in."

"Tell me about it," the teenager replied. "I'm looking forward to a few weeks' downtime."

"I'm sure you are. How is your father?"

Lottie's expression clouded over, her smile fading. "He's okay, I guess. Nanny Judy says he's just plodding through life."

"Well, he's been through a lot. You both have. Does he approve of your career choice?"

Lottie was cast back to the last conversation with her father, remembering his face when she told him of her wish to join the police force.

"He's not too happy about it. I guess he just wants me to get a regular job. After everything that's happened to us, I feel I need to put something back. To stop bad things happening to innocent people."

"Well, it's certainly a noble profession," Angie added. "But it's not all car chases and locking up the bad guys. There will be tons of administration, red tape and frustration."

"I know, Angie. And I accept that. I just want to help people."

"Well, that's the right frame of mind. And if you become a detective, like you've said you'd like to, you'll hopefully be doing some really great work keeping our streets safe." She looked at the clock on the wall, her stomach grumbling. "So, who is picking you up from school? Dad?"

"No. He's working today. Nanny Judy is probably already waiting for me at the gates."

"Well, you get yourself off. My work here is done, and I'll be closing your case down with a glowing report, Lottie. Be proud of what you've achieved and look forward to the future."

Lottie stood up, walking around the desk to embrace the older woman. Tall for her age, Lottie towered over the middle-aged woman, bending down slightly to hug her. "Thanks, Angie. I hope we remain friends. You've been so lovely."

Angie pulled away, holding the girl at arm's-length. "I'm sure we will. And I'm always here, whatever and whenever you need me. Now scram. I've a half-eaten meatball sandwich in the fridge. If I don't hurry up and eat it, one of the other teachers will scoff it."

Lottie scooted down the flights of stairs and walked across the playground towards the school gates, where fellow pupils and family members milled around. She spotted Judy, who was sporting a new hair-do, her steel-grey locks stylishly cut. She smiled at her granddaughter, walking towards her in clothes that Lottie had not seen before – a pair of dark jeans, with ankle boots and a shimmering silver top.

"Wow, Nan. You look amazing."

"Thanks, love. Bob took me shopping earlier. Thought he'd treat me to a few bits and bobs. You like them?"

"Are you kidding? You look fab!" she replied enthusiastically, hugging her nan.

"Aww. Thanks, love. Anyway, how did the last day of school go? Excited about the future?"

"It was okay. I was in with Angie for about an hour. She's really happy with my progress."

"And rightly so. You've done amazingly well, all things considered."

"Thanks, Nan. I couldn't have done it without you."

Judy was about to reply when a female voice called over to them. "Well, well, well. Look who it is?" Tracey Teale called, as she sauntered over.

"Who's this?" Judy asked, looking at the approaching woman, who was dressed in a grey tracksuit and faux leather boots.

"It's Alicia's mum," Lottie replied, a cold knot forming in her stomach.

"How's it going, Lottie? How's your dad?"

Lottie was about to answer when Judy stepped forward. "Our family's business has got nothing to do with you," she warned, her voice steady.

"You must be the mother-in-law? Still visiting your daughter's grave?" she goaded.

Lottie shrank back behind Judy as Alicia walked over slowly, a concerned look on her face. Judy smiled, holding her ground as the younger woman stepped closer. "Every few weeks. If you like, I can give you the number of my florist. In preparation for when John catches up with your scumbag brother."

There was a collective intake of breath as Alicia and her friends stared wide-eyed at the older woman, who'd just delivered a killer putdown. "You cheeky bitch!" Tracey spat. "Soldier boy will never find him, or Jerome. They're long gone."

"So, you're all on your own then, but still talking tough," Judy countered, sensing danger.

"I don't need any backup to sort you and your bitch granddaughter out. And I'll tell you another…"

Tracey's sentence was cut off as Judy slapped her hard across the face, knocking her into a nearby bus stop. The side of her face hit the corner of the metal structure, sending the younger woman crumbling to the floor. Lottie and the other girls stood there, unable to move as the older woman stood over her fallen adversary. "Disrespect my family again and I'll knock your bloody teeth down your throat. Do I make myself clear?"

The younger woman stared upwards, her glassy eyes barely focusing on the middle-aged woman who towered over her.

"Come on, Lottie," Judy said. "Let's go home. There's a bad smell in the air."

The headmaster, Mr Shawcross, appeared from the playground and stared down at the women on the floor. "What's going on?" he asked, looking at Judy.

"She fell and banged her head against the bus stop. Those bloody paving slabs. You should phone the Corporation and get them fixed. Dangerous, if you ask me," she replied, smiling sweetly at the man, before walking off with Lottie, hand in hand.

Shawcross stood there, looking down at the woman on the ground, who was struggling to get to her feet with Alicia's help. He turned on his heels, striding back across the playground, a wry smile on his face. *Couldn't have happened to a nicer person,* he thought, glad that another bad apple was leaving his precious school.

"You should have seen her, Dad. Nan is the boss!" Lottie exclaimed proudly, as the foursome sat around the table, enjoying fish and chips. The table was littered with chip papers, barely leaving room for the salt and vinegar that sat together in the centre, as dinner was consumed with gusto.

"Bloody hell, Judy," John exclaimed, trying to process the information coming his way. His dear mother-in-law had knocked out the local toe-rag, giving her the slap that she so dearly deserved. "I'm never tangling with you!"

Bob placed his hand over hers, smiling at his woman. "She's a feisty old boot, this one," he added, before stuffing a piece of cod into his mouth, the batter crunching loudly as the man chomped away happily.

"Less of the old," she admonished, squeezing his hand, a playful smile spreading across her face. "She just got what was coming to her. No one messes with or disrespects my family."

"Well, let's hope that she doesn't involve the police," Bob replied soberly.

"Let her," Judy countered defiantly. "In fact, I want them knocking on my door. They've never caught her scumbag of a brother, yet they'd cart an old lady off to the police station."

"I thought you said 'less of the old'?" John challenged, waving his fork at her.

"I know I did," she smirked. "But I'd play the little old granny in a heartbeat if they turned up."

John laughed, for the first time in what seemed like ages. He was smiling, the muscles in his face unused to the action, preferring the regular frown that followed him around. "Well, Lottie probably won't be seeing much of Alicia now. I wouldn't have thought she'd be going into the Sixth Form. So, hopefully, that's the end of it."

"I'll drink to that," Judy stated, hefting a large mug of tea from the crowded tabletop.

"I'm finished, Dad. Can I leave the table? Got a few things to do on my computer."

John looked at his daughter and smiled. "Okay, sweetheart. You can leave us old folk to tidy up."

"Thanks, Dad," she replied happily, hugging John. "I'll be back down in a bit."

A minute later, Lottie was sat at her PC, logging into Facebook, her fingers flying over the keyboard, before clicking *ENTER*. Next to her, a small notebook lay open, with a black biro placed on top. "Now, Detective Wilson. Let's do some digging."

She grabbed the pen, writing down four names on the page, leaving enough space, just in case she found anything out. She entered a name in the search bar. *Tracey Teale*. She found Alicia's mother after a few seconds, clicking onto her profile. *Damn,* she thought, finding very little information. Only one blurry picture and no friends listed was enough for the teenager to abandon that search. She typed another name into the search bar. *Dean Teale*. Lottie scrolled through various hits, finding nothing. She deleted the name and typed *Deano Teale,* mentally crossing her fingers, in hope of a result. After a few minutes, Lottie took a swig of Coke, her enthusiasm slightly deflated. *Shit. Nothing.*

"Lottie," John called from downstairs, "do you want a drink?"

"No thanks, Dad," she replied, minimising the internet window. "I've got a Coke."

"Okay."

She continued, typing *Jerome Marshall* into the search bar. After a minute of searching, Lottie tossed the pen at the screen, the plastic biro clattering back onto her desk. *This is harder than I thought*. She remembered Angie's comments earlier about the frustrations involved in police work. Blowing out a deep sigh, Lottie typed in her last option, *MJ Kerr*. There were only a handful of profiles, many without profile pictures. Her eyes drifted towards a profile, with a small photograph. Clicking on it, Lottie was taken to the profile page of MJ Kerr, which showed a picture of a dark-haired woman with a small mole on her face standing in front of what looked like a large building on a sunny day. *Hmm*. Her interest piqued as her eyes fell on a small pendant around her neck. She looked closer, her eyes widening when she realised what the pendant's design was. *Birmingham City*.

There were a few likes for the picture as Lottie clicked the mouse to see who had approved of the profile picture. The person at the top of the list drew her eye. Not because of her name, Gabrielle Phillips, but because of her profile picture. *Jesus!* Lottie clicked on the profile, her pulse racing as the main picture presented itself to her. It was MJ Kerr, formally Mandy Terry who looked back at her. There were many likes, loves and comments, which the teenager began looking through slowly. There were many *'thinking of you'* comments, along with, *'I'm here if you need me, hun'.*

"So, this Gabrielle must know her, maybe a family member," she muttered to herself, taking a swig of Coke to ease the dryness of her throat. She looked at Gabrielle's *About* tab, seeing that she lived in Leicestershire. Backing up a few clicks, Lottie opened a Word document, taking screenshots of MJ Kerr's profile, along with Gabrielle's. She then saved the document into a folder on her computer, finishing the Coke before sitting there in silence to take stock. *So, MJ and Gabrielle could be family. And if so, Gabrielle might know MJ's son. The man who killed my mother.*

45

Lottie and Sharon sat on the swings, the spring sunshine bathing the park in warmth. The small play area was almost deserted, save for a few toddlers and adoring parents a few feet away, blissfully unaware of the two teenagers. Sharon offered a packet of cigarettes to Lottie, who shook her head. "No thanks," the blonde teenager said politely. "You really shouldn't, it's bad for you."

Sharon blew a puff of smoke out of her nose, trying her hardest not to cough. "I don't really care. What's the worst that could happen? Cancer? I couldn't care less at the moment."

"Okay," Lottie acquiesced. "Just don't smoke too much."

"I won't. I can't really afford it. I only bought these because I stole some money out of Dad's wallet, not that he would bother to check. He's too busy texting his bitches."

"Is it still that bad?"

Sharon turned on her swing, looking at her best friend. "It's all the time. I even checked his phone when he went to the shops. Jesus! Some of the messages were disgusting."

"Like what?" Lottie asked, suddenly very curious. She'd never had a boyfriend or experienced her first proper kiss, but through the passage of time and school the teenager was very aware of matters of intimacy.

Sitting next to adolescent boys for the last few years, Lottie had picked up on many conversations about what went on, even if her classmates spun their tales in crude fashion.

"One woman, Jane, wants him to come over this weekend and punish her for being a naughty girl. When I read it, I was like, gross!"

Lottie laughed, feeling her cheeks begin to flush. "God! Do women actually talk like that?"

"These women do. It's disgusting. My dad's old. He shouldn't be doing stuff like this anymore."

"To be fair, he's probably the same age as my dad. It's just gross when it's your own parents, I guess."

"How is your dad?" Sharon asked.

"He's not the same guy anymore. He blames himself for your mum's death. Even though it's been two years since it happened, he's still heartbroken."

"It's not his fault," Sharon stated quietly. "I know he probably shouldn't have got involved. But you said yourself, that guy who killed Mum would never have left him alone. I just want him to pay for what he's done."

"I know. I do, too. And I've been doing a bit of detective work on Facebook. Found a few things out."

"Really," the other girl replied, a surprised look on her face. "Like what?"

"Nothing on the guy who killed Zoe. But I found a few more things out. The mother of the boys that killed my mum. As you know, she was killed by this Jerome and Deano. I found her profile. And she has someone, probably a family member who lives in Leicester."

"And?" Sharon replied, her surprised expression now a mask of confusion.

"And I don't know. That's as far as I got. But I'm hoping that this Gabrielle might know the man who killed Mum?"

"But isn't he in prison?"

"Well, yes," Lottie responded evenly, brushing a stray lock of blonde hair away from her face. "But he might get out one day."

"Okay. And then what? Are you going to hunt him down and kill him?"

Lottie sighed, realising how ridiculous her recent fantasies now sounded. "No. He'd probably kill me, too."

"So where is this leading?"

"I don't know," Lottie wondered, feeling uneasy. "I just wanted to find out about them, is all."

"Well, it looks like a waste of time to me."

"I know. Lame, right?"

"Totally. We just need to let it lie. We'll be starting Sixth Form or work soon. Dad says I need to concentrate on that."

"Maybe he's right?"

Sharon nodded, jumping off the swing. "One day, they'll catch Mum's killer. Then, I'll feel better. And hopefully, the man that killed your mum will never be released. Let's hold that thought, eh?"

Lottie nodded, linking arms with her friend as they walked out of the playground, a nagging doubt tugging at her mind. *But what if he does get let out? And how would I find him?*

Gabrielle stared at the laptop. A large glass of wine sat next to it. Beads of condensation dripped down the stem, slowly pooling on the pine coffee table. She took a large swig, enjoying the crisp taste of the Pinot Grigio as her eyes played over the screen in front of her. She ran her fingers through curly brown hair, pleased with what she'd been able to find out over the past few years, in between looking after her tribe of children and studying an Open University course. Since MJ had been killed, Gabrielle had spent countless hours trying to find out the whereabouts of her killers. The woman knew Jerome was one of them, the other was possibly a man called Deano. Gabrielle knew this, as she had been receiving texts from MJ shortly before she'd died. With that in mind, she'd started to scour the internet for them. She'd been met by a social media brick wall, unable to glean any information from Facebook, Instagram, Twitter and others.

However, that had recently changed. *Time has made them sloppy,* she thought, looking at the profile of Deano Teale. She'd found both him and Jerome as both of them had created Facebook accounts recently, a handful of friends and a very limited amount of photographs adorning their pages.

Wanting to keep hold of as much information as possible, Gabrielle had taken screenshots of pictures and friends lists, saving them to her laptop. From Marshall's profile, she'd been unable to find out anything pertinent to his location. His one picture was a close-up selfie of a dark-skinned man sporting a pair of black sunglasses and there was very little else to go on. No other information was listed. No friends, education or locations could be found over the past few weeks that Gabrielle had been looking.

She'd found out much more about Deano by studying his main profile picture and the one other photograph on his timeline. The picture was taken at a bar. Half of Jerome's head was visible on the right-hand-side. There was very little information, except one piece of information that had unlocked a significant door in the search for them. Behind Deano, a Mediterranean barman was sporting a bright yellow T-shirt with *Rui's Bar, Fuengirola* emblazoned across the back. When she'd first seen it, Gabrielle had opened up a search engine, finding the bar with relative ease. It even had reviews on TripAdvisor, which she'd saved to her favourites. Years before, Gabrielle had visited Spain, spending two weeks in Torremolinos with a group of her girlfriends. Now, she knew that it was merely a short drive away from the resort where Jerome and Deano may be residing.

Across the lounge, the baby monitor flickered, taking the woman's attention away from the screen for a few seconds. She watched the small plastic device, hoping that her youngest had merely stirred in her sleep. Satisfied that the child didn't need her mother, Gabrielle clicked onto Deano's friends list once more, finding his sister, Tracey Teale. She was listed as living in Rubery, Birmingham and Gabrielle remembered vaguely that she'd passed through the small suburb years before. An image flashed through her memory, a large flyover that she'd travelled along that led to the motorway a few miles further on. Tracey's friends list was small, only a handful of friends and very little activity, telling

Gabrielle that the woman from Birmingham wasn't a frequent user. Deano was one of her friends, but not Marshall. At least not yet.

She'd pondered what to do with the information, wondering if she should tell the police, who could hopefully track down the two men and bring them to justice. However, she had hesitated when she'd picked up the phone a few weeks before, opting to sit on the information. After all, she didn't want the police knocking on her door. She preferred to stay off their radar. *I'll keep this under my hat for a bit,* she thought, wondering if she would ever tell anyone else about what she'd found out.

46

MARCH - 2018

Lottie digested the news that John had just given her, not really knowing what to say. "So, what happens now, Dad?"

"Not sure," her father replied. "I've never really been made redundant before. I left the Marines when you were a little girl and have worked at this place ever since."

"Why are they letting you go?"

"They gave a big speech in the canteen, blaming Brexit and external forces. The usual crap. Anyway, I'm not that bothered. The house is paid off and I've been putting a bit away over the years. So, you've no need to worry, princess."

"Are you going to get another job?"

"Yes," John replied. "But I might take a bit of a break. There are jobs to do around the house, which I've let slip over the years. I might concentrate on that for a few months and then sign on with an agency when you return to Sixth Form in the autumn."

"Okay, Dad. Whatever you think is best. Will you get a pay-out?"

"Yes. But it's not much. Couple of thousand. Maybe, once you've learnt to drive, we could put the money towards your first car?"

"Really?" Lottie exclaimed, a surprised look on her face.

"Sure. You're nearly seventeen. You need to learn to drive as soon as you can. The longer you leave it, the harder it will be. Let's get you some lessons booked soon. Your birthday is only a few months away."

Lottie snuggled into her father on the settee. "You're the best, Dad."

He kissed the top of her head, the curls tickling his nose. "I'm just your dad and want to do what's right for you. Anyway, how was school today?"

"Sixth Form?"

"Sorry, my bad," he replied, half-smiling. "Sixth Form."

"It was okay. I think I'm all set for my exams in May."

"That's good. I'm sorry if I don't ask enough questions, sweetheart."

"Dad, that's okay. I know you are interested. But you've got work to deal with and you've been through a lot over the past few years."

"Tell me about it," he sighed. "How's Sharon getting on?"

"She's okay. Hates living with her dad. She said as soon as she can, she'll move out. Don't blame her. He's a right moron."

"I never met him. Zoe told me enough to know that he's really up himself."

"I still think about her, Dad. She was lovely."

John smiled, an image flashing before him of a dark-haired woman with an infectious smile. "I know. I miss her, too. I think we could have made a go of it. I think we could have been something."

"Would you have married her?" Lottie asked.

"Maybe. I only ever assumed I'd be married once. After your mum died, I never thought I'd meet anyone else, let alone marry them. But Zoe was great. I think we'd have made a great team, especially as you and Sharon are such good mates."

"Life's so unfair, Dad," his daughter replied, moving across the settee away from John. "Innocent people get hurt and no one really pays for it. It's total bollocks!"

"I know, Lottie," John replied, wondering what other swear words his daughter had as part of her vocabulary. "I wish I could turn back the clock. I wish I could have protected your mother and Zoe. But I couldn't, and I'll have to live with that."

"That's why I want to join the police. Even if I save one life, it will be enough, Dad. Even if I stop scumbags like that Deano from hurting anyone, I'll be happy with that."

"I know. And even though I'm not completely happy with your choice, it's your choice to make. I know you've done the right thing and I know you'll make a cracking policewoman. By the way, you've not mentioned Alicia for a while. Any more problems?"

"None. I never thought she'd make Sixth Form, but she's kept her head down and seems to be doing okay. Plus, most of her school friends have now left, so perhaps she's grown up a bit?"

"Or maybe the sight of Judy giving her mum a slap has made her think twice about messing with you?" John wondered, winking at his only daughter.

"Oh God! That was so cool. Nanny Judy is just the best. She certainly knows how to stand up for herself, and us."

"That she does," John replied. "I don't know what we'd do without her."

His expression dropped slightly as he recalled the conversation he'd had with his mother-in-law a few days before. *Please be okay, Judy,* he thought. *We need you.*

The man stepped off the bus, trying to get his bearings. It had been many years since he'd visited the area as new houses and shops confused him momentarily, before he spotted a familiar landmark. Walking past the public house with a large play area at the side, he turned left onto a long street, packed with terraced houses. He pulled a note out of his pocket, checking the address that was written down before continuing. His stride was loping, long arms swaying by his sides, his grey T-shirt clinging to a body that was totally devoid of fat. He dodged bins and bags of rubbish left strewn on the uneven pavement, trying to remember the house number. After a few minutes' walk, the man knocked on a front door, looking left and right until footsteps could be heard on the other side of the door.

A woman opened it, having to look up at the man standing before her, even though she stood on the front doorstep. "Yes?" she said, her face inquisitive.

"You don't remember me, do you?" he replied, his voice deep and gravelly.

She looked at him, a flicker of recognition dawning in her eyes. The man was tall, well over six feet tall, with a bald head, flame-red beard and piercing eyes. "Sean? Is it really you?"

"It's me, Aunt Gabrielle," he responded, his face impassive.

"Jesus!" she blurted. "Come in." Gabrielle stood to one side as Sean passed her into the tight hallway, his bulk barely fitting between her and the bare-plastered wall. "When did you get out?"

"A few days ago," Sean replied. "Mum sent me a note in prison, telling me to look you up if I ever got out."

"Go through to the kitchen. Most of the kids are out. My youngest, Clarissa, is asleep upstairs." She followed him into the small kitchen, noting how his wide shoulders almost brushed the two door jambs. *God! He's huge,* she thought as she nudged past him on her way to the kettle. "You fancy a brew?"

"Coffee, please. Black, no sugar."

"Okay," she replied busying herself with the drinks. Something about her second nephew unnerved her. It wasn't just his size or his piercing grey eyes. He seemed emotionless, almost robotic. "Pull up a stool," she suggested as the kettle began to boil.

"I went to Mum's house but someone else answered. Where is she?"

Placing a mug of black coffee in front of the man, Gabrielle steeled herself. "Sean, your Mum died."

He didn't flinch. "When?"

"A few years ago."

"Where?" His voice was monotone.

"Scotland," Gabrielle replied, her pulse beginning to quicken.

"What was she doing in Scotland?"

"She moved there once she was released, to start a new life."

"How did she die? Was she ill?"

"Sean. Prepare yourself. She was murdered."

Sean flinched, his eyes locking onto Gabrielle's "Go on?"

Gabrielle recounted MJ, formally Mandy's, story. How she'd been tracked down by two men, who'd then killed her, throwing her off a cliff. Sean sat impassive, sipping his coffee as the woman gave him the information. "She gave me a letter to give to you, Sean. She told me that if you ever turned up here, I was to hand it over to you, and you only."

"Okay. I will read it in a minute. The men who killed her, were they arrested?"

"No," she replied. "The police never found them. Hang on here. I'll check on Clarissa and get you the letter." She left him in the kitchen, sipping at his coffee as she padded upstairs to check on her daughter and retrieve the letter.

Gabrielle made her way downstairs, placing the white envelope in front of Sean. "Here you go."

He split the seal, gently pulling out a piece of lined paper. Placing his coffee on the counter, he began reading.

Sean

If you're reading this, chances are I am probably long gone. Gabrielle will explain what has happened. You're probably mad at me for never once visiting you? And I'm sorry, I just couldn't bear to see you in prison. I have thought about you every day since you were taken from me. What you look like, how you were getting on and whether you would ever be released?

My heart was broken when you did what you did. And then we lost Luke, which broke my heart even more. I know you both did wrong. But, you're still my boys and a mother never stops loving her babies. And I will always love you both, from the bottom of my heart.

I moved to Scotland to start a new life after I was released. Nan has been living with me and life has been okay. I recently met a man called Felipe, who is kind and has treated me well. He owns the local chip shop and we've kinda hit it off.

However, Jerome and his friends have found me, and he wants the money I took from him all those years ago. They've already tried to hurt me, but Felipe helped me fight them off. But I know they will return to take the money and do me harm. He'll never find it though. But you will, Sean. On the back of the note is where it's hidden.

Please don't think badly of me. We've both done bad things, but we're not bad people, deep down.

I will always love you, wherever you are and whatever you do.

Mum xx

Gabrielle watched him as he read the back of the note. She noticed a small scar, just below his right eye, a small white line in an otherwise unblemished complexion. The woman wondered how prison life had been for him… what he had endured and what kind of man had taken his first steps towards freedom a few days before.

He placed the paper on the table, wiping a stray tear from his cheek. "I need to go to Scotland," he stated matter-of-factly.

"I thought you'd probably say that," Gabrielle replied, rising from her stool. She walked over to a cupboard and took a small biscuit barrel from the top shelf. She removed the lid, taking a bundle of notes from the porcelain jar. "Here," she said, handing him a wad of cash. "It's not much. Couple of hundred, but that should get you there."

"Thanks," he replied, tucking the money into his jeans pocket.

As Sean folded his arms on the table, Gabrielle noticed the thick muscle and bulging veins on show across his freckled skin. "I know where they all live, Sean," she told him. "Jerome and Deano are in Spain. I'm certain of it. I found Deano's profile on Facebook. His main picture was taken in a place called Fuengirola. Deano's sister lives in Birmingham, near to where the old car factory used to be. If you find her, you'll find them."

"I want to know everything. And then I will find them."

"And then what?" Gabrielle asked, not really wanting to hear the answer.

"I'll make them pay. All of them."

47

Twenty-four hours later, Sean stepped off the local bus, shouldering a dark backpack. He'd bought it, along with a black hooded top, with the money that Gabrielle had given him. He knew the pack would come in handy. The sky was clear, the weather warm by Scottish standards as the man crossed the main road towards a convenience store. A few minutes later, he walked back onto the pavement, downing half a bottle of Fanta. Wiping his mouth, Sean took out the piece of paper from his pocket, reading the address on the rear of the note.

A young woman approached, pushing a buggy proudly in front of her. Sean stepped into her view, clearing his throat. "Excuse me, do you know where Cromarty Street is, please?"

The woman stopped in her tracks, looking up at the imposing figure in front of her. She pulled the buggy to one side as his grey eyes looked at her impassively. "Yes," she said, her thick Scottish accent pleasing to Sean's ears. "Go to the end of the street, turn left and it's first on your right."

"Cheers," Sean replied, smiling. He took a step back, letting the young mother carry on her way as he finished his bottle of Fanta. He finished his drink, discarding the empty bottle in a bin before striding towards his destination as seagulls flew overhead. He'd not heard them for many years, trying to remember the last time their calls had drifted to him on the breeze. He couldn't remember, knowing that it was probably when he was a small boy. *Probably Weston-Super-Mare,* he thought, knowing it was his mother's choice for a family holiday.

A minute later, he arrived at a small terraced building, divided into two flats. He pressed the bell, waiting patiently for a few seconds before the front door opened slowly.

"Yes?" an old lady said, eyeing Sean warily from behind the door.

"Hi. I am looking for my mum. She used to live here. MJ Kerr."

"Never heard of her," the silver-haired woman replied. "I moved in a few months ago. There was an old lady that lived here before, but she died."

"That must have been my great-grandmother," Sean countered. "When did she die?"

"No idea. I was just told by the council that the previous tenant had died and that the flat was available."

"Do you have a number for the council? I could give them a call and ask if they know any more details?"

"Sorry, but I don't and I'm about to go to the shops. I'm sorry, I can't help you more."

"Thanks anyway," Sean replied, walking away from the front door.

He headed along the street, waiting at the corner for a few minutes, his eyes fixed on the property. Sure enough, the elderly woman exited the flat a few minutes later, heading away from Sean along the street. *Now or never,* he thought, walking back towards the terraced building. He tried the front door, silently cursing that it was locked securely. Looking to his left, he noticed an entryway a few doors further down the street. *Bingo.* He hustled down the narrow space, turning right into a tight footpath with high fences on either side. Counting the buildings, Sean calculated the gate he needed to gain access to and smiled as it opened onto a small yard with barely a whisper.

He walked over to the kitchen door, shaking his head in disbelief when it, too, opened silently. *Silly old cow,* he thought. *You wanna keep your shit locked up. You never know who might be lurking around.* He found himself inside a small kitchen, the smell of cabbage overpowering, reminding him of prison. Shaking off the memory, he strode to the cupboard under the stairs and opened the door, the hinges protesting loudly. He felt around the cupboard, finding the light switch and flicking it down. The cramped space was immediately bathed in warm light and his eyes headed north towards the sloping ceiling. *Gotcha!* There was a small crack in the white panel where it met the stairs above. Sean prised it open with his fingers. A shoebox slipped forward, the big man pulling it from its hiding place.

"Please be in here," he whispered to himself. He removed the dusty lid and drew his breath in sharply as his eyes fell on the rolls of banknotes. "Thank you, Mum. I'll use this to set the record straight."

Placing the cover back onto the box, he refitted the wooden panel and two minutes later, Sean was heading back to the bus stop, his backpack considerably heavier than it had been when he'd arrived in Castletown thirty minutes before. His face was impassive, his insides the opposite. Building tension seeped through his body, fuelling another emotion. Rage.

Twenty minutes later, he stepped down from the bus, heading along a busy street in nearby Thurso. He stopped across the road from the local chip shop, his stomach grumbling. Sean walked across the street and as he pushed open the glass door, the smell of chips assailed his nostrils, setting his mouth watering. A Mediterranean-looking man appeared from the rear of the premises, smiling at the bigger man across the counter. "What can I get you?" he asked, his Scottish accent at odds with his olive complexion.

"Fish and chips, please," Sean replied, eyeing the man as he set to work.

"Salt and vinegar?"

Sean nodded in response. "Is your name Felipe?" he asked the man behind the counter.

"Yes. Why?"

"You knew my mother, MJ?"

"Sean?" Felipe exclaimed, his eyes widening.

"Yeah," was his simple reply.

Felipe placed the wrapped bundle of fish and chips on top of the glass-fronted display, wiping his hands on a white towel. "What are you doing here?"

"Just sorting a few things out before I head back down south."

"I'm really sorry about what happened to your Mother. MJ was a lovely woman."

"She wrote me a letter and said that you were together at the time she was killed. She said you were a good man and that you treated her well."

Felipe looked at the man, wondering what he'd been through during his years of incarceration. Although tall himself, the Spaniard was dwarfed by the younger man with the bald head and red beard. There was a look about him that made Felipe's insides constrict, making him nervous. "She was a real lady. And real ladies deserve to be treated well."

"You were there when Jerome sent his thugs to find her." It was a statement, not a question.

"Yes," Felipe responded, suddenly wary of the big man. *He may be police. I need to tread carefully.* "They roughed us up a bit, but we managed to fight them off. Then they came back a few weeks later. That's when they caught up with your mother whilst she was out walking. We were due to go out for dinner. I knew something was up when she didn't call or turn up for our date. I went to her flat and her nan told me she'd not seen her for hours and was getting worried. I'm really sorry for what happened to her."

"It's not your fault," Sean replied, a tiny part of him feeling sympathy for the chip shop owner. "But I'll find them. You can count on that."

"Do you know where they are?"

"Can I eat while we talk?"

"Sure. It's closing time anyway. Do me a favour and flip the sign on the door, please."

Sean did so, walking back to retrieve his lunch. He leaned against the wall, placing his lunch on the counter as he dug in. "Nice," he replied simply, taking a blue plastic fork from a dispenser next to the till. "There are three of them. Deano, his sister and Jerome. From what I've found out, the sister lives in Birmingham. Jerome and Deano are in Spain, I think."

"Spain. Whereabouts?" Felipe asked.

"Fuengi-something," Sean replied, trying to remember the name of the resort.

"Fuengirola. It's on the Costa del Sol. My cousin lives in nearby Malaga."

"Okay. Is it easy to get to?"

"Yes," Felipe confirmed, becoming animated. "If you fly to Malaga, there is a local bus that goes all the way to Marbella in the west." The Spaniard took out a pen and pulled a notepad from behind the till. He scribbled something down, handing it to Sean, who had almost finished his meal. "Here. This is my number. If you are going, call or text me a few days before. I will then call my cousin. He will put you up while you're down there. Just be careful, though."

"Careful, why?"

"Because the Costa del Sol has many criminals. And if these two men are there, chances are they're connected."

"I can handle myself. And I have the edge. I know what they look like, but they don't know who I am."

"Well, just take care of yourself. And remember to call me."

"How much for the fish and chips," Sean asked, reaching into his pocket.

"It's on the house."

Sean extended his hand across the counter. Felipe took it, attempting to match the bigger man's grip. "We'll probably never meet again. Thank you for being nice to my mum."

"Think nothing of it. Best of luck."

Sean walked out of the chip shop, becoming lost to sight a few seconds later. Felipe stood there, digesting what had just happened. *I'm glad he's not hunting for me,* he thought, an involuntary shiver running through his body.

~

Hours later, Sean stepped off the train at New Street station in Birmingham. Tired and achy from the journey, he walked stiffly out of the newly refurbished travel hub, heading into the darkened streets of Birmingham. *Need a hotel,* he thought. *Somewhere low-key that won't ask questions.*

He walked down ill-lit streets, heading towards Digbeth, with its bars and large bus garage. The Probation Service had fixed the man up with accommodation following his release. Sean had stayed there for a short time before informing his Probation Officer that he was going to visit family in Leicester for a few weeks. He knew that he would return there in due course and he'd made a mental note to stop off at a post office to grab a passport application form, Spain being his destination.

Just off the main drag, he found a tired-looking bed and breakfast and paid the Polish receptionist cash for his night's stay. Sean made his way up the stairs, fighting with the stiff lock on his door before it gave way. *Jesus. What a shithole. Makes my prison cell look like the Hyatt.* The double bed was the centrepiece of the room, with barely enough space around it for the big man to walk. A small en-suite shower room was to its right, appearing to be the newest edition to the tired hotel room. He stripped off, neatly folding his clothing before placing it on a small desk that sat underneath a flat-screen television. Sean scratched at his shoulder, his fingernails grazing an old stab wound, high up on his back. Two other puncture wounds just out of reach completed the set. "Let's hope the water is hot," he muttered, stepping into a small cubicle and firing up the shower. Sure enough, the water soon warmed up, pulsing against his skin, battering his bald pate. The minutes ticked by, Sean standing statue-still as the bathroom fogged up, the steam dissipating into the hotel room.

Leaving the hotel twenty minutes later, Sean found a local convenience store, where he bought a litre bottle of vodka and a selection of snacks to tide him over for his night's stay. As he lay in bed, a discarded sandwich wrapper on the bed next to him, his vodka bottle open on a bedside table, Sean took stock. *I need a bank account, a passport and a mobile phone,* he thought, as tiredness quickly overcame him. As he slid into slumber, the last images floating in his mind were of two men. Two killers who he'd set his sights on.

48

APRIL - 2018

"Sean, take a break," the warehouse supervisor shouted from across the goods-in area.

"Okay. Cheers," the bigger man replied, moving his fully-laden pallet truck out of the way of passing forklift trucks. He dug into the pocket of his high visibility vest, retrieving a packet of cigarettes as he walked towards the far corner of the warehouse. He stepped out, hunkering down as he strode across the yard, torrential rain battering him. Once inside the smoking shelter, he shook himself down, lighting his cigarette as a fellow employee sat on a plastic chair watching him closely.

"Lovely day," the young woman said, blowing smoke into the air.

"Sure is," Sean responded, pulling up another plastic chair.

"How are you getting on?" she asked, her eyes drawn to the muscled arms and tight-fitting work trousers.

"It's a job."

"I'm Mandy," the woman replied, holding out a hand.

Sean almost flinched, the woman's name giving him a split-second flashback to his mother. The moment passed and Sean took the proffered hand, shaking it briefly. "Sean."

"You settling in okay?"

"I guess. I'm just getting used to life on the outside."

"How long were you in for?"

"A long time," Sean replied evasively.

"Okay. I won't ask any more questions on that subject. That's your business. Just be careful of some of the other guys, though. You're not the first ex-con to work here. Many don't stick around too long."

Sean nodded, drawing on his cigarette. "Thanks for the advice."

"You live nearby?" Mandy asked neutrally, even though she wanted to find out more about the quiet man opposite her.

"Selly Oak," he replied. "I was staying in Lozells for a few weeks, but they moved me closer to work, which is good. Getting a bus across town every day would be a pain in the arse. I can pretty much walk to work."

"I take it you don't have a car?"

Sean shook his head. "I never learnt to drive. But I will." He looked at the woman, trying to discern if he found her appealing. She looked to be a few years older than him, her dark hair pulled back into a ponytail. Her bare forearms were covered in ink, another tattoo on her neck, partially hidden by her polo shirt. *Not bad,* he thought.

"Plenty of time, I guess," she replied. "Have you been out much?"

"Not really. There's a pub down the road from where I live. Popped in a few times."

God! He's not very chatty, she thought. *But I get it.* "Some good bars in Selly Oak, if you don't mind all the bloody students."

He blew out a stream of smoke, flicking the ash onto the wet tarmac. "I'm sure I'll get around to it once I've found my bearings. Where do you live?"

"Rubery," Mandy replied.

The hairs on the back of Sean's neck prickled to attention. "Rubery? Do you know a Tracey Teale?"

The woman considered the question, shaking her head after a few seconds. "Doesn't sound familiar. Why?"

"I went to school with her." The lie came out of his mouth seamlessly. "I heard that she lives in Rubery. Are there many pubs there?"

"Not really. There's the Rose and Crown, which is a bit of a dive.

Hollywood Bowl is just down the road but is packed full of kids at the weekends. I generally use the Hare and Hounds in Rednal. It's about a mile away from where I live. Decent pub, but it's always busy at the weekends, too. You should come for a drink sometime. Some of the lads from the warehouse have a Saturday afternoon session in there."

"Sounds like a good idea," Sean replied, an idea forming in his mind. "Let me know when you're going next."

"Okay, will do. Anyway, my break is up, catch you later," Mandy replied, before dodging puddles and raindrops on her way back into the warehouse.

"See you later." Sean pulled out his mobile phone, activating the device. He clicked onto the Facebook icon, scrolling through his very limited newsfeed. It was all new to him, the social media platform only coming to prominence once he was in prison. He understood how it worked and why people spent their days fascinated by it. For Sean, though, it was a tool. A way to locate a few key people. His friends' list was very select, only Gabrielle and a few ex-inmates a part of his network. He clicked onto the search bar, Tracey Teale's profile appearing at the top. Selecting her profile, he gazed at her picture, burning the image into his brain. *Stage one. Find this bitch. Then make her talk.*

John pulled up on Rubery's main street, parking his car in front of the local bookmakers. As he crossed the road towards the park, he unzipped his thin jacket. The spring afternoon was brightening up after the heavy shower that had battered the land a few hours before. He saw a group of teenagers gathered around the park's play area. Walking closer, he spotted his daughter's blonde hair in the crowd and made his way through a yellow gate.

"Hey," he called.

Lottie and Sharon turned around.

"Hi, Dad," Lottie chirped, walking over to him with Sharon and another girl, who looked vaguely familiar. "You remember Alicia?"

"Yes," John replied. The third girl gave him a brief smile. "You all friends now?"

"Yeah," Lottie agreed.

John looked at Sharon, who seemed a little more guarded. *You're not too happy about it, though. And who could blame you?* he thought.

"Okay, cool," John said. "Anyway. Are you ready?"

"Yeah," Lottie replied, turning to Alicia. "See you Monday."

Climbing into the car a few minutes later, John turned to his daughter. "How come you've become friendly with that girl? I thought you were sworn enemies?"

"She's okay, Dad. I think she was in with the wrong crowd at school. Anyway, most of them have now left and Alicia wants to do well in Sixth Form so she can get a decent job."

"And you, Sharon. How do you feel about her?"

"She's okay," the girl on the back seat shrugged. "I know her uncle did what he did. But she's not seen him in ages. And her mother is going off the rails, too. I think as soon as she can, Alicia will move out and go it alone. And who can blame her? Her Mum's either pissed or stoned most of the time."

Life's so simple when you're a kid, he thought. *They see things so differently.* "Okay. Well, what are you girls doing now?"

"Can Sharon come back to ours for a bit? Her dad can pick her up later," Lottie replied.

"Is that okay with you, Sharon? Does your father know where you are?"

"That's fine, Mr Wilson. I sent him a text earlier, saying I might go to Lottie's after Sixth Form. He can pick me up on his way home from the gym."

"Okay then," John replied, buckling his seatbelt. "I'll cook Spaghetti Bolognese. Does that sound good to you two?"

"Perfect, Dad," Lottie replied happily.

"Sounds good to me," Sharon concurred, from the rear of the car.

John pulled away from the kerb, heading away from Rubery towards home, a nagging doubt clawing at the back of his brain.

49

MAY - 2018

For the third Saturday in a row, Sean found himself riding a double-decker bus towards the Lickey Hills, an afternoon of drinking on the cards. On his previous two visits, he'd been keeping an eye out for Tracey Teale, but there had been no sign of her. He'd even walked the streets of Rubery after leaving the pub, popping into the Rose and Crown and Hollywood Bowl, in an attempt to find her.

The weather had warmed up considerably and the large man had opted for a pair of camouflaged combat shorts and a white polo shirt, new editions to his growing wardrobe. He stepped off the bus at the top of a tree-lined dual-carriageway and gazed across at the Hare and Hounds public house, gently nestled next to the forested hills above. As he approached the pub, he lit a cigarette, noticing several afternoon revellers in the pub's beer garden. Men were laughing and slapping each other on the back, women were sitting on sturdy wooden benches as various multi-coloured drinks adorned the tables.

He shouldered his way in through a set of double doors, walking over towards the bar where his work colleagues stood drinking. "Hey, Sean," Mandy chirped, gently punching him on the arm as he approached.

"Hi," he replied, attempting to make his smile genuine. It didn't come naturally for Sean. He'd spent twelve years in prison, mostly keeping himself to himself, or fighting off fellow inmates who wanted a piece of the murderer. Many had tried, a few succeeding in giving the young man a couple of souvenirs to remember them by. This new life seemed alien to him. People were nice, not judging him on his past. However, he understood that no one really knew what he'd done. How he'd snatched a young girl and then killed her mother. Not that he'd given them much thought over the years that followed. Or the family that had to deal with the pain and heartache of losing a loved one.

"Pint?" Mandy asked, looking a different woman to the one he worked with. High visibility clothing and safety boots had been replaced with a halter neck top and tight jeans. His eyes drifted south, liking the firm physique and pert breasts that were on display under his nose.

"Please," he replied, nodding to his fellow workers, whose conversation had suddenly dried up. *They don't like me. And that's fine. I don't like them.*

She handed him a pint of lager as Sean nodded his thanks. "Cheers," he said, smiling at the woman in front of him.

"My pleasure," she replied, her eyes lingering on him for a few seconds.

A burst of raucous laughter erupted behind them, making Sean turn around. Just out of sight, a table of women were already well-oiled, laughing at some unknown joke. *Looks like I'm in for a long afternoon,* Sean thought, as he took a long pull on his beer.

Another bottle of Prosecco landed on the table, Lorna elbowing Tina as she sat down. "Look at him," she exclaimed, pointing towards a tall, well-built man at the bar. He had a shaven head, a well-trimmed beard and a physique that made all four sets of eyes gaze at his rear end.

"He looks like that guy from *Vikings*," Charlotte replied, popping the cork from the wine bottle.

"Who, *Thor*?" Tracey asked.

"Thor is from The *Avengers*," Charlotte chided. "She means *Vikings*. It's on the telly. He's pretty fit, though, but not that old."

"He's probably pushing thirty," Tracey observed, eyeing up the mystery man. "He's big. I wonder if he's big all over?"

The foursome laughed, each thinking the same thing. "He's been standing there for a while, by the look of it," Charlotte added. "I heard a bit of chit-chat while I was getting served. I think they all work together, by the look of it."

"He's looking over," Lorna said excitedly. All four women looked up at Sean, his piercing grey eyes picking out Tracey. His stare lingering on her for a few seconds, a flash of something appearing in his eyes.

"He's checking you out, Tracey," Tina added, feeling a pang of jealousy towards her friend.

"He's not," Tracey responded. "Probably just people-watching. Hang on, he's coming this way." The four women looked up at him as the man walked past, heading outside towards the smoking area.

"He was definitely checking you out. He's gone for a fag. Go out and break the ice," Charlotte urged enthusiastically.

"Okay," Tracey agreed, grabbing her bag from the table. "If I'm not back in five minutes, you know I've hit the jackpot." She rose from the table, pulling her cigarettes out of her leather bag. A few seconds later, she was leant against the smoking area, its covered roof protecting her from the warm sun overhead. The man stood on the opposite side, engrossed in his phone. "Have you got a light?" she asked, even though her lighter was firmly ensconced in her bag.

"Sure," Sean responded, smiling as he walked over. He handed her his disposable lighter, his expression warm and friendly. "Here you go."

"Cheers," she nodded, lighting her cigarette before handing him the lighter back. "Not seen you in here before."

"I was here last week. My mates from work invited me out for a few beers."

"Well, I've not been up for a few weeks. We're having a girly night out, although we usually don't make it past seven. I'm Tracey." The woman extending a hand, smiling up at him.

Gotcha! "I'm Sean," he replied, taking her small hand in his, gently squeezing it. "Nice to meet you." He looked her up and down, noticing a small Chinese symbol on her bare ankle. His eyes ventured north, liking her firm legs that gave way to a short, stripy dress that showed him just what he wanted to see.

"Is your missus with you?" she asked, testing the waters.

"Nah," Sean replied. "I'm single." His voice was deep. Tracey was feeling more and more attracted to this man who loomed over her.

"Good-looking guy like you and no girlfriend? I thought they'd be queuing up!"

He laughed, his teeth white and even. "Well, if they are, I've not seen them."

"You from around here?"

"Selly Oak. And you?"

"Just down the road. Rubery."

"Is your fella waiting for you at home?"

"Not had a fella in ages. Been single for a few years. Men don't really stick around for single mothers." She left it there, to see how the man would react. She was expecting him to make his excuses and take off. Instead, he lit another cigarette, placing his lighter on the wooden table.

"Well, not all men are like that." He left it there, too, letting the woman know that being a single mum was not an issue for him.

Tracey smiled, her eyes narrowing slightly as she took in his words. "Well, I'd better head back in, or they'll be sending out a search party. Nice to meet you, Sean. Might see you back out here a bit later?"

"Hope so," the man replied, smiling at her before she headed back into the pub, pulse racing, her skin flushed.

He stood there, finishing off his cigarette, reflecting on the exchange. *That was easier than I thought. Let's see if I can reel her in?* He followed Tracey back inside, a plan hatching in his mind.

"Come on," one of the group urged as he held onto Mandy. "Let's get you on the bus."

"I'm okay," Mandy replied defiantly, her speech slurred.

The man, whose name was Wayne, looked at Sean, a wry smile on his face. "She'll be okay. We'll make sure she gets home."

"Okay," Sean replied, eyeing the swaying woman in front of him. He smiled, shaking his finger at her. "Early night for you. Hopefully, you'll be okay in the morning?"

"I'll be okay," she replied. "God! I think I'm gonna be sick." She weaved her way through the pub-goers, heading to the back of the lounge area where the toilets were located.

Sean looked at the others. "I'll see you Monday," he said, the alcohol coursing through his body. They nodded as he made his way outside, walking past the table where his new smoking partner sat with her giggling friends. He smiled at them, heading outside, the double doors closing behind him.

"Have they deserted you?" a female voice asked.

Sean looked up, seeing Tracey walking towards him, cigarette in hand. He pulled out his lighter, handing it to her. "Looks like it. One of them had too much to drink. So, I'm all alone."

"Are you staying for a few more or heading off home?" Tracey asked expectantly.

"Not sure. Do you think it's worth sticking around for a bit?"

"Buy me a drink and we'll have a talk about that," she replied huskily, blowing smoke into the air."

"Why not? What's the worst that could happen?" Sean replied, his simmering rage replaced by something stronger. Lust.

Tracey led him away from the pub, orange streetlights illuminating them. Turning right at the local chip shop, she pulled Sean up a private driveway towards the Lickey Hills, away from prying eyes. A few yards into the gloom, Tracey leaned against a garage wall, a wanton expression on her face as the man moved towards her. Their first kiss was fierce, clashing lips, teeth and tongues heightening their need for each other. She felt strong hands on her breasts and cried out as Sean pinched her nipples between forefingers and thumbs. "You like it rough?"

"Do you?" Sean replied, his breathing ragged.

"I'll let you know." They kissed again, Sean pressing himself into her, the backs of her arms grating against brickwork. She felt his arousal grinding into her as he kissed and bit at her neck, sending shivers running through her already tensed body. "Fuck me, Sean," she breathed.

He needed no further invitation as his hands snaked up her skirt, ripping her underwear off. She gasped, unbuckling his shorts, pushing them roughly to the floor. Sean stepped out of them, hitching her skirt up before entering her quickly. Her feet came off the floor as he lifted her easily against the wall. Tracey wrapped her legs around his hips, moving in synergy with the shaven-headed man as he bucked and rutted against her. They kissed again, each of them climbing towards the summit as their moans and grunts increased.

"God! I'm gonna cum," she exclaimed, feeling him stiffen inside her. Tracey dug her fingernails into his back, delighting in the rubbery muscle that moved underneath taut skin.

"Ugh," he grunted, burying his head in the crook of her neck as he tumbled over the edge with her. After a moment, her feet met the tarmac floor, both of them trying to catch their breaths.

"Jesus!" she panted, her heartbeat slowly returning to normal. "You were like a bloody caveman."

"Sorry," he replied, retrieving his shorts from the ground and pulling them up hastily. "It's been a while."

"Well, I hope that wasn't a one-off? I don't normally do that kind of thing," she lied, not wanting to sound easy.

"Me neither," Sean replied, and meaning it. He was twenty-seven years old, his virginity now broken forever. He liked it, craving more. "I'd like to see you again, Tracey, when we're not so pissed."

She smiled up at him, her hands straightening her dress. "Okay. I'll give you my number. Are you on Facebook?"

"Yes, but I don't use it much. Feel free to add me, though," he replied happily, post-orgasmic shivers still emitting small charges through his body. "Are you going back into the pub?"

"I should do, if only to let my mates know that I'm still alive. And you?" she asked.

"I'd better be heading home, I guess. I'll walk you back." They headed back down the driveway, avoiding the glances from passers-by before turning left towards the pub. After exchanging numbers, Sean kissed her fully on the lips with her friends looking on through the pub windows, mouths wide open.

"I'll text you tomorrow, babe," she said, making an effort to look presentable before turning towards the main entrance.

"Enjoy the rest of your night," he replied, before walking away from the pub, towards the bus stop a few hundred yards away.

What a night, he thought. *Broke my cherry and I've moved one step closer to finding her brother and Jerome.* His pace was steady, a serene look on his otherwise stern face as he looked forward to the next few weeks.

50

They saw each other over the coming weeks, Sean taking it slowly whilst waiting for his passport to arrive. They'd met on neutral ground, the Hare and Hounds and an old pub in Northfield being the chosen rendezvous points. When alone in his single bed, he'd scoured her Facebook account, finding out a few more interesting pieces of information about her brother. Because he was connected to Tracey on the social media platform, he could see more information about Deano. Not much, but enough to confirm that he was indeed living in southern Spain. There was even a photograph of the two half-brothers together. Sean took screenshots of all Tracey's pictures, which he saved to his gallery.

During the week, he continued to work, keeping himself off the radar and getting on with his job. A growing sense of unease was building within him as Mandy became more friendly, more flirtatious. For all his bravado as a teenager, Sean was a shy person now, feeling awkward and clumsy around women. Except for Tracey. He knew she was brazen, to which he tailored himself accordingly. She was a means to an end, another step towards reaching his goal.

As he sat at the rear of the warehouse, a thought suddenly came to him. *What do I do when I've evened the score?* He'd not planned that far ahead, avenging his mother being his sole focus, until that moment. *Well, I've got eighty grand burning a hole in my pocket. Maybe I'll stay out there? Never been to Spain. I might like it out there.* He also knew he could travel at a moment's notice, as his shiny new passport had arrived in the post a few days before.

"Penny for them?" Mandy probed, as she approached him from the rear.

"Huh?" he responded, snapping back from his thoughts. He squirmed inside, wondering if the persistent woman would keep on with her suggestions for meeting up. *If things were different, I'd take you out,* he thought. *But things aren't different and I've no time for this. I need to get you off my fucking case.*

"You look troubled, mate," she replied, pulling up a chair and lighting a cigarette. "What's up?"

"Nothing," he lied. "Just sitting here chilling."

"You've been quiet lately. You've hardly spoken to me since the pub. Have I done something wrong?"

"No. Why would you think that?"

"Because I was pissed as a rat. I hope I didn't show myself up?"

"Not at all, Mandy. I've just been busy, that's all."

"Okay. We're going up there again this weekend. You fancy it?"

He shook his head, stubbing out his cigarette. "Can't this weekend. Got a few things on."

"What's her name?" It was so blunt and to the point that Sean almost flinched.

"What makes you say that?"

"I'm not blind, mate. That day in the pub, there was a group of women all checking you out. And every time you went out for a fag, the women in the stripy dress followed you."

"You should be a detective," he stated, lighting another cigarette.

"Clearly," Mandy replied coolly. "So, am I right?"

Sean sighed, nodding his head. "Yeah. I've been seeing her for a couple of weeks. Nothing serious."

"Friends with benefits?"

"Huh?" he replied, not following her.

"Fuck buddy," the woman replied, almost spitting the words out.

"Dunno about that. I've never had one before."

"Well, it's a shame. I thought that maybe we could have hooked up?"

He looked at her, feeling something that he was familiar with. Pity. "I'm not a nice person, Mandy. You're too good for me and I'd probably end up hurting you. I'm good at doing that."

"I get it. It's not me, it's you. I've heard that one before."

"I'm just being…"

"Save it, mate. Maybe you're right. Perhaps I am too good for you? Laters," she grunted, grinding her cigarette butt underneath her shoe before walking away from the smoking shelter.

Fuck. Oh well. Better this way. No ties, no baggage, no comebacks, he thought, heading back to work.

The following Saturday was a blur for Sean. He'd arrived at Tracey's house at dinner time, to be informed that her daughter, Alicia, was staying over at a friend's house. Minutes later, they'd lain sweating in bed, before heading down to the Rose and Crown pub, the centrepiece of the village. Beer and wine were followed by shots as the pair chugged down drink after drink before staggering home, kebabs in hand. They'd hoped for some more sex. However, moments after staggering through the front door, giggling and crashing about, they were both asleep on Tracey's double bed, still fully clothed.

"Here you go," Tracey said, placing a cup of tea next to his side of the bed. "Not sure how you took it, so I went for milk with two sugars. My fucking head's banging," she groaned, walking around the bed before snuggling in next to him.

"Thanks," Sean replied, his voice croaky, the back of his throat feeling like sandpaper. He sat up, looking down at the garlic mayo stain that was smeared across his polo shirt. "Shit. I should have stripped off last night. I'm minging."

"Don't worry about it, babe," She replied. "Get that down ya and go and have a shower."

"Good idea. I didn't even bring a toothbrush."

"There's a spare in the bathroom cabinet. You can use that if you want?"

"Cheers," Sean replied as he took a sip of his tea, wondering how many other men had used the same implement. "That's better," he declared, peeling off his polo shirt and shorts. He sat there in just a pair of dark boxer shorts, Tracey eyeing his physique.

"You've got a great body. What gym do you go to?"

Shit, he thought, trying to think of a plausible answer. "I tend to work out at home. Or use a local gym. There's one in Selly Oak that's okay, pretty basic though."

"Well, I've never seen a body quite like it," she purred, running her hand over his chest and down his washboard stomach. An extended index finger traced the line of his boxers, causing a guttural sigh to escape his lips. She looked up at him, noticing the material of his underwear start to move under her touch. "You like that?"

"You know I do," he breathed, smiling across the bed at her.

Her hand slid slowly inside the front flap of his boxers, grasping him. "You fancy a bit of fun?"

He finished his tea, placing the chipped mug on the bedside table. "What did you have in mind?"

"I'll show you," Tracey replied quietly, shifting position on the bed. The woman's lips parted, her head slowly sinking down into his lap, the inside of her mouth still warm from the coffee.

"Jesus!" he sighed, interlacing his fingers behind his shaven head. Sean's eyes closed, the rest of the world fizzling out as the woman pleasured him slowly.

"Mum! I'm home," a voice called from somewhere in the flat.

"Bollocks," Tracey blurted, letting go of him.

Sean's eyes flew open as the woman ducked under the covers next to him, just as the bedroom door was thrust open, banging loudly against a pine wardrobe.

"Stacey's dad dropped me off early. I'm gonna make myself…" Alicia's voice died in her throat when she saw a large man lying next to her mother. "Oh. Sorry. I didn't know you had company?"

"Well, you do now. So, bugger off and leave us in peace."

"Okay. I'll be in my room. I've already had breakfast at Stacey's. My other friend is popping round in a bit to help me with some coursework."

"Jesus!" Tracey exclaimed. "It's Sunday morning. Can't we have some bloody peace?"

"It's nearly midday," Alicia stated defiantly. "I need help with it. She'll be here in half an hour."

"Fuck's sake!" Tracey cursed in frustration.

"It's okay," Sean replied, trying to placate her. "Tell you what, I'll grab a shower, then you can have one after. We could maybe go for something to eat a bit later?"

Her troublesome daughter was momentarily forgotten, the thought of a Sunday roast taking the edge off her. "Okay. I'll grab you a towel and put some stuff out for you," Tracey agreed, tossing the duvet off her legs. She headed out of the bedroom, leaving Sean and Alicia together, the atmosphere anything but familiar.

The teenager looked at him, not liking the way in which his eyes moved up and down her body while a smile appeared on his face.

"I'm Sean," the man said, the duvet slipping down his body.

"Alicia," the teenager replied guardedly, her eyes drawn to his muscular physique. "Are you sticking around? Or will you lose interest in a few weeks like all the others do?"

"Depends," he countered, squeezing his thighs together under the quilt. "Things just got a little more interesting."

Alicia had been intimate with a guy once, a forgettable episode of fumbling and grunting. She knew how guys looked at her, mainly due to her considerable chest that had sprung up out of nowhere over the past few years. Since turning sixteen, she'd been the focus of many local boys, none of them floating her boat, except one, who'd turned out to be an arsehole, as she'd delicately put it. Now, as she stood there facing the stranger, she suddenly felt uncomfortable, wanting to be anywhere but in her mother's bedroom. "Interesting how?" she asked, her words almost getting stuck in her throat, her nerves building.

"Here's a towel," Tracey said, walking back into the room. She tossed it on the end of the bed, sliding back under the duvet to finish her lukewarm coffee. “I’ve put some shampoo and shower gel out for you, along with a toothbrush. It’s women’s shower gel, but you don’t mind, do you?”

“Not at all,” Sean replied, climbing out of the bed. He stood for a moment, stretching upwards, his palms flattening against the ceiling. Both women stared at him before he grabbed the towel and shouldered his way past Alicia, the bare skin of his forearms brushing past her.

She watched him walk down the hallway until a cough brought her back into the room. “Eyes off, madam. He’s mine,” Tracey warned protectively.

“You’re welcome to him,” Alicia huffed, heading out of the room. She closed her bedroom door, walking over to her bed. *He’s creepy,* she thought, *I need to keep an eye on him,* wondering if the big man would be doing the same to her?

51

Sean lay on the bed, the duvet covering half his body as he listened for the sound of the shower from the bathroom. As the noise of tinkling water drifted through to the bedroom, the man waited for a minute, then quickly closed the bedroom door and slid into bed. He picked up Tracey's mobile phone from the side of the bed, unlocking the device with the code that he'd spied her using on a few occasions. She had not thought to hide it from him, never knowing the implications that would unfold. Reading through texts and WhatsApp messages, Sean tutted in frustration, unable to find what he was looking for. He logged into her Facebook account, selecting messages, then smiled, as a conversation with Deano appeared before him.

Two minutes later, he placed the phone back where it had previously sat, having used his own phone to take photographs of the entire conversation. One part of the conversation was what he'd come for. An address. He tried to process the other parts of the conversation. *Who's the woman he killed? It doesn't sound like Mum. What other shit has this guy been up to?* He closed his eyes, trying to figure out the best way forward.

"You fallen asleep?" Tracey asked, walking into the bedroom with a large grey towel wrapped around her.

"No," Sean replied, opening his eyes. "Just chilling."

She walked over to the bed, the wooden frame creaking as she snuggled next to him. "Well, I'll get ready and we can go out. Leave Alicia and her friend here to do their homework."

"Okay," he agreed, wrapping an arm around her. "We've hardly had a chance to get to know each other. I know hardly anything about you."

"Like what?"

Sean wanted to appear normal, not seem as if he was prying. "Y'know. Family stuff. The usual kind of crap that couples ask each other."

"Are we a couple?" she replied, raising her head to look at the man next to her.

"I suppose so," he responded, seeing a smile spread across her face.

"Well, what do you want to know?"

Play it cool, Sean told himself. "Have you ever been married?"

"God, no," Tracey huffed in reply. "I was with Alicia's dad for years, but we broke up not long after she was born. Not seen or heard from him since, the tosser."

"Any brothers and sisters?" he probed gently.

He sensed a change in her. Very subtle, but it was there as she considered the question. "I have one brother and one half-brother."

"Okay. Do they live around here?"

"No," Tracey replied. "They both live in Spain."

"Nice. What do they do there?"

Her lie was seamless, almost as if she'd rehearsed it. "They run an airport taxi company."

"Cool. I bet they are busy?"

"Very," she replied, almost too quickly. "How about you?"

Sean's face changed, the woman noticing it clearly. "My younger brother died when I was a boy. He fell over at school and banged his head. Freak accident."

"Oh no. I'm so sorry." She squeezed his hand,

"It's okay. It was a long time ago. "Mum died fairly recently. Cancer."

"Oh dear. It must be tough, losing two family members like that?"

"I know," he replied, feeling his emotions begin to bubble under the surface. "Anyway, let's get ready and go and get some grub. I'm starving."

"Okay, lover," she replied, kissing him full on the lips. "Then when we're back home, I can finish what I'd started earlier, with no interruptions."

~

"That's it, Dad," Lottie said, hefting her bag into her lap as she released the seatbelt.

"Okay," John replied, pulling his daughter in for a hug. "Give me a call when you're ready to come home."

"Will do," she replied happily, climbing out of the car. Lottie walked through the gate, turning to wave as her father tooted his horn before driving away down the quiet cul-de-sac. She walked along the uneven path, weeds and dandelions protruding through cracks in the slabs. After knocking the door, she took a few steps back, noticing the peeling paintwork.

"Hiya," Alicia chirped as the front door opened. "Come in. Mum's just about to go out for lunch with her fella."

"I didn't know she had a fella?" Lottie replied, the smell of grease wafting down the hallway towards her.

"Nor did I until about half an hour ago," Alicia remarked, ushering the other teenager into a large room.

Lottie stepped in, placing her bag on the sofa as her eyes took in the room. At the far end, a small kitchen sat, dirty plates piled high in the sink. There was a small, round table in the centre of the room with wooden chairs tucked underneath. The carpet was threadbare and stained in places. "How long have you lived here?"

"All my life," Alicia replied. "But not for much longer. I want to get out of here as soon as I can."

I can see why, Lottie thought sadly, suddenly thankful for the home that she had always lived in. "Come on then," she urged. "Let's take a look at your coursework."

"Hang on. I'll just go and get it." She left Lottie standing in the lounge as she headed towards her bedroom.

She turned towards the front window, peering out through dusty blinds as she heard footsteps behind her. "You must be Alicia's mate," a male voice stated.

Lottie turned around, mildly startled as a large man headed towards the kitchen. "Erm, hi. Yes. I'm Lottie."

"Hi," the man replied, opening the fridge. He pulled a bottle of Coke from inside, keeping his back to her as his large hands unscrewed the top. She looked at him as he stood there, naked from the waist up. Lottie noticed the thick muscle on his shoulders. She also noticed something else, a trio of scars, close to the base of his neck. The teenager suddenly felt awkward, not knowing what to do or say.

"Here we go," Alicia declared, placing a neat stack of paperwork on the table. "Do you want anything to drink?"

"I'm good, thanks," Lottie replied, as she walked over to the table.

The man turned around, heading towards the two girls from the kitchen, long arms swaying back and forth. As he looked at the blonde teenager, he frowned, a memory flashing before him. *I know her from somewhere?*

Lottie looked directly at him, noticing the colour of his eyes, grey and piercing eyes, as a memory flashed before her, too; a ginger-haired boy, dragging her along as she cried for her mother. Her eyes widened, her mouth trying to form the words that would not come out. "Y-you," she began, her throat constricting in panic.

Alicia looked at her, her own eyes widening too as she noticed a dark patch began to appear on her friend's jeans. "Lottie?" she began. "What's wrong?"

The teenager backed away, pointing a finger at the man across the table. "It's you. You're that guy."

"What guy?" Sean replied, also noticing a dark stain begin to spread down the girl's thighs as her bladder emptied itself.

"Lottie?" Alicia urged. "You look scared. What's wrong?"

"He killed my mum," she blurted, backing into the sofa next to the window.

Fuck, he thought. *It's her. Shit.* "I don't know what you're talking about. You must have me confused with someone else."

Tracey walked into the lounge, clipping a silver bracelet onto her wrist. She'd dressed in dark jeans with a loose-fitting top, hair tied up in a ponytail. She was ready for an afternoon of fun but her face began clouding in confusion as she looked at the three people in front of her. "What's wrong?" she questioned, noticing the girl next to the window. "You!" she exclaimed. "What are you doing here?"

"I asked her, Mum. We're friends now," Alicia stated.

Tracey looked at her, seeing the terrified look on her face. She followed her gaze, noticing Sean across the room, who was looking edgy and uncomfortable. "What's going on?"

"H-he killed my mum" Lottie stammered shakily, tears rolling down her face.

"I don't know what she's on about," Sean countered firmly, his grey eyes boring into Lottie's.

"You took me. You and your brother. And then you killed my mum." She was trembling, Alicia going over to her warily.

"I don't know what the fuck she's on about," Sean declared, trying to look indifferent. "Shall we go?"

"Hang on," Tracey replied, a sense of unease washing over her. "Lottie, Do you really think this man killed your mum?"

"It's him. I know it is."

"Whatever," Sean replied. "I'm outta here."

"MJ Kerr," Lottie countered, trying to keep her voice under control. The man flinched and Lottie knew that she was right. "She was your mother."

Something triggered in Tracey's brain. "What the fuck? Sean, Is that right?"

Sean looked at her, his shoulders sagging. "Yes. She was my mother. That's why I'm here, Tracey. Your brothers killed her. I'm here for them, not you."

"I'm calling my dad," Lottie interjected, pulling her mobile out of her rear pocket.

As her shaking fingers struggled to unlock the device, she didn't notice the man advancing on her. He snatched the phone out of her hand, tossing it across the room. "You're not phoning anyone, bitch!" he spat.

"Get off her!" Alicia hollered, trying to prise the man's hands from Lottie's shoulders.

Sean looked over, seeing Tracey run out of the room, heading for the bedroom. *Shit,* he thought, knowing that she was heading for her phone. In a blur of speed, the man grabbed both girls by the neck, slamming their heads together, a sickening crunch reaching his ears as he strode out of the lounge.

"Get the fuck away from me!" Tracey screamed as she tried to dial a number on her phone.

Sean was there a split-second later, slapping her hard across the face. She crashed into the wall, her head bouncing off the plasterwork as the man snatched the phone, ending the call before it could dial out. He tossed her onto the bed, punching her hard in the face. Tracey's eyes rolled back in her head as large hands circled her neck. "Your brothers are both going to die. Let that be your last thought," Sean hissed, as he applied pressure to her throat.

The woman tried to prise his hands away as the life was choked out of her. Tracey attempted to gouge his face with her nails, not quite able to reach him as her vision darkened. *Don't hurt my baby,* she thought, succumbing to the darkness. One that she'd never return from.

"Fucking bitch!" he hissed, letting go of her throat. "You had that coming."

Sean suddenly remembered the two teenagers in the lounge and hurried back in there. To his relief, Lottie and Alicia lay in crumpled heaps on the carpet. *Think Sean, think. I need to get out of here. Out of the country.* He'd never been on a plane but had spent the previous weeks researching how to book flights and how long he'd need to be at the airport before the plane took off.

"I need to conceal this," he said to himself. "But how? Start a fire?" *No. That would alert people too quickly.* He bent down, turning Lottie over onto her back, seeing a large purple welt growing angrily on her forehead. Moving over to Alicia, he did the same, noticing a dark depression in her hairline. He busied himself, running back and forth across the flat to conceal his crime. Ten minutes later, he shut the front door, making sure it was securely fastened before he walked casually away from the flat, his heart hammering in his chest as he realised what he'd just committed. Another murder.

52

John put down the phone, his third call to his daughter's phone ending the same way as the answerphone kicked in. He looked at the clock on the wall. *Almost six,* he thought, a growing sense of unease seeping into his bones. His mobile started vibrating on the mantelpiece and John snatched the device from the mahogany top. His hopes were extinguished when saw Judy's name on the screen. "Hi," he said dully.

"Hi, love," Judy replied. "How're things there?"

"Not sure. Lottie went over to her friend's house this morning. I've tried to call her a few times, but it's just ringing out. That's not like her. She always answers."

"Have you tried calling the landline?"

"I don't have it. She's not at Sharon's, either. She's at Alicia's."

"What!" Judy exclaimed. "The rough one from school?"

"Yes. They've become friends since they started Sixth Form. I was surprised, too, but Lottie said Alicia has grown up a bit."

"Maybe, but the whole family are trouble. What's happened to Sharon? Have they fallen out?"

"Don't think so. But you know what teenagers are like?"

"So, what are you going to do about Lottie?"

"Not sure. I could always take a drive up there?"

"Good idea. I'm sure she's fine, but just check," the woman suggested.

"Okay. How are you, by the way? Any update from the doctors?"

"I'm fine, love. It's just a bit of high blood pressure. Don't worry. You'll not get rid of me that easily."

"Good. Because we need you fighting fit," John replied, naturally concerned for his mother-in-law. "I'll give you a call in a bit, once I've picked her up."

"Okay, John. Speak to you in a bit. 'Bye for now."

"'Bye," John replied, ending the call.

He dialled Lottie's number one more time, pacing the living room as the dial tone rang out once more. *Shit.* The man scooped his car keys off the coffee table and headed out as rain-filled clouds hung over central England, the first spots of rain falling from the sky.

Ten minutes later, John pulled into the quiet cul-de-sac as a torrential downpour doused everything around him. He pulled up outside the maisonette, his wipers on full as he tried to spot signs of activity coming from the property. It was in darkness, the blinds appearing shut. Streetlights flickered on along the road, bathing the interior of his car in an orange glow as the rain began to relent. Climbing out, John jogged up the path, stopping underneath a small canopy above the tired-looking front door. He knocked, turning around to look back down the street. A few seconds later, John knocked again, harder than before. Still, no reply was forthcoming.

Something's wrong, he thought, stepping across to the bay window. He tried to peer inside, cursing at the shuttered blinds. John made his way around the back, the back gate protesting as he shouldered it open. At the rear of the property, there was a single window and a kitchen door that had also seen better days. He peered inside, angling his head in an attempt to see inside. Nothing seemed out of the ordinary to him. *The place is empty,* he thought, his pulse beginning to throb. He took a few steps to his right, peering through the bedroom window, drawn curtains blocking his view. *The top closure is open,* he observed, reaching up to slide his hand inside, moving the curtains to one side.

"Fuck!" John cried out, seeing the figure on the bed below him. It was Tracey Teale. Even in the diminishing light, John could see that she was dead, glassy eyes staring back at him. He turned, taking two steps towards the kitchen door, his boot connecting just below the lock. It splintered easily, the door slamming into kitchen units on the other side as he barged into the flat. Two figures lay on the floor in the middle of the lounge, bound together with washing line.

"No!" he cried, running towards them. Both girls lay on their side, appearing lifeless as he knelt down next to them. "Wake up, Lottie!" he urged, feeling for a pulse. It was there, but faint. John baulked when he saw the large lump on her forehead and a dried trickle of blood smeared across her face. Her mouth was gagged with a tea towel. The man removed the tea towel, his hands trembling. "Princess, wake up. It's Dad. Come on, please wake up."

He moved to Alicia, placing two fingers on her wrist. *Oh God! She's dead!* Tears fell from his eyes as he tried to undo the blue plastic washing line. After a minute, his shaky hands managed to untie both girls. Placing a cushion under his daughter's head, John called *999.*

"Hello. Emergency Services Operator. Which service do you require?" a female voice said.

"Police, and ambulance," John replied, his voice shaky.

"Okay, I'll connect you now." There was a double beep on the line as John walked out of the lounge into the bedroom.

"Police Service. What is the address you are calling from?" another female voice asked John. He relayed the address, checking in vain for a pulse on Alicia Teale. There was nothing, the body was already cool to the touch. "What is the telephone number you are calling from?" As calmly as possible, John relayed his number, conscious that his daughter's life was hanging in the balance. "Okay. Tell me exactly what has happened?"

"I'm at my daughter's friend's house. She's been here for hours and I couldn't get hold of her. I made a forced entry when I spotted a body in one of the bedrooms. My daughter and her friend were tied up on the floor. My daughter is alive but unconscious. Her friend and her mother are dead."

"Is your daughter breathing?"

"Yes."

"Okay. Stay on the line whilst I send for help."

John stumbled into the hall, unlocking the front door before heading back into the lounge. He lifted Lottie into his lap, cradling her like he did when she was a child. His tears splashed onto her upturned face as the orange hue from the streetlights was replaced by flickering blue as the emergency services arrived. *Please save her,* he thought, his already fractured heart shattering all over again.

Judy barged into the ward with Bob a few steps behind her. John looked up, his red-rimmed eyes making the older woman's blood pressure increase. "Where is she?" she asked urgently, embracing John.

"In theatre," he replied as fresh tears emerged at the corners of his eyes.

"She'll be okay," Bob added, grasping the younger man by the shoulder. "They'll fix this, John. You need to stay strong."

They all sat down, Judy holding John's hands in her own. "What happened to her?"

"I've no idea. I found the girls on the lounge floor, tied and gagged. Alicia and her mother are dead."

"Jesus Christ!" she exclaimed, then crumpled in John's arms, sobbing openly.

"Have the police spoken to you?" Bob asked.

"Just the constables that accompanied us. That was about half an hour ago. No one else has spoken to me."

"Well, just sit tight, love," Judy replied, wiping her eyes with a handkerchief.

"That's all we can do," John sighed heavily. "I just feel so helpless. I just want her to be okay. Nothing else matters."

"We all do, John," Bob reassured, wrapping his arm around Judy.

Two hours later, Bob nudged John and Judy. They came to, seeing a doctor stood before them. "Mr Wilson?" the middle-aged man asked.

"How is she?" John replied, standing up stiffly, rubbing his eyes.

"Your daughter is in a coma, Mr Wilson. She suffered a severe diastatic skull fracture, which led to swelling on the brain. We've managed to relieve the pressure, but the next few days are critical."

"*Coma*?" John cried, his legs beginning to tremble. Judy held onto him, her own grief clear for the doctor to see. "Will she come through this?"

"I cannot say at this point. Comas are unpredictable. She could wake up in twenty-four hours, or it could be a month. We just need to keep monitoring her. The swelling on her brain is our main concern. Hopefully, that will subside, Mr Wilson."

"Can we see her?" Tears fell from his eyes, the doctor steeling himself like he'd done a thousand times before.

"Yes. She's being moved to a private room. One of the nurses will come and get you shortly," the Asian man responded calmly.

"Thank you, Doctor," John croaked, trying to hold it together.

"I'll be back to check on Lottie soon. I suggest that you get some rest. It's been a long day for you all." He nodded, taking his leave as the others stood facing each other.

"Another twenty-four hours," John muttered, appearing to be on the brink of collapse.

"She'll be okay," Bob replied positively. "She's a fighter. I'm going to grab some coffees. Who wants one?" They both nodded absently as Bob headed off down the sterile-looking ward, leaving John and Judy alone.

"When will this ever end?" John started. "First Lucy, then Zoe and now Lottie. I want this fucking nightmare to be over."

"We all do, love," Judy replied, sitting down heavily. "Who could have done this?"

"I've no idea," John shrugged. "I've been racking my brains, trying to figure that out. Her brother is long gone, as is Jerome. But why would they want their sister dead? That makes no sense. Unless Tracey had enemies of her own. I can't lose my little girl, Judy," he cried, as raw emotions boiled over once more.

She clung to him, not knowing what to say. "I'll pray for her, John. I'll pray for all of us."

53

John slumped onto his settee, the last few days bringing him to the precipice of physical and mental exhaustion. He'd kept an almost constant vigil at his daughter's bedside, hoping that she would wake up. However, his hopes were fading as Lottie showed no signs of recovery. The doctor and nurses that came into the room had tried to reassure John and his family, telling them that it was early days as far as a coma was concerned. John could see the impact it was having on his loved ones. Judy and his parents all looked on the brink, too, tears and anger rising to the surface every time they gazed at their unconscious granddaughter.

On his parent's orders, John had returned home on a sunny Friday morning to get some fresh clothes and hopefully sleep. He rested his head on a cushion, quickly succumbing to the inevitable. A short while later, his eyes opened as he lay trying to figure out what the noise was that had woken him. *My phone*. He pulled out of his pocket. "Hello?" he answered blearily, praying it wasn't bad news from the hospital.

"John, it's DCI Blaney," a familiar voice stated.

"Hi," the ex-soldier replied, his throat feeling like a dried-up riverbed.

"I know that you've been through a tough few days, but I need to see you."

"Okay. When?"

"How are you fixed tonight?"

"I need to get back to the hospital in a bit to see Lottie. But yes, I could meet you later. What's up?"

"I would rather discuss it in person. How does eight o'clock sound? I could meet you at the Stone."

"Okay. I guess I could ask my parents to watch over her for a few hours."

"Great. I'll see you then."

The line went dead before John could agree. He walked into the kitchen, hoping that the detective had some positive news. A thought came to John as he flicked on the kettle. *But he's not in charge of the case?*

"John, good to see you." DCI Blaney walked over, extending his hand.

John shook it, pointing towards the bar. "Can I get you a drink?"

"I'll get you one," the older man replied.

"Lager please," John said.

They took their drinks and headed towards a far corner of the lounge. The pub was filling up with Friday night revellers, happy to see the back of the working week. Blaney looked at the younger man, noticing that he appeared older than when they'd last met. "I'm very sorry to hear about your daughter, John. How is she doing?"

John placed his beer on the table, shrugging his shoulders. "No change. They've said it could take a while before there is any improvement in her condition."

"It's not uncommon. Don't think the worst. I've seen many cases like this. It can be a day, six months and anywhere in between. You've got a good support network around you, John. Lean on them."

"Where's Jenn – I mean Detective Shaw? She's normally with you."

Blaney placed his pint of ale on the table, sighing. "She's taking a break from active duty."

"Oh no. Is she okay?"

"Hard to tell," Blaney replied. "Her husband left her about eighteen months ago. Claiming that her career had wrecked their marriage, which it probably did. So, she's taking a break to regroup and sort her personal life out."

"Oh no. Poor Jenn," John replied. "She was very good to me when Lucy died."

"She's a fine detective. The best I'd ever worked with. But the job does not go well with marriage. Long hours, broken promises. I think Leon just had enough and had his head turned by a colleague at work. It all got rather messy."

"I can imagine."

"Anyway, I didn't drag you away from your daughter's hospital bed to talk about Jenn's failed marriage," he stated brusquely. "I have some news."

"Go on," John urged eagerly.

"What I'm about to tell you is off the record. I'm not involved in the investigation, but I called in a favour. A big one, probably my last." John looked at the older man, noticing his waxy complexion and deep-set eyes. "Sean Terry is the man who assaulted your daughter and killed Alicia and Tracey Teale."

"Sean Terry?" John muttered, digesting the information.

"The man who killed your wife, John."

John's eyes widened, shaking his head in disbelief. "Tell me this isn't happening?"

"It's happening, John. Let me bring you up to speed. Sean was released from prison recently, having served twelve years for the abduction of your daughter and the murder of your wife. Her Majesty's Pleasure isn't worth the paper it's written on anymore. Thirty years ago, that would have probably meant a whole-life term. Not now, though. As soon as Sean was sent down, there have been people trying to get him out. The system is broken, with too many do-gooders getting involved these days. Anyway, it looks like he's found out what happened to his mother, who, as you know was murdered, possibly by Dean Teale and Jerome Marshall. Sean managed to hook up with Tracey Teale, who had no idea about the connection between her brothers and Sean's mother. That must have all come out last week before he did what he did."

"So, where is Sean now?"

"Spain," Blaney replied. "A few hours after the incident, he flew to Alicante on the east coast. From there, he's vanished into thin air. Local and national police have been made aware of his arrival, but to be honest, they're more interested in drug gangs and people traffickers. Sean would have to be pretty dumb to end up in a Spanish police cell."

"Okay. So, where is this going?"

"We were able to access Tracey Teale's Facebook account via her mobile phone. Sean's prints were all over it. There is a message from her brother, Dean, along with an address. My money is on Sean making his way there to settle the score and avenge his late mother."

"Why are you telling me this?" John asked as he eyed the older man.

"I've got stage four prostate cancer, John. Doctors are giving me six months to a year. I've spent over half my life chasing perps, only to see them re-offend and ruin people's lives. Sean Terry, Teale and Marshall are the kind of scum that should be behind bars for life. But they are all out of our reach and pretty much off the grid. I'm going to die, John. My wife doesn't give a toss and will happily keep the house and my police pension. My kids hardly ever speak to me and the best partner I ever had may never come back. I've not got much to show for a lifetime of police work."

John stared at him, not knowing what to say. "Shit. I'm so sorry, Martin. Really, I am."

"It's okay. I've known for a few months but only told the Chief Super a few days ago. They'll put on a bit of a party soon, with some flowery words about my commitment to the cause and all that bullshit. Then, I'll go home to die. I'll keep in contact with Jenn. She's more upset than anyone else. She sends her best wishes, by the way. To you and your daughter. Your case affected her more than any other. She was only a sergeant back then and a bit wet behind the ears.

"I don't know what to say?"

"You don't have to say anything, John," Blaney stated, sliding a brown envelope across the table.

"What's this?" the ex-soldier asked.

"Dean Teale's address in Fuengirola. What you decide to do with it is entirely up to you, John."

He stared at the envelope, not sure whether to open it. He looked up at the older man. "You're sure it's concrete?"

"As concrete as it can be. If Sean flew into Alicante a few days ago, chances are he'll be heading for the Costa del Sol."

Tension started building inside John, knowing that the men who took so much from him were now within reach. "Can I ask you a question?"

"Shoot," Blaney replied.

"If you were me, what would you do?"

"I'd want justice. Not by the courts. But by my own hand. Not exactly what you'd expect a Detective Chief Inspector to say, is it?"

"Not really. But thank you for answering truthfully."

Blaney drained his glass, standing up stiffly. He extended his hand, which the younger man took, rising from his chair. "Farewell, John. We'll probably never meet again. I wish your daughter a speedy recovery and I will remember you to Jenn."

"Take care of yourself, Martin," the younger man replied. "And thank you for coming to see me."

"I'm sure you'll do the right thing," he responded with a tight smile, before walking out of the pub.

John sat down, staring after the ageing detective until his eyes fell on the envelope in front of him. He took a swig of his pint and slid the object towards him as cold tentacles of apprehension danced over his skin.

54

Sean walked out of the *peluquería* sporting a freshly-shaven head and newly shorn chin, most of his beard now being swept up by the proprietor inside the establishment. He donned his sunglasses against the glare of the bright Spanish sun, directly overhead. Its warmth was a welcome feeling after the years he'd spent indoors. He walked down the tree-lined promenade, the Mediterranean to his left, white-washed buildings that clung to foothills on his right. The sound of the sea drifted to the man as he walked, calming him. *It's so nice here,* he thought. *I may never leave this place.*

Five days after arriving, he'd made his way along the coast, taking local buses that bobbed and weaved along the coastal roads of the Costa de Almeria until he finally entered the Costa del Sol. Sean had alighted in Nerja, a small resort with a sprinkling of tourists milling about. That suited him, as most of the people he'd passed looked like locals. *The fewer Brits, the better,* he'd thought as he looked for some digs. Now, as he stopped for ice cream at a local *heladería,* he started to plan his next few days.

Stay one more night here, then get the bus to Fuengirola. Then, watch them come and go, he thought, savouring the salted caramel ice cream. *Once I know their routine, I'll nail them both.*

He carried on walking, enjoying the beachfront with its restaurants and bars. He smiled as various owners tried to entice him in with promises of the finest catch or special of the day. "Maybe later," he said, his stride looping and carefree as he passed them by.

On impulse, Sean ducked into a local souvenir shop, having spotted a variety of football shirts hanging up underneath the red awning. He wandered inside, trying on a few baseball caps. Finding a red one with a gold eagle emblazoned across the front, Sean sauntered towards the till, grabbing a can of Coke from the large refrigerator. He smiled at the cashier, the old Sean seeming to melt away… the Sean who'd murdered three women, two of them only a few days ago. Here, he felt like a whole new person, having left his old self back in dreary Birmingham.

As he walked along the streets of Nerja, his future plans started formulating in Sean's mind. *A car. An apartment. Maybe buy a local bar and live out my days here?* he thought, walking casually towards his accommodation. Locking himself away in his room, Sean stripped off his clothing and headed into the shower. For ten minutes, he stood motionless, letting the lukewarm water pummel him before turning off the mixer tap. He padded back into his small room, wrapping a towel around his waist and diving onto the bed to check his phone. Nothing of interest presented itself, Sean still being a novice when it came to social media. Instead, he checked the BBC page to see if there were any headlines relating to his activity. *Nothing. Maybe something else has taken the headlines,* he thought. *That Brexit stuff is all over the news. Maybe I'm in the clear?*

Holding that positive attitude, he opened Google Maps on his phone, to try and work out how long the final leg of his journey would take him. *Not long. I could be there by tomorrow night,* he thought, a wide smile spreading across his face. Sean lay there, wondering how it would go down. He envisioned a fistfight in which he brutally took his two opponents down, strangling the last vestiges of life out of them with blood-splattered hands. He held onto that image as he drifted into his own version of the local siesta, succumbing to sleep as a warm Mediterranean breeze gently wafted the net curtains of the hotel room's window.

~

A few hours later, Sean's eyes fluttered open to find the warm sun shining directly into his face. He looked down the bed, noticing his state of arousal. "It's been a while since I had some action," he muttered to himself as he grabbed his smartphone from the bedside table, the endless portal of internet porn his destination. An hour later, freshly showered and feeling revitalised, Sean strolled along the promenade once more as the afternoon sun was about to dip behind far-off mountains. He walked into a British pub called The Rose and Crown and seated himself at the bar. A few fellow patrons looked over briefly before resuming their conversations, and tucking back into their British cuisine. He surveyed the countertop, seeing what drinks were on offer. A selection of local lagers stood proud on the bar, along with a Guinness tap. Sean's eyes drifted over the vast array of spirits adorning the glass shelves as an old Oasis song played quietly in the background.

A young woman walked towards him, a friendly smile on her face. "Hiya. What can I get you?"

"San Miguel, please," Sean replied, returning the smile. "And can I have a look at the menu, please?"

"Here you go," the woman replied, placing a laminated A4 piece of paper in front of him before attending to his drink.

Sean's eyes appraised her, liking her tanned skin and auburn hair. She was dressed simply, in denim shorts and a yellow vest top. "Nice place," he commented, attempting to make small talk.

"Thanks," she replied, placing a pint of beer on the counter, the glass clouding over with condensation. "It's my dad's place."

"Okay. Has he had it long?"

"Thirty years. He loves it here. We all do," she replied, her accent neutral.

"Well, I can see why. Nice place to live."

"Are you on holiday?" she asked, taking a step towards him.

"Not exactly. Just taking a bit of a break from work. So, I thought I'd travel around Spain for a few weeks. I've never been before."

"Well, I hope you enjoy it. It's fairly quiet here, but then we have plenty of Expats, who come here year-round. If you want a bit more action, head over to Torremolinos or Benalmadena. Plenty of clubs, if that's your thing?"

"Thanks for the info. Not really into clubs. I prefer a few pints and a decent meal," he stated. "I've heard that Fuengirola is nice. Have you been there?"

"It's okay. A few seedy characters around there, if you ask me. But if you head past there to Marbella or Puerto Banús, you'll find all the rich folk and footballers."

"I may check them out. But to be honest, I prefer it quieter."

"Well, you'll enjoy Nerja. What do you fancy to eat?"

You, he thought, surveying the menu. "I'll have the cheeseburger, please."

"Coming right up, hun" she replied, smiling before walking back through a small doorway at the end of the bar.

Sean took a swig of his beer, cooling his dry throat. *I like it here. I might come back once I've sorted those cunts out.* He sat there, a sense of calm descending over him. One that he'd never felt before. He knew what needed to be done. And Sean knew he would succeed.

55

"Come on, Bruv," Jerome snapped as Deano dawdled out of the apartment block. "We're late."

"Chill," the younger man replied. "I was just grabbing a coffee for the drive." He held up a silver travel mug, his eyes bleary.

"You're in no state to drive. I'll drive there, you drive back."

"Fair enough," Deano agreed, walking around to the passenger door and climbing in clumsily, his flip-flops catching on the sill.

"You look like shit," Jerome pointed out, as he started the ignition of the beat-up panel van.

"Late night, bruv. Didn't get in until two."

"Well, you need to lay off the booze when we're working. Saturday nights are for drinking. You know we have to do this every Saturday. It's a long way to Seville. I need you sober in future. Ron's been good to us, letting us run this operation for him. We don't wanna fuck it up."

"Okay, bruv. I hear ya," Deano huffed in annoyance. "I'll just have a few in future. No shots."

They pulled away from the apartment block, the streets of Fuengirola still relatively quiet. They passed a few store owners, sweeping and hosing down the pavements outside their shops and bars as similar-looking vans headed in the opposite direction, delivering the supplies needed to keep them well-stocked. "Let's hope the traffic is light. If we make good time, we can spend the rest of the day in Rui's bar."

"Should be. Four-hour round trip, half an hour to offload the fags. Piece of cake," Deano declared confidently, as they wound their way out of the resort onto the main highway. He lit a cigarette, handing it to the older man, who accepted it with a nod before Deano lit his own. They sat there, the windows wound down as the Spanish countryside scooted past, the van making steady progress.

"Are you still seeing that bird? What's her name again?"

"Trisha. Yeah, she'll probably pop by later."

Jerome looked at his younger half-sibling, noting his suntan and trimmer figure. "Spanish life suits you, bruv. You've lost a fair amount of timber recently. Is this to impress Trisha?"

"Nah. She'd fancy me whatever size I am. It's all this donkey work, mate. I've never worked so hard."

"It's worth it, though. We've got a decent apartment and life is good at the moment. Even if the Old Bill weren't after us, I'd never go back to the UK."

"Me neither," Deano replied.

"Have you heard from Tracey?"

Deano flicked his fag butt out of the open window, taking a sip of his coffee. "A few weeks ago. She's got a new fella. All loved up at the moment, she is."

"Well, let's hope she keeps a hold of this one. She could do with a bit of stability."

"Yeah, I know. Single mums find it hard to keep a fella. Too much bloody baggage."

"Yeah, but Alicia is sixteen. She'll be flying the nest soon and then Tracey can hopefully settle down with someone decent?"

"What about you? That Clara seems keen?"

"Too keen," Jerome replied. "She's a decent shag, but way too needy. I might bin her off soon."

"Fair enough. There's plenty of fanny around here. Not like Brum."

"Definitely not like Brum," Jerome echoed, using the colloquial name for his home city.

. . .

Two hours later, they pulled onto the main highway, opting to take their usual cross-country route which kept them largely out of sight of the roving police patrols of Andalucía. After a few kilometres, Jerome pulled onto a road that led to the small town of Dos Hermanas, pulling into a rutted roadway between two buildings. "Come on, let's get this done," he said to the younger man.

"Okay," Deano replied, opening the passenger door. He climbed out, stretching his back, before walking over to a roller-shutter door. He wrapped twice on the grey metal, waiting as the older man joined him on the gravelly roadway.

A whirring noise signalled the opening of the door as it slowly retracted into a mechanism above. After a few seconds, a large Mediterranean stepped out, spitting into the gravel. "*Hola*," he said simply.

"*Hola, Diego*," Jerome replied.

"*Abra la puerta*," he ordered, his voice low and brooding.

"Deano, open the door," Jerome responded, his grasp of Spanish proficient enough to hold a simple conversation with the locals.

"Okay," he replied, busying himself with the hasp on the van's rear door. After a few grunts, Deano lifted the roller shutter, pushing it all the way up to the roof.

Diego walked over, nodding as his eyes scanned the illegal cargo of cigarettes. "*Vamos*," he urged, pulling two large boxes towards him, hefting them close to his body before walking inside the building.

Deano hopped into the van, sweat breaking out across his forehead as he began moving box after box towards the lip of the load space. "Don't strain yourself," he grinned, winking at the older man below him.

"Up yours," Jerome replied, winking back as he grabbed hold of two boxes.

After twenty minutes, the van was empty, Diego lighting a cigar in the shade of the doorway. He handed Jerome a brown envelope, along with a box of local wine. "*Dale esto a Ron.*"

"*Si, por suppuesto*," Jerome replied smoothly. "*Hasta luego*." The

Spaniard nodded, blowing a stream of smoke into the air before disappearing inside, leaving the two men alone in the alleyway.

Deano lit a cigarette, leaning against the wall, grateful of the shade. "Shall we grab some grub before we head back?"

"Good idea," the dark-skinned man replied. "Usual place?"

"Why not?" the younger man agreed, walking over to the van. "I'm fucking starving."

Just over three hours later, the two men arrived back in Fuengirola, navigating the narrow streets before pulling up at their apartment building. They climbed out of the van and headed over to a side door with an intercom system imbedded in the wall. They went inside, the door slamming behind them as a figure emerged from an alleyway opposite. The man wore cargo shorts and a T-shirt, his red baseball cap pulled over his sunglasses. He put his phone away, intending to view the photographs later. Sean strolled across the street, his fingers running the length of the van as he sauntered past. A sign a few hundred yards away caught his eye. *Rui's bar. I'll get comfy and see if they turn up?* He walked along the shady pavement, his thirst already building. The knife in his cargo shorts pocket, thumping reassuringly against his leg.

56

"Get them in, bruv," Deano urged. "I need to get some fags from the machine."

"Two beers, please," Jerome said to the young barmaid, as he watched the younger man shovel coins into the cigarette machine. He took the drinks over to a table underneath the bar's awning, sitting down heavily. There was a football match on the television. A large man sat watching it as he sipped at his beer. Jerome had never seen him before and noted the bulky shoulders and muscular arms.

Deano sat down next to him, offering him a cigarette from his fresh packet. "Here," he chirped, picking up the pint with his other hand. "Who's playing?"

"No idea," Jerome muttered.

"It's Liverpool versus Brighton," the lone man answered. "2-0 to Liverpool at the moment."

"Cheers, mate," Deano replied happily. The stranger nodded before he resumed watching the match.

"What time's your bird arriving?" Jerome asked, as he puffed away.

"Not sure? Probably about three?"

"Plenty of time for some drinking then. Cheers," the dark-skinned man offered, clinking glasses with Deano.

"Cheers," the younger man replied, taking a long pull on his Estrella Dam. They sat people-watching, Deano occasionally glancing up at the football match. Customers came and went as the smell of freshly cooked food wafted out from the bar, prompting the two of them to grab two menus from the table's centrepiece.

"What do you fancy?" Deano asked, eyeing the menu.

"Calamari, bruv. And you?"

"Fuck that. I'll go for burger and fries."

"Okay. You go and order and get some more beers while you're at it."

"What did your last fucking slave die of?" Deano countered, stubbing out his cigarette.

"He never paid for dinner," Jerome replied, flashing his half-brother a smile.

Twenty minutes later, the men pushed their plates across the table, each lighting a cigarette. "That did the trick," Jerome stated, as his phone started buzzing in his pocket. He stood up, walking away from the bar, leaving Deano alone.

On impulse, he, too, pulled his phone out, dialling his sister in the UK. He held the handset next to his ear, watching his older brother who seemed to be embroiled in a heated discussion. *Women,* he thought, as the dial tone was replaced by an automated answerphone message, telling him to leave a message after the beep. *Strange, she normally answers...*

He quickly typed her a Facebook message, asking him to give her a call when she could, before returning to his pint. "Clara?" he asked, as Jerome walked back over to him, a light breeze ruffling the overhead palm trees.

"She wanted to see me tonight. I told her I was out with you and that she can pop by later. She wasn't happy with that, saying I only want her when I want to have sex with her," he replied.

"Fuck her off, mate. She seems high maintenance." He paused for a moment, remembering the failed call to his sister. "I just called Tracey, but she didn't pick up. I've left her a text to call me later."

The men didn't notice the lone man's head twitch, or see him glance over at them.

"She's probably out with her new fella. If I know Tracey, she's probably in the pub, swigging back Prosecco."

She's not. She's in the fucking morgue, Sean thought, enjoying his little secret that the two men had yet to discover. *But they will find out, and soon.*

~

"Are you on holiday, mate?" Deano asked the man at the bar; the same man who'd been there all afternoon.

"Kinda. Just travelling along the coast for a few weeks. I've never been to Spain before and thought it was time I checked it out."

Deano nodded. "Good plan. I'm Deano by the way. The moody fucker outside is Jerome."

"Luke," Sean replied. "Nice to meet you. Do you guys live here?"

The alcohol had loosened Deano's tongue, making him feel relaxed and confident. "Yeah. We've been out here for a while now."

"Cool. Are you working?" Sean probed, trying to coax as much information out of the man as possible.

"Yeah. We do a bit of this and that. All cash in hand, if you know what I mean," he answered, winking at the bigger man. Jerome looked around, wondering where his drink was. He was also finding it difficult to keep the conversation going with Trisha, as the young woman was glued to her mobile phone.

"Sounds like my kind of work. I may stick around a while. I'm after a change of scenery."

"Well, you've picked the right place, mate," Deano replied, belching as he wiped his lips after a swig of his pint. "You want one?"

"I'll have a beer, please," Sean nodded, his face a mask of friendliness.

"One more here, please," Deano shouted down the bar. The young barmaid looked up from the till before pulling another glass from underneath the bar. Once the beer was on the counter, Deano pointed towards the table. "Come and sit with us, mate."

"Okay," Sean agreed, following the man over to a table and chairs next to the street. As he sat down, a man passed him by on the pavement, weaving around the big man before crossing over the road towards another bar close by.

"Jerome, this is Luke," Deano began. "That's Trisha."

The dark-skinned man offered his hand and Sean took it. The older man's eyes narrowed slightly, feeling the younger man's grip and trying to match it. "Hi," he said.

"Hi," Sean replied, seating himself.

"You on holiday?" Jerome asked inquisitively.

"Kinda. I was telling your mate that I'm just travelling along the coast, seeing what opportunities come my way."

"Well, you'll probably find something that takes your fancy down here. There's lots going on. And lots of opportunities for the right kind of person."

Across the street, the man seated himself with a shandy. He sat there next to a large potted plant as he gazed across the street at the other bar. His eyes were locked on the four people seated around the table, his main focus the three men. He could see that the men were chatting amicably. *Just three guys enjoying a beer,* John thought. *They've no idea who he is. And that's how he'll keep it until he's ready to make his move. And when he makes his move, I'll be right there, ready to make mine.*

57

He watched the two brothers for five days, staying a few hundred yards away from them as they were walking down the promenade. He stopped to grab an ice cream when they stopped to light a cigarette, chatting to another man who was walking in the opposite direction. He was up early, his hire car parked a few hundred yards from the address he'd been given by Blaney. He'd followed them in his rental, keeping a fair distance behind them, until they'd turned off the busy highway onto smaller roads, heading into the countryside with its olive groves and low stone walls. At that point, John had dropped back, putting a kilometre between his car and the white panel van being driven by Deano and Jerome but still keeping them in his sights.

After a few hours, they'd turned left, heading towards a small settlement on the outskirts of Seville. Again, John had maintained a good distance, parking close by but in a hidden spot when the van stopped between two whitewashed buildings. He kept up the vigil, doing the same throughout the week until, on a Friday morning, something unexpected happened. The van pulled over at a busy junction next to a large family hotel, where a burly man in shades and a baseball cap climbed inside the cab. *Jesus,* John thought. *This is too good to be true. Are they roping Sean into the operation?*

He knew roughly what was going on, as his binoculars had been trained on the panel van every day, watching as Deano, Jerome and a big, local-looking man had unloaded the rear of the truck, an envelope changing hands before the brothers had departed. Now, as the car climbed into the Andalusian countryside, the ex-soldier wondered when the attack would happen. He had no idea what would unfold under the Mediterranean sun.

"Ron will be there today," Jerome stated. "I'll introduce you to him, but I'm not promising anything."

"That's fine," Sean replied, as he bounced about in the cab while the van navigated a rough stretch of road with potholes and broken tarmac. He bent forward, pushing his bulky backpack under the seat, wrapping the strap around his ankle. He felt comfortable, knowing it was close by.

"He's got his fingers in many pies, has Ron," Deano stated, winking at the bigger man. "I'm sure there'll be something you can do. He even owns a few clubs in Torremolinos and Marbella. Maybe you could work the doors for a bit?"

"I'll do anything," Sean replied evenly.

"Beats working in a warehouse," Jerome added.

"True." Sean had concocted a cover story. He had fed the brothers his fabricated life story over the past week as they drank beers at the bar. Both men had appeared to accept it readily. He felt confident that they had no idea what was about to happen as his hand slid into his shorts pocket. Without the men noticing, he opened the knife in his hand, gripping it tightly as the van levelled out. On their right, the ground rose steeply towards a tree-line, the steep incline of which was dotted with boulders. To the van's left, the earth fell away into a tight ravine, several hundred feet deep.

Sean peered through the dusty windscreen, looking at the ribbon of tarmac that stretched into the distance. He could see no traffic coming in the opposite direction, noting that the van had passed several lay-bys along the route. He pressed the tip of the knife into Deano's side.

The other man flinched and looked down, spotting the gleam of the blade. "What the...?"

"Keep quiet," Sean said calmly.

"Huh?" Jerome responded, looking across the cab and spotting the knife.

"Keep driving. There will be another lay-by shortly. Pull in there, or I'll gut this prick."

"You're making a big mistake," Jerome cautioned. "Any idea who owns the cargo? They'll find you. And when they do, you're a dead man."

"I'm not here for the cargo. I'm here for you two."

"What?" Deano blurted, a trickle of urine seeping into his shorts.

"Who the fuck are you?" Jerome spat.

"Mandy Terry? You know that name?" Both men flinched and the tip of the blade pressed deeper into Deano's flank. "She was my mother. And you bastards killed her."

"Sean," Jerome started, a cold shiver running down his spine despite the growing heat outside the cab. "Take it easy," he urged, trying to think of a way out of their current situation. "We can sort this out. I'll pull over, then we can talk."

"Try anything cute and your brother dies," Sean hissed. "Up ahead. Pull over."

Jerome did so, parking the car a few feet from a low wall, beyond which the ground fell away into the ravine. "Now what?"

"Give me the keys, then get out of the van. Both of you." The older man did as he was asked, tossing the keys into Sean's lap before opening the battered door and stepping out into the blinding mid-morning sun. "You too," Sean commanded, pulling Deano with him as he exited the cab. A car drove past the van a few seconds later and disappeared around a tight bend, lost from sight.

"Look," Jerome pleaded, "we never killed your mum. She threw herself off the cliff, rather than tell us where my money was."

"You mean *my* money. I found it, thanks to Mum."

"We never meant to hurt her," the dark-skinned man added, edging closer to Sean, who had Deano pressed against the side of the van.

"Really?" he replied. "You fucking sliced her face open. Like this." In a blur of speed, Sean swiped the blade across Deano's cheek, causing the younger man to scream in pain and anguish. Before Jerome could act, the knife was aimed at his face, while his younger half-brother slid down the van, bright red blood streaming from the wound on his cheek.

"What do you want?" Jerome pleaded, his voice faltering as he saw his blood-soaked brother whimpering on the floor.

"To get even," the bigger man countered, moving towards the older man.

Let's go out fighting, Jerome thought, launching himself across the space between him and his adversary.

Sean was ready for the attack, bracing his feet before shoulder-charging the dark-skinned man into the van's already pummelled side. His head bounced off the sheet metal, stunning him briefly. As Jerome's vision cleared, he was too late to see the arching fist sailing towards his head. The blow almost knocked him unconscious. He crumpled to the floor, vaguely aware of being dragged around the side of the van and tossed onto the drivers' seat. He sat there, breathing heavily, slumped against the steering wheel before a large arm slammed him into the cab's back wall.

"I hope it was worth it," Sean whispered, jamming the knife just under Jerome's right ear. The older man's body reacted as if it had received an electric charge. He stiffened, grunting in pain as the knife was dragged from the fatal wound.

"Fuck you," Jerome breathed, seeing his blood come spurting in jets across the cab.

"Brave words, old man," Sean mocked, watching as Jerome slumped once more onto the steering wheel, his last breaths ragged and pained. He wiped the blade on the man's T-shirt and walked back around the cab to finish off the younger half-brother. There was no one there, just a trail of blood, sporadically coating the single-track road.

"He went that way," a male voice said from behind Sean.

He spun around to see an older man standing at the side of the road. "Who the fuck are you?" Sean challenged, a sense of unease washing over him.

"You finished Jerome off. Now, you just need to chase down Deano to complete your mission, Sean."

The bigger man baulked at hearing his name. Not only his name, but the names of his targets, too. "You a copper?"

"No. I'm not a copper," the older man replied, taking a step forward.

"Then who the fuck are ya?"

"Funny thing about revenge," the man started. "You think it will give you closure, but it doesn't, because you're already dead inside. The thought of it has eroded your soul, leaving very little of the person you once were. But then again, you were a murderer before your mum was killed. Isn't that right, Sean?"

"Look, mate," the younger man replied, feeling a tsunami of panic building inside him. "I'm here for them. I don't have any quarrel with you."

"But you did with my wife," John stated flatly, "when you murdered her in cold blood. And you did with my daughter, who you tied up and left for dead last week."

Sean's eyes widened as the man removed his cap and glasses, placing them on the bonnet of the van. "What the fuck are you talking about?"

"Lucy Wilson. My wife. You killed her, Sean. Then you put my little girl in a coma. That's what I'm fucking talking about!"

"What?" he blurted. "How did you find me?"

"Because you're not as clever as you thought you were. But I am."

Sean lunged at him, the blade missing John's ribcage by millimetres as he shifted to his right. They came together, the older man shocked when he collided with a wall of muscle which almost knocked him off balance. Instinctively, the ex-soldier caught Sean's wrist as the knife scythed towards his face, stopping its trajectory before it could slice through flesh and bone. John knew there and then that he was no match for the younger man's strength, and felt his arm quivering as the blade inched towards his face. He stared into Sean's eyes, seeing something he didn't expect. Desperation. He was scared, and John knew it, the blade edging closer as the larger man bore down on him. Taking a step backward towards the blood-smeared van, he braced his foot against the gravel, attempting to push the blade away, while the younger man doubled his efforts to finish it once and for all.

That was what John was hoping for. His free hand grabbed Sean around the neck, heaving his bulk towards him as he shifted to one side. Then they were on the floor, blood trickling from a slit on Sean's eyebrow.

"Come on, old man," Sean bellowed, scrambling to his feet. But the older man was faster as his left foot connected with Sean's jaw, snapping his head back.

John picked up the knife, tossing it out into the ravine as the larger man floundered on the ground beneath him. "Get up," he panted, hefting Sean against the van and delivering a blistering right hook, which rocked the younger man so that he struggled to stay on his feet. "You killed my Lucy. You ruined my life!" he shouted, taking his eyes off Sean for a second, thinking he was beaten.

In the twelve years Sean had spent in prison, he'd never been beaten. No one had come close. In all his life, this was the sternest test he'd ever faced. And he was not beaten yet as he rugby-tackled John to the ground. Both men vied for superiority, Sean quickly gaining the upper hand as he pinned John to the ground, punching him hard behind the ear, stunning the older man. "You should have left me alone, old man. Now, I will finish this. No more comebacks," he spat, as he clamped his large hands around John's throat, applying unrelenting pressure.

John's hands tried to beat at his opponent, his fists bouncing off rubbery muscle as his vision began to darken. He could feel the life ebbing out of him as the younger man bore down on him, thick fingers and thumbs constricting his windpipe. He closed his eyes. Lottie appeared before him as a little girl, her blonde curls bouncing up and down, her infectious smile focusing his mind. The sun beat down from above, the countryside unprotected against its onslaught.

Both men were sweating, John especially. He began to force his chin downwards, causing Sean's hands to slowly slide close to the ex-soldier's mouth. With his eyes still closed, John felt a stray finger touch his lip and instinctively clamped down on the digit with his teeth.

Sean hollered in pain as his left index finger snapped loudly. Blood dripped into John's mouth as the bigger man gave way. Before Sean could react to the man underneath him, a dusty thumb hooked itself into his eye, gouging the eyeball, forcing him to fall to his right, landing painfully on the gravel.

John was on him, dragging him towards the open passenger door. "This is for Lucy," he panted, smashing Sean's face into the door sill. He grabbed the door, slamming it shut over and over again on the back of Sean's head until he suddenly stopped and collapsed to the ground, gasping for breath, his sobs not heard by the younger man who was motionless. After a minute, the ex-soldier climbed to his feet and heaved Sean into the cab, seating him against the dark-skinned man whose life had ended slumped over the dashboard.

Two down, one to go. John turned, following the blood trail across the road. His trainers slipped over the gravelly incline as he found himself scrambling on all fours into the tree-line above, his heart hammering in his chest. He began to climb. No trail of blood was evident on the bracken-strewn ground. He was relying solely on instinct, on the training he'd received almost twenty years before. He weaved through evergreen trees, snagging his already ripped shirt and scratching his arms on low branches. He blocked it out, focusing on finding Zoe's killer.

He didn't have long to wait. A few hundred yards ahead, he spotted a sobbing Deano sagging against a tree, his face a macabre mask of fresh and dried blood. Suddenly, he spotted the man who was approaching steadily.

"You!" he blurted.

"Yes. Me. Didn't think you'd ever see me again, did you?"

"I never meant to kill her. You gotta believe..."

His pleas were cut off as John kicked him in the side of the head, knocking Deano to the floor. His eyes rolled back in their sockets as the younger man blacked out, two weary hands pulling him to his feet. John had not physically carried another man since Afghanistan and he found his vision clouding as he hefted the bulk of Deano onto his shoulders in a classic Fireman's Carry. He stumbled and lurched through the trees, his feet digging into the soft bracken underfoot until he was on the lip of the slope back down to the road. Here, John offloaded the man, watching as he tumbled down the incline to land awkwardly on the road.

Two minutes later, after dragging the mumbling man across the cracked tarmac, John loaded him into the van next to Sean. He looked at the steering column. *Where are the fucking keys?* he thought, opening the van door. He rifled through pockets, finding them in Sean's possession. John slammed the door once more, putting his cap and shades on before walking around to the drivers' side. Leaning in through the window, he dragged Jerome's body backwards, starting the van first time. *It will look like an accident,* he thought, opening the door to release the handbrake. The van started to lurch forward slowly towards the low wall. A car shot past, causing John to shrink behind the van, thankful that the large silver SUV sped along the road back towards the coast without slowing. He turned his attention back towards the van, cursing when he saw it had come to rest against the wall. *Shit.*

Twenty yards further on, the wall had been damaged and loose rocks lay on the gravel lay-by. "I can do this," he breathed, opening the door and shoving Jerome into the unconscious Sean. He depressed the clutch, putting the vehicle into first gear before piloting it towards the rent in the wall. Turning the wheel to full lock, John climbed out of the cab and let gravity take hold of the vehicle as it perched precariously over the lip, the ravine below beckoning it to fall. It did, the van toppling sideways, rolling and crashing over and over for several seconds until it disappeared from John's sight.

He stood there as silence fell over the countryside. *Is there anything left of the old me?* he thought, reflecting on his previous words. John turned away from the edge and walked back to his car, his steps pained, his body battered like the white panelled van that he'd sent on its final journey moments before. He finally had closure. But at what cost?

Two hours later, John walked stiffly along the beachfront of Fuengirola, his clothes changed, his scars hidden, watching as holidaymakers milled about in souvenir shops and played on the beach. He kept walking until the hotels gave way to rocky scrub as the footpath took him onto a headland above the sea. His phone beeped in his pocket. John took it out and read the text from his mother-in-law, telling him to call her.

He dialled, his stomach constricting as he feared the worst. "Judy?"

"Daddy?" a voice sputtered over the line.

"Lottie? Is that you?" he croaked.

"Yes. I'm here with Nanny Judy. Where are you?"

John broke down, landing heavily on the rocks as he sobbed openly. "Oh, princess. I thought I'd lost you. I'm so happy that you're awake," he answered shakily.

"Hi, John," Judy interjected. "We've got you on speakerphone."

"Hi, Judy. Is anyone else with you?"

"No, just us two. She's been awake for an hour or so. The doctor has been in and he's coming back in a bit to check her over."

John sat there, happy tears cascading down his stubbly face as his breathing returned to normal. "I'm so glad you're awake, Lottie. Daddy misses you."

"I miss you too, Dad. Where are you?"

"I've just had to take care of something. But I'll be home real soon."

"Take care of what?" his daughter asked.

"It's over, princess. I got them. I got them all."

"Oh, John!" Judy exclaimed. "Are you okay?"

"I'm fine," he lied. "No one will ever hurt us again. I've made sure of that." Fresh tears sprang from his eyes as sobs echoed down the line. He cried with them, the feeling of release a welcome friend.

"Thank you, Daddy," Lottie whispered as John pictured the smile on his daughter's face, although he couldn't see it.

"I love you, Lottie."

"I love you, too. Please come home. We need you."

"I'll be there real soon, princess. Then we can begin our lives again."

He heard sniffles before Judy cleared her throat. "Thank you, John. You're a good man. Now, come home to your family."

Moments later, John walked back towards the hotels and holiday-makers, his stride more relaxed now, a smile on his face. He felt at peace, knowing that the record had finally been set straight. Knowing that the two women he'd lost had finally been avenged.

SIX MONTHS LATER

The Rose and Crown hotel sat majestically under the autumn sun, its manicured grounds resplendent as the wedding party walked across the roadway towards its vibrant colours. Judy held onto Bob's hand tightly, hoping that her tears had not turned her into a steely-haired Alice Cooper. She wore a stylish grey trouser suit, the white carnation in the buttonhole ruffling slightly in the balmy breeze. She was glowing inside and out, a goofy smile etched across her tanned face. Bob was trying to look equally jovial, though he was not used to wearing fitted suits and his trousers felt a bit on the snug side. However, he was happy, knowing that he'd found someone special to grow old with; a life partner whom he couldn't live without. This was his second chance and he couldn't wait to take it.

Derek beckoned them towards the gardens, his SLR camera hanging proudly from his neck. "Let's start with a shot of the bride and groom," he said jovially, guiding the happy couple over to a flowery trellis. The thirty or so guests stood watching, all decked out in their finery, as Lottie's grandad began snapping pictures.

"They look so happy, Dad," Lottie beamed, wrapping an arm around John.

"They sure do. It might not be Cyprus, but the setting is perfect."

John replied. On his daughter's orders, he'd visited a local shopping centre, buying a dark blue suit and matching tie with a crisp white shirt. Over the past few months, John had decided to grow a beard, which was sculpted to perfection for the special occasion, parts of it shot through with silver. Even his hair was waxed and tousled, Lottie having done the honours for her father an hour before, as they got ready to leave the house.

"Grandad wants you," he pointed out, noticing his father pointing towards them. She scooted away, John loving how her blonde curls bounced up and down. *She'll always be my little girl*, he thought, noticing a few teenage male guests checking out his daughter in her figure-hugging bridesmaid's dress. He cast the thought aside as a drink was presented before him.

"Champagne?" the dark-haired woman offered, presenting him with a slender flute of bubbly.

He looked at her and smiled, accepting the drink gratefully. The woman wore a red knee-length dress with matching shoes, the colour complementing her milky skin and dark hair perfectly. A dash of makeup was all that was required, as she had a fresh complexion. Her nose was adorned with freckles. He'd never really noticed them before. But now he did, and more besides. He'd been in contact with her over the past few months, since the funeral of Martin Blaney. They'd talked often, sending and receiving messages, and sharing numerous coffees when time allowed it. It was an unexpected development, but it was slowly blossoming as they spent more and more time in each other's company.

"Thanks, Jenn," he replied, turning towards her as most of the other guests began moving towards the lawned area, under Derek's orders.

"They look so happy."

"Sure do. They've both had tough times, but Bob's a great guy and I know Judy will keep him happy. And in check," he affirmed.

"Maybe there's hope for us all, eh?"

"I'm sure there is," John agreed. "Shall we?" he asked.

"Why not?" Jenn replied, linking his arm. Then the two of them walked towards the rest of the wedding party as laughter drifted across the Lickey Hills country park.

His eyes fluttered open, the light drapes allowing the sun to penetrate the cool stone room. His throat felt like sandpaper as the man looked to his left, seeing a warm beaker of water within reach. Sitting up slowly, he shifted himself on the bed, grabbing a plastic cup half-filled with warm water. The liquid barely quenched his thirst, rivulets of it running down his chin as he gulped it down. He grabbed the crutches and stood up from the bed stiffly. Progress was slow as the man hobbled towards a full-length mirror, its surface dusty and slightly warped, making the reflection even more macabre. He looked at himself, his scarred face impassive. His right leg had been amputated below the knee, crude purple stitching crisscrossing the stump. It had healed well enough though, a local vet having performed the procedure off the record. He'd also reset a break in his left arm, where a purple welt added to his collection of battle wounds. Another scar ran from the top of his skull, down the left-hand side of his face to his chin, giving him a distorted, lopsided appearance, his one eye drooping slightly at the corner. The rest of the injuries had also healed to a degree, so the man was now able to move around the small cottage that lay a few hundred yards from the white panelled van. The van that hadn't been seen or moved in months, two desiccated corpses still inside, frozen in time. *A few more months and I'll be well enough to travel,* Sean Terry thought. *Once I've got my strength back. And I'm going to need it. No mistakes next time. No comebacks.*

THE END

ABOUT THE AUTHOR

Phil Price was born in Sutton Coldfield in 1974. He lived in various places in the UK until his family settled in Rednal, a suburb on the outskirts of Birmingham in 1979. Growing up with an older brother and sister, he always flirted with reading, his home always littered with books. Then in 1997, Phil embarked on a travel expedition that took him from Greece to Thailand, via East and Southern Africa. Sitting in dusty bus stations in Kenya, Tanzania and Malawi with Wilbur Smith and James Herbert accompanying him, his imagination was sparked into life. Since those far-off days, he has never been without a book to read.

Phil started toying with the idea of writing a book in 2009. After writing a few short stories, he caught a whiff of an idea in his head. It started to evolve in 2010 until he had enough to begin his writing journey. Marriage and two children came along, with the story being moved to the back burner for periods of time. However, during those periods of writing inactivity, the story continued to manifest until it just needed one thing. To be written down.

The story was littered with places that had influenced Phil's life. From the Lickey Hills in Birmingham to the Amatola Mountains in South Africa, with other many other locations, in-between and far beyond.

The book was finished sometime in 2014, left on his computer until a chance conversation with an author friend made Phil take the bold step to publish his story, Unknown.

From there, Phil's love for the first book spurred him on, creating The Forsaken Series. A vampire/paranormal/horror trilogy set in our world, and others too. His love of horror and all things supernatural, inspired by authors such as King, Herbert and others, helped create the epic series.

Aside from his writing, Phil lives on the edge of a small town in Worcestershire, UK. A wife and two sons keep Phil happily occupied as he steers his way through life, playing the husband, dad and world creator in equal measure.

Find out more about the author at:

https://www.amazon.co.uk/Phil-Price/e/B019LK4QFY/ref=dp_byline_cont_ebooks_1

https://twitter.com/philprice19?lang=en